Satellite

The Satellite Trilogy Part I

Copyright © 2013 Lee Davidson
All rights reserved.
ISBN-10: 1479235318
ISBN-13: 9781479235315
Library of Congress Control Number: 2012916673
CreateSpace Independent Publishing Platform
North Charleston, South Carolina

For Heather.

Your unwavering support has brought

my make-believe world to life.

Thank you.

Contents

1. I'm not going in there   1

2. Here come the little stunners   17

3. Use that great charm to make some friends, Casanova   37

4. You're a stalker, is what you are   55

5. You live in a sad world of denial, kid   77

6. If I'm right, you owe me dinner   101

7. It's like a jolt of electricity, but worse   121

8. A punch in the face would be more subtle   141

9. You're not going to yack, are you   155

10. You were destined for this   173

11. If I hear that one more time, I'm gonna hurl   193

12. There's a whole world happening around you   209

13. We'll eventually fix that mind of yours   223

14. You weren't meant to find out this way   249

15. You really are Captain Oblivious   267

16. It won't stop hurting   283

17. I'm all about doing the impossible   301

18. She almost burned the house down   323

19. You guys look like you're lost   345

20. Why couldn't you have shut up like this months ago   361

All goes onward and outward, nothing collapses,
And to die is different from what any one supposed, and luckier.
—Walt Whitman, Song of Myself

Prologue

Progression, twenty-two years ago...

After re-inking his pen (the one he refuses to retire despite the push to go digital), Jonathan Clement diligently scribbles on a thick page. In contrast to the thousand-year-old books wallpapering the ceilingless, octagonal room, the stacks concealing Jonathan are crisp and dust free. At a squealing sound, his dancing feather pen halts.

"Good evening, Beaman," Jonathan guesses.

Beaman, overly muscled in a green tracksuit, adjusts his ball cap before sighing. "Looks like the week to make babies." He cranes his neck to see the piles disappearing into the black, star-littered sky. "Have you finished with them all?"

"Finishing the last now. We have a Satellite from today's conceptions," Jonathan says.

"About time. The pool's been dry for a while."

"Indeed." Jonathan dips his pen into the inkwell and resumes writing.

Beaman neither breaks a sweat nor topples the swaying towers while transferring books to his long industrial cart. When Jonathan finally comes into view, Beaman looks at him expectantly.

Jonathan, holding a book, rolls his chair back a few

feet and removes an iron rod from the fireplace. "Beaman, I would like you to keep tabs on this one. I think he will prove to be quite extraordinary," he says, scorching the leather book cover with the gold branding iron.

"Sure," Beaman replies, taking the still-smoking book from Jonathan and throwing it onto the only available space on the cart. Light bounces off the book's cover, making the name *Grant Bradley* and the gold pair of wings shine impossibly bright.

1. I'm not going in there

I'm dead. This much I figure.

Certainty jabs into my side like a knife. The glare is too bright; the black forms will not focus. I strain to hear something, anything, besides the echo of air gasping through my lungs. *I'm dead, I'm dead, I'm dead!* screams every breath. This is really happening.

After a few minutes, my breathing level chills out, and I open my eyes to a transformed setting. A...college campus? I *did* land in Hell. Super.

Surrounded by hundreds of others looking much too attractive to be dead, I ask the guy to my left, "Any idea what's going on?"

He's built like a lion (clarification: a lion on steroids) and his angular jaw becomes even sharper when he clamps down on his toothpick. "Uh-uh. I've never seen anything like this," he answers, rubbing stubble on his chin that's as short as his dark hair.

Overwhelmed by the Harvard-type landscape (as if I actually know what Harvard looks like), I close my eyes and think of Tate. Turns out she was right about the whole life-after-death thing. I should have figured, seeing as she's right about everything. Until now, that is. She swore I wouldn't die. Guess that's finally a point for me.

"Think we're supposed to go in?" the Toothpick Guy asks.

I open my eyes, hating the utopian landscape and equally perfect weather, and stare across the crowded lawn at a massive gray castle. "I don't know," I say, though what I mean is, *I don't care*.

He flips his toothpick with his tongue. "I'm not going in there. Not without an invitation, anyway." He pulls the stick from his mouth and offers me his free hand. "Marcus Riggins. Call me Rigby."

"Grant," I mumble. When we shake, the calluses on his hand make me feel better, like I'm not the only one who isn't polished enough for the grandeur of this place. I scratch both of my hands through my hair. (My hair's back!)

"You all right, dude?" Rigby asks with an interrogating look.

"Yeah!" My voice screeches out as high as a girl's. Nice.

To play it cooler, I lower my hands from my head and clear my throat before assessing other changes. My jeans now fit my waist and butt; my chest fills out my blue sweatshirt. I wasn't in these clothes when I died. In fact, I hadn't worn these clothes in months. This hoodie was gracing Tate's closet at last check and still smells like her. A hollowness spreads inside me like thick syrup.

"Welcome," a deep voice booms, silencing the low murmurs of the crowd. The voice's owner stands on the balcony above the open doors, sporting a red pullover and a five o'clock shadow not quite as thick as Rigby's. "As some of you may have concluded, you have passed on from Earth. Or died, if you prefer the informal definition."

You don't say? I think, shaking my head. Surely everyone's figured this out, but the shifting crowd says otherwise. OK, maybe not.

Rigby laughs at who-knows-what, and those within earshot turn to offer their disapproving stares. He answers a cute redhead with a wink and flips his toothpick. She rolls her eyes and twists back around.

"You are here to fulfill a momentous purpose," Mr. Red continues, pushing up his fleece sleeves. "If you would be so kind as to join me inside, I will explain further." His smile stretches even wider, and he disappears into the building.

"Guess that's our invitation," Rigby says dryly.

Excuse mes and *thank yous* drop like confetti as the crowd pushes into the building. Finding no reason to hurry, Rigby and I bring up the rear like herding dogs and finally pass through the golden doors.

Once we're inside, Rigby murmurs "dude" and almost loses his toothpick.

Hating that my breath is taken away, I rehinge my jaw before it hits the marble floor. I'm pretty sure places like this don't exist even outside Missouri, though having a limited number of "been there, done that" experiences under my belt, I couldn't say for sure.

I run my finger over the black wall, hoping to leave a smudge. As if to mock me, the wall shines more brightly. I consider spitting, but think of my mom—she'd be mortified if I did something so disrespectful. My dad, however, would probably laugh. As usual, I side with my mom, but push harder against the glittery marble.

After wondering how the seams were hidden so perfectly, I shift my attention to the lighting. A person doesn't have to be an electrician to know that the candles in the chandeliers, even if there are thousands of them, aren't enough to light a room the size of two football fields.

The crowd leading the way rubbernecks like tourists. Smaller groups of people who don't appear to be new to this place linger in and around the halls, staring like we're the afternoon entertainment. A few girls ten feet away point at Rigby and me and giggle. We eventually spill through one of the three doorways into a heavily columned church and slide into a pew toward the back.

"Check it out," Rigby says. I follow his eyes up to the ceiling, or, more appropriately, the lack thereof. A swarm of red, orange, and yellow birds darts across the sky like fire. I push my fingers through my new hair and sigh, hoping I don't get dumped on by one of them.

At the front of the room, Mr. Red leans against a podium and looks up. The birds scatter in the sky and settle on the cap molding high above us, as if on cue. "Congratulations," Mr. Red announces while I mull over the ridiculous coincidence. "You are among the chosen few to join our select team of Satellites."

Was I just congratulated for being dead?
Everyone's frozen, sighted in on Mr. Red. I wish I had a pin to drop. In the silence, seven haunting words pop into my head. I try to push them out, but like always, I fail.

"I'll die if I ever lose you," Tate had said. I was expecting an "I love you" or some other cliché. I should have known better. Tate had no idea how those words would stick with me—how they would later cut my heart in two. How could she? I hadn't even been diagnosed yet. She'd never said them again after my death sentence, as if not saying it would keep it from happening. My parents were the same. They could talk about my disease, my treatments, even my weight loss, but never my death. Denial is easier than reality, I guess. I wonder what my mom thinks about her miracle baby now, dead at twenty-two.

And my dad...getting close to him was like hugging water. Still, I know he loves me, even if the words never came from his mouth (which they most certainly did not). This past week, he spent most of his time "secretly" crying in the hospital hallway. Since my dad is one of those loud, slobbery criers, his little fits were not as hush-hush as he thought. My mom and I played the pretend game as usual because, quote, *men don't cry.* This according to my father.

"My name is Jonathan Clement. I realize most of you are feeling disoriented," Mr. Red says, snapping me back. "You have much to learn about your new life as we prepare you for your purpose. Let me begin by saying we've waited many years for your arrival and are so pleased that you are here. You have been selected because you possess a chromosome arrangement that perfectly suits you for our distinguished team of Satellites."

Perfectly suited? Right. I've never been perfectly suited for anything, not even Tate. Now she'll finally realize how much better she can do. I swallow instead of hurling.

"Immediately after conception," Mr. Red, er—Jonathan, goes on, "your lives were carefully and strategically planned, leading you on the necessary path to your arrival here. Although you were chosen based on your unique genetics, your life experiences have also played a significant role in preparing you for your purpose."

When he pauses, my eyes dart around. Why is everyone so calm? Rigby looks at me and unclamps his jaw to pull out his toothpick. *What?* he mouths.

I grit my teeth and turn back to Jonathan, who's looking directly at me. After five awkward seconds I lose the staring contest, and he continues.

"Your purpose as Satellites is one of paramount importance: to keep Tragedies, those who have faced great adversity, on their life's course. You will each be paired with a Legacy—your mentor, so to speak. There is much to learn in preparation for this new life. Your journey will be difficult, but we know you can succeed. Each of you was, after all, built for this. Are there any questions?"

Yes, actually. I have a million, but none are very nice. To keep myself quiet like everyone else, I bite my tongue until my mouth fills with blood. After swallowing down the iron taste, the sting is gone. My teeth scrape over skin that should be split, but isn't.

"Excellent," Jonathan says, clapping his hands together. "Please make your way back to the lobby and form orderly lines corresponding to the first initial of your last name. Thank you, everyone."

"It's hideous," I retort.

She thinks this is funny. "Well, that's subtle."

"I'm not subtle," I say.

"So I've seen."

"What does that mean?"

She shrugs and says nothing else.

I make my way toward the atrocity, the old hardwood floor creaking under my feet, and sit beside a guitar that's seen better days. Sheet music littered with scribbles and a chewed-up pencil lay on an aged trunk turned coffee table. The ache in my chest burns.

"You a musician?" I ask over my shoulder, glad that she can't see my face.

"Observant. That'll come in handy as a Satellite. So, what brought you here?"

"Cancer." I force my eyes away from the yellowed paper.

"Well, isn't that just a kick in the crotch. Tea?"

I twist around to see her. Do I really look like a guy who would drink tea? "How about a Coke?"

"Dude, that crap'll kill you." She smirks at her own joke. "Water, then," she decides, hurling a bottle in my direction. After years of my father throwing things at me, I catch it easily.

She bounces over and plops down in the guitar's place. The instrument hits the floor with a groan. "So, kid, tell me what you know so far." She picks at her electric-blue fingernails, completely oblivious to how obnoxious she is.

I take a deep breath. "I know I'm dead, I've abandoned

my fiancée, and apparently I'm supposed to watch over some stranger. This blows, if you want my two cents."

"I don't want your two cents, but you should feel honored to be chosen. Being a Satellite is major. Very few people are cut out for it."

"Lucky me," I snap.

"You can sulk all day, but it's not going to change anything. It will, however, make me crazy, so get over it already."

Deflated, I sink into the couch even further. "I don't want to be dead."

She stares at me. "Done?"

"For now."

"Don't worry about your fiancée, kid. You'll forget all about her soon."

I sit back up. "Forget?"

"Uh-huh. Most of your memories will be gone within a week," she says, as if it's no big deal.

"But I don't want to forget." Panic causes my voice to hitch.

She laughs. "Nobody wants to forget, but it's part of the process. I lost my memories of my husband and daughter, so I get it." She looks at the bookshelf across the room. "It's necessary, though."

I try to keep my breathing in check. "Do you remember anything about them?"

She looks back at me. "Just their names, mostly. It's critical for us to forget. As Satellites, we can't afford to be distracted by our pasts."

Suffocating, I tug at the collar of my sweatshirt and keep the acid in my throat at bay with a swallow. "Will you ever see them again?"

"Of course. As a matter of fact, my husband, Troy, is joining me soon."

"What about your lost memories?"

"There's a department called Programming that brings them back."

Even though I'm internally freaking out, I'm able to raise an eyebrow.

"Your memories don't die, kid," Willow explains. "They just get buried."

Oh, OK. That makes perfect sense. I don't even bother to ask.

"Moving on to Tragedies," Willow continues.

"Me being here is tragic," I say under my breath.

"Wrong context," she says matter-of-factly. "'Tragedies' is the term we use for those being protected."

"Of course it is."

She glares at me, repositioning herself on the ugly cushion. "Look, kid, you need to get over yourself. You're connected to a much larger purpose now. Someone out there is going to need your help."

"That wouldn't be necessary if everyone had a fair shot at living," I shoot back.

"Well, isn't that all rainbows and lollipops," she mocks, pouncing up like a cat.

When her mug clinks on the counter, I twist to look over the back of the sofa. "What's wrong with everyone dying of natural causes?" I try to keep the resentment out of my voice.

"Natural causes? Come on, kid—really?" Willow laughs when my eyes narrow. "There's no such thing as natural causes. Every person's life is planned beginning to end, period. Your genetics make you built for this."

"I don't buy that. I'm as average as they come."

She moves a tea bag up and down in her mug. "If that were true, you wouldn't be here."

"Well, someone made a mistake."

"There are no mistakes." She flings her spoon into the sink and shakes her head.

Since we're clearly getting nowhere, I change the subject. "Can we be Satellites for someone we know?"

She leans against the countertop. "No."

"That's stupid! Why not?"

"Nice vocab, kid." She comes around the counter and walks back to the sofa. "For one thing, it's against the rules. For another, you've gotta be on your best game. Devastating things can happen in an instant. Get it?"

I scowl as my own D-day replays in my head: Tate clutching my clammy hand like I might die right there in the sterile office, the yellow lights making my skin look sickly and transparent, the doctor explaining all the medical terms and then dumbing them down. My brain was frozen on just one part: "Your cancer is aggressive."

Willow interrupts my trip down memory lane. "It helps to remember that sometimes the living need to lose someone to find their purpose."

Right, like that makes it easier to swallow. "I seriously hope you can come up with something better."

"I'm serious. My daughter would have been a different person with me in her life, and Troy a different kind of father. Neither of us would have become what was intended. Tragedy alters people, and that change is necessary for each person to fulfill his or her purpose."

My eyes stay fixed on a dark knot in the floor, and I bury my anger more deeply with each breath, pretending the fury won't return. "I still say it sucks."

Willow unfolds her legs from under her, pats my knee, and then pushes herself up from the sofa. With half an ounce of pity playing in her voice, she says, "I know it seems that way, but try to stay open minded. Being a Satellite is totally stellar. Trust me, you're gonna love it."

2. Here come the little stunners

Willow returns from going down the hall and tosses a musty-smelling blue book onto my lap. Pushing the music sheets aside, she parks herself on the trunk and rolls a pencil between her palms.

My eyes scan the thin book that's certainly second-hand…or third…or hundredth. *Satellite Basics* is in cracked text on the curled cover. "Some title," I sneer.

"Hey, kid, I didn't write it. Besides, you look like the type who needs simple instructions. Think of it as Satellites one oh one."

I frown at her cheerfulness and open to the first page, discolored and stained with spots.

"Read aloud," she instructs.

I stare at her, realizing she's serious. I hesitate before reading the black typewriter text. "Rule number one," I recite mockingly. "Satellites must keep their Tragedies on course." I look up from the book.

"Seriously, kid. I thought that one would be self-explanatory."

"Yeah, I get it," I snap, insulted. "They have to make this a rule?"

"I told you—one oh one."

"More like *Handbook for Dummies*," I mutter.

"That's quite perfect for you, then."

I throw her my dirtiest look.

She sighs. "Listen, it's written because it's important. The Schedulers tend to frown upon rewriting the future because of a Satellite's carelessness."

"The Schedulers?"

"It's exasperating that you know nothing."

Tell me about it. "I assume that's what you're for, as my…whatever you're called. So enlighten me."

"I'm your Legacy." She stares at me as if considering the best way to torture me. "The Schedulers write every person's life course."

"Including mine?"

"Including yours. Don't go hating on them for it."

I wonder if I'll get to meet these Schedulers. I smirk, thinking of the choice words I'd share. When the dramatic performance in my head is over, I flip to the next page. "Satellites cannot protect Tragedies they have known in their mortal life." I look up at Willow. "No explanation needed."

Because her expression resembles a clown high on cotton candy, I have to bite my cheek to keep from smiling. This turns out to be a big, fat fail.

"That's the spirit!" Willow sings.

I shake my head and turn the page. "Satellites are forbidden to share information about their assignments with other Satellites." I pause. "This seems easy enough. Keep my mouth shut."

"That one seems to be the most difficult rule to obey

around here," Willow says, half to herself.

I ignore her and move on to the fourth. "Blocking will be used only to protect one's Tragedy or under supervision in training." I look up from the book. "Should I even ask?"

"You'll learn all about that one in training." At my questioning expression, she adds, "We can't send you dimwits out there blindly."

Biting my tongue, I turn to the last page. "The Schedulers have outdone themselves."

Willow twirls a frizzy dreadlock. "Just read it."

"Satellites must allow themselves to separate from their pasts." I stare at the page. "What do they mean by 'allow'?" I ask evenly.

"The quicker you accept your new life, the easier you will transition. You've gotta let go of your past, kid."

I can't look away from the words. "And if I don't let go?"

"Fighting it will only slow the inevitable," she says quietly.

I inwardly rebel. The Schedulers may have cut my life short, but they won't get my memories without a fight. Keeping my expression level, I look up and follow Willow's eyes to her unusual watch. She catches me staring.

"It's a calimeter." She extends her arm toward me.

Regardless of what it's called, it's impressive. The oval face fits inside a thick leather strap. A silver disk floats above a gold disk, and a tiny triangle is cut into the edge of each circle.

"You'll receive your own with your first assignment.

The discs move in opposition. When the notches are aligned, it signals the beginning of break." She pauses. "We do get breaks around here, kid."

"And that's a good idea? Leaving all those Tragedies unprotected?" I can't believe the conversations I'm having.

Her arm muscles sharpen when she stretches. "There's a lapse that occurs—a sort of time warp. Anyone on Earth within an eighth-mile radius of a Tragedy freezes while we break. Anyone not frozen who stumbles into the radius will freeze, too. Our break is two hours, but in Earth time, it's just seconds. There's one break cycle per day. It's plenty of time to rejuvenate your mind."

Now I'm laughing. "What are you—some kind of New Ager or something?"

Willow yanks an orange pillow off the chair beside us and launches it at me. "Honestly, you have to be the most irksome person ever!"

"Funny, I was thinking the same thing about you."

Her mood lightens. "Come on, kid. I'll show you around Benson and introduce you to the crew. You have the distinct honor of hanging with me, which is sure to make you überpopular."

"That's doubtful," I mumble.

Her elbow meets my ribs, and the playful gesture brings bittersweet thoughts of Tate to mind. My sudden attitude change doesn't go unnoticed by Willow.

"Let it go, kid." Her voice carries a warning that infuriates me, and I glare at her in defiance. "Understood?"

I swallow and push myself up from the sofa. "Yeah,

I got it," I spit back in a tone that matches hers.

Willow's fist hits my cheek and I stumble backward.

"What was that for!" I yell, shocked that someone so tiny could knock me off balance. Plus, aren't girls suppose to slap? Fitting, I guess, since nothing about this chick screams *girl*.

She drops her arm. "I'm not kidding. Let it go."

"It's none of your business." I rub my jaw as I head for the door.

"Don't walk away from me! If your head is not in this game, everyone loses. As your Legacy, I'm not willing to have that on my conscience."

"Oh, well, in that case…I wouldn't want to go messing with your conscience or anything," I sneer, twisting the doorknob.

"Would you want someone in your condition guarding Tate?"

My fingers fall from the knob. On one hand, I get Willow's point, but on the other, much heavier hand, I'm not capable of letting Tate go. Not yet. No—not ever. The thought of such emptiness brings me to my knees.

"I can't do it," I whisper, not even caring that my hands are trembling. "I can't be without her."

Willow's suddenly on the floor beside me. "I know this is difficult. Trust me, I get that. But I need you to promise you'll try."

I pause for a long time, and then shake my head. "I'll think about trying. It's the best I can do. I'm sorry."

"You have no idea how important your decisions

ahead will be. If a distraction causes you to falter, even once, the results could be devastating." She keeps her eyes on me and stands. "Come on, let's see what's cooking in Benson," she says, pulling me up by my arm.

My hand rubs along my jaw. "You've got some uppercut."

"You're not going to whine about that for the rest of the day, are you? We heal three hundred times faster than when we were human, so that means"—she looks up at the ceiling, mentally calculating—"you shouldn't even feel it anymore."

I continue rubbing, hating that she's right. It doesn't hurt at all.

She uses her toes to flip over one of the dingy purple flip-flops by the door. "You should be thanking me. I think I made an improvement to that pretty-boy face of yours."

"You are such a flake."

She misinterprets this as a compliment. With both feet shoved into her beach shoes, she digs through the contents of a brown corduroy bag before lifting the strap over her head and across her short body. Then she throws a green backpack at me.

"Where'd this come from?" I examine the familiar frayed bag.

"I'm guessing your house."

"How did it get here?"

"Must have followed you," she jokes. "Convenient, huh?"

"No, seriously."

"I am serious. You're going to need a bag for your stuff.

You should have some clothes in the hall closet as well." She pulls her collection of dreads into a ponytail while I stare at my bag in confusion. "Just put your rulebook in there and let's go already."

I do as she says, following her out the door and down the copper hall. The elevator opens the instant she touches the button. We're delivered to the ground floor at a speed not quite as fast as my ride up.

"Have a fabulous day," GPS Jeanette pipes after us.

"What's with the birds?" I ask when we pass by the three doorways on the far side of the lobby.

"You mean in Alogan?" She pauses. "That's the room you were in with Jonathan," she explains, reading my puzzled expression.

"Oh, right. The birds?"

"Scarlet tanagers. Beautiful, aren't they?"

"They're loud. I bet they leave one heck of a mess."

She snickers. "You have a lot to learn about this place. On Earth, they're secretive and prefer flying high in the canopies, out of sight. Here, they don't have to hide."

"I still say they're loud."

"They're not nearly as annoying as some people I've met."

I bite my bottom lip to keep my grin from escaping.

The smell of something baking—cookies, maybe?—fills the air as Willow leads me through a forty-five degree opening off the corner of the lobby. *Benson*, written in various shades of earth-toned glass, spans the length of both walls. The stone floor is similar to my parents' patio back home—the one I single-handedly installed with Tate serving as "foreman." These tiles, however, are easily five times larger and must have been a nightmare to install.

Through each of the four archways, the weathered plank floor goes on forever, but the noodle rugs and leather furniture make the extensive space welcoming. The smell of food is so overwhelming that my mouth waters, even though I'm not the least bit hungry.

I stop and stare at the hundreds of iron-and-glass lanterns overhead, all scaled proportionately to the massive room. My mouth hangs open. "Are those floating?" I finally ask.

"Mmm-hmm," Willow replies from a distance.

I pull my eyes from the ceiling and jog around the fireplace before snaking through a maze of curvy wood tables.

"So this is Heaven, right?" I say when I catch up to her.

She keeps walking. "Progression, actually. Thousands of bases are spread over the Earth, grouped by languages and regions. This is the American English base, obviously."

"Obviously," I mutter, but Willow ignores me.

"It does seem perfect, doesn't it?" She looks around as if seeing it for the first time. "Don't be fooled by the extravagance. Appearances can be deceiving. A Satellite's job is difficult. Remind me to teach you coding after break."

"Teach me what?"

"Coding. It's the closest thing we've got to sleep. It's kind of like meditation."

"We don't sleep?"

She shakes her head. "No, we code."

I do my best not to laugh, thinking of my mom's "find the cure" phase. I quickly explain to Willow that a "doctor" once recommended that I burn incense in addition to meditation, since meditation alone wasn't working (big surprise). When I declared at the follow-up visit that the incense smelled like cat urine, Tate replied with an elbow jab to the ribs. Yes—Tate, too, insisted on subjecting me to nonsense remedies.

"I hope you're not a fan of incense," I say to Willow, as straight-faced as I can muster.

"Don't be a hater." She measures me for a few seconds before adding, "But please tell me you didn't think meditation would cure your cancer."

"Hey, it wasn't my idea."

She cracks up. "I can assure you, the point of coding isn't to 'cure' anything. It's to put you in a balanced state of mind, to help you cope with the job stress." She sits at one of the larger tables, far enough over that we can see three of the four entryways around the fireplace.

I hop in a heavy chair beside hers and search the awed faces entering for Anna and Rigby. The redhead who caught Rigby's attention earlier glances in our direction before sitting with another girl a few tables over.

Willow leans forward, putting her chin on her laced fingers. "Here come the little stunners."

My fingers drum nervously on the smooth table and the muffled hum grows until...holy mother! Someone opened the floodgates!

In seconds, the entries and seating areas are hidden by a sea of bodies washing over them. A group of steroid-heads pushes to the front, laughing and hurdling over the chairs and sofas. They race to the back of the room and disappear through a doorway in the corner.

Willow follows my stare. "Wanna eat?"

"I'm not really hungry," I say, bringing my attention back to the table.

"You'll never be hungry. You're dead, remember? Food is just a comfort from our human life. Oh, and bonus— calories don't count!" she mocks.

Ugh, I hope she's not one of those girls. One of the (many) things I love about Tate is that she's never been overly consumed with her weight and appearance. Ironically, the few parts of her body she was unhappy with were the ones I loved the most.

"So what'll it be, kid? You wanna eat or what?"

Whatever. "Might as well check out the grub."

"Trust me, one look at the spread and you won't be calling it grub."

Willow's right. When we enter the back room, I have to pull my jaw off the floor for the umpteenth time today. The food spread is even more impressive than the picturesque mountains and 200-foot tall pine trees visible beyond the back glass wall. Some of the foods are so vibrant I actually have to squint. Upon closer examination, I realize that for every steak, casserole, or doughnut, there's a not-so-appetizing choice. I turn away from the raw seafood and slimy things and go to the more appealing things like bread and—

Stew!

I beeline to the scent and grab one of the red ceramic bowls.

Willow appears from nowhere. "So that one's yours, huh?"

The ladle in my hand freezes over the venison stew. "Huh?"

"Everyone brings a food with them. Family recipe?"

I nod in shock, and my mouth is unhinged again. "Uh, my mom's."

"Well, let's give it a shot and see how they did."

After filling my bowl, I add lasagna, a brownie, and some chicken wings to my tray. "So let me get this straight. All this food is from other Satellites?"

"Yep. Studies done centuries ago found that we benefit from a little taste of home." She winks at me. "Stew and coding—they'll be your two favorite things."

I continue piling a little of everything on my tray. "Which food's yours?"

"The lime Jell-O."

Of all the food in the world, her favorite is lime Jell-O? I shake my head. "You are such a weirdo."

She ignores my comment and pulls me across the room. A bowl of jiggly green squares appears on my already full tray. Still, I succeed in adding a roll, a can of Coke, and a piece of cheesecake onto it. No one would ever know that I wasn't the least bit hungry.

"How'd you know mine was the stew?" I ask on the way back to the table.

Willow adds even more bounce to her step; it's obvious that she's enjoying herself. "New Satellites are so predictable."

Our table made some friends while we were away. Two guys and a girl stare at me as I sit down.

"Who's your pet?" a guy with an English accent asks Willow. He pushes a hand through his dirty-blond hair and looks sour faced at my overflowing tray.

"Grant." I match his glare and quickly add, "I thought this was the American base."

"Liam," he finally says, smirking. "British transplant to the States when I was thirteen. How are you fancying Progression?"

The others relax and he flashes a wider grin, compliments of a good orthodontist.

"The food looks great, but I got paired with this nutcase." I point my thumb at Willow. "Is there any way to trade up in this Legacy program?"

"You're gonna wish. She's raving mad, that one. Looks like you pulled the short straw."

Willow chimes in. "Liam, you could only wish you had a rock star like me as your Legacy."

The blonde girl at the table clears her throat; her wide, clear-blue eyes are fixed on me. She's supermodel hot, but much too thin. "I'm Clara," she says in a quiet voice.

"Hi." I lean over the table and shake her hand, which is child-sized inside mine. "Nice to meet you."

Her eyes dart down, and her green turtleneck compliments the blush on her light skin. Her polished, stick-straight hair is a stark contrast to Tate's reddish-brown, unruly hair, but her lips are glossy like Tate's always were.

Willow continues with the introductions. "Grant, this is Owen. Owen, Grant."

"What's up, man?" Owen says to my nod. He looks and acts so much like an excited dog I'm afraid he might pee down his own leg. His plastic-looking hair, black as oil, is flattened against his head. His eyes are not deep-set like mine, but they are the same generic brown shared by half the world. "Don't worry about remembering names. It took me months to learn them all," he says, still pumping my hand up and down.

"Good to know. How long have you been here?" I ask, jerking my hand out of his.

"Sixty-three years," Owen says.

I cough back my shock. "How old are you?"

"You mean how old was I when I died?"

"Uh…?" I shake my head and look at the others, who offer no help.

"Thirty-one, but I'm physically twenty."

I cock my head in confusion.

"I was thirty-one when I died. I reverted to twenty when I got to Progression," he states simply, as though I've just asked him about the weather.

Willow jumps in. "Our bodies reflect our best physical form, which typically falls somewhere in the late teens or early twenties."

"Unless you're a bloody decrepit like Wilhelmina here," Liam says, carelessly juggling a Matchbox car.

I choke on my drink. "What did he call you?" I ask

Willow.

She tsks. "Ignore Liam. He died way too early."

"Seriously, Willow. Case in point—you still use the word 'groovy'," Liam says.

She shrugs. "What can I say? I'm forever a product of my generation."

"Yeah, except for your dreads and tats." Liam gives me a sympathetic look. "Willow was influenced by the grunge scene of the nineties. But I guess the clothes are better than the eighties garbage she used to wear."

"Aren't we supposed to be just souls when we die?" I shift uncomfortably when the others laugh at my question.

"It'd be tough to do much without a body, mate," Liam says, mocking me.

Willow shoots him a dark look. "Our bodies give us a sense of normalcy, making the transition to Satellite smoother." Willow puts her hand on my chest for a second. "Even our hearts beat. I'm particularly fond of that detail."

"And who wouldn't want all this?" Owen flexes a meaty arm at Clara. From her response, that kind of humor is not Clara's bag.

"Having our physical bodies means we can still feel pain, but we heal quickly, as you've already experienced," Willow says.

"He just got here. What could he have possibly experienced already?" Liam asks.

"I punched him," Willow states flatly.

The others roar with laughter. Could Willow be more irritating?

"The exhaustion—don't forget about that one," Owen adds, after the hyenas have settled down.

Willow nods. "Right. We get tired, too."

Still trying to make sense of the age thing, I ask Willow, "How old are you?"

"Twenty-seven." Her face brightens, and she pushes her chair back from the table. She raises her shirt high enough to reveal her tiny stomach. Before I can stop it, my face cringes at the white vertical lines marring her skin.

Liam smirks at me. "Not hungry anymore, are you?"

Willow's still smiling. "Haven't you seen stretch marks before, kid? They're from my baby girl."

I continue to stare at her bare stomach, horrified. "Did she try to claw her way out?"

Willow howls with laughter and rubs her hand across the white scars. "I love them. They're one of the only reminders I have of my daughter." She pulls her shirt down and hops her chair back to the table. "And as you'll soon see, they haven't affected my strength one bit."

"How old are you?" Clara asks me in a small voice. Her blue eyes dart back to the table after briefly meeting mine.

"Eighteen." I shock myself with my immediate response. That explains my disease-free body. I was diagnosed at twenty-one, six months before I was supposed to marry Tate.

"You're just a pup!" Owen says.

"The bloke's barely old enough to vote," Liam adds.

They are nowhere near as funny as they think they are. "This comedy show sucks," I complain.

"How about a gun show, then?" Owen flexes his arm again.

"Ha! More like freak show."

"Says the tatted girl with the dreads," Liam replies. "Grant, don't sweat it about being so young. Looks like Clara finds you pretty fit. You two could be the next Ken and Barbie."

"Liam!" Clara turns tomato red. She clears her throat and regains her composure. "You're only nineteen, so you don't have much room to talk."

He was kidding, I remind myself, and unclench my fists. *I can't imagine being with anyone else...* Stop! Don't even think it.

I focus on my food, which is as delicious as it looks. The hot stew is a perfect match to my mom's, and I'm scraping the bottom of the bowl too soon, not caring in the least about the heat burning my throat. Owen distracts me from going back for more by teaching me a card game called "Sats." The game is similar to Spades, and Liam is, by far, the best player at the table.

I'm picking the eight of diamonds out of my hand when Liam announces, "Catch you cats on the flip."

When I look up from my cards, Liam's gone. I look around, wondering how he made his escape so fast.

Clara looks at her wrist and touches the tiny oval on her beaded bracelet. "Nice to meet you, Grant." She blushes and slings on a gold bag as big as her before mumbling something under her breath. Then she vanishes. Literally. Into thin air, like a frigging magician.

I squeeze my eyes closed to clear the deception. When I open them, Owen forms a gun with his hand and playfully shoots me before vanishing as well. Around the room, others vaporize the same way, minus the gun gesture.

"That's our cue, kid. May as well get a jump on some coding," Willow says.

"Where'd they go?" I ask, after putting my eyes back in my head.

"I'll explain on the way." She stands and pushes her feet into her flip-flops. I grab my tray from the table, impressed that I ate everything but one chicken wing.

"Don't bother." As soon as Willow says this, my tray is gone, along with all the other trays on our table.

"What happened to everyone?"

"Break's over. They went back to their assignments." Probably noticing that I'm losing patience, she elaborates. "It's called displacing. It's how we travel to our assignments. You'll learn all about it in training."

"What's it feel like?"

"It's a major rush," she says in a no-big-deal kind of way.

She isn't paying attention to my inquisitive look. "And my tray?"

She flips her yarnlike hair over her shoulder. "It's Progression, kid."

I follow her out of the room, which is now—conveniently—as clean as when we arrived, and I wonder aloud how two hours could have passed already.

Just steps into her room, Willow returns to bare feet and then disappears at the end of the short hallway. "You coming or what?" she shouts.

I follow her voice into a small doorless room. This is not looking good.

"Clearly you're super stoked. Please, try to control your enthusiasm." She's already settled on one of the two black mats like she's either about to meditate or do yoga.

I cross the hardwood floor to reach her. "I would have never guessed you were a ballerina," I joke, sitting on the other thin mat. The only thing missing in the empty room is a ballet bar along the mirrored wall.

Willow ignores me.

I freeze on my reflection. It's as if the past year never happened—like my brown eyebrows and messy hair had never fallen out and my skin had never looked like ash.

"The purpose of coding is to find serenity by disconnecting from your physical body," Willow says while I flex my arm in the mirror to confirm that my muscles are really back. "Come on, kid, stay with me here. Close your eyes and imagine your perfect place, thing, or smell—anything that will help you relax."

When I realize she's being serious, I squeeze my eyes shut and then laugh.

Willow stands and smacks the back of my head. "Come on!"

"I'm sorry. You have to admit, this is stupid."

"Show a little effort. This is no walk in the park for me, either," she snaps.

To shut her up (because this is absurd), I close my eyes and think of Tate—of the way we used to lay together on my bed and talk for hours. Soon I can picture my arms folded around her perfect curves and her head on my chest. I'm twirling one of her curls around my finger. After another minute, I can even smell her shampoo and feel her finger mindlessly doodling designs on my defined abs.

She lifts her head and the sunlight streams through the window, making her wild hair glow red. I trace my index finger down her cheekbone to her full, soft lips. She playfully nips my fingernail before stretching to kiss me. Her tongue moves with mine in the same dance we've done thousands of times before.

She pulls back and I bite my bottom lip, tasting peppermint. Her hazel eyes darken to smoldering when she stares back at me. She's more stunning than ever. I cling to her and bring her lips back to mine, but when she gives in, the kiss is rushed, urgent.

I try to grab for her when she pulls away, but my arms won't work. "No," I whisper, but no sound comes. I can't move; I can't breathe.

"Why did you leave me?" Tate's raspy voice floors me and my eyes pop open instead of my mouth.

"What's wrong?" Willow asks, quickly looking me over. I claw at my chest and gasp for air.

"Grant, answer me!" Willow shouts two inches from my face.

"What happened?" I pant. My muscles sting when I reach up to wipe the sweat from my forehead.

"You tell me! You blanked forever. I couldn't wake you up."

No, she's wrong. It was just minutes.

"Where'd you go?" she asks.

"I was with Tate." I scrub my face despite the torturous pain the movement sends through my arms. After a long silence, I look through my fingers to be sure Willow is still in the room and find her glaring at me. "Hey, you said to choose a place of peace!"

The red in her face dulls a little and she turns away. "Certainly your memories are fading by now," she says, but not really to me.

"Willow, I don't think that was a memory," I answer quietly.

She turns around. "What do you mean?"

"Tate…talked to me."

Willow locks her eyes on mine. "What did she say?"

I don't answer. I should have kept my mouth shut five seconds ago.

"What did she say?" Willow demands.

"She asked why I left her."

Willow turns away too fast for me to gauge her reaction, then paces the room and chews her thumbnail down to nothing.

"What's happening?" I finally ask.

She stops and looks up at me, shaking her head. "I don't know. Whatever it is, I don't think it's good."

3. Use that great charm to make some friends, Casanova

I zone on a sofa stain to keep still because my muscles remain ticked off at me. "Are you sure you're all right?" I ask Willow after hearing the dishes clink even more loudly in the kitchen.

"I said I'm fine." Like Tate, she's a horrible liar. If I wasn't so uneasy about what just happened, it would be comical seeing Willow so scattered.

She finally walks into the living room, holding two mugs. I take one from her and she sits on the other side of the sofa, her hand curled around her cup like she's cold, which is absurd here in Perfectland.

"OK, kid, here's the deal. What happened in there"—she nods down the hall, toward the coding room—"keep your trap shut about it. Got it?"

"Fine by me." I take a drink and wince. "Blech!"

"Sorry. I needed something strong."

"Well, this should do it. This could thin paint." I wipe my lip and set the mug of poison on the trunk. Willow stares at the floor.

"So I failed miserably at coding, huh?" I ask to break the

the silence.

"You could say that." She lifts her eyes. "What happened in there was just a forgotten memory."

She's wrong. In fact, my memory feels sharper than ever. But no way am I going to share that with Willow.

"We're going to take a few days off from coding. Just stick to the stew, OK?"

I cross my ankle over my knee, fidget with my bootlaces, and nod.

"I'm heading to Programming. You can hang out here or down in Benson. Other Legacies will be in Programming, too, so there's bound to be some newbies around. Use that great charm to make some friends, Casanova. You'll need the camaraderie once you start your assignment." Willow pats my leg before pushing herself up. I twist to look over the back of the sofa, watching her walk slower than usual into the kitchen to pour another cup of battery acid.

When she's almost to the door, her free hand claps against her forehead. "Shoot, I almost forgot. Viscal. I actually won't be seeing you for a few days."

"Viscal?"

She pulls her gaze from the ceiling. "Twice a year we spend three days in Viscal with our loved ones. You don't get to partake in the festivities until you've got five years under your belt."

"Our loved ones?" I ask, feeling hopeful.

"Our dead loved ones."

"Oh." Certainly she heard my heart hit my stomach. "But if you've forgotten your memories, then how...?"

"When people from your life die, your memories resurface automatically. If they're already dead, you won't lose them at all."

Grandpa. My mind quickly compares my memories of him with my memories of Tate. They're equally strong. I try to downplay my relief, though I'm not sure if I succeed. "What about Programming? I mean, what's the point if your memories return on their own?"

"Lots of events happened in our lives that we forgot even before we died—things from when we were very young, memories of that sort. Programming brings back everything." Willow gets quieter. "When you're about to be reunited with someone, Programming brings back memories of that person in advance. This allows us a little time to adjust, I guess." She fiddles with a charm at the end of a dreadlock.

"What happens to the Tragedies while you're away?" I ask, because she's clearly uncomfortable with the Programming subject.

"Same as break. Time stops for everyone within an eighth-mile radius of a Tragedy. Again, it's the time-warp thing—three days for us, less than a minute for them."

"Is three days enough time in Viscal?"

"Plenty. Trust me. Seventy-two hours is substantial when you're not sleeping through any of it." She rummages through her bag, and then slings the strap over her shoulder. "We're all usually ready to get back to our assignments, or at least our routines, after so much time away. If you get bored, feel free to clean the place up. It'll be yours soon."

She's out the door before I can argue.

Great. Just what I wanted: Willow's hippy lair. First thing to go is the sofa. That I can guarantee.

In the kitchen, I watch my coffee cyclone down the drain. I dump the remaining toxin from the coffeepot as well, surprised that it doesn't eat through the red finish on the sink.

What the heck am I supposed to do now?

I walk past the sofa for a better look at the built-in bookcase. My hand traces over the remarkable craftsmanship of the ornate wood, searching for just one puttied hole. I can't find any, of course, not even on the undersides of the shelves or hidden behind the multiple picture frames.

Housed in a Popsicle-stick frame is a photo of Willow. The blonde girl she's standing with has such sharp features she may as well be sculpted from ice. One shelf down, in a shiny silver frame, the same blonde girl poses next to a surfer guy. All he's missing is a stripe of sunblock down his dirt-brown nose. And to think, I was the one who got skin cancer.

I wade through the sea of faces, stretching to reach a buried frame on the lowest shelf, and my throat tightens. It's exactly the same as I remember, but the picture of Tate and me is gone. A white square fills the photo insert area instead. Gracing the black wooden frame are Tate's metallic-silver stick people (which she declared were her and me) standing under a sun; the rest of the frame is decorated with Tate's silver doodles. I trace over her handwriting—*Love and a Little Sunscreen*. The joke doesn't seem so funny anymore.

Tate made sure the frame was with me while I was doing time in the hospital. Once, I hid it from her as a joke, but of course she found it. The frame was waiting for me in the sterile room I returned to after treatment. I'd had a particularly bad reaction to the chemo that day. I never told her having it there made me feel better. Why hadn't I ever told her?

The pain in my chest is like a tightening fist around my heart. A high-pitched ringing fills my ears, and the walls shrink. The frame drops back to the lower shelf when I dig my fingers into the bookshelf for support.

I don't remember leaving the room, but I'm already in the elevator, using the wall to keep myself upright. I punch the *L* button and the doors close on two pairs of wide eyes staring at me like I'm a madman. Their assumption is probably not too far off.

Downstairs, I stumble out of the elevator and lean against the hard marble. My chest rises and falls until the pressure finally dissipates. When my dinner no longer threatens to make an appearance, I cross the lobby to Benson.

A few people are scattered around the enormous eating hall, but nothing compared to the earlier crowd. Apparently, the Satellites are all busy saving the world. My posture straightens when I see Anna. Alone, she's curled in one of the leather chairs close to the fireplace.

"Hey Anna," I say when I reach her.

After she jumps, her expression brightens. "You scared me! How's it going?"

"OK, considering." I fall into the chair beside hers.

"Oh my gosh, I know. Isn't this a lot to take in?" She looks around and combs her fingers through her dark ponytail.

"That's stating it mildly." I watch three people enter and sit at one of the tables in the middle of the room.

"It's good to see you. I know we've just met, but you remind me of my brother." Anna bites her lower lip. "I've been trying to recall my last conversation with him. We were fighting…" She pauses, thinking. "And I can't remember if we made up." Her eyes bore into mine like she'll find the answer in them.

I have no idea what to say, but want to make her feel better. Strange, considering I hardly know her. "I'm sorry about your brother. I'm sure he knows how much you love him," I reply awkwardly. "Feeling talk" has never been my thing.

"Jordan explained the memory loss, and I get that it's necessary, but it's just so frustrating."

Rigby appears in one of the doorways, and I nod to him. The faded motorcycle on his black T-shirt distorts across his chest, making him look even bigger than before. Add to that his crew cut and the guy may as well have just walked off a military base. He strides over and plops into an empty chair.

After I introduce him to Anna, he pulls the ever-present toothpick from his mouth. "Crazy place, huh?"

Anna and I agree.

"How are you guys adjusting to your memory loss?" Anna asks.

"It sucks," Rigby says.

Odd. My memories still feel strong. "I'm not so bad.

Maybe you should try to hang on a little harder," I suggest.

"Dude, there's nothing left to hang on to." Rigby's obviously deflated. He rolls his toothpick between his thumb and index finger.

"I've been trying." Anna gives a discouraged huff and fidgets with the cuff of her sweater. "How are your Legacies?"

I roll my eyes. "Willow's a lunatic. We couldn't be more opposite."

"Huh. She's got to be better than mine," Rigby says. "Shane's a techie. Computers are all he talks about. I have a few choice places he can shove his terabyte. His throat, for starters, to shut him up."

"Don't hold back," I joke.

He shakes his head. "He's annoying as all get-out, man."

"Funny, I thought the same thing about Jordan. Except the shoving part. Seriously, Rigby, that's harsh," Anna remarks with disapproval. "Jordan's kind of a loose cannon, but I'm learning a lot about this place. He says we'll be getting our assignments soon."

"But we're not ready, are we?" I ask.

They both shrug. At least we're all bobbing in the same ocean of the unknown. Though maybe drowning is a better word.

We sit for a long time while the fire crackles. I study my hand, amazed that I can make a strong fist again.

"Any luck with coding?" Anna asks a while later. I lift my head and rub my palms nervously along my thigh.

"Yeah. It's wild," Rigby says.

"How about you?" Anna directs to me. Not knowing how much I'm allowed to share, I shake my head.

"Oh, thank goodness! I mean, I'm glad I'm not the only one."

I sit up straighter, hopeful that maybe she had a similar experience.

"I just can't let myself go. I've tried to find my 'happy place,'" she makes mock quotations, "but my head won't clear. I'm trying so hard to hang on to my memories, I just can't relax. You get it, right? I mean, that's why you can't code, either?"

I work to keep my face even. "Pretty much." I hate lying to her. "Did you guys try the food yet?"

"Yes! It's amazing, right?" Anna's obvious enthusiasm tells me crisis averted.

"It's definitely that," I agree.

"What'd you guys bring?" Rigby asks.

"Deer stew," I say.

"Gross!" Anna wrinkles her nose, and the image of my mom pops into my head. *Try this*, Mom would say, leaning over the stove, making me take a taste from the community spoon.

I snap back to reality because the memory of my mom lends itself to missing her, and my heart begins hurting more than I can bear.

"—with my dad on the road all week," Anna is saying, "and every Sunday we'd have fried chicken." She pauses, deep in thought. "It's funny, I can still remember some things so clearly, but not any actual conversations."

Rigby huffs. "Consider yourself lucky. I'm completely blank. I brought boiled peanuts."

"If you're blank, how can you remember which food is yours?" I ask.

He looks confused and then shrugs. "I have no idea. I just know, which sounds ridiculous, I'm sure. The peanuts are phenomenal, by the way. Even better than I remember." He cracks up, but I find his joke more scary than humorous.

"You seriously can't remember anything?" I ask.

He shakes his head and bites harder on his toothpick. "Apparently I win the amnesia award."

Anna tries to console him. "If it's any reassurance, I think it's completely normal."

"I don't get how it works. Willow still remembers having a husband and daughter."

"Jordan says each person's memories vary," Anna explains. "Some retain names, even conversations or memories of certain events, while others may not remember anything at all."

"Doesn't sound fair, if you ask me. I wonder if anyone ever remembers more than that," I say.

"Sounds like that's as good as it gets. It does kinda makes sense. We're not going to be very good Satellites if we're distracted by our past."

I lean back, crossing my arms. Anna's way too indifferent about this whole mess. "But it's part of who we are. Who will we be if we lose that?" I'll be just Grant—without Tate. This scares me beyond words.

"Satellites. Hope you enjoy your new life."

Unlike me, Anna finds humor in Rigby's statement. I, on the other hand, keep my mouth shut. I don't want to be a Satellite.

In the ensuing silence, I lean my head back and mull over the floating lanterns. From an engineering standpoint, there must be an explanation, but it goes beyond my construction knowledge.

A muffled hum comes from the corridor. "Sounds like it's break again," Anna says.

Already? I pull my eyes from the ceiling and watch the doorways. In no time, the hall is filled with people.

"Hey, Owen!" I yell. The blushing Clara is with him, and together they push through the crowd.

"How's it going?" Owen asks. His eyes become rounder when he sees Anna. He turns back to me, looking again like a dog, but this time he's waiting impatiently for the ball to be thrown. I introduce him to Anna before he licks her face.

"It's a pleasure to make your acquaintance," Owen says to her.

Is this guy for real? He's transformed into a goofy, smirking clown.

"Nice to meet you," Anna replies.

Clara breaks their weird connection by shaking hands with Anna. When Clara looks back at me, her pale cheeks turn red. I use the opportunity to shift Clara's attention off me by introducing her to Rigby. Rigby's whole demeanor changes and his upbeat vibe tells me he finds her attractive, but he plays it much cooler than Owen.

"I saw you in here earlier with Jordan. How's that

going?" Owen asks Anna. He pets the top of his hair like he's fixing it, despite the fact that the black plastic wouldn't move in a hurricane.

"We certainly have our…differences," Anna replies diplomatically.

"Ah, such is the life of a Legacy. I dread the day. Don't worry—nobody likes their Legacies. Jordan's cool once you get to know him."

"We have nothing in common," Anna admits.

"That's the point. You're paired with your opposite so you won't be distracted by common interests," Owen says.

"That explains a lot," Rigby scoffs, kicking at the rug.

"Who'd you get?" Owen asks.

"Shane."

"Techie Shane?" Owen asks in disbelief.

Rigby's desolate expression answers the question.

"Dude, tough luck!" Owen sympathizes.

"Tell me about it."

"Well, try to cut them some slack. Even Shane," Owen hesitantly adds. "It's a tough job being a Legacy."

Rigby looks doubtful.

"Seriously, it is. On top of training new recruits, Legacies are soon to be reunited with someone they probably don't remember. Plus, their lives as Satellites are about to end, which is major suck city."

"Why would that suck?" Anna questions.

"Because being a Satellite is hardcore! I hope I'm lucky enough to be a Lifer."

"A what?" Rigby asks, biting on a new toothpick.

"A Satellite who never has to give this up. One of the lucky few who gets to be in it for eternity."

"I'm guessing there's no significant other from your past?" I ask Owen.

"No way, man. I'm not a fan of being tied down. Yet," he adds, his eyes glued back on Anna. "What about you? Any significant other?" he asks her, sounding hopeful.

She shakes her head.

"Really?" Owen almost yells.

Anna smoothes her ponytail with her hand. "None that I remember."

"Where's Liam?" I ask Clara, trying not to vomit.

"Not sure. I saw him in the lobby and he looked bad."

"Dude, he was a hot mess!" Owen adds. "Rough day in the field, probably. I'd guess he's doing some serious coding right now."

"Do Satellites have a lot of rough days?"

Owen misses Anna's worried tone and shrugs dismissively. "Sometimes. A bad day for a Tragedy equals an exhausting day for us. Anyone wanna eat?"

"I hear the chicken is phenomenal," I say.

Owen perks up excitedly. "Fried chicken?"

"That's the rumor." I wink at Anna.

"Sweet! I've been craving that since Pete left."

"Why?" I ask.

"Dude, when you go, so does your food."

I think of the vast food selection. Thousands of other Satellites must be here. All of whom are in Benson today, by the noise level.

Despite a lack of appetite, my mouth waters when we reach the buffet. I grab two pieces of chicken, stew, and a handful of boiled peanuts. By the time we're walking out the door, my overflowing tray includes an iced tea, manicotti, a biscuit, chocolate cake, and—at Owen's suggestion—some kind of dessert that looks like mud. Did I mention I wasn't hungry?

We sit at one of the smaller tables. Owen only looks away from Anna when he needs to pick up a new piece of food. He inhales the chicken like a savage until finally he's licking the bones and then his fingers. Though the chicken is fantastic, as is everything else (besides the peanuts, that is—those are seriously gross), Owen states this to Anna twenty-three times. I know. I count.

The comfortable conversation puts me at ease. Making friends was never my strong suit, and that's an overstatement. Aside from playing football, which my father strictly limited to practice and games only, I didn't interact much with the kids at school. Even during the season, I kept to myself. Some of the players tried to befriend me—whether out of sincerity or because I was one of the better players, I don't know—and I was never a jerk when declining their invites to hang out, but I just didn't see the point. While they were out partying every weekend, my free time was consumed by working for Bradley Construction. Until I met Tate, that is. Much to my dad's dismay, becoming a carpenter got pushed down a notch on my list of priorities. "You're wasting your talent," he'd said. He would have changed his mind if he'd taken the time to really get to know Tate.

Clara, Owen, and Anna are talking about things they remember from their life—favorite movies and food, what their parents looked like. Rigby and I stay silent, but for very different reasons.

"Why isn't everyone's clothing dated?" I ask when Clara is finished talking about some eighties' fashion trend.

Excitement fills Clara's face. "Willow didn't tell you the best part? We get new clothes whenever we want. Anything!"

Anna squeals. Apparently, she's the only other person at the table who gets it.

"Our assignments allow us to keep updated on all the latest fashions," Clara says, just like an infomercial host. I can't help but overhear Clara explain to Anna that she just needs to speak into her closet whenever she wants new clothing.

I shoot Owen a look that says, *Seriously?*

"Dude, I know. They're all crazy." He circles his ear with his finger. "If you don't put in any requests, your closet will be filled with your usual threads."

"Thank goodness," I say in relief. The past few years, I'd been relying on Tate to dress me. She'd drag me to the store when she deemed my tattered clothes "inappropriate." Now shopping for her, that was worth the trip, especially during swimsuit season.

Liam interrupts our fashion conversation when he shows up wearing a half-tucked wrinkled shirt as purple as the circles under his eyes.

"Hey, Liam—this is Anna and Rigby," I say.

He flops into a seat across from me and stares down at the table without answering. Clara gives him a sympathetic look and then resumes gabbing with Anna about clothes and bags and whatever else girls talk about.

Liam fidgets and then pushes himself back up after only a minute. "I'm going to go code again." His voice is hollow and he slumps back out of the room.

This time Owen catches Anna's worried expression. "He'll be fine," he reassures her. He pulls a deck of cards from his bag. "I'll teach you and Rig Sats." He flashes what I assume is his happy face. "I taught Grant earlier, but don't worry about him. He sucks bad."

"Hey!" I rebuke him.

Owen shuffles the cards. "Dude, it's true. You're terrible."

"I just learned!"

"Then I suggest you practice some more," he says, dealing me in.

We play a few games, and I can tell I'm getting better. I lay down my winning hand just as Owen looks at his calimeter. A second later, Clara does the same.

"Viscal, here we come. See you guys in a few days." Owen winks at Anna, and then he and Clara join the herd exiting the room.

Anna pushes up from the table. "I'm going to go practice coding. I get the feeling it's rather important. See you guys later?"

Apparently stuck in Perfectland with my new BFFs, I say, "I'm sure you will."

Rigby nods his good-bye to Anna. After a few seconds, he says, "So, that Clara chick is pretty hot, huh?"

I barely hear him because watching Anna skip out of the room gives me an idea. What Willow doesn't know won't hurt her. "Yeah, sure," I answer. "Think I'm going to go practice coding, too, man. I'll catch you later."

In the elevator, adrenaline pumps through me at the possibility of seeing Tate again, even if it isn't real.

I beeline to the coding room to avoid catching even a glimpse of my frame. Sitting cross-legged on a mat, I close my eyes.

I visualize Tate how I remember her: warm and soft. I can see her in my head—piercing hazel eyes and unruly hair, a thin cotton shirt clinging to her. It doesn't feel real like before, though. I can't feel or smell her. She's just a frozen photograph in my mind.

After a deep breath, I try again.

Nothing but my imagination works, and the void in my chest grows impossibly bigger. I take a different approach and picture my bedroom instead—my bed, specifically—and my heart pounds in excitement and relief.

Tate traces along my torso, outlining muscles that have been absent for so long. I suck in the faint smell of peppermint. She looks up at me like before and holds my gaze. I memorize her heart-shaped face, as if I could ever forget it. Then she destroys me with a kiss. I want to freeze time, to stay with her forever. I silently plead to be given this one gift. I'll never ask for anything as long as I...I...

There's no bargaining left. I'm already dead.

Tate pulls away and bites her bottom lip. Her finger stops moving at my ribs, and her face contorts with a sadness

I've never seen before, not even when I was sick. Afraid of waking, I don't dare move, despite the pain from the invisible blade hacking my heart into pieces.

She crushes another kiss on me before her beautiful, soft mouth trails up my jaw. Goose bumps spread across my neck and arms from the heat of her breath.

"Please come back," she whispers when she reaches my ear, sending the chills into overdrive.

I open my mouth to tell her I'm here, but there's no sound. As if in a nightmare, I try vocalizing again and again, only to be met with infuriating silence.

"Grant, please. I need you," she begs, louder than before and sounding frightened.

My eyes fly open, and I'm back in a place that's more like Hell than Heaven.

4. *You're a stalker, is what you are*

When I finally stop panting, I take a minute to study my sweaty reflection in the mirror. I look exactly as I had in life—as of a year ago, anyway. Even the scar cutting through my eyebrow, a souvenir from a victorious football season, is unchanged. Still, I hardly recognize the person staring back at me. The best part of me is gone. I'm incomplete without Tate.

I ignore the pain in my muscles and dry my face on my sleeve. Everything about Tate was so real: her feel, her smell, her taste. Could my imagination have gone that far? Maybe Willow's right. Maybe forgetting is better—or, at the very least, necessary. At that traitorous thought, I shoot my reflection a narrow look and push myself up off the floor.

After trading my sweat-soaked clothes in the closet for some fresh duds, I hit up the kitchen for relief, concede that no amount of cold water splashed on my face will help, and turn to caffeine instead. As luck would have it, the fridge has been stocked with Coke. Go figure. Willow's going to love that.

Too exhausted to code again, I chug down the soda and opt for a change of scenery. My feet drag me to one of the empty pews in Alogan. A twinge of jealously tugs at me as the careless birds dart back and forth overhead. What I wouldn't give to soar happily with them, to be free from this emptiness in my chest. Tate's words, "I need you," play over in my head until the anxiety becomes unbearable. I'm helpless at a time when she needs my protection the most.

To stop thinking of Tate, I think of Tate's brother. Elliott was the only one who had truly accepted the reality that my life was going to end, though I doubt my death was any easier on him. We had viewed each other as brothers already, even though I hadn't married his older sister yet. Elliott had given me the greatest gift I could ask for under the circumstances: a promise that he would push Tate to move on after my death.

Part of me hoped that Elliott and Fischer (Tate's youngest brother) could keep Tate occupied enough to eventually forget me. A larger part of me feared that she would. Today, I was siding with the larger part.

Something I haven't thought about in years surfaces. The memory is sharp—maybe even sharper than it was before I died. I try not to get too excited, knowing my memories could still evaporate any minute.

Less than a month shy of graduation, I was working for the warden (a.k.a. my father), as I did every Saturday. If it had been up to my dear old dad, I would have dropped out of high school my senior year, just as he had done. "Eleventh grade is more than sufficient for a carpenter," he'd argued to my mother. That spring was the company's busiest and best yet, and with every other construction company in the area equally swamped, full-time bodies were hard to come by. He needed mine.

He was right, though it killed me to admit it. Without

question, I would take over my father's company someday, and what I was learning in class wasn't relevant on the job site. Even at seventeen, construction came as natural to me as breathing, and I had no qualms about hard work. I would have sided with my dad about dropping out, but agreeing with the old man publicly was something I could never bring myself to do. That would be conceding that the two of us were alike. No thanks.

Our nail guns had run out of ammo that humid Saturday. It was ninety degrees outside, an unseasonable temperature in April, even for Missouri. In true Midwest form, the spring was a wet one, meaning the house we were working on, along with every other job we had lined up, was behind schedule. I was the official chump nominated to restock the nails. Visiting a home improvement store on a Saturday was not my idea of a good time.

My already sweaty clothes were even nastier by the time I'd finished my shopping and was slamming the tailgate up. Like the doors, the tailgate loudly displayed *Bradley Construction* in bright red letters. Free advertising at its finest. I didn't complain; this vehicle was loads better than my own truck. *Was* being the key word. The AC had stopped working the week before, and the air circulating through the cab was thick enough to cut with a knife.

I pulled out of the contractors' bay, cursing the Mulch Loader Man moving at a snail's pace. My diesel truck was neither invisible nor silent, yet Mulch Loader's flatbed cart continued to hog the entire narrow lane. I saw the taillights of Tate's Jeep before I actually saw her. I slammed into reverse just as she slammed into my front fender. Mulch Loader Man looked up at the damage, wiped casually at his brow, and proceeded to load his purchase.

To say I was angry would be an understatement. Not only would it take me longer to get back to the site, now I had to explain a bashed fender. The first issue was enough to raise my dad's blood pressure; the second would give him a coronary.

I recognized Tate as soon as she jumped out of the Jeep. In almost four years together at Weldon Spring High School, we'd had only one class together, Introduction to Art, our freshman year. She stood out as the teacher's pet, and I, without a creative bone in my body, was only in the class to satisfy elective requirements. I watched every guy in our class gawk at her. I was not oblivious to her beauty, but I was much too introverted to be so blatant about my thoughts. Besides, what would a girl like her—who could have her pick of anyone—want with a guy like me? My family was not like the other wealthy families in the area and my future carpenter career would never afford to give her the kind of life she probably expected.

I had known Tate was different from the other pretty girls in school, though. Her personality actually matched her appearance, which made her even more appealing. In art class, she ignored the guys vying for her attention and, instead, befriended a strange and quiet girl who was the punchline of many bad jokes throughout our campus.

Assuming she came from a wealthy family, like most of the kids in our school, and figuring the Jeep was a birthday gift handed to her just for existing, I had forgotten all about the Tate from art class in that second after our bumpers met. "Are you mental?" I yelled, before I'd even shifted into park.

"Oh my gosh! I am so sorry!" she exclaimed, flustered. "You're not hurt, are you?"

Barely hearing her, I continued with my rant. "This is my frigging luck! Just give me your insurance information. I don't have time to deal with this," I snapped.

I followed Tate to her Jeep, where she ransacked the glove box, scribbled down her information, and apologized again. I snatched the paper from her and slammed my truck door before reversing out of the aisle, because Mulch Loader Man was moving unnervingly slower.

When I got back to the site, I forgot all about Tate when my old man broke his own yelling record and got creative with some new words. When he finally shut up, his curses were replaced by the stink eye. I tuned him out and sweated through the remainder of the long afternoon.

That night—starving, exhausted, and in desperate need of a shower—I pulled Tate's note out of my pocket. I stared at the damp paper and shook my head in disbelief. As if the obnoxious purple ink wasn't bad enough, the notepaper had a winking koala bear in the lower left corner. Below her insurance information, address, and phone number was a message asking me to please consider accepting a cash payment instead of turning the accident into insurance.

Before crushing the note in my fist, I checked my watch and decided eight o'clock was still an acceptable time to call. A woman's voice answered the phone, and I asked with all the politeness I could muster if Tatum was available.

Tate picked up a few seconds later. "Hello?"

"This is Grant Bradley. You hit my truck today." My voice was flat. Better than the alternative, which would've be a colorful cocktail of yelling and cursing. Like father, like son. Ugh. No, I was better than that. I could control myself. Usually.

"Oh my gosh! Grant, again, I am so sorry."

"So let me get this straight. You don't want me to turn this in?" I said.

"I have a decent amount in savings that should cover the damages, but if it's not enough, I could make up the difference in payments."

Maybe my reaction was because I was hungry and tired. Or maybe it was because I was so good at being a jerk. Whatever the reason, her response put me over the edge. "You think I'm a bank? Maybe your perfect world works that way, but I'm not one of your little rich friends who gets handouts just for breathing. I have to work for my money. Nice koala paper, by the way. What are you, five?" So I was a little dramatic. OK—a lot. But I was so steamed.

Tate surprised me with her rebuff. "Look, I'm on my parents' policy, and my dad just lost his job. The last thing I need is for their rates to go up because of me. And for your information, the paper is from my little brother. It's all I could find. You were obviously in a hurry, so I was trying to be quick. Forget it. Just turn it in to insurance."

I snapped my mouth closed and stared at the humming receiver. Having misjudged her, I redialed.

"Hello?"

"Tatum, this is—"

She hung up before I could finish. In a huff, I tried again.

She didn't hesitate this time. "Listen, stop calling. My little brother is trying to sleep. Just turn it in." *Click.*

When I called the following day, a deep-voiced man told me she wouldn't be home until late that night. I was stuck waiting again.

With my words rehearsed, I paced outside of Physics on Monday morning. Tate's wild curls were easy to spot among the other heads.

"Hey, Tatum! Can I talk to you?" I yelled, jogging to her.

She and another girl stopped. In an odd reaction, Tate's partner-in-crime stared at me with her mouth hanging open. Tate's response involved less jaw-dropping and more shooting daggers. After two seconds, she pushed past me and cleared her throat to beckon her sidekick, who attempted a dirty look before obediently scurrying away.

I chased after her. "Tatum, wait up!"

When she turned, red crept up her face. Not the good I'm-embarrassed-because-I-like-you red, but the I-could-kill-you-right-now red. The expression looked so wrong on her, I almost laughed. Just a few years earlier, I was sneaking daily glances at her in art class. At that moment in the hallway, because my temper had simmered, I realized how much I had forgotten about her: the red tint in her brown curls, her intense eyes, and her body...well, her body had changed quite a bit from freshman year.

I kept pace with her and rambled off my rehearsed speech in the crowded hallway. Our peers took notice as I made a fool out of myself, either because none of them had ever heard my voice unless I was answering a teacher's question, or because the prettiest girl in school was being followed by a maundering idiot. "I'm sorry about the other day. I was a jerk. I was already late getting back to the job site, and my dad…well, if you knew my dad you'd understand. I know that's no excuse and usually my manners are better, I swear." The words didn't sound as convincing as they had in my bathroom mirror the day before.

When my monologue failed, I resorted to apologizing profusely. *Who the heck am I, and what did I do with Grant?* was all I could think as our peers gawked at us.

Tate again insisted that I turn the accident into insurance and increased her stride. I would have followed, but the first bell rang. One more tardy in Calculus would buy me after-school detention, which also meant I'd be showing up late to work. My dad would have my neck.

When the final bell released us from school, I ran directly from World History to Tate's Jeep, planting myself there until she arrived. Her bumper resembled a crushed aluminum can splotched with white paint. She tried once more to shrug me off. Imagine that.

"You're going to have to talk to me eventually. I'm annoyingly persistent," I assured her.

"You're already annoying me."

"It's safe to say it's only going to get worse."

"Just turn it in and leave me alone, Grant." Tate climbed in her Jeep and slammed the door.

Now she was irritating me.

I couldn't make it through another night working out ways to get her to talk to me. With only ten minutes left to get to the job site, I took half a second to juggle my options.

In my truck, I followed her Jeep past the convenience stores and strip malls of Weldon Spring, knowing my dad was going to kill me. She turned right on Harvester Road, putting me even further from the job site. Finally, she pulled into Harvester Retirement Home.

Trying to be quick, I parked only a few spaces away and was jogging across the hot asphalt before she even had her door open. Watching her bend over while rummaging through her backseat put being late for work completely out of my mind. She emerged clutching a maroon shirt and jumped off the side step. Her shocked expression was worth a million dollars.

"What are you doing here?" she demanded.

Suddenly, I felt nervous. "Hello to you, too." When her glare grew even darker, my words spilled out in a rush. "You wouldn't talk to me at school. I warned you I was persistent."

"You're a stalker, is what you are!"

"Whatever you want to call it. Either way, you're going to have to talk to me eventually."

"Sorry, chump, today isn't going to be the day. I gotta get to work."

I turned and assessed the building. "You work with old people?"

She looked me up and down, clearly not in a high regard. "They're better company than most."

"Huh. Well, what time do you get off?"

"None of your business."

"That's cool. I'll just wait out here for you." Yes, my dad was going to kill me.

"You wouldn't!"

I crossed my arms, and though I was internally freaking out, I calmly said, "Want to test me?"

"Oh, come on!" she yelled to the sky and then looked back at me. "Look, if you need something to do, run home and make an insurance claim."

"I'm not making the claim," I stated simply.

She stared at me, confused. "What?"

"I'm not making the claim."

Her wall was back up as quick as it fell, but it did fall momentarily. That had to count for something.

"Well, don't do me any favors." Her tone didn't quite match her words.

"Oh, I'm not. I'm still going to make you pay for it." I said, stifling a smile.

Some of the tension left her shoulders, though she still looked uncertain. "OK. Let me know how much I owe you."

"I've already gotten an estimate. The damages come to four thousand and twenty-one dollars."

"You're lying!" she yelled indignantly, struggling to put her eyes back in their sockets.

I was all-out grinning now. "Yeah, but I had you."

Unexpectedly, she punched my arm, and I detected a

momentary crack in her resistance. "Not funny," she said, looking past me to the building. "I've got to get in there. Thanks for doing this. Seriously. Let me know what I owe you, and I'll take care of it right away."

She started to jog away, but I didn't want her to go yet. "Have dinner with me!" I yelled across the lot, not exactly sure what I was doing.

She was almost to the glass doors, but she stopped and turned. "What?"

"Have dinner with me!" I yelled again, like she'd want anything to do with a carpenter who was more than a little rough around the edges. I couldn't even ask a girl out properly. Clearly, I had lost my mind.

"I don't even know you!"

"Get to know me during dinner." A million things were going through my mind, with imbecile gracing the top of the list.

"I have to go," she said, shaking her head. "You have my number. Call me with the costs."

When she disappeared into the building, it took everything I had not to follow her inside. She may have been onto something with the stalker thing.

The next day, I waited outside of Physics. Without the luxury of time, I had to get right to the point.

"Have dinner with me," I blurted out when she passed by.

"Did you hit your head in the accident?" she asked pointedly, then continued walking.

Probably. "Maybe. So, how about it?" I doggedly

followed her down the hall.

"You have lost your mind," she said, and then she left me staring into the Communications classroom while she settled in her seat. I could have used that class right about then.

On Wednesday, I proved my persistence once more. Well, my stalker tendencies, anyway. "Have dinner with me," I said, cutting her off in the hallway.

"Why won't you let it go?" she asked, exasperated.

Because I can't stop thinking about you. Because I want you to see that I'm not a complete jerk. Take your pick. "Come on, I'm not that bad, am I?" I mockingly smelled my armpits.

She looked at me with a mix of curiosity and disgust, like I was a new species of rodent she'd never seen.

I folded my hands together in supplication. "Pleeeaaase?" I gave her what I thought was a persuasive expression, but it's more likely that I appeared to be in pain.

She blushed. "I have to warn you, I'm probably the most uninteresting person you'll ever meet."

The first bell rang loudly, but that wasn't why my heart skipped a beat. "Is that a yes?" I blurted out.

She paused for so long that I thought I was going to explode.

"When?" she finally said.

"Friday," I answered, before she even finished. Nothing like coming across as desperate.

She shook her head. "Can't. I have to work."

"Saturday, then?"

"Fine." She was probably only agreeing so I would leave

her alone. "Pick me up at six."

A sudden thought seized me. *Crap! Crap, crap, crap!* "All right," was all I could say.

"Do you have my address?"

I swallowed, hoping to relieve my dry mouth. "It was with your insurance information."

"Oh, OK. I guess I'll see you then."

When she disappeared around the corner, I raced to Calculus, receiving a slew of funny looks along the way. I yelled an apology to Coach Neal after almost knocking him down.

Again…crap! Why had I picked Saturday? The foundation pour was going to take all day. Even if things ran smoothly, which they never did, we wouldn't be done until five thirty. But Tate had said yes. To *me.* No way was I going to change plans and risk her coming to her senses.

Just as I figured, my dad was not understanding about my date. The Cliffs Notes' version was this: when given a choice between making money and spending it…well, one guess which side of the fence he was on.

When Saturday came, we were surprisingly moving ahead of schedule, and by three o'clock I was sure I'd be out of there on time. That was, of course, before the last concrete load showed up an hour late. I had to bite my tongue to keep from sounding like my father.

It was six forty-five when I finally left the site. I saw the old man in my rearview mirror shooting curses at me because I took off before helping the guys roll up the tools and equipment. I clenched my teeth at his one-fingered gesture.

(It was not a thumbs up.)

I anxiously dialed Tate's number to explain, mentally noting that apologizing to her was becoming the norm. When no one answered, I felt terrible. Certainly she realized a guy like me would never stand up a girl like her? I was lucky enough to get a yes in the first place. Though covered in mud, I opted out of a shower and instead went straight to her house. Tate's mom answered the door. Her resemblance to Tate was striking, but, unlike her daughter, she looked warmly at me and didn't try to flee.

"Mrs. Jacoby?" I offered my hand out of habit, but retracted it quickly when I remembered the cracked dirt around my knuckles. "Sorry," I said, unable to shake her hand properly. "I'm Grant Bradley. Is Tatum here?"

"Oh. Hi, Grant. Tate said you were suppose to meet at six."

"Yes, ma'am, we were. I was held up at work. I tried to call, but no one answered."

"We were out back and must not have heard the phone. Tate took her brother out to dinner."

I could picture it already, once again trying to explain myself back into Tate's good graces. "Do you know where they went?"

"Juju's Arcade," she said.

Fifteen minutes later I was inside the arcade, questioning my decision to not stop for a shower. The mud had woven a nice home into my arm and leg hairs. I effectively separated a few clumps from my white shorts, but not nearly enough to make a difference.

The place was wall-to-wall animals disguised as kids. A pack bolted by and almost took me down. I was surprised to see that kids weren't hanging from the ceiling—they were certainly everywhere else. How I was going to find Tate in this asylum was beyond me. And I had no idea what her brother looked like.

My plan of attack was to start at the tables and hope that Tate would be sitting at one while her brother played. People stared as I passed by, which was no surprise. I was caked with mud. If I ever found Tate, I was going to leave quite an impression. Not the impression I was going for, but an impression nonetheless. The evening was not going the way I had hoped. At all.

With no luck at the tables, I scanned the play area. Hello, sensory overload. Between the squealing kids, blinking lights, and the loud ringing from who-knows-what, concentrating on any one thing was impossible. I had almost given up when I heard her name.

"You can't get me, Tate!" The voice belonged to a brown-haired boy who was all arms and legs. He stood on the blue cushion bordering the ball pit.

I grabbed the netting and stared through it. Tate popped out of the colorful balls and grabbed the boy. He fell onto her and giggled hysterically when she tickled him.

"My turn!" he shrieked.

Tate ran like she was in quicksand and clutched the net to balance herself on the padded edge.

The boy flew after her. "You're mine!" he yelled.

"You'll never take me alive!" she said playfully, jumping

back into the pit. She was amazing to watch. The girls I knew would never play like this; they were too wrapped up in trivial matters, nonsense like what they were going to wear to an upcoming party—things that would never matter in a month.

When her brother caught her, she pulled him into a bear hug. He squirmed to wrangle himself free.

And then she saw me.

Her arms fell off her brother, and her smile melted. "Hey, Fish, give me a sec, OK?" she said, pushing herself upright.

"Where ya going?" he asked.

"I just have to take care of something."

Disappointment replaced the boy's excitement.

Even though Tate was burning her glare into me, she caught her little brother's discouragement. She turned back to him and said in an upbeat voice, "I'll be back before you know it. Then it's death by tickling!"

He screamed with delight and cannonballed into the center of the pit.

Tate climbed awkwardly through the net opening and stomped in her pink socks over to me. She pushed her finger into my chest so hard that dust puffed off my shirt. "You! You have a lot of nerve," she hissed in a lowered voice.

"Tatum, let me explain—"

"So is this how you do it, then? You go through life being an ass and then just apologize?"

"No, it's not like that. I—"

"Don't even!" She whispered her yell and pushed her

finger into my chest again. "Others may let you get away with that awful behavior, but I was raised better. I don't know why I agreed to go out with you in the first place."

At least she saw it my way. I didn't know why she'd agreed, either. Certainly one of the rich boys from school wouldn't have been late if they had gotten the chance to take her out.

"Tatum, just listen, please! I got stuck at work."

"And I guess you've never heard of a phone?"

"We were in the middle of a concrete pour. I called as soon as we were finished."

"It would have taken two seconds to call."

"Conversations with you seem to last a bit longer than that." I cringed when I realized that my statement, at that particular moment, wasn't the smartest thing to come out of my mouth.

"We're done here." She stormed away, climbed the steps, and jumped back into the pit.

"Tatum, come on! Give me another chance!" I pleaded through the netting.

She completely ignored me. With nothing to lose, I pulled off my mud-caked boots and jumped into the pit, losing my balance. After nearly falling on Tate, I managed to get down on my knees.

"Tatum, come on! Look, I'm literally begging you. Please, please, please forgive me!"

"Knock it off, Grant. You're doing that stalker thing again and scaring my brother."

"Please, Tatum. Please!" I mockingly begged. My

attempt at humor was ridiculous, but my options were limited.

"Tate, what's wrong with him?" Fischer loudly whispered. Shoot, he did look frightened.

She kept her eyes on me when she answered. "Fish, you remember your hamster that couldn't figure out how to run in his wheel and Mom said he was a little slow?"

"Yeah."

"Well, Grant's kind of like that hamster."

I smirked. She was so bad at being mean.

The boy's eyes turned to baseballs. "Ohhh!"

"Let's go, Fish," she said.

"But I want to stay!"

"Fine, but we're finding somewhere else to play. It's too crowded in here."

In a desperate move to stop her, I swung my arms around her waist. She squealed and fell onto me, throwing my balance off. We fell into the middle of the pit, buried in plastic balls.

She tried to push away from me, but I tightened my grip. I chewed on my lower lip, but couldn't hide my amusement, which made her even more angry.

"Let me go! What is wrong with you?" she yelled, pushing against my chest.

I easily overpowered her, pulling her against me until my mouth was at her ear.

"Come on, just one more chance?" I whispered in what I hoped was a convincing voice. Still, I prepared for a slap to my face. When there was no blow, I pushed away to see her expression. Not having a lot of experience with girls, I could only guess, but her cheeks didn't seem to be flushed from anger.

It took a full five seconds (I was counting) before she responded. "You can buy Fish and me dinner. That's all I'm agreeing to."

"Deal."

When I forced myself to let her go, she pushed off me and we climbed out of the pit. I was able to get my boots on without leaving too much dried mud behind, and the three of us stood quietly in line to order a pizza.

It was Fischer who spoke first. "Tate, why is he so dirty?" he whispered, obviously not wanting me to hear.

"Apparently no one told him it's polite to shower before taking a girl to dinner," Tate answered indiscreetly. "Do you think we should make him eat outside?"

"No, I think he should eat with us," Fischer whispered. I was starting to like this kid. I had no doubt Tate would have made me eat outside, though I can't say that I would've blamed her.

Fischer distanced himself from me as if I smelled bad (probably true), using Tate as a shield. I knelt down and peeked around Tate's legs to talk to him. "How old are you?"

"Six," he answered shyly.

Knowing nothing about kids, I took my best stab. "Do you like construction stuff?"

He barely nodded, but from the size of his eyes, I knew I had him.

"Yeah? What's your favorite machine?" I asked.

"I like the diggers."

The kid liked heavy machinery. I could work with that. "Do you like the ones with the big buckets on the front?"

"Yeah," he answered so quietly I almost missed it.

"Ah, the skid loaders." I nodded sagely. "My dad's company has one of those. I'm sure I could work something out if you ever wanted to drive one."

"Really?" He was finally coming around from behind Tate's legs.

"Oh yeah, totally. We could even let your sister give it a try."

When I glanced up, Tate was giving me a speculative look.

"But she's a girl," Fischer stated, perplexed.

"I think she can hold her own," I answered, still watching her.

Just when I thought I was finally going to get a positive reaction out of her, Tate turned her attention to Fischer and the moment passed. "Watch it, Fish. This girl had you schooled back there."

"No way! I totally had you," Fischer argued.

I stood and asked Fischer a minute later: "You think Tatum will ever forgive me for being late?"

"Sure. She acts tough, but she's a real softy. That's what Dad says. Why do you call her Tatum?"

"What else would I call her?" I asked.

"Tate, of course. She's only Tatum when she's in trouble."

"Oh?"

"Yeah, everyone calls her Tate."

I leaned a few inches closer to her. "Tate it is," I said emphatically, feeling victorious that I knew something else about her.

She looked up at me briefly then, and I saw an uncertain optimism in her eyes. Her face turned cherry red before she placed our order.

5. *You live in a sad world of denial, kid*

"There you are! I've been looking all over for you."

The voice makes me jump. Not ready to return from memory lane yet, I drop my head to hide my disappointment and struggle to use my nicest voice. "Hey, Anna. What's up?"

"Not much. I'm exhausted." She sinks beside me into the pew. "I just can't get coding down. What are you doing in here?" she asks, looking around Alogan.

"Just thinking."

She leans her head back. "Seems like a great place for that."

I rest my head against the hard pew as well. Being with Anna is easy, like being with Tate. Emptiness tears at my insides like cancer. I swallow and try to focus on the swarming birds.

Rolling my head to the side to study Anna, she exhales dramatically. Her eyes are closed like she's sleeping. She's too tiny, too sweet, too unzombielike to be dead.

As if sensing my gaze, she opens her eyes. "Wanna grab a bite in Benson?"

"Sure," I say, standing. I'm not hungry, but apparently I can always eat.

"So, what else have you been up to?" she asks on our way.

I think about my second attempt at coding and decide to lie. "Nothing. It's been a pretty uneventful day."

We fill our trays and grab an empty table in the mostly deserted room. When Liam, who's looking much better now, joins us, I'm surprised.

"I thought you'd be at Viscal," I say to him.

"Nah. All my family and friends are alive and well."

"That's good, right?" Anna asks.

Liam grins. "Yeah, that's good. How are you guys adjusting?"

"Mmm," I answer noncommittally, thankful to have a mouth full of mashed potatoes.

Anna jumps in. "Not bad. I still can't get over the amazing food."

The conversation stays light while we eat and then the three of us play Sats. When Rigby joins us, I deal him into our fourth game. Liam wins as usual. By our fifth game, a rumble grows from down the hall.

Liam looks toward the archways while he shuffles the deck. "The slackers are back."

I choke on my drink. "Already?" There's no way three days have passed.

He smirks. "Time flies."

As if to prove him right, Willow bounces into the room ahead of the herd.

"What's up, losers? Did I miss anything?" Jovial, she plops into the chair beside mine.

Liam points his thumb at Willow. "Honestly, I don't know how you stand this one."

I'm barely listening. *Three days already?*

"Her? Shoot, he's got it easy!" Rigby barks before cannibalizing another toothpick.

When a throat clears behind him, Willow's smile grows so big it nearly cuts her face in half. "Hey, Shane," she says, looking above Rigby, whose face is now burning red.

"Hi, I'm Jordan," the lanky guy beside Shane says, smacking Rigby on the shoulder. "So, uh…you guys excited about training today?" he asks before grabbing a chair and squeezing himself into a position at the now crowded table.

Training? My eyes bulge in disbelief and I give Willow "the look."

"Oh yeah. I probably forgot to mention that," Willow says in her most aggravating voice. I heave an exaggerated sigh.

"Wait till you see the field." Owen's voice comes from behind me. He drags a chair close to a beaming Anna and leans over her to talk to me. "So, Grant, you know Clara's totally digging you, right? You should ask her out; she's a major babe." His eyebrows dance up and down. "But she's nothing compared to you," he whispers to Anna.

Willow's paying attention now, as is Rigby. She looks indifferent. Rigby looks curious.

"You gonna hit that?" Rigby asks.

"No!" I say too loudly. Willow shakes her head, though she's clearly not surprised by my sudden outburst.

"Mind if I do? I mean, not *hit that*—sorry girls, that

was disrespectful. But I'd totally ask her out if you're not going to."

"Be my guest." Please.

As if choreographed, the Satellites begin pushing their calimeters, saying their good-byes, and vanishing from the room as quickly as they arrived.

"Thanks for the heads-up on training. A little notice would have been nice," I say to Willow on our way out of Benson.

"You gotta check your schedule or something?"

"Funny. Is being annoying intentional or a natural gift?"

"Hmm, I'd definitely say natural. Good to know I still have my charm after all these years."

We stop at a hallway where *Orders* is spelled out in stained glass overhead. I stand to the side of the line in an effort to see around the crowd in front of us. "What are we doing?"

"Picking up your assignment." Willow may as well finish her sentence with "Duh."

My mouth drops into an *O*.

"Shoot. Did I forget to mention that, too? Sorry." There's nothing apologetic in her tone.

On the verge of hyperventilating, I try to keep my cool. Willow will never let me live it down if I crack right here in front of everyone.

"Don't worry, kid. You won't begin your assignment until you're cleared from training. That's a couple of weeks out still," she assures.

The hall is similar to the others, constructed of dark marble. I nervously tap my boot on the floor while more people file behind us. The classical music being piped in makes me think of Tate, which heightens my nerves. I can't place the melody, though Tate could likely recite the title, composer, and probably even the date after just a few seconds of listening. She's ridiculous when it comes to things like that.

"You'll have some time to review your assignment after training," Willow says as we move a step forward.

"What's training like?" I ask.

"And kill your initial reaction?" She shakes her head. "Uh-uh, no way."

"Another one of Willow's surprises. Excellent!" I say with exaggerated sarcasm.

"Hold still, kid." She brushes my shoulder. "Got it."

"Got what?"

"The chip."

"Seriously, Willow. Your jokes are bogus."

She sticks her tongue out.

When it's finally my turn, the girl behind the gold desk smacks her gum and then blows a huge pink bubble that matches her hair color. She sucks in and pops it. "Name?"

"Grant Bradley."

She tries to straighten her T-shirt over her pink tank top, which is difficult because the green-striped fabric, slashed with diagonal lines, appears to have been in a scuffle with a mountain lion.

I look at Willow, hoping she'll help me out when my staring contest with Bubble-Gum Girl is almost to the one-minute mark. Of course, she doesn't.

"Is something wrong?" I finally ask Bubble-Gum Girl, irritated.

"Nah. You just don't look like a Grant." She cocks her head. "Maybe a Sean or a David." She smacks her gum again.

"Sorry, it's Grant. My assignment?"

"Oh, right." She spins in a circle and disappears into the marble floor. An instant later, the floor spits her out, making her hoop earrings swing back and forth even though she's now standing still. "Here you are, then." She hands me a heavy book.

I mumble my thanks. This place is so ridiculous.

"You should consider changing your name!" she yells after me.

Willow and I walk back to the lobby. "She's as weird as you," I say.

Willow nudges me in the side. "Watch it, kid, or I won't go easy on you in training."

"Who are you kidding? You won't go easy on me, anyway!"

"True that. When you complete your first assignment, you'll meet Jonathan in the same place to get your next one. His approach at retrievals is a lot different than Eve's back there."

"What do you mean?"

"Let's just say he's much more…traditional. To each their own."

I study the book as we walk. On the cover, *Grant Bradley, Assignment One,* is stacked in gold text and bracketed by wings. The cherry red book is about the size of the ones Tate always had her nose stuck in before her reading material switched from fiction to medical texts. She was always trying to uncover the next miracle treatment for me.

"I'm hopeless, Tate. Give it up," I'd say.

"You're hopeless, all right," she'd tease back.

I wonder who she's trying to save now that I'm gone. I pray it's herself.

At the end of a short hallway, towering French doors made from a mess of tree branches greet Willow and me. The word *Courtyard* is formed from the limbs in the center. Willow grabs the giant stick handles and gives them a push. After chuckling at my reaction, she grabs my elbow and pulls me onto the stone pathway. If I could force my eyes to stop bugging out, I'd squint from the vibrancy.

My dad would have heart failure if he saw this. The lawn is even more manicured than ours, and that's saying something. One time, my dad cut the grass along our driveway with scissors. It was sick the way that man loved our lawn. One look at this place, and he'd never want to leave. He'd probably request a pair of scissors and ask if he could be the groundskeeper.

"You coming, kid?"

Willow's voice registers, but I can't stop staring.

"Earth to Grant." She snaps her fingers two inches from my eyes. "Hellooooo? Can you hear me?"

I grab her tiny wrist, and in an instant, I have her arm pinned behind her back. "Yes, I hear you, but I prefer to ignore you," I say into her ear.

She jerks unexpectedly, and before I know what's happening, she has my arm behind my back. "Well, you'd better listen up, because you're about to get schooled by the Almighty Willow."

I struggle lightly, not wanting to hurt her. "Certainly you've already taught me everything you know. I mean, how much can that little head of yours hold?"

"Save it for the field," Jordan jokes as he walks past us.

Willow smacks a kiss on my cheek before releasing my arm. "Watch and learn, kid."

"You are seriously touched in the head!" I yell after her. "And keep your lips to yourself!"

I follow her and the others along the sloped, winding sidewalk. Spiraling pine trees border the path in pots the size of compact cars. Down the hill at the end of the sidewalk, the ground levels into the greenest field I've ever seen. By comparison, Benson is matchbox size.

I climb the cedar bleachers to Anna and Rigby. From behind, Willow flicks my ear when I sit. I give her a dirty look as the last group of Satellites straggles onto the crowded bleachers.

Jonathan walks onto the field and scans us. He's clean-shaven now but still casual in a T-shirt, jeans, and flip-flops. His whistle and clipboard actually calm my jitters; it's like I'm back on the football field (or, more appropriately, a dozen football fields). Maybe this won't be so bad.

"Welcome, everyone. I've spoken with your Legacies, and it appears you are all settling in nicely thus far. I trust you are finding your accommodations acceptable."

They could be, if I got rid of Willow's sofa.

"Today we begin your training. In addition to being exhilarating, it will be challenging and exhausting. Be mindful of your body through this process. If you get tired, rest. Training is not the time, nor place, to be ostentatious. Your purpose here is to learn." His pacing, slow and measured, heightens his dramatic delivery. "Before we begin, let's first discuss your purpose. Your one—and only—job is to keep your Tragedy's life on course. You have all received your assignment books, which I ask that you begin studying later today. This book, in addition to detailing your Tragedy's past, will precisely guide you through their future."

I glance at Anna. She looks as relieved as I feel.

Jonathan continues. "The Tragedies are so named because they have experienced just that—tragedies. You must realize that every individual reacts differently to misfortune. Some will face depression, ranging from mild to severe. Others may act out, harming themselves or those around them.

"Having millenniums of experience, the Schedulers are rarely wrong when gauging a Tragedy's reaction. However, you must be prepared to handle even the smallest deviations, as they could have ruinous effects. If a Tragedy strays too far off course, they are deemed a Rebellion. Since the formation of the Satellite department centuries ago, Rebellions have been a rare occurrence; however, it is crucial that you understand failure cannot be an option. Failure is catastrophic."

After a dramatic pause, he places the clipboard under

his arm and rubs his palms together.

"Now, let's get down to business and learn how to avoid such devastation, shall we? Are there any volunteers who would like to start us off today?"

Bodies shift uncomfortably in the bleachers. I sink down lower, hoping to make myself invisible.

"We will!"

I groan. Please tell me my ears have deceived me.

"Come on, kid," Willow beckons, stepping between Rigby and me.

Somehow, I refrain from pushing her down the bleachers and instead follow behind her with much less enthusiasm, meaning that I'm *not* skipping. Being the center of attention, especially in a crowd this large, does not make my list of favorite things.

"We will begin with a demonstration." Jonathan happily looks down at his clipboard and flips through a few pages. "Grant Bradley?" he asks when Willow and I step onto the field.

"Yeah."

"Excellent." He flips the papers back over. "I'd like you to attack Willow, please."

I clear my throat. "Excuse me?" Not that I haven't fantasized about this, but she's a chick, for crying out loud.

"I'd like you to go after Willow. Knock her down. Punch her. Get creative," he urges.

"I...I can't." I sigh weakly, feeling hundreds of eyes burning into me.

"Sure you can."

How can I make this clearer for Mr. Sure-You-Can? "I can't hit a girl. Not even Willow."

Along with Willow, the crowd laughs at my unintended joke.

"Come on, kid. You know you want to," Willow provokes.

She's right. I do. I may have even come close earlier in her room (and maybe a few other times, too). But I wouldn't. Ever.

"Fine. Catch me, then." She's much less enthusiastic about this plan.

Jonathan approves. "That will work. Thank you, Willow."

I'm totally confused when Willow begins running in place. "Come on," she whines, sticking her tongue out.

I mentally curse her for volunteering, and then I sprint. Even with her head start, her short legs can't carry her across the field as fast as mine. I'll have her in two seconds.

"Haze!" she yells, and darkness curtains around me like black ink. The temperature plummets to ice.

Almost before my mind can register the chilling claustrophobia, my sight is back and the temperature has returned to normal. I'm overcome with such an urge to sit down that I'm afraid my knees are going to buckle. My own voice screams in my head to park it. I willingly fall onto the soft grass.

Willow, stopped just a few feet away, is happily panting.

"Wonderful!" Jonathan places his clipboard under his

arm to clap. "And that, my friends, is what we call blocking."

The gaping crowd applauds while I remain utterly baffled. What the heck is going on?

"Excuse me?"

Jonathan turns to me, smiling. "Yes?"

"Am I missing something?" The crowd, quickly becoming as exasperating as Willow, cracks up, even though I know I haven't said anything funny this time.

"Please, Grant, take a seat on the bleachers. Things will become clearer when you witness blocking from the outside."

I climb the cedar planks back to my spot as another pair is selected: a Legacy named Shyla and the redhead who gave Rigby a dirty look on our first day. In a Southern accent, she corrects Jonathan that it's "just Whitfield" when he calls her Janie Whitfield.

"Sounds familiar," I whisper to Rigby.

"Hardly," he hisses back, but then grins.

"Whitfield, do you have any problems attacking your Legacy?" Jonathan asks.

"None, sir," she replies.

A few things happen at once. Whitfield lunges for Shyla, who in turn yells, "Haze!" A bubblelike wall of rippling water materializes around Shyla and then extends out to Whitfield, obscuring both girls.

"Block!" Shyla shouts a second later.

The water splashes to the ground, and the droplets bounce on the grass before evaporating. Whitfield freezes in midstrike, like a cow looking at a new gate. She drops her arms to her sides.

"And there you have it," Jonathan says. "Through the haze, the Legacies are transmitting their thoughts and, in effect, changing their subject's mind."

Everyone responds with applause. Except me. If Willow blocked me, how do I not remember something about it? My muscles tense at the chilling thought.

Jonathan selects three more unfortunate pairs for demonstrations, and when the applause ends, he addresses us again. "This will be all for today. Thank you for a wonderful session. Tomorrow you will have the opportunity to practice blocking. Please return to your quarters and begin studying your assignments. But first, feel free to take a short break and enjoy this lovely day."

"So whatcha think, kid?" Willow asks on our slow walk back to the doors.

"I think you're a madwoman. You volunteered!"

She disregards my insult. "I'm asking about blocking."

I stare back at her for a few seconds and cross my arms. "It's creepy."

She considers this. "Maybe, but it works."

"I have my doubts," I mumble.

"Do you remember anything from my block?"

"I'm not convinced that you blocked me."

"Of course I did. Remember? You sat like an obedient dog. That is, unless you truly couldn't catch me?"

"Oh, I could have caught you!" I dispute. It would have been easy.

"See. That's the beauty of a block. There's no trace in the subject's head that it ever happened."

"Stop gloating. You're embarrassing yourself."

As if she knows her overly chipper attitude irritates me, she offers me a cheeky grin and practically starts skipping. She beams when we catch Rigby at the doors. "Yo, Rig, did you catch that killer block?"

"Yeah, that was sweet!" He pops a new toothpick into his mouth.

When I speak, my tone is caustic. "I'm glad you both enjoyed it."

"Get over it, kid. You'll like it from the other side. I gotta check in with Programming, so I'll catch you later. Start studying your assignment."

"Sure thing, Momma Willow."

She winks at me before being absorbed by the passing crowd.

"She's right, you know," Rigby says.

"About what?"

"I bet you'll think blocking is sweet once you do it yourself."

"Doubtful." There's nothing sweet about mind manipulation.

"You gotta admit, it's cool to watch."

"Not from the inside."

"Well, anyway, it's still sick. Willow was, by far, the best blocker. Completely seamless. You're lucky you're not stuck with Techie Shane." Rigby looks over his shoulder to make sure no one is behind us.

"Try spending more than an hour with her. You'll disagree," I scoff.

"What's it feel like to be blocked?" he asks.

"Like nothing, really. I mean, all I can remember is wanting to sit down."

"Seriously? That's it?"

"Well, there was something else. It was black and cold for a second. Although, who knows, my head could have just made that part up." My head has been known to make up crazier things, like seeing my fiancée while I code.

Anna bounces over to us, beaming. I sullenly wonder if she's the spawn of Willow, minus the dreads.

"Hey, guys!" she crows. "Willow's block was outstanding!"

Sigh.

"I hope Jordan blocks me so I can see what it's like," she adds.

"I prefer to have people *not* invade my head."

"Dude, it's mind control. That's got to be the best superpower ever!" Rigby acts like he's just won an all-expense-paid vacation to a tropical island.

"Really?" Anna turns and gives Rigby a disgusted look, which he then mimics behind her back. "Anyway, it's necessary for our Tragedies," she continues. "I'm at least glad to know we have a way of keeping them on course."

"She's got a point," Rigby concedes, flipping his toothpick over in his mouth.

I guess she does, but I don't say this aloud.

Anna and I leave Rigby at the R hall. When we reach our own elevator, I turn to her. "Did you have any luck remembering the conversation with your brother?"

We step inside the lift, and Anna twirls the end of her dark hair. "Huh?" she asks, choosing her floor number from the gold wall of buttons.

"You were trying to remember your last conversation with him," I remind her.

"I was?" she doubts, obviously still puzzled.

"Do you remember your brother at all?"

"Oh, absolutely. I miss him. But we'll see each other again. Until then, I plan to be an amazing Satellite!"

The doors ding open, and GPS Jeanette wishes her well. Anna says good-bye and steps out.

"Anna?"

In the hall, she turns back to me. "Yeah?"

"What does your dad do for a living?"

Anna stares at me blankly before the elevator doors close.

———

Back in Willow's apartment—or I guess I should say *my* apartment—the smell of coffee hangs in the air. My body collapses onto the sofa I hate; I feel deflated by Anna's memory loss. As I sink further into the cushions, it kills me to admit the sofa is comfortable. I look around, doubting this place will ever feel like mine.

I pull my assignment book from my backpack and set it on the trunk. I stare at the unmarred binding and wonder what lies ahead. Then, like clockwork, my thoughts go back to Tate. Deciding the assignment can wait, I push myself up to take advantage of Willow's absence.

In the room down the hall, I sit on a black mat and face the mirrors. My shock at my reflection has lessened, but I still run my hand through my hair for good measure.

Closing my eyes, I picture my bedroom and Tate as I did before. After just one breath, she's lying on my chest, humming quietly and tracing my abs. Her familiar, sweet scent impales me, making my insides scorch like burning coal. The desire to stay with her forever crushes me.

"Tate," I whisper, surprised and elated that I can talk this time.

Her finger pauses and her breathing stops for a second. She pushes her hand under my T-shirt, and a deviously tracing fingernail paralyzes me. When she raises her head, I suck in a sharp breath at her appearance.

A pooling tear in her sunken, bloodshot eyes rolls down her face and hits my chest. The moisture burns through my shirt, but I can't look away from her raw eyes. She contemplates my hair, twirling a strand around her finger.

I lean forward to kiss her, and she responds as urgently as she did during the kiss after my diagnosis. One hand grips and tugs at my hair while the other clutches the back of my neck. She wraps her right leg around me. I run my hand down the length of her arm and over the curve of her hip, stopping under her thigh. She pulls back but my arms react and draw her closer, refusing to let her go.

"Tate, please, stay with me," I plead when she breaks free.

Her face contorts. "Why are you doing this to me?" she demands.

I open my mouth to respond—to ask what she means—but before my words come out I'm back in the coding room, panting and covered in sweat.

No! I have to go back! I squeeze my eyes closed and think of my room. Nothing. Nothing, nothing, nothing! I need more strength from my worthless, drained body.

After three more attempts, I give up and fall back on the mat in defeat. Sweat drips down my face and neck while I glare at the wood beams overhead. My hand rubs at my stinging chest, and despite the exhaustion that hits me when I sit up, I manage to crawl to the mirror.

A small hole graces my T-shirt at the source of the stinging. After wrestling myself free from my sweaty shirt, my breathing stops. My finger traces over the burning, tear-shaped lesion on my chest.

Tate's tear did this.

"Hey, kid—where you at?"

Crap!

With no time (or strength) to put on my shirt, I use it to wipe my face instead. The wet fabric is about as helpful as drying off with a water hose.

"You back here?" Willow calls, her voice just outside the door now.

"Yeah," I answer, but she's already in the room.

"What are you doing?"

"Nothing." Of course, she doesn't buy my answer.

"I thought we agreed you'd chill with the coding."

Busted, I know continuing to lie will only make things worse. "I'm sorry, Willow. Here's the thing, though—I need to learn it, don't I? I mean, I'm going to need to code once my assignment starts." I hope my argument is convincing enough.

"But after last time…" She exhales deeply. "Why'd I get stuck with the stubborn Satellite?" she says to the ceiling.

"I prefer persistent." I almost laugh.

"I guess I can't say I'm surprised. Honestly, I'd probably be more surprised if you hadn't tried. So, out with it. How many times?"

"Just twice," I respond, biting my lip.

"And the results?"

"Huh?" Playing stupid has worked a time or two in the past, but she just stares at me shrewdly. Apparently, it won't work this time.

"Yeah, the results were the same. But it wasn't…it wasn't…What's the big deal?" I stammer.

"Oh, come on, Grant! Even you're smarter than that."

"All right, fine—but I'm not intentionally reaching out to Tate." It's not entirely a lie. I don't have much control over the outcome.

"I'm not blaming you, kid. It just doesn't make sense."

She chooses the dry mat for her seat. I opt for the hardwood floor, leaning my bare, damp back against the mirror.

"So you saw her again?"

I nod and stare at the frayed ends of my jeans.

"Did she talk to you?"

"Yeah." My head raises. "There's no way it's real, right?" I hate to be hopeful, but I am.

Willow slumps her shoulders and looks at her bare feet. "I don't know."

"Well, you're a lot of help," I jab, trying to make a joke.

"This shouldn't be happening. Even Reed agrees."

"Who's Reed?"

"Another Satellite."

I give her an accusing look. "I thought we weren't talking about this."

"Reed's cool. Anyway, he's never heard of it, but he doubts that you're the only one who's ever experienced this."

"Why?"

"No offense, but can you honestly believe your situation is unique to our entire Satellite history?"

"Well—no. I guess not."

"Reed thinks the Schedulers keep experiences like yours under wraps."

I shake my head. "I don't understand."

"Satellites have one focus. Even you should know that by now. If all the newbies worried too much about their transitions, they'd have difficulty focusing on their Tragedies, wouldn't you agree?"

After considering, I nod, though I don't necessarily see the problem. Except, I guess, that I've yet to open my assignment book.

"I may have you code again. Under my supervision," she adds pointedly. Seeing my expression, she goes on. "Settle down, kid. Not now. You need to rest—you look terrible. If you don't code the right way soon, you won't be strong enough to watch over anyone."

I think better of letting Willow in on how truly wrecked I am. Chemo doesn't even compare. At least I'm not puking, though. Yay for small favors.

"Speaking of Tragedies," Willow continues, "have you even looked at your assignment?"

I bite my lip and study the dirty creases in my leather boots.

She huffs. "Do you realize how bad you're going to make me look? Go. Sit. Rest—for the love of Pete!"

I get up. It's probably best to not make her tell me twice.

"And put a shirt on!" she demands behind me.

The closet, not just larger than my old bedroom but my old living room and kitchen, too, is filled with clothes that are obviously not all mine. My earthly wardrobe would hardly fill one corner. I pull an unfamiliar green shirt over my head as I walk past Willow in the kitchen. She chucks my assignment book at me. Still tangled in the shirt, I fumble to catch it.

The coffee scent follows me into the living room, and Willow's sitting beside me with two mugs a minute later.

I take a cup from her and nod at the bookcase across the room, trying not to think about the empty frame on the bottom shelf. "What's up with the pictures?"

"That's our Satellite family tree, so to speak." She places her coffee on the trunk, crosses the room, and grabs the Popsicle-stick frame I was scoping earlier. "This is me with my Legacy. Julia was seriously vexing, but she was a rock star, which is why I'm so good."

"From what I've seen, you're not that good."

She tsks. "You live in a sad world of denial, kid. Anyway, the frame itself is mine. My daughter made it." She traces the bright Popsicle sticks before exchanging the frame for another. "This is Julia with her Legacy, Madden. Her frame is much more polished than mine, pun intended. When you're cleared as a Satellite, we'll have a photo taken together for your frame." She bends down and scans the shelves, stopping at the lowest one. "Very nice. Yours looks homemade as well." She straightens herself and turns my frame over in her hands.

I swallow and focus on my calloused thumbs instead of the frame. "Yeah. Tate said it was supposed to make my hospital stays more cheerful. Can you believe that? Like a hospital stay could ever be cheerful."

I look up at Willow when she doesn't reply.

"You still remember that?" she asks after a few seconds.

"Sure, why wouldn't—?" I stop, realizing I just outed myself.

"Why haven't your memories faded?"

"I don't know. They just haven't," I blurt out defensively.

"At all?"

I decide honesty is the best way to go. I shake my head and brace myself for her wrath. When she comes toward me, I succeed in getting my mug to the trunk—though coffee splashes over the lip—before leaping over the back of the sofa.

"What are you doing?"

"Getting away from you!" I yell.

She's obviously confused.

"You were going to hit me again, right?"

"What? No! Seriously, kid, you need to get your head checked."

"Me? You're the one who goes around punching people!"

"You should have forgotten most of your memories by now, regardless of whether you were trying to or not," she whispers.

"So what's wrong with me?"

"Where do I begin?" She squeezes the bridge of her nose. "Truthfully, I don't know."

All this time I thought Willow was the mental one. Turns out, it's me.

"I'm gonna track down Reed again. Maybe he's come up with a theory by now," Willow says, checking her calimeter. "Shoot. I gotta go. Would you please study your assignment?"

"Yeah, yeah."

"And keep your mouth shut about all this," she orders.

"Fine by me," I agree, but she's already disappeared out the door.

6. If I'm right, you owe me dinner

After Willow's gone, I lounge back on the sofa and trace the gold wings on my assignment book. The binding creaks open, delivering a musty smell. Like the cover, printed in bold text on the first page is *Grant Bradley, Assignment One.* I flatten the inner spine with my palm before reading the handwritten letter on the next page.

Dear Grant,

It is with great appreciation that I welcome you to the Satellite program. You have been chosen because you possess the unique genetics that make you perfectly suited for this lifestyle. Your remarkable qualities of integrity, empathy & kindness will assist you in protecting your Tragedy in the coming months, as well as in future assignments.

Being chosen as a Satellite is a very high honor, and it is my hope that you find the program to be rewarding. If you should need assistance at any time, please do not hesitate to contact me.

All My Best,
Jonathan Clement

I skim back over the penned note, and those three words specifically: integrity, empathy, and kindness. These are my so-called remarkable qualities?

Integrity. OK, yes—that I have. Though these past few days, my behavior probably hasn't been exactly top notch. My father would flip if he knew the lies I've been telling. He would certainly take the opportunity to spew his famous phrase: "No son of mine is going to grow up to be dishonest."

The kindness is from my mother, no doubt, and I'd like to think I've done a decent job there (minus my first meeting with Tate, anyway), but I wouldn't consider this quality anything special. Both Tate and my mom are much kinder than I could ever hope to be.

I can't think of anything that would pertain to empathy, aside from my extended hospital stays. I formed dozens of relationships while I was doing time, and certainly I empathized with the other patients, but it'd have been impossible not to, since I was going through the same hell myself. The Satellite pool must be pathetic if I'm the kind of guy they're looking for.

I turn to the next page, titled "The Beginning." Below the bold text is the outline of a hand with simple instructions: place hand here.

I flip through the rest of the pages, which are blank, offering nothing more than a stronger musty smell. Half laughing because I'm forced to play by the rules, I backtrack.

Nothing happens when I put my hand on the page. Just as I start to pull away, though, a tugging starts at my palm and extends to my wrist, followed by a hard yank.

My arm is practically ripped from its socket and my stomach drops. Forced through a tight black space, a stinging pressure grates against my body, like needles scraping my skin. For what seems like an eternity, I squeeze my eyes closed and give up gasping for oxygen that's not there.

I finally land with a thud and open my eyes, panting. Hunched over, using my knees for support, I take in the dirty encircling stone wall that's punctuated with rusty doors. The damp earthy scent here levels my breathing, unlike the blackness high above me.

"Welcome, Grant Bradley. Please hold while I configure your assignment." Oh, super. GPS Jeanette is back.

The circular wall spins into a blur of dull colors while the floor stays stationary. Dust cyclones around my legs. I focus on my boots, which, for the first time, don't look so out of place.

Thirty seconds later, the wall abruptly stops and a ding echoes off the stone. Instead of, "You are now free to move about the cabin," GPS Jeanette says, "Your assignment begins in the year 1988, with your introduction to Tragedy Ryder Collin Beckmann. Please proceed through the door ahead."

Contrary to the previous wall of doors, now only one remains, appropriately labeled 1988 in iron numbers. My hand grips the oxidized handle and a light current shocks me. I quickly push down on the lever and the door swings open.

A sterile smell burns my nostrils, and I shudder at the memories the sensation brings. I step across the threshold, and the door clicks closed behind me. My breath curls like smoke from my mouth, but the hospital hallway is not the least bit cold.

Under fluorescent lights, a man and an older couple are peering through a glass window. A little girl bounces on her tiptoes beside them, hanging onto the narrow metal sill in order to gape into the room of babies.

"Ima big sistah!" she declares in a Boston accent.

A passing nurse stops and kneels down to the brown-eyed girl. "You are?"

"Uh-huh. Today is my brother's birthday."

"How exciting! I bet you're going to be a wonderful big sister."

"Oh yeah. I've been practicing."

"What's his name?"

"Ryder Collin Beckmann," she recites. "Dad says he weighs seven pounds and forty ounces—right, Dad?"

"That's right, honey," her dad says in the same thick accent, neither looking away from the glass nor catching the weight mistake. His daughter didn't hear the tremble in his voice, but I did.

The little girl also doesn't notice the nurse's face waver because, once again, she's beaming through the window.

The nurse stands and touches the man's arm. "I'm so sorry," she whispers. "If there's anything I can do…" She turns to the little girl. "Honey, would you like to get a snack from the nurse's station?"

"Dad, can I?" The girl's dress comes to life when she bounces up and down.

The man turns in my direction, away from his daughter, and wipes tears from his glassy, red eyes. "That'd be fine," he answers.

The little girl skips at the nurse's side. When they disappear around the corner, the man says to the older couple, "Ryder will never know any different, but how are we going to tell Mya her mom is dead?"

My feet are sucked out from under me, and a second later, I land (somehow still upright) back on the dirt floor. The metal door thunders closed. Inhaling the earthy scent to slow my pulse, I barely have time to process the scene because the wall spins into a blur.

With a ding, another labeled door is presented. "Please proceed to 1990," GPS Jeanette instructs calmly.

I take a deep breath before the shock of the handle zings up my arm. When I step into the campground before me, my breath hangs in the air like the smoke over the fire pit beside the faded canvas tent.

The man from the hospital is different in this scene— he happily chases a shrieking boy. The little girl from the hospital has changed, too. She's taller, and her face is less round. She casts a fishing pole into the glassy lake while the little boy runs behind her.

"Mya, fish!" her dad yells when he passes by her.

She jerks her head up and frantically reels the line.

"Come on, Ryder, let's see your sister's fish!" Breathless, he scoops up Ryder and circles back. He sits Ryder down beside him before working on freeing the hook from the spotted fish's mouth.

"Dad, can we come here every year?" Mya asks, never looking away from her newly caught prize.

"I don't see why not."

I'm sucked away from the smiling trio and hear the metal boom of the door. After a light rumble, the wall circles around me again.

The motion finally halts. "Please proceed to 1993," GPS Jeanette says.

I step through the door and breathe heavily scented air. I try to force thoughts of Tate out of my head, but the overwhelming peppermint smell makes it difficult. A spindly Charlie Brown-looking Christmas tree fills the tiny room. On the floor beside it, Mya is painting her already clownlike face with more makeup. Her dark hair is to the middle of her back now, and her face looks even thinner when she pouts into the lighted mirror.

Near Mya, Ryder pushes a truck through an explosion of wrapping paper. His spaghetti arms and legs are too long for his red pajamas. As he plows the paper into a pile, he vibrates his lips to effectively produce the motor's noise.

"Ryder, I think Santa left something else for you," their dad says, sporting plaid pajamas and more gray in his hair. "Look what I found in the garage." He holds up a squirming ball of fluff.

Ryder rockets up. "No way! Is he really mine?" he asks, grabbing the yellow puppy from his dad.

His dad grins. "He's all yours."

The dog drenches Ryder with slobber. Yuck.

"You did good," Mya whispers to her dad, who sits beside her on the floor.

He winks back at her. "How about you? You made out

decent, huh?"

"Best Christmas ever!" she exclaims, smiling. Then she asks Ryder, "What are you going to name him?"

"Granite," Ryder says immediately.

"That's a great name." Mya looks away from her dad when she sees him blink away tears.

After being unceremoniously yanked away and dumped back inside the stone room again, I yell, "Is it necessary to remove me so abruptly?"

I'm answered with a spinning wall. When the door positions itself, GPS Jeanette instructs me to proceed to 1995.

Metal spoons clink together in an otherwise quiet room. Ryder's dad and Mya are behind a table with three others, filling plates for a long line of haggard faces. Granite, now huge, almost runs through me. Ryder, lankier than ever, follows him. They stop at one of the tables, and the people shoveling meat and bread into their mouths pause expectantly. Granite's tongue hangs to the side, and his tail beats against a metal folding chair.

Ryder pushes a dark curl behind his ear and removes a stack of cards from his vest pocket. He places one of the cards into the ribbon of the top hat he's wearing. After everyone pulls a card from the deck, he pulls his own from his hat and turns it over to show the crowd. He asks a girl with a dirt-smudged face if her card matches his. Her reveal wins him applause.

After a formal bow, he and Granite move to the next table, and I'm sucked away.

My next year, 1996, puts me back in the soup kitchen.

The room has changed. It's now covered in all things red and green, including a scrubby tree in the corner. Now it's the lack of peppermint in the air—because the scent would be appropriate here—that has me thinking of Tate. Oh, how that girl loved Christmas!

The large crowd around me converses in accents so thick I may as well have landed on Mars. Granite sits patiently while Mya folds a large red bag and puts it under her arm. She pulls a bone from her pocket and tosses it in the air. Without moving from his spot, Granite snaps up the bone before it hits the ground.

"That was a great idea, Dad," Mya praises.

"I'm still amazed at how many gifts we collected. We're fortunate to be part of such a giving community," her Dad says. Mya agrees.

"How about you, Ryder? Did you have fun?" their dad asks.

"Yeah! Did you see how many families showed up for presents?" Ryder, even taller and skinnier than before, plays keep-away with Granite by jerking a red ribbon up before the dog snaps it.

"I sure did. I'd say it was a great success."

"Do you have the flowers for Mom?" Mya asks more solemnly.

"I'll go grab them." Their dad disappears into a room in the back.

Ryder gives up and lets Granite have the ribbon. "Do you think Mom watches over us?" he asks Mya in a whisper.

"Are you kidding?" She nudges his side. "I bet she's

totally trying to figure out how you do those great magic tricks."

Ryder squares his shoulders and lifts his chin proudly. "They are pretty good, huh?"

Mya hugs him. "Absolutely."

"After we visit Mom, I'm going to show Gramps my newest trick. I bet he'll never figure it out."

"I bet you're right," Mya agrees.

I'm pulled backward through the door and it slams closed. The wall finally settles with a ding.

"Please proceed to 1997," GPS Jeanette says.

"Shut up, you little wimp—or I'll punch your face in!" I hear, before I even step through the door.

Next to the slide, a red-faced, husky boy towers over a boy half his size.

"Leave me alone," the smaller boy says, more to the ground than the giant.

"Or what?" Husky demands.

"Or I'll tell." The small boy's voice hitches.

Husky pushes his finger into the boy's chest and warns, "If you do, I'll make you wish you hadn't."

"Leave him alone!" a new voice shouts.

Husky tosses a glance over his shoulder. "Stay out of it, Ryder."

"Leave him alone," Ryder yells again.

"This is between me and him. Go back to where you came from."

"He didn't do anything to you." Ryder places himself between the boys. Size-wise, he's the perfect combination of the two.

"Look at you," Husky growls to the smaller boy. "You deserve to be punched just for looking so stupid."

Ryder shakes his head and puts his arm around the frightened boy. "Come on, let's go."

Husky grabs the small boy's shoulder and pulls him back. "I said butt out!" he barks at Ryder.

Ryder frees the boy from Husky's grasp and pushes him gently to the side. "And I said let him be!"

After Husky shoves Ryder, Ryder launches himself at Husky, taking him out at the knees. After shuffling back up, red-faced Husky hurls himself at Ryder again. This time, Ryder catches him in a bear hug and throws him to the ground.

A whistle blows in the background. "Boys! Boys! Stop it!" a woman commands, running to them. "Both of you, come with me—now!"

Before I can judge how much trouble Ryder's in, the vacuum sucks me from the scene.

"Thank you, Grant. This completes your first session. Please return after training," GPS Jeanette states calmly after the door thunders closed.

Her words don't register until I'm yanked into the blackness overhead. Like before, I twist through the invisible needles, my lungs screaming for air. Not soon enough, I land on my feet, gasping. As if I dropped it, the book smacks against the wood floor and flops closed.

After catching my breath, I grab the book and toss it on the trunk. I'd swear it feels lighter.

———~~~———

I pour a cup of coffee and consider coding, but then Willow's face replaces Tate's in my mind. The little freak would have my neck for sure. Although, being dead already, how much damage could she really do? I rub my jaw. Her punch did hurt the other day.

I decide I might as well check out Benson for lack of anything better to do. My mind is still contemplating Ryder when I step out of the elevator.

"Hey, kid—watch it!" I hear when my chest smacks Willow in the face. She's traded her flip-flops and jeans for steel-toe boots and cargo pants. I can only assume the lace on her black tank is suppose to make her feel girly.

"Sorry, lost in thought," I mumble.

"You're lost, all right."

"Whatever."

"I was just coming up to get you. Figured you could use a diversion," she says.

I puff out a breath. "You're not kidding."

"Aw, this isn't proving to be too much for poor little Grant?" she sings, as if I'm a three-year-old.

Tuning Willow out, I follow her into Benson and then to the back of the room. Leaving her standing at the green Jell-O, I cross to one of the meat tables and bump Rigby's elbow.

"What's up, man?"

"Getting some fuel. What's up with you?" he asks.

"Same. Any luck with Clara?"

"Eh, can't tell. She seems uninterested, but isn't that what girls do? The whole playing-hard-to-get thing?"

"Beats the heck out of me." I pause, thinking. "My girl, Tate, seemed that way at first. But, I'm sure her attitude wasn't an act."

Rigby chuckles at that. "You're being cool about me and Clara. I mean, I'm not complaining, but how could you not want her? She's frigging hot!"

I smirk. "She's got nothing on Tate."

"Your former girlfriend?"

My stomach clenches. "No," I try to answer calmly. "My current fiancée."

"You mean previous fiancée," he corrects, making me flinch. "Wait—you still remember her?"

I look around to be sure no one is listening and nod. "Everything, man. But I'm terrified that my memories are going to dissolve any minute."

I definitely have Rigby's attention now. "How about other stuff? You remember your parents?"

I contemplate this for a minute. "My dad was an ass. Does that count?"

Rigby considers. "Is that all you've got on him?"

"No. I remember working with him."

"What about your mom? What's she like?"

"She's a saint. I still remember her and the things we did together. My mom and I have always been much closer than my dad and me."

"Well, if you do lose your memories—and from the way things sound around here, you will—you'll adjust.

Everyone else is all right. I mean, look at me," he jokes. "I've still got my swag."

I swallow, ignoring his wisecrack. The idea of forgetting my family—or even worse, Tate—is scary. I can't imagine life without her.

"I hate this place," I say quietly.

"It'll get better. Give it some time," Rigby assures me, but he's wrong. No amount of time will make it better.

After we go through the food line, we join the others already sitting at one of the tables.

Liam glances at me. "About bloody time you showed up. We were just discussing your first day of training."

Rigby coughs his laugh into a camouflage sleeve, and I give him a dark look before addressing Liam. "I can leave if you'd like to continue."

"I told you." Anna smirks to Liam. "He didn't think it was so great."

I playfully push on Anna's shoulder. "You selling me out now? You're supposed to be my girl."

"Your girl?" Owen interjects.

"Chill, Owen. Not like that." What I should have said is, *Heel, boy.* I strategically sit beside Willow so Rigby has to take the empty seat next to Clara.

"He's still in denial about being blocked. I'm that good." Willow winks at Clara.

"Don't sweat it, Grant. I was chosen to be blocked in my first session, too." Clara throws her white-blonde hair over her shoulder and moves her chair to put an extra inch between herself and Rigby.

"We weren't chosen," I sneer, noticing Rigby's disappointment a second before he recovers.

"I volunteered." Willow disguises her amusement behind the thumbnail she's biting.

Liam and Owen cackle like hyenas.

"I always knew you were off," Owen says when he catches his breath.

"You should have seen his face. It was priceless." Shane unbuttons a starched cuff and rolls it meticulously over his forearm. "Seriously, though, Willow—who volunteers for that?"

"I thought it would be a good learning exercise for the kid."

"More like you thought you'd show off your brilliant moves," Liam argues. "Better watch yourself, woman. The tables are going to be turning soon."

Willow snickers. "I doubt that."

"Yeah, probably not with you as his teacher," Liam agrees.

"Watch it, Liam. You know I have mad skills."

"That's right, I almost forgot. Willow the Amazing, is it?" Liam asks.

"The Almighty," I correct.

Owen joins in the fun, circling his ear with an index finger and then pointing at Willow.

"Don't be haters just because I'll be leaving behind a reputation you could only dream of."

Clara laughs. "She's got you there."

"Catch up with me on the field, kid," Willow orders,

leaving behind a full tray of food minus the green Jell-O. She walks toward someone I don't recognize.

"Who's that?" I ask, aiming my stare at a modern-day Hercules with an eyebrow bar.

"That's Reed," Clara answers.

Willow and Reed whisper something and then disappear through one of the archways.

"Duty calls," Owen says, touching his calimeter. He winks at Anna and vanishes.

"Smell you cats later," Liam says, also disappearing.

"Let's head out. I'd like to speak with Jonathan before training today," Shane directs to Rigby.

Before leaving, Rigby flashes a Hollywood-worthy smile at Clara, even taking the toothpick out of his mouth to do so. Clara's oblivious, though, because she's staring at me. I'm beginning to notice she does this frequently. Apparently, by Rigby's now sour expression, he notices, too.

Jordan and Anna follow Rigby and Shane out of Benson.

Clara sighs reluctantly when it's just her and me left at the table. "I'd better head back, too."

"Can I ask you something?"

Her crystal-blue eyes widen. "Sure, anything."

"What's up with Willow? I mean, I don't doubt her skills, but what's this talk about her reputation?"

"She hasn't told you?"

I give her a blank look.

"I guess I can't say I'm surprised. She talks big, but in reality she's pretty modest." Clara pauses. "She is amazing, you know?"

I hold back a laugh. "I've been hearing that a lot."

"Because it's true," Clara retorts. "A few years back, Willow fell off the map. Three weeks without a single word from her, if you can imagine that."

I wish!

"When she returned, we drilled her about it so incessantly that she began coming around less and less. One day, Owen overheard a conversation between her and Jonathan. Maybe 'overheard' is the wrong word. Anyway, Willow threw out the word Rebellion. You've heard of that, right? When Tragedies go bad?"

"Yeah." I half laugh and bite into my bottom lip. "But why's this Rebellion thing such a big deal?"

"Tragedies are so called because they're teetering between the right and wrong paths. That's why we're needed. If they start heading in the wrong direction, they could alter many lives along the way, not just their own. Once a person becomes a Rebellion, the world around them has already begun to shift. Think of a Rebellion as a domino. Then push it over when there are thousands behind it, each representing another life. Get the picture?"

I lean back in my chair with my hands knitted behind my head. "Certainly one person's actions can't affect that many people."

"Oh yes, they can. And once those dominos start falling, the task of standing them back up becomes harder and harder. In no time, that single line of dominos branches into two and then four paths, eventually stemming out like a starburst. At that point, the task becomes impossible."

"All right, I think I get it. So what's this have to do with Willow?"

"So, Owen—well, he can't keep a secret if his life depended on it. I still don't know how he keeps his own assignments under wraps. Anyway, he told anyone who'd listen what he'd overheard. Willow denied it, of course, but we all knew it was because she had to. After that, she disappeared again."

"So you're saying Willow was on a Rebellion assignment?"

Clara nods and pauses when a girl walks by. "A few days later, Jonathan called our group to a meeting on the field and admitted just that to us. He said there would be no details given and then basically told us to stop pestering her so she could start coming around again. He also added that if she stayed locked away much longer, she was going to lose her mind." Clara frowns thoughtfully, staring down at the smooth tabletop. "I think he was kidding about that part."

Interesting. Maybe that explains why she's such a head case. "What happened then?"

"We kept our mouths shut about it, that's what. When Jonathan talks, you listen," she states matter-of-factly. "It's been long enough that we can joke about it now. Willow hasn't, and never will, spill the details about the assignment, but she likes to rub in how good she is to the guys. I can't imagine the kind of toll a Rebellion assignment must take on a Satellite, both physically and mentally. You should consider yourself lucky. You've scored yourself a major Legacy."

Clara looks down at her calimeter. "I need to get out of here." Before she slings her blue canvas bag over her shoulder, she pulls a small tube from its front pocket and spreads shiny lip gloss over her lips. The scent hits me. Please tell me she's not wearing…

"Peppermint?" I croak, and then I mentally slap myself for saying it out loud.

Her face brightens. "I'm impressed." Then, her eyes narrow on me suspiciously. "Wait—are you gay?"

What? "No! Why would you think that?"

"Most guys don't know anything about makeup. Plus, you've got the whole good looks thing going on."

Whoa, she can stop right there. I put my hands up, palms out. "Trust me when I say I know nothing about makeup." Peppermint, on the other hand, is something I've had lots of fine experiences with.

"Hey," I mutter when Clara stands up, figuring that since I'm already feeling awkward, now is as good of a time as any to help a friend out.

She eagerly looks at me and presses her highly glossed lips together.

"What do you think about Rigby?"

He eyes fall to the tabletop.

"Don't look so disappointed. The guy's not that bad," I tease.

She looks up, embarrassed. "Oh, I know. It's just—he's…there's someone else who…never mind. I'll see you later, OK?"

"Um…OK." Weird. "Thanks for telling me about

Willow."

Her face brightens again. "No problem. I bet you're the only one who didn't know she had a Rebellion assignment."

"That I doubt."

"Seriously, ask around. If I'm right, you owe me dinner."

I shake her tiny hand to accept her bet, hoping she's wrong. Not only would Rigby disapprove of us spending time together, I'm getting the vibe that dinner means something entirely different to her than it does to me.

7. It's like a jolt of electricity, but worse

Prepared for the landscape this time, I open the doors to the courtyard and try to keep my jaw hinged. I do wish the old man could see this. When I asked him three months ago if he believed in Heaven, he gave me the same answer he always did to every non-work-related question: "Shouldn't you be talking to your mother about this?" Yep, that was my dad.

After walking down the stone path, I climb the bleachers to Anna and Rigby. "Did you know about Willow?" I whisper to Anna.

She knits her brows. "About Willow?" she repeats, thinking for a minute. "You mean the Rebellion assignment?"

"You knew?" I whisper harshly.

"You didn't?" Thankfully, Anna's volume doesn't match her bugged-out eyes. Looking down, I shake my head.

"Seriously?" she says in disbelief.

I don't reply.

"Wow, I can't believe she never told you. It's pretty major."

Rigby leans over Anna and asks, "What's major?"

"He didn't know about Willow and the Rebellion assignment," Anna whispers.

Rigby pulls the toothpick from his mouth and grins. "You're kidding."

It looks like I have a date for dinner. Super. Maybe Rigby can take my place.

The whole Willow-leaving-me-in-the-dark routine is getting old. Speaking of, here's Miss Loon now. She stomps her boot between Anna and me and then sits behind us. "Hey, kids, whatcha talking about?" She ruffles my hair.

I swat her hand away and turn around to face her. "Is there something you think I should know?"

She purses her lips at me before responding. "Yes. Your hair looks terrible today."

Rigby cracks up when my hand raises to smooth my hair.

"Come on, Willow. You know what I'm talking about. Why didn't you tell me?"

She feigns ignorance. "I don't know what you mean."

"Man, I can't believe you didn't know." Rigby shakes his head.

"I'm sure she had her reasons for not telling you," Anna whispers.

"Oh, I get it. This is about the Rebellion, right?" Willow asks.

"It's a big deal!" I blurt out.

"How does it affect your training?" When I don't answer, she says, "That's exactly my point."

"It would have been helpful to know," I whisper

angrily.

"Why?"

"Oh, I don't know." I sigh dramatically. "Maybe because I seem to be the only person who *didn't* know." And because I now have a date with Clara, which Rigby is surely going to be ticked about. Maybe I should tell him and wipe the annoying smile off his face.

"And that's a problem?"

"Yes, it's a problem!" I yell.

Everyone within earshot stares in our direction.

"Look, kid, I have bigger things to worry about than your ego. Like your training, for example." She looks over my head to the field. "Now pay attention, will you?"

Still angry, I turn around as Jonathan begins. "Welcome back. It's wonderful to see you all again. Today you will be performing drills with your Legacies. The exercise will teach you the fundamentals of blocking. Remember, blocking requires great effort and skill. Practice and patience are key." He pulls the clipboard out from under his arm and flips a paper over. "Legacies, please pair off with your Satellites and begin your training."

The crowd disperses across the vast field. I follow Willow like a sulking brat, still loathing her for being so insanely maddening. She stops thirty yards away from the other pairs of Satellites.

"Ready to learn?"

"That's why I'm here."

She ignores my sarcasm. "Thanks to my volunteering us yesterday, you're a step ahead of the others. You already know how it feels on the receiving end of a block."

"Yeah. Bad."

"You should work on your vocab, kid."

I cross my arms. "Fine. It was destabilizing."

Willow seems pleased. "Better. First things first. The most important element of blocking is timing. You have a very small window for a successful block. If you want to master this skill, the key is getting your timing right."

I answer with "OK," but only because she's obviously waiting for a reply.

"Now, to the action itself. You need to focus on the outcome you want. For example, when I blocked you, I focused on you sitting instead of catching me. Following so far?"

"I was, until you brought up the part that I apparently don't remember."

Unamused, she says, "Just keep up, kid. So you focus on the outcome you want after centering your energy around your thoughts."

"Centering my *what?*"

"I knew this part was going to be tough for you to grasp." She looks at the ground, taps her finger on her chin, and then looks back at me. "It's like this: you possess an energy that's in constant motion throughout your body. You need to focus this energy, because you will be transferring your thoughts to your Tragedy through it."

Clearly she's mental. "OK, go on," I say, humoring her.

"At first, it can be helpful to bring your hands into a position like this." She poses like she's praying. "Once your energy is tightened, give the order 'haze.' This will produce the necessary filter that clouds your Tragedy's mind. It's then that you focus on the desired outcome. Your thoughts will transfer to your Tragedy through the haze. Still following?"

No. "Yeah."

"You'll feel the moment your Tragedy accepts your thoughts."

"Feel?"

"Yeah. It's like a jolt of electricity, but worse."

"That sounds…uncomfortable."

"Quite, actually. Now, following that jolt, you will need to break the connection by giving the order 'block.' This is important, because it will clear the haze and complete the process."

"And what if it's done incorrectly?"

"Well," she rolls her eyes, "that's why we're here. One more thing—all of this needs to happen within a few seconds. You can only maintain the haze for a short time. If the haze evaporates before your thoughts are transferred, the opportunity is lost."

"Which equals a fail."

"Ding, ding, ding! And I guess that now you know what too many failures leads to."

"I've just recently been told," I say, feeling crabby again.

"Get over it." She looks around the field. "Whitfield's about to give it a shot. Wanna watch her before you try?"

Whatever will buy me some time. "Sure."

We pass by groups of working Satellites to get to them. Shyla's telling Whitfield she's going to walk left, and Whitfield needs to make her go right instead.

"Go," Shyla instructs, unbuttoning the sleeves of her shirt before swinging her arms loosely at her sides.

After Whitfield tucks her flaming-red hair behind her ears, she takes a stance like she's praying and shouts, "Haze!" A light blur surrounds the girls.

"Block!" Whitfield yells, but it sounds more like a question than an order.

Unaffected by Whitfield's attempts at persuasion, Shyla walks to the left. "You're not quite there yet, but that was a decent first shot," Shyla adds with encouragement. "With enough practice, you'll own this."

"Ready to take a stab at it?" Willow asks.

"I guess so," I mumble, realizing there's no delaying the inevitable.

We move back to a free area on the lawn.

"Since you refused to hit me," she mocks, "I guess I'll offer you the same courtesy. Let's duplicate Shyla and Whitfield's block. I'm going left. Make me go right. Got it?"

I nod and close my eyes, looking for my so-called energy. I open my eyes before a grin slips out. "You're going to have to give me a little more guidance concerning this whole energy thing."

"You're so high maintenance." She looks up to the sky. "OK, this is how it was explained to me. Try to be open minded." She lowers her glare to me, waiting for a response.

"OK!" I say to pacify her.

Unhumored, she keeps going. "My energy is a color. I visualize it and form it into a tight ball."

I crack up.

"Shut up! I'm trying to help you here. Now go, already."

I close my eyes, but I only laugh harder.

"Come on!"

"Fine. But just one question," I say evenly.

"What?" she snaps.

"What color?"

"Forget it. Let's go."

"Please." My expression is controlled. "I think it would help."

"Purple." She pushes a braid out of her face and exhales deeply. "Now, do you think you can at least act like an adult?"

"This coming from a woman with purple energy?"

"Shut it, kid. Let's go." She turns her face away from me.

"Is that a smile?"

"Just concentrate, will you?" she says, but her composure is breaking, too.

Finally, we both can keep a straight face. "All right, I'm ready."

"Good. Same drill."

With my eyes closed, I search for this energy: a color—any color—as Willow suggested. At first there's nothing. Then, slowly, a very faint blue forms behind my eyelids. When it darkens, I open my eyes. Everything around me is covered in this sapphire filter. I concentrate on pulling the color in. It retracts slowly at first, but then pulls in faster, eventually forming a small translucent ball. Forgetting to bring my palms together, I shout the order: "Haze!"

A rippled glasslike filter forms around me before extending out to Willow, and my hearing is muffled like I'm underwater. My senses fight against the claustrophobia while my brain screams the directions: *Go right, go right, go right, go right, go...*

Ahhhhhhhhggg!

Every nerve in my body is assaulted and paralyzed by pain. I can't think; I can't concentrate. My jaw clenches against the electric current, and the torture radiates through my teeth so intensely I'd swear they were about to fall out. How do I make this stop? Think, think, think!

"Block!" I yell.

The pain evaporates with the filter. I gasp in relief as my muscles twitch. I look to Willow for an explanation. She turns to her right, and thunderous applause breaks out around us.

"Grant, that was killer! I've never seen someone block that well on their first shot," Shane calls to me.

Willow is frozen.

"Willow?" I manage to say, even though my muscles still hate her.

She stares back at me. For once, she is speechless.

"Willow?" I ask again, starting to get a little worried.

Only her eyes move. "What happened?" she demands of Jordan.

"You should have seen him—he's a natural!"

I can't help but gloat when Willow stares at me in disbelief. Blocking her was downright torturous, but now I'm thinking it may have been worth it. "Huh. It's funny when the tables turn—"

She cuts me off. "Again!"

"What?"

"Again! Let's go. I'm coming at you. You should probably make me turn and walk away," she orders.

My eyes all but jump from their sockets when she gets into position. She's not kidding—she's going to attack me.

My energy comes faster this time, despite my trembling muscles. I look at Willow through the blue mask and tighten the filter as fast as I can. "Haze!"

The muffled hum doesn't throw me off as it did before.

Turn around, turn around, turn—holy mother!

The agonizing current swallows me. I try to remember what I'm doing while the jolt suffocates me. Think already!

"Block!" The paralysis stops, but this time I stumble forward. My knee catches me before I face-plant into the grass.

Willow turns and walks the other way, but this time my audience's response is more subdued.

"Did he block me?" Willow demands of the silent crowd. "*Did he block me!*" she yells.

A voice I don't recognize answers. "Yes, but—"

"Again."

"Willow, he needs a break," Jordan interjects.

"Again!" Her glare blazes through me. "I'm going to punch you. Come up with whatever you want."

I somehow right myself, knowing if I don't she's going to hit me—hard. My muscles scream in protest when I close my eyes and try to find my energy. Its color is very faint, but I'm able to center it. "Haze," I mumble.

Under the waterfall, Willow comes at me too fast. Her eyes are wild and her white knuckles grow bigger and bigger…

Sit, sit, sit, sit…

The pain crushes me. She moves in slow motion while I'm held hostage by a jolt that's ripping my muscles apart. I welcome her fist—anything that will make the current stop.

I force out the words, "Block!" and crumble to the ground. My flaming muscles seize uncontrollably.

When I can finally focus my eyes, Shane and Jordan are at my side, and Willow is sitting on the ground a foot in front of us. She doesn't ask this time. My beaten body must be proof to her that I performed another successful block.

When she pushes herself up, the look in her eyes is terrifying. "Again!" she yells.

"Enough!" a commanding voice shouts from behind me.

Willow stares over my head, considering her challenger. Then, she marches off toward the building. I try to relax my shaking muscles. She's lost her mind!

"That was brutal," Shane says.

I push off the ground, but my legs buckle under me. Jordan grabs my waist and hoists me up. As much as I hate to, I lean on him for support. "Was that normal?"

"No. I've never seen a new Satellite block so easily. That was sick, man."

"It wasn't easy," I manage to tell Jordan, but don't have the strength to clarify what I meant by "normal."

Anna looks like she's about to cry. "Why can't he stand

on his own?"

"He'll be fine. He just needs to rest," says a voice behind me. "Jordan, I can take him from here."

I'm passed off to Jonathan and left wishing that I could walk on my own. No dice, though, since my legs are the consistency of wet noodles.

"That was quite a show out there," Jonathan compliments, which makes me defensive.

"I didn't mean for it to be."

"Oh, I'm not coming down on you. Quite the contrary. Your blocking skills are impressive. I have no doubt great things are in your future."

My lack of energy makes the rest of our journey to the apartment a quiet one. By the time we reach the elevator, I am relying on him less than before. Still, I've never been more ecstatic to see the dreadful sofa.

"Thank you," I say when Jonathan lowers me onto the cushion.

"You're welcome. You should feel well after some rest. Can I get you anything before I go?"

"No, I'm OK."

Jonathan nods and crosses the room, but turns back when I call his name.

"What do you think got into Willow?" I ask. "I mean, I've never seen her like that before."

"Willow likes to be in control. I believe this afternoon's events left her feeling a bit out of sorts, with someone so new getting the upper hand."

"Has anyone else ever reacted that way?" If so, I pity

whoever was on the receiving end.

"No, not that extreme. That's Willow, though. Go big or go home."

I'd like to laugh, but I haven't recovered from my beating.

Jonathan continues. "It's important to consider the internal struggle that takes place throughout a Legacy's transition. Embracing the promise of the future means letting go of the past. This doesn't come easy. One day, you may find yourself faced with the same difficulty."

I'm facing it right now, I think.

"I hope you can forgive Willow for her actions. I'm certain that she feels bad about today's events."

Uh-huh. Right.

I stay on the sofa when Jonathan leaves, because unless I want to army crawl across the room, I have no other choice.

———

An hour later, I trust my legs enough to carry me to the kitchen. When I return to the sofa, the assignment book on the trunk catches my attention. I hesitantly set my coffee down, open to the page with the bad glove drawing, and push my hand down. The book yanks me in without pause this time, sending me on the blind, oxygen-free roller coaster of needles. Thankfully, I land more quickly than I did on the previous ride.

Because she's such a lovely hostess, GPS Jeanette extends her welcome, and like before, the wall spins to present a single rusty door.

After the handle sends the expected jolt, I step into 2001. The chirping crickets are deafening, and my steaming breath seems to float even longer in the air. Ryder's sitting on the grass beside a blonde girl. Behind them, Granite lifts his head when the street lights blink on.

"Only a week left, you know. Are you ready to go back?" the girl asks.

"I dunno. It's been great hanging out with you this summer," Ryder answers.

"Yeah?"

"Yeah!" he says, but then adds with less confidence, "Don't you think?"

Oh yeah, she's definitely into him. An airplane skywriting her feelings across a clear sky would be subtler than her current glowing expression.

From across the street, a woman yells in the thickest New England accent I've heard yet. "Hannah, honey, time to come in!"

"Be right there, Mom!" the girl shouts back. The woman closes her front door. "See you later?" the girl asks Ryder.

Ryder looks disappointed, but then his face brightens a little. "I'm working on a new magic trick. Wanna see it tomorrow?"

When the girl unexpectedly hits him with an open-mouthed kiss, I laugh. "Shut your eyes, Ryder!" I yell, though obviously he can't hear me.

Hannah pulls away and bolts across the lawn. Ryder's

goofy expression stays on his face until Granite scoots up and leans against him.

"Don't tell Dad," Ryder whispers to Granite.

I'm pulled away in a quick jerk, and the metal door slams shut.

As instructed, I step into 2004 when the spin cycle is complete. Ryder, now as tall as me, exits a brick-faced building in a historic district. He fidgets with his keys under the streetlight, locks the front door, and unties his apron.

"Ready?" his father asks from inside the rusty truck parked on the curb.

Ryder slides into the passenger seat and slams the door, but his voice carries through the open windows. "Uh, yeah!"

"It needs a lot of work. You realize that, right?"

"Come on, Dad, we've been over this how many times? It's a Shelby, for crying out loud! You said you'd help, so don't start flaking out on me now."

"I won't. I just want to be sure you understand what a big project this is going to be. You had to cut an awful lot of lawns and make hundreds of pizzas to come up with that money."

Now annoyed, Ryder grumbles, "Can we go now?"

"OK, if you're sure."

"Dad!"

After a deep chuckle, the truck roars away, and I'm sucked back into the room.

"Please proceed to 2005," GPS Jeanette says after the ding stops the wall. When I step through the door, the combination of gasoline fumes and loud music makes me homesick for the days Tate accompanied me when I worked on my truck.

"Hey, Dad, hand me the ratchet!" Ryder yells from under the Mustang's faded red hood. His grease-covered forearm hangs out the side, hairier and thicker than ever.

His dad, almost fully gray now, adjusts the radio's volume before rummaging through the toolbox. He steps around Granite, who's aged the most, and passes Ryder the ratchet. "Is Madison stopping by?"

"Yeah. Is it cool if she stays for dinner?" Ryder murmurs from under the hood.

"Sure. She seems like a great girl."

"She is."

"Does she make you happy?" I'd have fallen over if my dad ever asked a question like that. No, I would have gotten something more along the lines of, "Why were you late to work?"

Ryder's reply is strained, like he's tightening a bolt at the same time he's talking. "Mmm-hmm."

"That's what it's all about." His dad walks around the car and bangs his fist on the trunk. "You should have this thing purring by next week."

I'm jerked away, but this time, I don't land in the dirt. Instead, a force shoves me back through the same door, where antiseptic replaces the smell of gasoline. In a small room, Ryder hovers over Granite. I look down at the fur-covered animal on the linoleum floor, already knowing what's coming.

"The blockage is in a difficult area," a graying woman

in a white lab coat explains to Ryder. "Even if he tolerated the anesthesia, I honestly don't know if we could get to it."

"There's got to be something else we can do," Ryder pleads into Granite's wiry fur.

The woman squeezes Ryder's shoulder. "I'm so sorry. You gave him a full life."

When Ryder chokes out his OK, she leaves the room and closes the door. Granite pants and trembles. I look at the ceiling tiles, wishing I couldn't hear Ryder's profuse, sobbing apologies to his dog.

The doctor comes back a few minutes later. "Are you ready?"

My breath creates miniclouds in the suffocating room. I squeeze my eyes closed until the cold slam of metal tells me it's OK to open them.

I mash my palms against my eyes while the room spins. As instructed, I step into 2006.

"That's great." Ryder talks into his cell phone in a modest but bright kitchen, then thumbs through a stack of mail while he listens. When he gets bored with the envelopes, he moves to the outdated fridge and grabs a carton of milk. "This is what you wanted. We'll figure it out."

Mya looks up from a stack of magazines spread across the round table and watches Ryder. If it weren't for her familiar brown eyes, I probably wouldn't recognize her. She's prettier than ever.

"I know. Don't worry about it...OK, I love you, too. Bye." Ryder hangs up and locks the screen on his phone.

"What's up?" Mya asks lightly, not acknowledging that

Ryder has just slammed his glass of milk on the counter.

"Madison got into NYU."

"You don't sound too excited."

"It's a long way from Dartmouth."

"You guys will make it work."

"I know," he says, but his tone doesn't match the certainty of his words.

"I need a guy's opinion. Do you think Lucas would like this dress?" Mya asks, flipping her magazine around so Ryder can see.

"I'm not so sure you should be wearing white," Ryder jokes.

Mya hurls her pen at him before I'm jerked backward.

The stone room spins to 2008, and I step into another kitchen—this one even smaller than the last. It's crammed full of weird artsy stuff.

Ryder slumps through the back door. "What's wrong?" Mya asks him. The question should, more fittingly, be directed at her, because she looks like she swallowed a watermelon.

"Madison and I called it quits tonight," Ryder mumbles, hugging his arms around himself. "How are you feeling?" He eyes the growth where her stomach once was.

"Look at me—how do you think? I'm sorry about Madison. I know you were worried that this was coming."

"She thinks that by having a boyfriend, she's missing out on the whole 'college experience,'" he says, making mock quotations in the air. "Apparently her idea of college includes sleeping around."

"Stop it. Madison's not like that."

"I know." He combs his fingers through his black hair, which looks like it hasn't been cut (or washed) in years. "This just sucks. I love her."

Mya crosses the kitchen in three waddles and rubs his shoulders. "Hungry? I always feel better when I eat."

He points his stare at the giant bump in her belly. "That's obvious."

She squeezes his shoulder until he shrinks in pain.

"Kidding! Jeez, woman! I'm not hungry, but I'll stick around. Where's Lucas?"

"Late shift tonight. He should be home in about an hour."

Mya digs around in the fridge for a long time. "Nothing looks good," she says from inside the box. She comes out with a bottle of orange juice and then gasps.

Ryder jumps up from his chair to get to her. "What happened?"

"Uh…I think my water just broke."

Ryder, instantly changing his mind about helping his sister, leaps back until he's pressed against the wall and gawks at the puddle under her feet.

"Wipe that look off your face! It's not like I just peed myself!"

"That's disgusting! Can I call Lucas or something?" Ryder inches further away.

"Yeah, on our way to the hospital. Go grab my bag. It's up in my room by the dresser." Comically, she tries to bend over to sop up the fluid with a towel. Ryder stares, repulsed.

"Go!" Mya shouts.

Ryder disappears up the stairs, returns less than a minute later, and announces, "We're taking your car!" He flings a bath towel at Mya and then throws her flowered bag (which is bigger than her) up over his shoulder.

Mya rolls her eyes. Funny, she looks just like—

The yank through the door cuts off my thought, and I forget to look down. The stone wall makes me dizzy.

"Please proceed to 2010," GPS Jeanette says when the spinning stops. "This will be your final door."

The huge crowd throws me off, and it takes a second before the loud speaker registers. "Joseph Alexander Becker...Ryder Collin Beckmann...Julie Rene Behlman..."

Ryder's dad, Mya, and another guy (presumably Lucas), jump from their seats around me, whooping and hollering like banshees. A two-fingered whistle almost blows my eardrum.

"Lennon, look! That's Uncle Ryder!" Ryder's dad exclaims to the little boy in Lucas's arms, and then proudly points over a sea of black square caps to the stage. No way would my old man have been this enthusiastic about his son receiving a college diploma. Heck, the only reason he was excited about my high school diploma was because he got five more days of work out of me every week.

"Ry-ry!" The boy, Lennon, has Mya's eyes.

"Yeah, Ry-ry!" Mya shouts.

I'm yanked back into the stone room, and GPS Jeanette says, "Thank you for your time," as if I had a choice. Then, to be even more polite, she says, "Best of luck with your assignment."

I'm jerked painfully into the oxygen-sucking darkness, though I stay calmer this time, knowing it will end eventually.

I catch my balance in front of the sofa and the book jumps away from me, landing on its spine and flopping closed. Grateful to be done with all that, I grab the book and put it on the trunk before settling into the worn sofa cushion.

A minute later, Willow barges through the door.

So much for relaxing.

8. A punch in the face would be more subtle

"OK, kid, let's get this over with," Willow's voice barks from behind me.

I lift my head. "Well hello, Willow," I say with feigned politeness. "I'm fine. Thank you for asking."

"Just shut up and let me get this out."

I kick my legs off the cushion before she plops down on them.

"I'm sorry about what happened on the field today," she starts, wringing her hands together. "I don't know what got into me. You have every right to be angry."

"You're giving me permission?" I plan to fully relish her apology.

Willow continues talking to her lap. "Look, I realize I made a fool of myself out there. I never react like that; I was out of control. Being a Satellite is everything to me. It's all I know—I mean, really know." She shakes her head. "I don't remember my life, and to make things worse, my husband and I are expected to have this magical reunion or something. I barely know who he is!"

She lays her head back and stares at the ceiling. "Sheesh. I'm rambling." After a minute, she looks over at me. "I'm sorry, kid. It's inexcusable what I did out there. Can you forgive me?"

Just to make her sweat, I pretend to consider before agreeing.

She seems surprised. "That's it?"

"That's it."

"Wow! That was way easier than I thought it was going to be."

"Oh, come on, Willow. I'm not heartless."

"I know, but I expected a little more resistance. Wait—did Jonathan get to you?"

"What do you mean?" I ask, pretending innocence.

"He did! I should've known. Too bad. I had a whole slew of things I was planning to say."

"Well, let's hear them," I urge her.

"Fat chance now. I'll store them away for another time."

"So you're planning to go crazy again? Super. Give me a heads-up next time."

"We'll see."

After sitting in silence for a while, she says, "I really am sorry."

"I know."

She smacks my knee before pushing up from the sofa and sauntering to the kitchen. "So I talked to Reed, and he thinks I should observe you while you code," she announces.

"When?"

"You totally look like crap, so the sooner the better. You feel up to it now?"

"Sure, but can we do it from here? I'm super

comfortable," I joke, resting my head back on the cushion.

"Isn't that sofa the best?"

"If you're blind."

"Ten to one says you keep it after I'm gone."

"No chance," I say.

"You don't want to lose another bet, do you?"

"Another?"

"I hear your having dinner with Clara tonight," she says.

I twist around to look at her. "How did you know about that?"

"News travels fast, kid. Everyone loves new gossip."

Un-frigging-believable.

"Should I go ahead and spread the word that you're off the market?"

"No!" I yell harshly and then level my voice. "I mean—no. We are definitely not a couple. I barely know her." Not to mention there's no way I could ever be with someone else. The thought ignites like a match behind my ribs. I push up from the sofa and storm past Willow. "I'm ready," I declare, anxious to see Tate again.

Willow catches up, and soon we're sitting on the black mats. She faces me while I stare at my fists in the mirror.

"Reed said you should do everything just like before. While you're under, I'll see if anything seems off."

This entire situation is off. "Good luck with that," I retort, closing my eyes.

It's easier than I expect to tune Willow out. I visualize my room—and Tate—and the scene comes even faster than before. Tate's body is curled into my side; her arm sprawled across my chest. Her shallow breath feels hot on my neck. To prove she's awake, she sighs heavily.

When she raises her head, her eyes give away that she's been crying. She brings her mouth close until our lips and tongues are moving together. She clings to me, and I tighten my arms around her.

"Tate, please stay," I whisper when she pulls away, tracing my finger on her lower lip.

Her reaction doesn't change. It's as if she didn't hear me.

"Tate, please. Stay with me!" I beg.

She leaps up and grabs her favorite pink T-shirt from the floor and then violently rips the cotton in half at the collar.

Ice floods through my veins, and blackness covers me for less than a second. It's long enough for me to recognize the feeling, but it doesn't make any sense. Not now.

When I blink, I'm back in the coding room. I bolt up and snatch Willow's arm. "We're not on the field anymore!"

Her eyes dart down to her biceps. "Grant, stop! What are you talking about?"

"Observe? Was this your idea or his? Probably yours—you're so twisted!"

"Stop! Let go!" She jerks her arm out of my grasp.

How could she? How dare her! Enraged, I pace in the room. She follows behind me, wisely keeping a considerable distance between us.

"Calm down and talk to me."

I spin around. "How could you block me in there?"

Willow freezes. "What? I didn't. What do you mean, block you?"

"This isn't one of your little training exercises! This is my life!" I growl.

"I don't know what you're talking about."

I continue pacing until she grabs my shoulders and forces me to stop. "I didn't block you! Come on, let's go into the other room and figure this out. You need to sit down. You're shaking."

I try to make fists to steady my hands, but my muscles are too weak. She wraps an arm around my waist and leads me into the other room. On the sofa, my trembling increases and sweat drips down my face.

"Tell me what happened."

"You honestly didn't block me?" I ask weakly.

She looks directly into my eyes. "I swear I didn't."

But the feeling—it was exactly the same: the blackness, the temperature drop.

"Tell me what happened. Start from the beginning."

"There's not much to it. I was in my room with Tate. We were kissing. Everything went black and cold, and now, here I am."

"Why do you think you were blocked?"

"It felt the same." I shake my head in frustration. I'm missing something. "Did you notice anything off?"

"Other than you were out a long time? No."

"It was just a couple of minutes," I say, correcting her.

She studies me. "No. It was a long time. An hour, or

maybe longer."

"That's ridiculous."

Willow looks as puzzled as I feel. "I'm at a loss here. I'm sorry, kid."

"Don't apologize. It's not your fault that I'm eternally jacked up."

"Oh, you're jacked, all right, but for reasons way beyond this. I just wish I knew why." She looks down at her calimeter. "Go clean up so you don't look like a hobo on your date."

Clara. My stomach drops. "It's not a date!" I yell and then level my tone. "I mean, uh, it's definitely not a date. There's nothing we could possibly have in common." Plus, I would never do that to Tate. "How awkward do you think this will be?"

"If your enthusiasm is any indicator, I'd say extremely. She's a nice girl. At least try to act like you're having a good time."

I strip off my sweat-soaked shirt in the closet and search for the right words to explain it to Willow without coming off like a jerk. "It's not that I don't like her. I just don't like her like *that*," I yell into the kitchen.

"Seriously, kid. How old are you?"

"Sorry," I murmur, embarrassed. "I suck at this stuff. I just get the feeling she wants to be more than friends." I pull on a new pair of jeans and bring my boots and a new shirt into the kitchen.

"You get the feeling? A punch in the face would be more subtle. She's been ogling you since you arrived."

"Did you seriously just say ogling?"

"Yeah—so?"

"Dude, you are so old."

She dramatically clears her throat. "Timeless and wise, thank you very much."

"A wise something," I say, pushing my feet into my boots.

Willow snorts and then eyes my chest before I get my shirt on. "I bet Clara would get a kick out of that look."

I shoot her a deadly look before putting my arms through my shirtsleeves. "Why can't she be into Rigby?" I complain.

Willow shrugs and slings her bag strap over her head. "Because she's obviously into you. Next time don't make bets you're guaranteed to lose."

"It's your fault! If you had told me about your past, this wouldn't even be happening."

"Oh no, don't pin this on me! Besides, she would have found some other way to pull you in. Clara's a persistent little thing," she snickers.

———————

"Looks like she didn't forget," Willow says when we walk into Benson, crushing my last bit of hope.

I follow Willow's stare to Clara, who is sitting in the corner at a table for two. Alone.

"Try to be a gentleman, kid."

Willow bounces off to the table I wish I was joining,

leaving me standing by myself. Rigby glares at me, which sucks. I'd be glad to trade him places right now.

On my way over to her, Clara stands and waves. Holy hell, she's wearing a tight red dress and high heels. I sigh, knowing I should feel underdressed in my jeans and work boots, but instead, I'm thankful for my wardrobe choice. Maybe she'll realize this isn't a date. At least, it's not to me.

I force a smile. "Hey, Clara."

"I was starting to think you weren't going to show. Looks like you lost, huh?"

"You knew I'd lose," I joke.

She throws her arms up. "Guilty."

"Do you wanna get something to eat?" I ask.

"Nah, I'm not hungry."

"Is anybody ever hungry here?"

Clara laughs. "No, I guess not. You all right? You look tired."

She sits rigidly, like she's nervous, and crosses her legs. I pull out the chair across from her and sit. "I'm good," I lie. "What are you drawing?" I ask to change the subject.

She blushes and conceals her sketchbook even further under her arm. "Nothing."

"It looks like more than nothing."

"Just doodling."

"Can I see?"

She reluctantly pushes the book across the table, and I flip through the pages, growing more impressed with each sketch. "This is great stuff. Seriously, Clara, this is really good!"

"Thanks," she replies, blushing. "Most of them still need a lot of work." Despite her opposite-in-every-way appearance, she's artistically more like Tate than I would have guessed—and humble like her, too.

"They look finished to me," I argue, fanning through the pages of landscapes. "Are these places you've been?"

She stares at the page I've paused on. "Previous assignments. That one is of a bay in California."

"It's amazing."

"If I had known before I died how beautiful California was, I would have insisted on going there while I was still alive," she says in a softer voice.

"How'd you die?"

"Heart failure. I was on a transplant list by the time I was three. Having an uncommon blood type made finding a donor difficult. In my case, impossible." She looks up at me and blinks her long, dark-painted lashes.

"How old were you?"

"Nine."

"How are you so much older now?" I ask, surprised.

"We take our best physical form when we die." She pauses. "I never made it to mine, which turns out to be seventeen." She looks down at the table and shakes her head. "I can't believe I'm about to tell you this, it's so embarrassing, but I was happy about my new body when I got here. Stupid, right?"

"No, I totally get it. I was, too." Getting rid of my diseased body is one of the only good things about this place. "I can see why you wouldn't be disappointed." *Crap! Why did*

I say that?

Clara blushes again. That's what I get for trying to be nice. I bite my tongue to avoid paying any more compliments.

She talks while I flip through more of the sketchbook. "My mom prayed for a new heart, but the ugly truth is, she was praying for someone else to die. I heard her tell my dad that she felt like a monster for that. That's the word she used. But I was the real monster. It was all my fault." She looks away. "That's one of the few memories I got to keep."

"It wasn't your fault."

She looks back at me. "Wasn't it? It was my genetic makeup, after all, that made me this."

"Were you angry when you got here, when you realized you were never meant to get another heart?"

"I felt regret more than anything. My parents were too afraid to let me do much, like my heart might spontaneously combust or something."

"What would you have done?"

"Danced. Taken gymnastics. Gone to California." She turns her head to the side and her blonde hair falls from her shoulder. "Lived. Really lived, you know?"

I nod.

"Would you have done anything differently?" she asks.

My deepest regret would totally kill the mood, so I keep it to myself. "I'll get back to you on that."

"Fair enough. I'm holding you to it, though. So, cancer, huh?"

"Melanoma. Who knew something as small as a mole

would eventually kill me?" I say dryly.

She slides her index finger along her glossy lower lip. The action is not sensual, yet my eyes lock on her mouth. "The Schedulers."

"Sorry?" I question, mentally punching myself in the face for fixating on her lips.

"The Schedulers knew that mole would kill you."

"Oh. Right." Hoping I'm not getting red, I dart my eyes back to the sketchbook and flip through a few more pages. "How many assignments have you had?"

"I'm on my eighth."

"How long do they last?"

"Depends. My first assignment lasted a little over a year. My second was over three years. It varies by Tragedy."

"Do you miss your Tragedies when your assignments are done?"

She looks confused. "Miss them? No. Didn't Willow tell you about Maintenance?"

I shake my head. "I guess we haven't gotten to that yet."

"We still check in a couple of times a month. I'm surprised Willow hasn't told you. What have you guys been doing, anyway?"

"Coding has been giving me some trouble." That's not completely a lie.

"Huh. From what I hear about your blocking skills, I would have thought coding would be a breeze."

From what she hears? What's with this place?

"You've heard what the others are saying, right?" She

gauges my expression. "You haven't? I feel another bet coming on."

"No way! I'm not betting with you anymore," I say, hoping my voice sounds like I'm joking.

"Word is, you're the most promising blocker we've had. No other Satellite has ever performed three blocks on their first day. Sounds like Willow really put you through the wringer."

"You could say that."

"That's so unlike her."

"What—being insane?" I ask.

Clara laughs. "Seriously, I don't know how you lasted three times."

"I didn't have a choice. Willow was trying to kill me."

"Now you're being dramatic."

No, she definitely wanted me dead. "Maybe a little." I close the sketchbook and slide it back to her.

"I'd better get going," she says unexpectedly. "I need to code before heading back to my assignment."

"Oh, OK." I'm surprised to feel a little disappointed.

"Thanks for hanging out with me."

"I enjoyed this," I say, my words astonishing even me.

"Don't sound so shocked," she teases.

"I'm sorry. I just…I don't want to give you the wrong impression about us. I mean, me…or me and you," I stammer.

"Are you seriously giving me the it's-not-you-it's-me speech?"

"No. Well—yeah, I guess so. But I do mean it. Any guy

would be a fool not to want you."

She remains way cooler than me. "So I guess you're a fool, then?"

If I had a dollar for every time I heard that. "I'm just not looking for a relationship right now." *Or ever again.*

"I can appreciate that. You're a nice guy. And hot, for what it's worth," she adds. Sincere amusement overcomes her, and her eyes crinkle at the corners. "It's nice to see *you* blush for once."

She presses her lips against my cheek before I've even realized she's gotten up from the table. The faint scent of peppermint makes my stomach tighten and for just an instant, it was like Tate was the one kissing me.

"Thanks for the nice conversation," she says.

My index and middle finger slide across my skin where her lips were pressed. When Clara disappears through the archway, whistles and catcalls come from the middle of the room.

"Grow up!" I yell to Willow's table when I find my voice, turning quickly away when I see the scowl on Rigby's face.

9. You're not going to yack, are you

"How was your date?" Willow asks on our way to the field, because I successfully avoided her table after Clara left. Getting food and hiding at a deserted table in the back of Benson was a smart decision, considering Rigby's foul mood.

"It wasn't a date, and it was surprisingly decent," I reply.

"I told you Clara was cool."

"Have you seen her drawings?"

"Yeah. Incredible, right?"

I agree and hold the courtyard door open for Willow.

"Looks like they haven't forgotten our spectacle," Willow says when everyone parts like the Red Sea for us.

"I was trying not to notice," I mumble under my breath. I keep my eyes down and follow Willow's stomping feet to the highest row of bleachers, making sure not to look at Rigby.

"Nice try," I say. "I would have picked the first row." At least then we wouldn't be subjected to watching everyone stare.

Willows barks at the rubberneckers, "Your faces are going to get stuck like that if you're not careful."

The spectators couldn't care less and continue to gawk and whisper.

An unfamiliar woman, who by her attire just dismounted a horse, shuts them up. "Good afternoon. For those of you who don't know me, which is most of the new Satellites, I'm Wynn. I'll be standing in for Jonathan today. He sends his regrets." She paces the edge of the field while she talks and her long ponytail bounces with each step. Her tall, curvy build is similar to Tate's. "Legacies, continue working with your Satellites on blocking. I will be available if you need assistance." She looks down at her clipboard. "Willow and Grant, please join me."

After rudely stealing a few more glances, the crowd disperses, and Willow and I hop down the cedar planks to Wynn. Crossing the field with Shane, Rigby looks over his shoulder at me and his glare is so nasty, I can feel the burn of it even when I look away.

"Grant, it's a pleasure. Jonathan tells me that you did exceptionally well with blocking," Wynn says. Her handshake is stronger than most men's. "Willow, fantastic work thus far. You've been cleared to begin displacement training."

"Sweet! Let's go, kid."

"Fantastic work thus far?" I repeat to Willow when we cross the field, grateful to be heading in the opposite direction of where Rigby and Shane are working.

"Not bad, being cleared after one day. I'm sure that's a record," she says, a compliment I'd swear she was giving herself.

"Does this mean I don't have to block you today?"

She nods, and my shoulders relax. *Thank you, thank you, thank you!*

"Today we're displacing," she says.

"Which is what, exactly?"

"It's how we travel. We're going to visit one of my Tragedies."

"That reminds me," I interrupt. "Clara told me about Maintenance. What happens with you, since you'll no longer be a Satellite?"

Defensively, she answers, "I'll always be a Satellite," then lightens her tone. "I won't be getting any new assignments, but I'll still continue Maintenance."

"For how long?"

"Until the end."

"The end of what?"

"My Tragedies' lives, ignoramus," she says.

I don't have the energy to acknowledge the insult. "Then what?"

"Then I enjoy eternity with my husband, I suppose. Even then, I'll still come around to check in on the other Satellites. Being a Satellite is forever, kid." She pushes her shoulder against mine while we walk. "Even you may realize how cool it is one day. Now, back to displacing. You'll need a personal belonging from your Tragedy—a 'tocket,' as we call it. One will be supplied to you when you're cleared from training." Willow stops, reaches into her bag, and pulls out a plastic beaded bracelet. "This belongs to one of my previous Tragedies, Hope."

Willow grips one side of the bracelet and extends her arm. "Go ahead," she urges me.

Reluctantly, I wrap two fingers through the small loop.

Willow winks. "I think you're going to like this. Displace."

The grass drops out from under us, and we plummet like skydivers without parachutes, connected by the cheap bracelet. Wind howls in my ears. I'd scream, but thankfully, my voice has been stolen. The last thing the lunatic beside me needs is more ammunition to razz me.

When I'm half a second away from tossing the contents of my stomach, my feet hit the ground hard enough to throw my balance. Willow leaps in front of me, grabbing my shoulders. After a minute, she asks cautiously, "How are you feeling?"

"A little sick," I groan, swallowing down the lingering nausea and breathing in the smell of worms.

She jumps back. "You're not going to yack, are you?"

I shake my head. "I don't think so."

"Good, because I so hate that!"

When I step forward and lose my balance, Willow grabs my shoulders and pushes me back. "Easy, kid—let your body adjust. Displacing takes a little getting used to. Kinda wild, huh?"

"You could say that."

A minute and a lot of deep breaths later, I successfully step from the shiny pavement onto a leaf-covered lawn. My head jerks to the large house to my left when the front door opens. A trail of people come out, saying good-byes and carrying small coolers and foil-wrapped dishes. Not one of them acknowledges our presence.

"I gotta say, you're proving to be a natural," Willow

says, gaining my attention back.

When Willow starts walking, I follow. Oddly, the wet leaves don't move under our feet. She stops and looks up at one of the skyscraper trees close to the two-story house.

"This is my favorite place to watch Hope." She bends her knees and then disappears.

"Willow?" I ask into the still air.

"Come on up, kid." She's perched on a high branch with her legs swinging under her.

"How?"

"Jump."

It seems too simple. "That's it?"

"Would you prefer a ladder?" she sneers.

Hesitating for a second, I push off the wet ground, rocketing skyward.

Willow's hand closes like a vise around my ankle. "Easy. You're stronger than you realize." She yanks me down to her branch.

"So, no one can see us?" I ask, jumping when a squirrel runs overhead.

"Nope, we're invisible. Phenomenal, huh?"

"Not sure about phenomenal. Weird, for sure."

"There you go again with your extensive vocabulary."

Sheesh. "Unconventional, then."

Willow smirks. "Follow me." She steadies herself on the branch like a gymnast on a balance beam before leaping through a glass window.

I'm barely familiar with displacement and she's throwing this at me? Repeating her movement with much less grace, my mind calculates the improbability and stops me before going through the window. My feet land on the narrow sill, and I lose my footing.

Willow's hand appears through the glass and catches my arm. "Careful, kid." Her voice sounds muffled through the window. She tugs my arm hard enough to drag me through, and I like the constricting pressure about as much as being dropped from the sky.

I right myself in the lime-green bedroom. The smell of what I guess to be pizza lingers in the air. "Couldn't we just use the door?"

Willow, too busy beaming at the teen couple sprawled across the oversize bed, doesn't answer.

The emptiness in the pit of my stomach spreads out like a thick puddle of dirty oil. Tate and I would do this same thing, especially after my treatments increased. In our case, there was less flirting and more vomiting.

"She's doing so great!" Willow says proudly.

"It must be hard, huh?" I ask, hoping to take my mind off missing Tate.

Willow stares at the giggling girl. "Hmm?"

"Leaving all this."

"I'm not leaving," she argues. "I get to check in."

"I know, but it's going to be different, right?" To spare my own feelings, I've plainly hurt Willow's. Ugh, me and my big frigging mouth.

Her gaze shifts to the fuzzy pink rug at the foot of the bed and she chews on her lip. "Yeah, it's going to be tough."

"You're going to see your husband again, though. That's

gonna be pretty excellent." I go overboard with my enthusiasm.

She looks up at me and whispers, "What if I suck?"

"What?"

"I mean, what if I'm a terrible wife? It's been so many years…" She trails off.

"Come on, you're an overachiever by nature. You'll be great," I assure her. "Although you're probably going to annoy the snot out of him. Poor guy."

Willow's expression brightens about half a notch. "I'm a little jealous of you."

"Me? Why?"

"You haven't forgotten her," she says in a whisper.

I silently pray that I never will. "That's just because I'm broken or something." I smile to try and lighten the mood.

"Part of me wishes it had been like that for me with Troy. There are still so many holes in my memory. What if some pieces are lost forever?"

"They'll come back," I encourage. I hope, for her sake, that they really will.

She looks back at the girl, and I maintain my silence to avoid saying anything else that might upset Willow.

She elbows my ribs. "Let's check out before I get all emotional. How about some more maneuvering practice?"

Anything to get out of here. Make-Out City is making my chest ache even more.

"Follow me." She winks and disappears.

Now or never, I decide, before running headfirst into the pane of glass. *Pain* of glass is more like it.

When my feet are clear, I turn sharply to avoid the oak branches stretching toward me. I land in the neighboring yard with a thud; felt, but not heard. At least I'm standing. I stay rooted in place for a second, trying to grasp how differently my muscles work here.

When I jog across two lawns to Willow, my body feels light, like it doesn't want to stay grounded.

"Nice dismount, but your landing could use some work. Overall, though, not bad. Ready?" she asks, pinning her dreads into a knot. The yellow glow from the streetlight makes her look even more freakish. "Take my hand," she orders.

When I do, she says, "Displace."

We hurl upward so fast that I'm nauseous again. If the g-forces weren't pinning my arms down, I'd cover my ears to shut out the screaming wind.

"Woo-hoo!" the frigging maniac yells.

I don't open my eyes until we stop. Abruptly.

My feet are planted like concrete on Willow's floor when she releases my hand and circles around me, inspecting me like I'm an alien. "You good?"

Doubting that my voice will work, I nod my answer.

"Cool, let's jet," she says, and it's back to the training field we go.

Pairs of Satellites are blocking, or at least trying to, on the expansive lawn. Even from across the field, Rigby's face is easy to read. I'd guess this wasn't his only missed block today. Either that or he's still upset about Clara. I'm hoping it's the former and not the latter.

Wynn catches us at the bleachers. "Welcome back! How was your displacement?"

"It's an interesting way to travel," I reply.

"The kid's a natural," Willow beams.

"Fantastic. Keep it up and you'll prove Jonathan right." After a pause, she looks at Willow. "Although, he's rarely wrong."

"Rarely?" Willow questions.

Wynn smirks and grabs my right hand with both of hers. "Wonderful to meet you," she says, bowing strangely. "That's all I have for you both. Willow, please oversee him in displacing to his Tragedy later today. I expect Jonathan will be back for your next session."

We say our good-byes, and Willow and I walk back to the building.

"Feel up to coding again?" Willow asks when we're through the lobby.

Is she serious? Like I'd pass on an opportunity to see Tate. "Sure."

"You sound surprised."

"I didn't think you'd be in a hurry to let me try again."

She presses the elevator button. "I'm not. Unfortunately, time is no longer a luxury."

In her room, Willow kicks off her combat boots and heads down the hall. I can't believe she's being so cool about this.

I sit on the thin mat, close my eyes, and an instant later, I'm in the place I'm meant to be. I kiss the top of Tate's head and she sighs. Her hair smells so familiar, so good, but is messier than usual. When she lifts her head to kiss me, I immediately pull back.

I gasp and push against her shoulders. "Tate, your eye!"

Her hand reaches up to her left eye as if she's understood me. Her bruised, swollen flesh is an awful combination of purple, black, and blue. What the hell happened?

With feather lightness, I rub my finger along her swollen skin. My hand jerks back when she launches from the bed and rips wildly through the room.

"Damn you, Grant! You left me when I needed you!" She violently snatches a frame off my dresser and groans, but when she looks at the picture, she becomes calm again.

Dear God, she's going all Jekyll and Hyde on me.

I jump off the bed and look over her shoulder at the ridiculous photo. Like always, she looks too amazing in the photo to be with a guy like me. I complained profusely when she made me board the children's train at the zoo and the look on my face shows that I was not happy. How and why she tolerated my whining is still a mystery.

With her head down, Tate cries softly and a tear splats on the glass.

Her hair curtains her face and I pull the curls back to rest my head on her shoulder. Goose bumps raise on her arm and I try and rub them away. "I'm here," I repeat in whispers. Desolation and guilt dig into me like eagle talons grip prey. I would do anything to take Tate's pain and add it to my own, anything to stop her tears.

"No!" she yells, suddenly violent. The frame hits the wall with the sick crunch.

A shiver quakes through me before the lights go out.

———~~~———

"Come on—snap out of it!"

My eyes spring open to find Willow fiercely shaking me.

"You look terrible," I manage.

She huffs. "Are you all right?"

Still panting, I push my fingers through my wet hair. "I think so."

"What happened?" she demands.

"Tate had a black eye and then—I don't remember." *I don't remember!*

"You were out a long time," she says.

Panic floods through my veins. "What's happening?"

She looks at the floor and won't answer me.

———~~~———

After a little bit—OK, a lot—of effort, Willow calms me down and insists I rest. So here I am on the ghastly sofa, still feeling drained.

"Do you ever code, or do you just trash the kitchen to relieve your stress?" I ask after twenty minutes of nonstop racket. "If it's the latter, I was thinking maybe I could give it a try." Although, by the sound of it, she's already rearranged the cabinets a hundred times.

"Huh?" She pauses, making me remember how much I love silence. "Oh, sorry—nervous habit. You feeling better?"

"Sure. Relaxing is easy with you around."

She ignores me. "Think you're ready to displace?"

"Why not?" Anywhere is better than here. I push myself into a sitting position and spin to watch her over the back of the sofa. A dozen coffee cups of various colors are lined up along the dark counter.

"You're going to be on your own this time. Are you cool with that? If not, we could go back to Hope's for more practice."

The image of Hope and Lover-Boy swirls in my head. "I'll be fine. Why can't you go with me?"

"Privacy policy."

"Oh. Right."

"Remember that when you return. You're probably going to want to blab all about it."

"You know me—such a blabber," I tease. "So, is this officially the beginning of my assignment?"

"More like a dress rehearsal. If you do well you'll be released soon, though. You're far ahead of schedule. Expect some jabbing from the others."

"For what?"

"For being an overachiever," she says, running the water in the sink.

"Great. One more thing to draw attention to myself."

"As if the good looks weren't enough," she jokes.

"Funny."

"You know, Clara's not the only one around here that's into you. Plenty of girls have been drooling since you got here."

"Yeah, I've been beating them off with sticks."

"I'm serious. I'm constantly being asked what it's like to be your Legacy." Willow puts a few of the mugs into the sink and turns the water off. "It gets old."

"I can only imagine your response," I reply, still not believing her.

"I tell them that when you open your mouth, it cancels out all the good looks."

I pretend to be wounded while I stand. "Thanks a lot!"

"Hey, kid, that's what I'm here for." She dries her hands on the checkered towel hanging on the fridge handle and then reaches into one of the cabinets, taking out something small enough to fit in her fist. "Ready?" she asks, walking over to me.

"I guess. I hope my good looks don't get in the way."

She punches my arm and then passes me a smooth, pocket-sized stone.

I roll the sparkling granite over in my palm and then juggle the light stone with one hand. "What is it?"

She snatches it from the air. "Your tocket. Don't lose it." She holds the rock between two fingers, an inch from my face. "This is your lifeline to your assignment. Got it?"

"Yep." I steal it back from her. "The size is convenient."

"The Sorters try to be mindful of the fact that we have to carry these things around all day. Can you imagine a surfboard or giant teddy bear?"

Willow really is funny sometimes. "Who are the Sorters?"

"Tocket hunters. It's no easy feat, either. The item must be important to your Tragedy yet go unnoticed when it's missing. Being size-appropriate is another obstacle."

"So they're thieves, basically?"

"No, they're not thieves!" she sneers.

"What would you call them?"

"Convenient."

"Thieves," I repeat, mostly because it bugs her. I toss the stone in the air. "So how, exactly, do I do this?"

"Getting there is easy—you just need to say the word. The physical adjustment is the most difficult, but you've already fared well in that area."

"And the word?"

"'Displace.' You don't need to say it loud—a whisper works just as well. As long as you're holding the tocket, it will take you to its owner. Just remember to take a minute to adjust after you land."

"How do I get back?"

"Same word, but no tocket. When you're holding nothing, displacement will bring you home."

I flinch at the word. Willow notices.

"This is your home now," she says levelly.

I swallow and bite the inside of my cheek.

"Try not to throw up," are her last words of encouragement.

I tighten my grasp and say the magic word. The hardwood floor disappears and gravity takes hold. The wind screams louder and louder until I'm sweating in panic. When my feet finally hit solid ground, Willow's warning rings in my ear. I steady myself, and my breathing, before making any sudden movements.

Despite the dark, my sight couldn't be better, and I focus on the glistening terrain burying me from the knees down. Because the temperature feels mild, even in my thin T-shirt, it takes a second to register.

"You've got to me kidding me," I say under my breath. I'm barely comfortable maneuvering through normal terrain. This is sure to be disastrous.

After assessing the situation, I lift my foot as high as I can out of the snow and take a step. I fall face forward, buried up to my shoulders in crystal powder.

Pushing off the ground in frustration, I apply too much force and go flying through the air with my legs and arms spinning like a windmill. The plowed street passes under me in slow motion, and I land in a neighboring yard, knee-deep again. This is ridiculous.

I sight in on a driveway and push off the ground, using much less power this time. My judgment is better, and I land at the edge of a high drift, barely on the pavement.

Across the street, the door of a shoebox-sized home with an extra steep roof opens, and Ryder steps under the porch light. He pulls on a stocking cap and buttons his wool coat. "See you later. Lennon, go easy on your mom," he calls back to the boy in Mya's arms.

He walks down the sidewalk. In a role reversal from the last time I saw him, it's now his breath that's visible.

I judge the distance, jump, and land directly in front of him on the cleared sidewalk. Not bad. He keeps walking and passes right through me. Not good. The sensation feels worse than going through the window, and I lose my balance. I fail to catch myself and land on my butt.

I leap up as Ryder climbs into a gorgeous royal-blue Mustang. The engine purrs rhythmically. I would love to get behind the wheel of that thing. When he backs out of the driveway, the garage light reflects off the New Hampshire license plate. Guess that explains his accent. And all the snow.

It doesn't occur to me that I should be with him until the taillights shrink in the distance. *Crap!*

I start running—as if I'm actually going to catch up with a car. Surprisingly, my legs move fast. Extremely fast. In less than a minute, I'm jumping headfirst through the passenger door. I overshoot and land awkwardly, almost in Ryder's lap. Obviously, practice is still in order. I lean back into the passenger bucket seat, noticing that my breath is unusually even. If I had sprinted half that distance when I was alive, I'd be hurling by now.

The Black Keys blares through the speakers, but despite Ryder's decent taste in music, he drives the Mustang like my grandma, being excessively cautious even though the roads are clear. I wish he'd break the tires free—she deserves to be driven better. When he turns the car off the deserted road, the headlights illuminate the tops of gravestones. Great. Nothing like partying with dead people after dark.

With the engine cut and the music off, his door squeaks loudly in the still night. My side of the car is pinned by a huge snowdrift. Not that it matters, because I don't have the luxury of exiting the conventional way, anyhow.

I should probably head back before Willow wigs out, but I have to see why Mr. Morbid is in a cemetery so late. Plus, more practice moving through this absurdity of winter couldn't hurt. Opting for the side without the wall of snow, I jump through the driver's door and land gracefully. Well, almost.

I jog along the cleared path, trying to keep myself grounded. My body still feels too light, like it's going to float away. I stop a few feet behind Ryder.

"Hey, Mom," he says, kneeling down by one of the headstones. So much for my Mr. Morbid theory. "You should see Lennon. I swear he doubles in size everyday. Dad says he has your eyes. And Mya, she's so great with him. I wonder if that's how you would have been with me." He pauses and rubs snow off the top of the stone. "I know I say this all the time, but I do wish I had known you." He stands and digs something out of his coat pocket. "Happy birthday."

Snow crunches under his feet on his way back to the car, and I stare at the headstone. I should head back to Progression (Miss Dreadlock's surely in a conniption by now), but curiosity pulls me closer to the grave marker to see what Ryder left for his mom. If I hadn't seen him lay it down, I probably wouldn't have noticed the object. I pull its twin from my pocket, rolling the granite rock over in my hand. Like the snow, the speckles shine like glitter under the moonlight. Remembering I don't need it to get back to Progression—I refuse to call it home—I put my rock back in my pocket.

Freezing in horror, my breathing hitches and then stops altogether for a full minute.

When I can finally move, I bend down to the headstone. My eyes blink frantically. The image is wrong. It must be!

I lean against the stone for support and gasp for air. Despite my pleading, the writing stays the same.

May You Rest In Eternal Peace, Wilhelmina Ann Beckmann, January 6, 1959 – November 27, 1988. Forever Willow—Loving Wife, Mother, and Daughter.

10. You were destined for this

"Oh jeez! You look terrible!" The birthday girl places the back of her hand on my forehand, like my mom used to do to check for fever. "Seriously—worse than usual. Say something."

Not trusting my voice, I stare back at Willow in silence.

"If you don't talk soon, I'm calling Jonathan. You're freaking me out."

"I'm fine," I say, praying she doesn't catch the hitch in my voice.

"Did you displace all right? Please tell me you didn't have any trouble. The last thing I need is you ending up God knows where, especially on your first solo."

"No—no trouble. It was fine," I assure her, feeling a little steadier.

"All right. Well, don't tell me any more. Remember the rules."

A loud breath of relief escapes me. Saved by the Handbook for Dummies. The rules hadn't even crossed my mind.

"Chillax, kid. You really do look awful." She checks her calimeter. "I've got to head to Programming. You're gonna be on your own for awhile."

My mouth is dry when I try to swallow.

"It's almost break, if you want company. Jonathan wants to see us today, so I'll find you later, OK?" She continues to study me.

"Good luck in Programming," I say, wishing she'd leave already so I can drop the act.

"Thanks, I could use it."

When Willow's finally gone, I try to relax, but pacing frantically doesn't seem to be doing the trick. I can't will away the image of her headstone.

Of all the Satellites, how did I end up with Willow's son? This is a huge mistake—it has to be. I'll just pull Jonathan aside when we meet up with him later, and he can get this mess straightened out. There. Easy.

Squeezing the bridge of my nose and praying that I'm right, my eyes stop on the bookshelf. The faces in the photographs stare back at me. Were any of them responsible for protecting someone so close to their Legacy?

"No, they couldn't be. This is just a mistake," I say aloud, because apparently, I *have* lost my mind.

My eyes stop on the frame Tate made and my thoughts begin to shift, remembering my dreadful hospital stays. Tate refused to leave my side, even through the worst of my cancer-ridden days. My mom was so grateful that Tate could always raise my spirits a little. Even my dad got closer with Tate during that time. My dad! The man who couldn't get close to a blanket full of static.

When an idea hits me, I glance around the room, expecting someone to be there, watching. Could it work?

If I'm fast enough, I can be back before Willow even knows I'm gone.

Before I change my mind, I grab my empty frame from the shelf. "Displace," I whisper.

The floor falls out, and my stomach drops when I plummet down. I squeeze my eyes closed, pushing both nausea and consequences out of my mind. I open them cautiously when my feet hit the ground, unsure of what to expect.

I'm in my room. *I'm in my room!* I was hoping for Tate's, but I can make this work.

An unsettled feeling slides through me. The room hasn't changed at all. Even my bed is unmade. I'd feel better if the space were transformed into an office or something—anything that indicated my parents were moving on.

As I'm about to jump through the back wall, my bedroom door clicks open behind me. Expecting Willow or Jonathan, I play possum (though I guess I'm not really playing).

I finally turn and then have to remind myself that my mom can't see me. Thank God, because my mouth gapes open at her appearance. She's aged at least ten years.

My mom grabs a frame from my dresser, sits on my bed, and brushes her hand along the photo of Tate and me. "Be good," she whispers and then she cries. A lot. Like she's going flood my bedroom. She curls on her side, hugging the frame, and buries herself under the mess of covers.

As I sit beside my mom while she sobs, my jeans become spotted with my own tears and my blood boils, because there's nothing I can do to comfort her.

"Mary?"

My head jerks up, and my mom is returning the frame a second later. She dries her eyes on her sleeve and slips out the door.

I hear my dad's muffled voice through the wall. "What were you doing?"

"Just putting some things away," my mom answers, sniffling.

Long pause. "Do you need any help?" My dad's voice is laced with concern—an alien emotion for him.

"I just need a minute."

Their bedroom door clicks closed, and a second later, I hear heavy footsteps go down the hall.

Suddenly I'm anxious to get back—worried that Willow will catch on to my absence. Or maybe I'm not ready to face Tate yet. Either way, I can't risk getting caught now, knowing that I can get here. I'm partly relieved. I don't think I can stand any more sadness today.

I displace with an upward jerk, and I'm so numb that I hardly notice the discomfort.

"I'm so sorry, Mom," I whisper after my feet hit solid ground.

The clink of Willow's bag hitting the floor fills the silent room, followed by Willow's overenthusiastic voice. "Hey, kid —you ready to go check in with Jonathan?"

"Sure," I say over the sofa, watching my thumbs race

around each other.

She pushes my feet off the trunk. "Cool. Let me grab some tea. You're looking better. Oh, heck—who am I kidding? You look like rubbish still. Did you head down for break?"

"Nah, I just hung out here. I was tired after displacing," I say, a little disconcerted at how easily the lie comes.

"It takes some getting used to. You're doing well, though. Better than I expected. Ready?"

I push myself up, feeling weaker than ever, and pull on my bag. Willow does the same, with mug in tow.

"Where are we meeting Jonathan?"

"Back on the field."

She walks fast, but it's easy to keep up with her short legs. The others have already starting training by the time we reach the grass. In the far corner, Jonathan spots us, smiles, and holds his finger up. Not the one my dad always used.

Willow and I watch the others. Surprisingly (at least to me), many of the Satellites still don't have blocking down yet —Anna, especially.

As promised, Jonathan comes over in less than a minute. "How's Programming going?" he asks Willow.

She answers in a very un-Willowlike way, meaning her enthusiasm is only about a seven on a scale of ten. "All right."

When he turns to me, his face fills with concern. "Grant, you look exhausted. How are you holding up?"

"Fine." My eyes drop to the ground. I hope he's not suspicious about my coding problem.

"Tell me—how was your solo displacement?" he asks.

I clear my dry throat. "I made it there and back."

"He's being modest. He did great!" Willow keenly praises. If she only knew.

"You have excelled in your training, so it's no surprise that you are the first to be released."

"Huh?" I ask, bemused.

Willow smacks my back. "He's clearing you, kid."

"Congratulations," Jonathan says. "I have no doubt you will prove to be an asset to our team."

"Are you sure?" Panic raises my voice too high. I feel like I've been punched in the gut. "I mean, I'm not ready."

Willow, clearly entertained by my response, chokes her tea down. "You're ready."

"Please know that I wouldn't clear you if I had even the slightest reservations about your abilities. Now, I believe there's only one thing left to do." Jonathan pulls a small box from his jacket pocket, gives it to me, and shakes my hand.

"Thank you," is all I am able to say.

He reaches into his other pocket and pulls out a square object no bigger than a postage stamp.

"Say cheese!" Willow wraps her arm around my waist and squeezes my side. "At least try to appear happy."

I laugh from her tickling pinch just as Jonathan clicks the tiny silver square.

"Willow, I'll see you in Programming. Grant, if you need anything at all, please don't hesitate to ask."

"Um, there is this one thing. Do you have a minute?" My mind races for an excuse to get rid of Willow.

"Willow, I have a private matter I would like to discuss

with Grant as well. Please excuse us," Jonathan says.

Well, that was convenient.

"Sure thing. Catch you guys later." Willow bounces across the field to a group of Satellites.

Jonathan turns his attention back to me. "Please forgive me. I don't, in fact, have anything to discuss with you, but I gathered that you preferred to talk in confidence."

Uh-huh, I bet you did. This guy is seriously a mind reader. *Don't think about Tate, don't think about Tate, don't—Crap!*

"What can I do for you?"

Remembering what I need, I say, "Here's the thing— there's been a mistake. My assignment…" I trail off when I notice Willow laughing animatedly with Jordan and Shane.

"Is this about Willow's son?"

When I back look at Jonathan, he doesn't need to be a mind reader. The shock on my face says everything. "How'd you know he was my Tragedy?"

"I know about every assignment."

Is that even possible? Of course it is. Man, I hate this place! "That's a lot to keep track of," I murmur.

"I do all right. I can assure you that no mistake has been made. You were destined for this particular assignment, along with all the others that will follow."

"What if I slip up and say something to Willow?"

"You don't give yourself enough credit."

"And if I make a mistake?"

"You could make a mistake with any Tragedy— Willow's son or otherwise. I have faith that you will not." He pauses. "Of everyone you have met in Progression, who would you hate to disappoint the most?"

I don't answer because it's obvious.

"I understand your concern; however, I believe you are the perfect choice. Your love for Willow will serve as significant motivation to succeed."

"Trust me when I say I have *no* love for Willow."

His comical expression says he doesn't believe me. "This plan was laid out before you were born. I promise you this assignment is not a mistake. You were destined for this."

"Thanks." I struggle to use my friendly voice, since he's clearly not changing his mind.

"Anytime. I sincerely mean that. I look forward to following your progress." He stares at me for a minute, says, "Happy Thanksgiving," and then walks away.

"Uh…you, too," I finally call back, but he's already moved across the field, observing a pair of Satellites. Certainly he would have said something if he knew I tried to get to Tate's. At least, that's what I'm going to tell myself.

"Well, let's see it!"

Willow's perky voice scares the crap out of me. I snap my eyes off Jonathan.

"Sorry." There's zero sincerity in her tone. "Let's see it!"

"See what?"

"Your calimeter, genius."

"Oh. Right." I open the black box I forgot I was holding. The sun glints off the calimeter's square face.

"Sweet!" Willow messes up my hair.

Sweet is right. Even sweeter, though, is that the notches

of the silver disks are still far apart. They could freeze right now as far as I'm concerned.

I don't care when Willow looks at me funny for sniffing the brown band. The smell of the leather is a reminder of home: my parents sofa (which happens to blow Willow's away—at least, aesthetically), my tool pouches, Tate's corded bracelet…

Willow interrupts my trip down memory lane. "We've got the rest of the day to kill. Want to hang out here and watch the others?"

With no way of escaping, my chances of seeing Tate are zilch. "Why not?"

We sit at the edge of the field, out of the way of the practicing Satellites. Willow kicks off her shoes and rolls onto her stomach. "You gonna gawk at it all day or put it on?"

Unaware that I had been staring at my calimeter, I strap the thick band around my wrist. Perfect fit. Go figure.

"It looks great on you. How's it feel to be official?"

"I don't know. I mean, it doesn't seem official yet."

"It will. After break you'll head to your assignment just like all the other Satellites."

Anxiety and fear grab hold of my insides. "What if I screw up?" I ask Willow. Thinking about her son makes the urge to vomit even stronger.

"You won't."

"How can you be sure?"

"Because you've been trained by the best," she states matter-of-factly.

"You have a skewed image of yourself," I try to joke,

swallowing down bile.

"Sticks and stones, kid. Happy Thanksgiving, by the way. Got anything you're thankful for?"

She can't be serious. "No," I say dully.

Oblivious to my attitude, she turns her face toward the sun like she's enjoying the nonexistent heat. "Try to relax and enjoy the entertainment, kid."

I find Rigby and Shane on the crowded field. After three tries, Rigby succeeds in making Shane sit on the ground. A little further down, Anna and Jordan are hard at it. Jordan's beyond patient, but Anna, on the other hand—not so much. After watching four attempts, I can no longer take her disappointment and fall back on the grass, thinking about Ryder and my upcoming assignment.

To avoid getting sick, I shift my thoughts from Ryder to Tate. My stomach does a nervous flip at the thought of seeing her—the real her, not the angry, black-eyed Tate from my dreams. But what if she's physically changed like my mom, or worse, what if she's a train wreck, too? I'm unsure if I'm prepared to see her in that condition. My worried mind goes into overdrive and the guilt of my secret tugs at me. I push the guilt away, close my eyes, and let my imagination run wild with a happier Tate.

"Congratulations!" a breathless voice says, pulling me from a memory that was just getting to the good part. "They're saying you've beat some record or something—the quickest Satellite to go through training."

I push up into a sitting position and shade my eyes to see the dark silhouette hovering over me.

"That's because he had the best trainer ever!" Willow gloats to Anna.

"Fat chance it had anything to do with the trainer," Jordan says, walking up with Rigby and Shane.

"I don't know. If Willow was my trainer, I would have blown through training as fast as possible, too," Shane says.

Willow shrugs them off. "You boys," she smirks, "always intimidated by strong women."

Anna's the only one who finds humor in Willow's statement.

"Nice cali," Rigby says, pulling the toothpick from his mouth. Not catching the sarcasm at first, I hold out my wrist so Rigby can examine it. His eyes narrow. "How was your date?" he asks sourly.

"You're so lucky. I can't wait to start my assignment," Anna says, clearly uncomfortable.

"Newbies," Jordan jokes, shaking his head.

Having scarier things on my mind, I ignore Rigby's glare. My nerves make my laugh come out wrong, but no one seems to notice.

In Benson, everyone eats but me—even Clara, whose diet usually consists of a single can of Dr. Pepper.

"You're missing out," she says. "The Thanksgiving feast

here is the best in the world!"

I longingly scan Clara's plate. It's overflowing with turkey, sweet potatoes, a couple of rolls, dressing, and cranberry sauce. I swallow, wishing I could enjoy the food from one of my favorite holidays. I don't dare fuel my stomach, though. Instead, my palms wear out the thighs of my jeans while my leg bounces up and down. Twice, Willow places her hand over mine to stop me and gives her best "chill out" look.

After what seems like just minutes, the room thins out. Terrified, my knee bounces higher.

"I'm outta here, guys." Clara bounces around the table and plants a quick kiss on my cheek. "Best of luck, Grant. You're going to be great." She vanishes an instant later. The warmth crawling up my face is not from embarrassment this time, but rather from Rigby's emanating hate for me. His chair slides loudly behind him and he stalks out of the room.

Liam ignores Rigby and says, "Good luck, pansy," before disappearing.

Owen kisses Anna and whispers something to her. Now that they're public, we all have to suffer through their PDA. "Dude," Owen says to me when they're finished, and then he vanishes too.

"You'll be awesome, I know it," Anna encourages.

"Ready?" Willow asks, placing her hand on my knee again to stop the bouncing.

"I guess so."

"When you arrive, be sure to read up on your assignment. Your book will give specific details of what you need to do."

"What will you be doing?"

"I'll be in Programming. They tell me my husband will be joining me soon. That's good news, right? I mean, something I should be thankful for?"

Ryder's dad. I try to smile, but it doesn't work. My insides twist into a tighter knot thinking about Ryder's loss. My old man and I weren't nearly as close and I miss the grouch more than I would have ever thought possible. Ryder, having a much better relationship with his dad, is surely going to be a mess.

"Dude, relax. You're getting all pale on me again," Willow says, but she's nervous, too. I can hear it in her voice. "I'll be waiting for you at the next break. You're gonna be stellar, kid."

I dig into my backpack, wrapping my hand so tightly around the rock that my fingernails dig into my palm. "Displace," I force out, only because I can't face Willow for another second.

The floor disappears, finally giving the sick feeling I've had an excuse for being there. I hear a new sound this time—a higher-pitched whistling—but I keep my eyes closed and ignore my stomach.

When I land, I strain to find the source of the distant rumbling. Wet snowflakes hit my face and arms. Their temperature is that of bathwater.

A dark blur slides around a corner and screams past me. Another brushes my side. A third goes through my left hand and more rumbling is coming. I jump out of instinct and float ten feet over the bluish-white path while the last snowmobile races by underneath me.

Floating feels natural to my body, but not to my head. I focus on the ground below, and my body slowly drops. I jump again, wobbly, but then more controlled, and stay suspended above the earth much higher than before while my head grows accustomed to the feeling.

When I was alive, the glare from the lowering sun would have been blinding, but now my vision isn't affected. Paths weave throughout the precipitous mountain of evergreens below me.

The engines cut in the distance. Aside from my own breathing, it's like someone hit the mute button. A few branches drop their loads of snow, but even that is eerily silent.

Remembering my purpose, I mentally slap myself for being such an idiot. Ryder has to be one of the snowmobilers, or I wouldn't have displaced here. I lower to the ground and sprint along the trail, but there are too many forking paths, and with the engines cut, there's no sound to follow.

On my next stride, I push off the ground and soar into the air like Superman. The trees blur below me, and I catch the faintest hint of voices. I slow down by leaning back and follow the left trail. It opens to a flat, white field. Eight snowmobiles and their riders (and hopefully my Ryder) are parked along the far edge.

"You're full of it—there's no way you got that kind of air!" a guy says.

"Seriously, man. It was unbelievable," another guy

answers.

"Figures it'd have to be when I was in class."

"Carter, you always miss the good stuff," a girl says.

"Someone's gotta get an education around here."

"Hey, watch it, man." I recognize Ryder's voice easily. Now just a few feet away, I lower to the ground.

"I wasn't talking about you, Mr. Grad School," the guy says, and the snowball he's formed splats against Ryder's head.

Ryder brushes away the remains of the attack. "Oh, you want to start that? You know your mom's turkey always makes you slow."

"Hey, don't talk about my mom!" The guy launches himself toward Ryder.

In an approach similar to his playground attack years ago, Ryder bear hugs the guy, and they both hit the ground. Ryder pops up with a snow goatee and shakes his long hair like a wet dog.

"Oh, you think it's funny?" he says to one of the laughing girls, rocketing up and chasing her across the field.

"I wish they'd just get together, already," one of the guys says, while Ryder's target squeals in the distance.

"Seriously. He's all Hannah talks about," a girl's voice adds.

Shoot! I haven't read the book!

I drop my backpack from my shoulders, retrieve the assignment book, and skip ahead until I reach the newly titled page, "The Present." The paragraph narrates what's going to happen—or rather, some of what has already happened (snowball fight). Ryder will be receiving a call. After that call, it is essential that Hannah goes with him.

I flip to the next page, and another situation is explained. Instead of reading it, I fold the corner down and close the book. In the distance, Ryder is already on the phone and flattening the snow where he paces.

Damn! I'm across the field in less than a second.

"I'll be right there," Ryder says urgently before shoving the phone into the pocket of his thick coveralls. He takes off running.

"What's going on?" Hannah asks, sprinting behind him.

"I have to go!"

"What is it? I'll come with you."

Block, you moron! Block!

I hastily drum up the blue filter and bring it in as quick and tight as possible. "Haze!" I shout.

*Take her with you, take her—*ahhhhh!

As I experience the excruciating current, my thoughts can only focus on one thing: I must stop the pain. My muscles are in knots. *Think, Grant—think!*

"Block!" The electrocution halts the instant the word flies from my mouth. Relief spreads through my burning muscles. Does blocking have to be so ridiculously painful?

Ryder stares at Hannah in a daze and then yells, "Fine, but we need to go now!"

Whew, success.

They run back to his snowmobile and Hannah jumps on behind Ryder, wrapping herself around him as the engine roars to life. They jet across the field, leaving the others staring, open-mouthed, at their hasty departure.

My feet move under me, leaping to soar above the snowmobile. I easily keep pace above them, even around the sharp turns.

Flying is a rush, no doubt, but being on one of those machines has to be even sicker. Having Tate's warm body hugged around me the way Hannah is holding Ryder would be the cherry on top. The closest Tate and I ever got to this kind of fun in Missouri was ATV riding, but we never reached speeds like this. Letting my imagination go, I can almost hear Tate's shrill of excitement in my ear.

Ryder doesn't hit the brakes until the trail opens into the parking lot.

"Whoa, what's going on?" a man working on one of the machines asks when Ryder nearly takes him out.

Ryder cuts the engine. "I think my dad had a heart attack," he says, running to his car with Hannah two steps behind.

While Ryder and Hannah argue over who's going to drive, I hurl myself through the side panel of Ryder's car and land almost gracefully, though my knees bend awkwardly into my chest to keep from ghosting through the front seats.

In the passenger seat, Hannah strips off her heavy coat and hideous rainbow sock hat. I realize she's the same blonde girl from Ryder's past, although she's much more… developed.

"Mya drove Dad home from my grandparents' house about an hour after I left. She said he collapsed in the kitchen after they went inside. An ambulance took him to Portsmouth Regional," Ryder explains while driving the Shelby like it should be driven.

"He's not—" Hannah starts to ask.

"I don't know."

I do.

"He'll be all right." Hannah tries to sound convincing.

No, he won't.

"He's all I have," Ryder says, his voice pleading.

I pull out the book and open to the marked page. The paragraph says that Ryder is going to insist on driving. Hannah needs to drive instead. Panicked, my eyes shoot to Ryder and back to the page. The words disappear and new text emerges. I read as fast as I can, which isn't impressive.

New scene: I must make Ryder stop the car before running through a red light. A handwritten sentence follows:

Please do try to keep up with your reading, Grant. We wouldn't ask if it wasn't important.

—S

I look ahead to the stoplight. At this speed, we'll be there in no time. I concentrate on my energy and the blue filter clouds my vision. "Haze!"

Red light, red light, red light…

Even though I know it's coming, there's no way to prepare for the torment. The bolt electrifies me. This time, however, it's easier to remember what I'm supposed to do.

"Block!"

The pain subsides, but my muscles tremble. I hope this guy's not going to be like his mom in the blocking department.

The tires squeal and the car's back end fishtails when Ryder slams the brakes. When we abruptly stop, an SUV passes an inch in front of us.

Hannah finally closes her mouth, then opens it again and yells, "Get out!"

"You're not hurt, are you?" Ryder asks, as if he didn't hear her.

"I said—get out!" Her door squeaks open and she storms around the back of the car. "Get out!" she demands, jerking his door open.

Ryder's expression morphs from disbelief to frightened before he wisely obeys. When Hannah falls into the driver's seat, he gapes down at her. She stares narrowly back until he goes around to the passenger side.

I can't help but laugh. If I didn't know better, I'd think I was watching Tate.

I read during the rest of the drive, not eager to make another mistake. Scene three, Cliffs Notes' version: go to the hospital and keep Ryder calm.

When I flip ahead for more, the next page simply says "break" and the pages that follow are blank. I look at my calimeter and internally deflate. The notches are nowhere near each other.

It's dark when Hannah drops Ryder off at the emergency doors. I jump out of the side of the car and land on my feet. I'm getting better at maneuvering, especially through objects, though it still seems ridiculous. I jog beside Ryder into the hospital.

"I'm looking for Troy Beckmann," he says to an old woman at the front desk.

A girl's voice rings from down the hall. "Ryder!"

We both turn to Mya. She's the spitting image of Willow, minus the dreadlocks and tattoos. How had I missed that before?

"Oh, Ryder!" She collapses to the floor and covers her mouth with her hand.

Ryder closes the distance. "What's going on? Where's Dad?"

"They tried." Her whole body is shaking. "They tried to save him."

"What?" He falls to his knees as if he'll hear her better from down there.

"They did everything they could. They tried…" She trails off and sobs into his shoulder.

Hannah's voice sounds far away. "Ryder?"

No one answers.

"Ryder, what's going on?" Hannah asks again.

"He's gone," Mya whispers. "Dad is gone."

Thinking about my own dad, I blink back stinging tears.

11. If I hear that one more time, I'm gonna hurl

"No! Where is he?" Ryder bellows and sprints past the child-sized hand turkeys lining the hallway. "Where is he!" he yells again. His shoes squeak on the linoleum when he flies around the corner and runs into a supply cart.

Now more familiar with the process, I concentrate. "Haze!"

Calm down, calm down, calm down...

It takes longer for Ryder to accept my persuading this time. The shock hits me, but my adrenaline burns away some of the pain.

"Block!"

Ryder, almost to the twin elevators, smacks his palms against the glossy-painted cinder-block wall. He turns and slides down it until he's sitting.

"Ryder!" Mya shouts, running to him. She kneels at his side.

When Hannah kneels, too, I cringe. Seriously, do people not realize hospital floors are contaminated with more than just dirt?

While Mya and Ryder sob together, I wonder what the scene after my death was like. Did my parents or Tate break down like this? I hope they were able to keep themselves together. The thought of them crying over me—without being able to console them like I would when they broke down during my harsher bouts of cancer—is haunting. Tate would know better than to sit on the floor, at least. She saw me hurl in too many places.

Ryder stares through Mya. "What are we going to do?" he finally asks.

After a long time, Mya answers through her tears. "We're going to survive. That's what Beckmanns do."

Mya helps Ryder up and we take the elevator to the second floor. The walk down the hall is a quiet one. Mya grabs and squeezes Ryder's hand before they disappear into one of the rooms. I step around Hannah, who's parked herself on the germ-laden floor, and enter cautiously with a plan: keep my eyes on Ryder. Ironically, I hate death and don't particularly care to stare it in the face (I guess I should stop looking in mirrors). My plan of course fails, and—like a car wreck—I can't help but look immediately at Troy's corpse. Surprisingly, he doesn't look so bad. My grandpa was way more pallid and emaciated.

I missed details about Troy in the flashbacks of Ryder's recent past. The creases around his eyes are deeper, and his hair is even grayer. He and Ryder share many features, including their sharp noses and olive-colored skin. Unlike Willow, who is widely inked, he has just one visible tattoo: *Willow,* in script, where a wedding band should be. It figures that it's purple. I'd bet money it was her idea.

I wonder if Troy's joined Willow yet—if there's some kind of protocol on how soon they are reunited. Ryder and Mya's devastation, which has taken the form of loud sobbing, must be a stark contrast to Willow's emotions. Will she realize how screwed up her kids are going to be from losing their dad?

When the sobs increase, I go to work on calming Ryder, since he's now beating Mya in the emotional department. Ryder falls off the cliff when a pastor comes in and prays over Troy's body.

Four blocks later, after things have calmed a bit, I back out of the room and slide to the linoleum next to Hannah. Screw my hospital floor rule; I'm wiped out. I close my eyes and listen for any signs of a freak-out while my arms and legs twitch. I've never been much of a texter, but Hannah's rhythmic tapping relaxes me. She clicks away on her phone with the skill of a master thumb wrestler.

An hour later, we both leap up and Hannah jams the phone into her pocket.

"I thought you'd left," Ryder says in a grating voice. His eyes could use some Visine, stat.

Hannah shakes her head. "I wanted to be sure you were all right."

"Thanks, but you should go."

"I can stay. I don't mind."

Ryder finally persuades her to leave. I'd leave too if I got to take his car.

"You'll get through this," Hannah whispers as she hugs

him.

"Will you tell the guys?" he asks quietly into her shoulder.

She agrees, and they say good-bye.

"Come on, kid." Mya, clearly exhausted, drags Ryder down the hall to the coffeemaker.

God help us. She's Willow incarnated.

Ryder and Mya stay through the night, chugging coffee, signing papers, and trying to grasp the nightmare. Lucas and Lennon make a quick visit. Lennon is one of the cutest kids I've ever seen, although that's not saying a whole lot, as I don't know many people under three feet. I see a lot of Willow in Lennon, especially in his eyes. Willow's parents stop by, too, and are both as broken up as Ryder and Mya. I'd guess the couple to be in their upper seventies; they seem to get around well, considering. Willow shares her mom's compact size, though Willow's intellect and smart mouth are clearly passed down from her dad.

It's far beyond lights out by the time Mya drives Ryder home. I sit much more comfortably in the minivan than Ryder's backseat, though Mya is obviously not someone who cares about cleanliness. Lennon must eat all three meals back here. The quiet, dark drive reminds me of heading out for an early morning hunt, as five in the morning is about spot-on for deer season. After Mya parks her van, I follow her and Ryder into the fully lit house.

"Are you sure you won't reconsider?" Mya asks.

"Seriously, sis, sometimes you can be so annoying." Huh, I wonder who she gets that from.

"I guess you might as well get used to the empty house. It's yours now."

Ryder drops his coat on the kitchen table. "What?"

Mya slowly turns the pie plate on the counter in a circle, talking to her hands. "Dad updated the will after my wedding. Lucky break for you. I tried talking him into leaving it to Lucas and me. He didn't buy the 'It's nicer than our house and your grandson would love the extra room' bit. I was a little surprised—you know how he usually caved with Lennon."

"You're kidding."

She shakes her head.

"But you have a family. You need it more."

"That's what I said. But you know Dad." She makes mock quotations with her fingers, scrunches her face, and uses a stuffy voice. *"It's good for you and Lucas to work your way up. Handouts don't build character."* The voice isn't anything like her dad's, but the effect works because Ryder half laughs.

"This is really mine?"

"Unless you want to trade." Her joke lacks enthusiasm.

"And live in that matchbox of yours? Fat chance." Ryder buries Mya's neck under his arm, and she leans into him.

"What are we going to do without him?" Ryder asks a minute later.

"We'll figure it out." She wipes away a tear. "I'll pick you up tomorrow around eleven. Nana and Gramps will be here later tonight. Try to get some sleep and call if you need anything. I love you."

"I love you, too."

The door clicks behind her, and Ryder stays frozen in the kitchen for fifteen straight minutes while I watch the second hand of the wall clock make its rotations. I jump a foot in the air when he yells, "You can't be dead! You're all we have!" The next thing I know, his fist is pummeling repeatedly through the yellow wall.

I stare as he pounds away until it occurs me that I should probably be doing something to stop him. I focus and command the haze in under a second, a new record for me. Of course, this would have been more beneficial ten seconds ago.

Calm down, calm down, calm down, calm down…

And…there it is. Ouch!

"Block!" I yell, freeing my paralyzed muscles.

Ryder finally shows mercy by backing away. He bends over and pants while staring at the peppered drywall. I'm no doctor, but I'd take a stab and say his hand is broken; his knuckles are already the size of a golf balls.

Ryder walks into the living room, wiping his eyes with his good hand, and pulls the curtains closed to block out the peeking sliver of sun. *Please fall asleep soon,* is all I can think when he slumps into the tan recliner. My muscles hate him right now.

I unhitch my bag and fall onto the pink sofa, which is as comfortable as it is wretched. I'm sensing a pattern here. The photograph collection across the room is a little over the top. In addition to pictures of Ryder and Mya at various ages, there are also wedding photos of Mya and Lucas and tons of pictures of Lennon.

Set apart from the other frames are the photos of Willow—at least, I think that's Willow. I can't be sure because she looks so…*normal*. It's strange seeing her inkless and dreadlock-free in the photos, looking so alive I expect her to move. What a waste of a potentially great family.

After four and a half hours of sobbing fits, not quite ramped up enough to be worthy of a block, but frequent enough to be tiresome, Ryder finally gives into sleep. His thunderous snores are louder than his car. After an hour or so, they lessen into quiet, shallow breaths, until the ticking mantel clock is the only noise in the room.

Still staring at the Beckmann's wall of memories, I wonder what it would have been like to have a family with Tate. My meager carpenter's salary never would have given Tate the life she deserved, even if I had taken over my dad's company. Still, Tate insisted she didn't need or want material things, always trying to convince me that we were meant to be together. And, after a while, I stupidly believed that. This makes me feel like a fool. I'm glad her dream of kids didn't die with me, but to think of her with someone else…I just can't.

From our many conversations about kids, one specific discussion pops into my head. Following a day of bad fishing (bad for me, anyway—she caught seven), I was jabbing her about the fish biting her line out of pity.

"You're a sore loser," Tate had teased.

"Am not."

"Are too. And so what? It still counts. You keep biting as well, by the way."

I threw the tackle box in the bed of my truck and

hopped onto the tailgate beside her. "True, but not out of pity," I said, nipping her bottom lip.

She laughed and then stared across the lake for a few minutes. "Look how cute he is," she said, pointing.

A guy a few years older than us was trying to coax his two-and-a-half-foot kid into holding his own fishing pole.

"Oh, come on. I'm better looking than him," I said, to which she slapped my arm. "The poor guy has to keep up with two fishing poles. It's like fishing with you," I joked.

"Ha! More like fishing with you." She looked down at her swinging legs. "Do you think we'll be like that?"

"I hope you'll be more helpful than her," I said, watching the boy's mom laugh at her husband trying to wrangle their son.

Tate turned her head and gave me a look that said she wanted a real answer.

"Don't you think we should get through the wedding first?" I don't think she caught the hitch in my voice. Even then, I somehow knew the cancer was going to rip away our chance of a family.

Her face remained even. "I'm serious."

That's what scared me, but I played the part. "Babe, you want eight kids! Not that I don't look forward to making that many with you, but"—I beat on my truck for effect —"construction salary, remember? We'd need a motel to house them all. And don't even think I'm sharing our room with them. I have too many reasons to keep you to myself in the dark." I bumped my shoulder against hers and wore my best game face, because inside I was splintering apart.

"You're a big talker. As soon as our first is born, you're going to be putty. Just watch."

"Not if they're anything like their mother," I lied, earning another slap on the arm.

"They will be beautiful, our kids," she whispered, after I thought the conversation was over.

And of course they would have been beautiful, because Tate would have been a part of them.

Beep, beep, beep, beep! screams through the room like my old alarm clock. *Make it stop!* is all I can think. When I finally realize the source of the pesky noise is my calimeter, I trace my finger along the face for a knob. Nothing.

Shut up, already!

By accident, from tapping on the glass too hard, I learn the face is also a button. Ahh, at last—some relief!

The kitchen light flashes and then shuts off, but brightness from the late afternoon sun still streams into the darkened living room. I freeze in panic from the eerie silence. Even the mantle clock has stopped ticking, with the small hand frozen on number five. That much time has passed already?

I jump up and lean into Ryder's unmoving chest. My heartbeat overcompensates for his until it occurs to me that he isn't dead. Time has stopped. Literally.

I let myself breathe before hitching my bag on my shoulder and then say the command. The air whooshes past, and I force my eyes open to find the source of the high-pitched whistling. My sight is clouded by a blue filter that's identical to my energy's color. All around me, a rainbow of colors that are bright even through my filter streaks the atmosphere, like shooting stars in reverse. The paths of glowing lights merge too close. We're going to collide.

A fluorescent green streak morphs into the blurred face of a girl I don't recognize. She winks at me before looking back up. I squeeze my eyes closed, certain I'm going to hurl. A second later, the vacuum releases me. I open my eyes in—I guess it's official now—my room.

"Hello? Willow?" I call, checking the coding room. After no sign of her, I head to Benson. The hallway and elevator are full of other Satellites with the same idea.

"Grant! Hey, Grant!" Clara pushes through the crowd when I step off the elevator.

"Hi. What's up?"

"Not much," she says, a little out of breath. "Man, you look beat. How'd it go?"

"Not bad," I answer while we walk, now remembering how exhausted I am.

"I knew you'd be great. Willow's headed back to Programming. She said to tell you she'd catch you on next break."

"Oh. OK."

"You wanna grab a bite?" She bumps my shoulder, getting close enough that I faintly smell peppermint, which I guess to be from her highly glossed lips. She is hot, though I've never been into blondes. No, not just blondes. I've never been into anyone except Tate, and I plan on keeping it that way.

I force my eyes from her shiny lips. "Actually, I just

remembered I left something in my room," I lie. "I'll see you later?"

"Yeah, sure." Her disappointment makes me feel terrible.

"Clara!" I yell from the elevator. When she turns, I say, "Snowmobiling."

"Huh?"

"That's what I regret never doing while I was alive."

Her porcelain face lights up as the elevator doors close.

I blow through the room, dropping my bag on the way to the bookcase. Searching for my empty frame, I almost miss the surprisingly good photograph of Willow and me. I stare at it for only a second. "Displace," I say, out of breath. Stoked to see Tate, I hardly notice losing my stomach in the fall.

I don't hang out in my bedroom this time. I miss my parents terribly, but I don't think I can stand seeing my mom break down again. When I'm through my wall, I jump into the air to cover the mile as fast as possible.

The street we walked a million times (because Tate stubbornly insisted the exercise was good for us) looks different from up here. Even the trees have betrayed me, their branches transformed into twisted, skeleton arms reaching up to me. Or maybe warning me to turn back.

I lower myself to the deck and push away my panic. I can't go back without seeing her.

After mustering the guts to walk through the wall, my

breath hitches. It's like I've just dropped by after school. When Elliott walks into the bright-blue kitchen, I stumble backward. *Breathe, Grant, breathe!*

"Hey, Fish—where's Dad?" Elliott asks.

"In the garage," Fischer answers.

"Cool." Elliott bites off half of Fischer's sandwich and drops the rest back onto the plate.

"Hey!"

"Thanks," Elliott mumbles with his mouth full. I step out of his way and the back door swings shut behind him.

I jump when a loud rumble faintly resembling music cuts through the silence. Typically the only noise around here is cartoons from the television. But even that is rare, as Fischer is usually building something or playing a game with Elliott or Tate. Fischer appears aggravated when he looks toward the stairs. He grabs his plate and stalks into the living room.

She's up there. I'm so close now.

Taking the steps two at a time, I freeze when the knot in my gut tightens. My legs don't want to go, but I force myself through the bedroom door. When I see her, even from behind, I feel…everything. Empty and full, all at once.

She nods to a rhythm that doesn't exist and turns.

Oh. My. God.

I gasp and fall backward through the door, thudding against the wall in the hallway. After three breaths, I go back in.

I can't find Tate through all the makeup. The thick lines around her eyes, as black as her T-shirt, are especially disturbing. Her ribs jut out in a sickly way. She makes Clara look obese.

She shakes her iPod and skips through four songs before stopping at one I recognize. The song is slow, heart wrenching—a guy belting out emotional lyrics accompanied by an acoustic guitar. I silently plead for her to change it, but the song continues, flooding the room with sadness.

When I reach out, my hand ghosts through her and makes me shiver. She picks up a photo I hate—one that makes me look even less deserving of her. Tate is glowing, so happy and full of life. Me, on the other hand—not so much. My cheeks are sunken from the chemo, and my Cardinals hat can't hide my missing eyebrows. This was the last baseball game we went to before I died.

She pulls her arm back and then the frame crunches against the wall. She yanks the picture out of the shards of glass. "How could you leave me?" she yells, ripping the photo paper. Goose bumps cover me, followed by darkness, but Tate's room instantly comes back. My jaw clamps down to control my chattering teeth.

Something crunches under Tate's foot before she throws herself on her bed. I study a fragment of a shredded photo on the carpet. For the life of me, I can't—

"Oh, honey!"

I jerk my head up and more emotions run through me. Tate's mom is thinner too, but at least she's opted out of the black makeup and clothing trend. "You have to stop destroying these things," she says, moving a red pillow out of the way so she can sit on the bed beside Tate.

"It's too painful," Tate whispers.

Her mom looks around the room. "Let's box them up, OK? We can put them in the basement," she suggests.

"I won't act like he never existed!" Tate yells.

"That's not what I'm saying. You just need—"

Tate interrupts. "I need his things around me." She sniffs and leans against her mom.

"Will you at least consider talking to someone?"

"How many times do I have to tell you? I'm not going to some shrink."

Her mom rubs Tate's scrawny arm.

"What did I do to deserve this?" Tate moans, pinching the bridge of her nose.

"Look at me," her mom says, pulling Tate's chin up. "It's not your fault. Everything happens for a reason, even if we may not understand it."

Tate flails off the bed and stomps across her room, avoiding the shards of glass on the carpet. I jump out of the way before she goes through me, and she spins around. "Come on, Mom! I am so sick of the BS, 'Everything happens for a reason,'" she mocks. "If I hear that one more time, I'm gonna hurl!" She shrinks to the floor and hugs her knees.

Fischer clears his throat quietly in the doorway. "Hey, Tate—wanna play a game?" he asks. His voice is soft and hopeful, but he looks scared.

"Not now," Tate barks.

Fischer flinches from Tate's verbal blow before ducking out the door.

Tate's mom pushes herself up from the bed. "At least

consider packing these things away before you destroy them all," she urges, closing the door behind her. "I'll play a game with you, Fish," her voice muffles through the wall.

Tate has never refused Fischer. Ever. I kneel beside her and try to push a curl away from her face, but my hand ghosts through it.

Infuriated, I growl and charge through the room, yelling things my dad would say. Stupidly, I assume Fischer's soccer ball in the corner will respond differently and almost fall over when I try to kick it. After my fit, I sit in front of Tate on the floor and bounce my foot up and down in frustration, knowing I need to go back to Hell (a.k.a Progression) before I get caught. I bend close enough that our faces almost touch, and she stares at me. No, *through* me.

"I love you," I whisper.

A tear rolls down her cheek and hits my knee, spotting the light denim. I can feel the warmth of the moisture through my jeans.

"I'm so sorry, baby. What have I done to you?" I say, before whispering the command that steals me away.

12. There's a whole world happening around you

My muscles feel like jelly, but relief washes over me when I see Clara. I may have pulled this off. "Hey," I say, sinking into a chair at the empty table.

"Hey, yourself." She looks me over.

Mental head slap. I should have at least changed out of my wrinkled clothes so I'd look less like a train wreck.

She marks her place in a book that has some muscled guy on its cover and drops it into her bag. "You were gone awhile. You all right?"

I swallow. I can't get caught now.

She reaches over and massages my shoulder. "Relax. All the new Satellites need to code a lot in the beginning. It'll get better."

"Good to know," I say with a gulp.

"It's a lot of responsibility. I don't think any amount of training can prepare you for that. So—how many blocks?"

"Sorry?" I ask, thinking of Tate's disturbing makeup job.

"How many blocks did you do today?"

"Oh." I count them in my head. "Eight."

Clara laughs. "Oh, come on." I give her a puzzled look, and she asks if it was one or two.

"Neither. It was eight." *Like I just said.*

She stares—measuring me, I guess—before cracking up again. "Grant, no one performs eight blocks their first time. Heck, most Elites don't even do that."

Getting miffed, I repeat, "It was eight," and give her a wide-eyed nod to drive the point home.

Her glossy mouth falls. "You're serious!"

"Uh, yeah." *Jeez!* "Who are the Elites?"

"You're not serious?" She pauses. "Unbelievable! Do you live under a rock or what?"

Awesome. My Legacy left me in the dark. Again.

"The Elites are only the most talented team we've got. It's the highest rank you can achieve here. Every Satellite wants to be one."

"Why?" I ask, getting tired of her looking at me like I've grown a second head.

"Because they're elite!"

Oh, right—of course. I keep my real thoughts to myself and ask instead, "How many are there?"

"Seven. Where have you been? It's all the buzz, now that there's a spot available. It's been fourteen years, for crying out loud! How's Willow taking it? Leaving the team must be killing her."

"You've gotta be kidding me," I mumble under my breath.

When Clara's finally able to recover, she says, "You didn't know?" but the shock stays on her face. "You need to get out more. There's a whole world happening around you."

"Apparently. Is there anything else I'm missing about Willow?"

"Hmm." She bites her lower lip. I so wish she wouldn't do that. The traitor in me begins wondering if her lips taste like peppermint. "Her husband just got here. That's pretty significant."

Finally, something I do know. Figures I can't admit it.

I force my eyes off her lips. "Any word on how that's going?"

"Good, I think. She said her memories returned all at once." A worry line creases between Clara's eyes.

"Is that a problem?" I ask, suddenly concerned about the little loon, even if she never does tell me anything.

"I think it was just unexpected. She said she had a killer headache, but she was beaming when I saw her. Even more than usual, if you can imagine."

Just the thought exhausts me.

Clara pushes on the face of her calimeter when mine starts buzzing. I mimic her by pushing on the glass face of my own. "Good luck on your next round," she says, tying her hair into a ponytail.

"Thanks," I reply, wishing I was going back to Tate instead of Ryder.

Clara hikes a pink bag over her shoulder and winks before vanishing. She didn't kiss me, at least. Figures Rigby's not around to see that we really are just friends.

"Hey, you!"

I turn to the familiar voice. "Hey, yourself," I holler to

Anna, who's halfway across the almost-empty Benson.

"Man, you look tired. Tell me everything!" she says when she reaches me.

"Wish I could," I joke and dig in my bag for the rock.

"Oh, right. This is why I'm not a Satellite yet."

"Seriously, Anna, it's only been a day. Has anyone else been released?"

She shakes her head.

"You're fine," I assure her.

"I know. I'm just so excited to start."

"Well, you shouldn't be. It sucks."

She looks me up and down. "You appear to be coping all right. Aside from looking drained, that is. I think I've almost got blocking down," she continues. "Seriously, I don't know how you did it with Willow. My muscles are so fatigued after just one block."

"You'll get it."

"I hope so. It's good to see you. It gets lonely around here when everyone's out saving the world."

I smirk. "The world is going to be in a sad, sad state when I'm finished with it. How's Owen?"

Her face lights up. "He's fabulous! You think he's great, right? I mean—as a Satellite, of course."

"Cut the crap, Anna. You're totally into him."

She blushes and gives me a spacey grin while fidgeting with her skirt.

"Not that my opinion matters, but I think it's nice that you two have each other."

"Thanks," she says, still vacationing in la-la land.

"You're welcome." I look around the empty room. "I should head out."

After we say good-bye, I hitch my bag onto my shoulders, clutch the rock, and say the magic word. A colorful collection of blurred streaks whistles far below me. I must be getting better at this because I can keep my eyes open without tossing my lunch. Or maybe it's just because I didn't eat lunch. Either way, I'll take it.

The living room is eerily still when I land. After I park myself on the Pepto-Bismol-colored sofa, the kitchen lights flicker on and the mantel clock resumes ticking. Ryder gasps once before his breathing falls into a strong rhythm.

I pull my assignment book out and flip to the appropriate page.

A handwritten note has been added since yesterday:

Welcome to your second session. Thus far you are doing an excellent job. Keep up the good work.

—S

By the time I read the entire span of the day's events (partly to kill time, but mostly so I don't miss anything again), the sun is setting. Aside from a couple of documented outbursts, the instructions for the upcoming day mimic yesterday's: keep Ryder calm. I glance over at the mouth breather. Looking forward to that.

Willow's parents show up with an overnight bag. They try, with no luck, to get Ryder to eat something. Eventually they throw in the towel and retreat up the steps to Ryder's dad's room. Ryder opts for the chair again and he floats in and out of consciousness through the night. Occasionally I have to block him when he gets too upset.

Terrified about the possibility of losing my memories (to the point of making myself nauseous) my mind stays on Tate in my down time. My memory still seems intact, even full of events I wish I could forget.

"I don't understand why we can't go on with the wedding," Tate had once uttered from my bed while I messed with the cable wires behind my TV.

"I'm not going to let you marry me like this. It's not fair to you," I'd said coldly, frustrated because my hands no longer worked like they should.

"*Not* marrying you is unfair to me!" Her voice raised an octave. "You're not dying!"

I dropped the wires. "Please," I begged. "I don't want to do this now."

When her tears started, I went to her. "Listen, the chances of me dying are—" I shot a dirty look at my hands. "You'll be glad we never got married. Trust me."

"That's not true," she whispered, trailing her hand from my disgusting bald head to my sallow cheek.

"Do you honestly want to be a widow at twenty-three?" I asked, still unable to look at her.

"Grant, you're not dying!" she cried.

When I finally raised my eyes, she was truly broken.

"I get it. You don't want to marry me anymore. Stop blaming the disease," she whispered.

Fighting against the pain, I held her as tightly as I

could. "I do want to marry you. I love you."

"Then why won't you?"

"Because I'm dying. I know you don't want to believe it, but I am. I can feel it."

"How can you say that? How can you just give up?" True to form—always the glass-half-full girl—she had fooled herself that there was still hope for me.

"I'm not giving up—I'm being realistic!" I barked in frustration. I was fighting, but an exceedingly stronger force kept defeating me. Her tears softened my anger. "I promise we'll get married if I beat this." Lying to her was nearly impossible, but I knew I'd never see her walk down the aisle.

She'd buried her head in my shoulder then, and I had silently cried with her. Not marrying her was painful, but making her a widow was…I couldn't do that to her. I loved her too much.

My biggest regret, the one I couldn't tell Clara earlier, claws at my insides. Why hadn't I just gone along with the wedding plans? Knowing it was never going to happen anyway, knowing deep down that I was going to die, I could have at least postponed killing Tate's dream. Failing in her attempt to save me, she'd had so little to hold on to. I should have given her that.

I push away my stinging tears with the back of my hand and suck in a deep breath. Early morning light cuts through the gaps in the living room curtain, and Ryder's breathing has reached chainsaw volume. If he ever gets married, his snoring is going to make his wife crazy. Willow's mom tiptoes in to check on Ryder and then retreats back up the stairs.

I stretch and rub my palms against my jeans, but a small hole makes my hand stop. Springing up, I unbuckle my belt. A second later, my jeans are around my ankles. My finger trails over the raised, tear-shaped lesion on my right knee and then jerks back from the heat of the scar. It's a twin in every way to the new scar on my chest.

Laughing out loud seals that fact that I'm officially crazy, but I don't care. Tate's tear burned me again, which means we still have a physical connection, however screwed up it may be. It also means that seeing her while I code is every bit as real as seeing her in person.

I yank my jeans up when I hear keys jingle in the door.

Mya stomps the snow off her boots on the kitchen doormat while I'm still buckling my belt. "Hey, Ry—wake up! It's almost eleven o'clock."

Already? I glance at the mantel clock. Maybe this day isn't going to drag after all.

She curses before coming into the living room. "Hey, kid—get up," she says, shaking Ryder's shoulder.

Both Mya and I leap back when he comes to. "What?" he shouts, spinning around the room.

"Chill. It's just me."

"Oh. Hey, twerp." He rubs his eyes, but then the color drains from his face and he falls back into the chair.

"We need to be at the funeral home in an hour," Mya says.

He pushes himself up slowly this time, like he's made of concrete. "Let me get a shower," he says with zero enthusiasm.

She glances at his hand. "I'm guessing you didn't even ice it."

Ryder pretends to not hear her and walks out of the room.

Mya mumbles her disapproval on her way to the wall of pictures. She traces her finger along one of Willow's photos. "Please take care of him," she whispers before exiting the room.

I resume my place on the sofa and focus on the rhythmic clock, trying to keep Tate out of my head. From the kitchen, Mya's conversation with her grandparents spills into the living room. Ryder and I join them in under ten minutes.

"I like what you've done with the place," Mya says dryly, glancing at the peppered wall as she passes by.

―――♒♒♒―――

Feeling more prepared than yesterday, I wait in the small office for Ryder's forecasted outburst. I picture my mom and dad in place of Mya and Ryder, planning my funeral. After a while, I have to shut my imagination off because my thoughts become too painful.

"We would like a lot of hydrangeas placed around the casket," Mya tells the funeral director, a diminutive man with a bad comb-over.

"Mmm, that's sweet. Red roses will be more appropriate," he responds smugly, scribbling in his leather notebook.

Mya leans forward to see what he's writing. Her tone is harsher when she says, "I appreciate your input; however, we would like hydrangeas."

"My dear, hydrangeas are difficult to get this time of year. Roses will be the most suitable."

I only know two things about flowers: they are a waste of money (those were Tate's words; ironically, she always beamed when I bought them for her), and roses are insanely unoriginal (also Tate's words). I'm not sure what Mya's deal is, other than she's a woman.

Mya forces her sour expression back and takes a deep breath.

Ryder jumps in. "No, the most suitable flowers for my dad are hydrangeas."

"How about white roses, then?" the man offers.

"We said hydrangeas," Ryder manages through clenched teeth. My muscles tense. Here it comes.

The director looks up from his notebook. "It's going to be very expensive. Certainly you have a budget to maintain."

Ryder bolts up, dumping his chair behind him.

I focus and give the order that puts the rippled filter around us.

Stay calm. Stay calm. Stay calm.

Zap! My mind freezes in pain before I yell the severing command. "Block!"

Ryder reaches behind him and rights his chair. "We would like hydrangeas," he says firmly, sitting back down and burning his stare into the funeral director.

"Hydrangeas will be beautiful. How many?" The

director's voice hitches, and he offers what I think is supposed to be a smile.

———

I block Ryder two more times: once for road rage and once before he kills the kitchen wall again during an emotional outburst.

When Hannah returns his car, she insists (demands) on taking Ryder to the ER to get his hand checked. He's smart enough not to argue. We're all back two hours later, with Ryder bandaged and sporting a high-fashion sling.

"What am I going to do without him?" he groans.

Beside him at the kitchen table, Hannah comfortingly rubs his arm. "I'm so sorry. I can't imagine what you're going through."

"He's all I had. He was my best friend."

I think about my own dad. Best friend is the last title that comes to mind.

"You have Mya and her family."

"Exactly. *Her* family. She has her own responsibilities to keep her busy."

"They're your family, too," Hannah says in a softer voice. "And don't forget about your grandparents."

Ryder looks around the room. "I feel so alone." He pauses and then whispers, "I've never felt so alone."

I know the feeling. Unlike Ryder, though, I keep my tears under wraps. My old man would be so proud. This almost makes me want to cry just to spite him.

Poor Hannah looks like she doesn't know what to do. She rubs Ryder's back and stays quiet.

I push the shut-up button when my calimeter buzzes. The lights go off, and Ryder and Hannah freeze at the kitchen table like wax sculptures. Ryder's expression is so desolate, his eyes so dead. He no longer resembles the guy I watched in the flashbacks.

For the first time, I wish the rapid pull would carry me faster. "Willow!" I yell when I land.

No answer.

Wasting no time, I trade clothes (choosing Tate's favorite dark blue hoodie), dump my backpack on the sofa, and grab the picture frame. With the magic word, it's back down I go. When I land, I notice my previously disheveled bed is now made, the dark green comforter smooth and perfect the way my mom always wished I could make a bed. Seeing my room back in order makes me hopeful that maybe my mom is doing better.

Knowing I have to go, I don't waste another minute. I'm in Tate's backyard after a quick flight. I pass through the empty kitchen and bound up the steps, but the violin stops me. I spin and thunder back down the stairs and into the study.

Tate's arms aren't much wider than the violin bow, and her face is still marred by the black makeup. Still, it's encouraging to see her writing. After she scribbles a few notes in her book on the music stand, the bow screeches across the strings at a speed I've never seen. When she whips it away and freezes, the hairs on my neck raise.

I spend too much time watching the music sheets float under the desk. Even before the first vase has finished crunching, she's grabbing another one.

I don't remember pulling my energy in, but I'm yelling, "Haze!" an instant later.

Stop, stop, stop…

I groan from the fire and try to claw at my new scars, but the paralyzing current won't release me to extinguish the flames. Frozen, I clench my teeth and force my eyes on Tate.

She falls to her knees after I finally spit the word severing the command. The vase rolls from her hand and thuds on the floor. I stagger back and slide down the wall, even more wrecked than when I blocked Willow. Thankfully, the fire in my scars is gone, because I don't have the strength to lift my arms to rub them.

Paralyzed by exhaustion, I watch Tate return to her violin and, as if the situation could get any more twisted, I pretend I'm alive with her. "I wish I could have married you," I whisper when she finishes her song.

She lifts her chin. "Grant?" Her voice is so quiet. Did I imagine it?

She closes her eyes and breathes through her nose.

I use all my energy to crawl to her. "I'm here, Tate. I'm here!" She opens her eyes, and my heart thunders into overdrive.

"Can you hear me?"

She swallows, puts her chin on the violin, and plays another song.

Willow's nose is touching mine when I open my eyes.

I stumble back, and the sofa clotheslines me at the calves. "Jeez, woman! You scared me!" I say, looking up from my crooked position on the cushion.

She swings my backpack on two fingers. "Forget something?"

Gulp! "That's actually what I came back for." My dad would have a conniption if he knew all the lies I was telling lately.

She juggles the granite rock in her other hand. "Cut the crap, kid. You have some explaining to do."

13. We'll eventually fix that mind of yours

"Can't you just drop it?" I say to Willow, trying to play it cool while frantically scrambling for an excuse.

"You don't know me at all, do you?" she asks, pacing back and forth.

"Apparently not, Elite."

She flings around and points a finger at me. "Don't even try to turn this on me. Where were you?"

"On my assignment. Where else would I be?" *Please buy it. Please buy it.*

She, of course, doesn't buy this, and juggles my tocket again. "Spill it, kid."

"I went to see Tate." Did those words just come out of my mouth? I've lost my mind! I shrink back in preparation for Willow's wrath. This moment was clearly not the best time for my integrity to make an appearance.

"You what?"

Unless I want her to sock me, it's probably best not to repeat it.

"What? I mean—how? Wait—what?" she stammers, twisting her fingers through her dreads.

"You're blubbering," I point out.

"You're killing me here!"

"Technically, I'm not."

"Stop making jokes!" Her face grows two shades darker.

I try to maintain a calm and collected demeanor by sliding my hands into my hoodie pocket and casually shrugging my shoulders in a "it's no big deal" kind of way.

"Why? How?" she demands.

"Which one do you want me to answer?"

"Both!"

"Because I had to see her. I used my picture frame."

By her expression, the lightbulb just flicked on. Odd. I thought the idea seemed like a given.

"I can't believe it!"

"You can't believe I did it, or you can't believe you didn't think of it?" I am relaxed now, relieved to have the secret out of the closet.

Her eyes narrow. "That you did it!"

"Oh, come on. Admit it. You wish you'd thought of it first."

"No, I don't! It's against the rules!"

"I don't remember that rule." And who cares, anyway? It's not like the Schedulers cared when they ruined my life, so why should I follow their absurd rules?

"Hello? Rule number five. You're still connecting to your past."

"Oh. Huh." I look up at the ceiling. "Yeah, I guess there's that. I thought you were going to say rule number four."

"Oh, please tell me you didn't block her?"

Because Willow's reaction is seriously funny, I have to bite my lip to keep from smiling.

"You did?" She twists her hands tighter into her nest of hair and paces. "What were you thinking? Do you know how bad this makes me look? I'm your Legacy, for crying out loud! You're preposterous—absolutely preposterous! You're not cut out for this. Satellites don't run around breaking the rules. What is wrong with you?"

"Are you finished?" I ask when she finally shuts up.

"No, I'm not finished! You're supposed to be on your assignment. What was your Tragedy doing while you were playing house with your fiancée?"

"I wasn't playing house!" I take a deep breath to bring my voice back to a normal level. "I went during break. Come on, I'm not that stupid."

"Pffttt."

"Why doesn't Tate have a Satellite?" I whisper. The thought hadn't even occurred to me until now.

"She must not need one."

I hardly hear her over my pounding chest. I lunge out of the sofa, convinced I'm going to vomit. When Willow pushes me back down, I throw my head between my knees and suck deep breaths.

"Calm down, kid. This is a good thing," she says from beside me, rubbing my back.

"She needs one," I muffle into my knees. I lift my head and stare at the bookshelf. "You should see her. She's a frigging wreck. I had to block her so she wouldn't destroy the study."

"Listen to me—you cannot ever do that again. Do you understand? You're too green to realize the effects this could have."

"She needs someone protecting her," I protest.

"If she needed someone, the Schedulers would have given her someone. An impressively high number of people can get through the grieving process on their own." She pauses for a long time. "You can't go back there."

When I don't answer, she says, "I'm serious. You don't even have her book to know her path."

My heart jumps. Turning slowly to Willow, I try to control my heartbeat. "She has a book?"

"Of course she has a book. Everyone has a book."

"How do I get it?"

"Well, let's see. You could just march up to the Schedulers and demand it."

"Really?" I would love to have some words with them anyhow.

She smacks my arm. "No, not really!"

"You're awfully testy for someone who just reunited with her husband."

Willow darn near bursts with joy at the new topic. She can't contain herself, though she tries. "Don't change the subject."

A subject change is exactly what I need. If this conversation continues, so will the lies, because I'm not staying away from Tate. "Is he just like you remember?"

"Yeah." She bites. "My memories came back like a

punch in the face. Only good."

I snicker at her metaphor and follow her into the kitchen.

"Want one?" she asks, holding up a mug.

"Sure."

She dunks a teabag in the hot water and passes me the cup. I figure now is probably not the time to argue for coffee.

I nod at the colorful new addition on the counter. "What's that?" I ask, taking a tentative sip of my tea.

"It's a hydrangea. Beautiful, isn't it?"

I nearly spray hot water out my nose, but choke it down instead.

Willow looks concerned. "You all right?"

"Mmm-hmm," I mumble, looking away from the bluish-purple flower in the vase. "Wrong pipe." I fake a cough, and she gives me a funny look. "Where'd you get it?" I ask.

"Troy. They were our wedding flowers." She taps her head with her finger. "I remember," she says, obviously thrilled. "So, Reed had another thought about coding. He thinks you're trying to reach Tate, which I now realize you are," she adds narrowly.

I open my mouth, but she cuts me off.

"I don't want to hear it. You need to code before you collapse. You look rotten, kid. Are you up for trying again and maybe not thinking of Tate this time?"

Now that I can see Tate for real, I'm open to trying something different. "Why not?"

Willow drops her spoon in the sink and when she

heads down the hall, I dump my wretched tea down the drain.

When we're seated on the mats, she says, "OK, let your mind go blank. I'd love to make a joke, but apparently that actually is difficult for you."

"Funny."

"I know, right?"

I close my eyes and after a couple of minutes, I confess, "I can't get her out of my head."

"Try counting backward from one hundred."

This is her advice? She may as well have said start counting sheep.

"You don't have to do it out loud," she says to my expression. "It gives your mind something simple to focus on."

Reluctantly, I do as she suggests, and the last number I reach is seventy-three before the blackness around me changes. I recognize where I am immediately and shift to look at the tree stand supporting me. Twenty feet below, the wooded area opens into a vast field covered with dead leaves. Birds and squirrels go about their business as if I'm not here. Then, what has to be the world's highest-scoring buck walks into the clearing. He moves slowly, and I watch his muscled body, entranced. I've never seen a buck like him, except maybe in a dream.

I want to stand, to draw my bowstring back, but my muscles are jelly. Surprisingly, not being able to shoot the creature doesn't bother me. Just watching him is enough.

"Come back, kid," Willow's voice eerily echoes from far

away.

I take a deep breath, squeeze my eyes closed, and then open them.

"Well?" Willow asks, wide eyed and just a foot from my nose.

I flinch back, a little more dramatically than necessary. "I think I did it."

"No Tate?"

"No. No Tate." I swallow and remind myself to calm down. I'll see her soon.

Willow bounces up and pulls me with her. "Awesome! How do you feel?"

"Good." Physically, anyway.

"Yes!" Willow throws her arms up in victory. "We'll eventually fix that mind of yours."

I roll my eyes. "My mind is fine."

"Your mind is definitely not fine! In fact, your mind is probably the furthest thing from fine I've ever seen. Now your body—Clara seems to think that's pretty fine."

"Willow!" Heat crawls up my cheeks.

"What?" she asks innocently and then snickers. "Clara told me that was a surefire way to embarrass you."

"Yeah, speaking of Clara—what's up with the Elites?"

"What's that have to do with Clara?"

"She's the only one around here who tells me anything. She may as well be my Legacy."

"She'd love that."

"Come on, Willow—first the Rebellion and now this? How come you don't tell me this stuff?"

"It's not important to your training," she says, all businesslike.

"And?"

"And what?"

"What's up with the gag order? Tell me more about them."

"Not much to tell. There's a team of seven. When one's close to retiring—in this case, me—this place goes crazier than Mardi Gras. It's all the rage," she mocks. "Anyway, the Schedulers watch everyone extra closely since all the little stunners are preoccupied with who will be selected. So you'd better start following the rules."

"They're watching us?" I hope she doesn't hear the panic in my voice.

"Kid, someone can always be watching. By your performance in training the other day,"—she looks away from me—"you are proving to be very good. If they haven't started watching you yet, they will be soon. So no more trips to Tate!"

"Being an Elite sounds a little self-serving," I say, ignoring her demand. "No offense."

"None taken. It's nothing more than a title. For me, it's been more of a curse than anything." Seeing my questioning expression, she continues. "There were loads of others more worthy of the position, so I've always felt like I need to prove myself."

"Who chooses the Elites?"

"The Schedulers. Which is kind of funny, with all the buzz around this place." I obviously don't get the joke, so she elaborates. "Since being an Elite is decided at conception, the Schedulers could stop squashing everyone's hopes by just posting an eternal list of them. It would spare everyone a lot of unnecessary anxiety."

"Why do you think you were chosen?"

"I'm not sure. Maybe so someone else wasn't." She smirks and jabs my arm. "Anything else, while you're picking my brain?"

"Yeah. I fell through a door at Tate's house."

Willow sticks her fingers in her ears and sings, "Not listening." She removes her fingers and looks around like she's checking if the coast is clear. "I don't want to hear about your illegal adventure."

"Fine, whatever. For the sake of argument, let's say I was on my assignment. How's the movement thing work? I mean, I can lean on a wall, but walk through it a second later."

"You're overthinking it, kid. Take a chair, for example. You approach it knowing that you're going to sit on it, so you need that object to be solid. If you needed to pass through that same chair, your mind would no longer consider it a solid object. Mind over matter."

"That makes sense, I guess. But what about people? Consciously and subconsciously, I'd prefer them not walking through me."

"I know. It's creepy, right? I'll never get used to the confirmation that I'm a ghost. People, as well as animals, are different. Mind over matter only works on inanimate objects."

"So say, hypothetically, that you wanted to move an object. Can it be done?"

"Hypothetically?" she questions.

"Yeah."

"Right." Willow's not convinced. "In that case, you're talking about something different." She shakes her head. "I can't believe I'm even telling you this."

"Come on—share the goods." I hope my smile is innocent enough to be persuasive.

She takes the bait. "It requires a boatload of concentration. You need to hone in on your energy like your blocking and wrap the filter around the object you want to move. At that point, you can physically touch an object. Smaller, lighter things are obviously the easiest."

"What's the largest object that's been moved?" I ask out of curiosity.

"I've heard it was a boulder, but that's all hearsay. Moving is difficult. I'm not saying it's impossible for someone to move something so large, I just have a hard time believing it. The concentration and strength needed would be fierce."

"A boulder. That's awesome!"

"You're such a dude. Anyway, if—hypothetically—you wanted to try something like this, please be careful. It's extremely important that we stay invisible. That's a tough thing to do when objects start floating through the air. Got it?"

I cross my fingers behind my back. "Yeah, sure."

She studies me for a few seconds. "What am I going to with you, kid?"

—⁓—

Willow dumps me at Benson on her way to Programming, but not before making me change clothes and brush my hair.

"Behave," she warns at the arched doorway.

I mischievously wrap my arm around her neck. "You know me."

"That's what I'm afraid of." She appears contemplative, like leaving me alone may trigger the next world war. Finally, she says, "See you later," and ducks under my arm, disappearing down the hall.

When I'm sure she's halfway to wherever the heck Programming is, I bolt. I'm almost across the lobby when I jump at my name being called.

"Hey, man." Willow's pierced and tatted advice guy (who's clearly spent too much time lifting weights) says when he reaches me. "I'm Reed." He shakes my hand before I've fully extended it and then leans into my ear. "By the looks of you, I'm guessing you got that problem ironed out?"

I hope my face doesn't show my guilt for not being where I'm supposed to be. "Um, yeah. Your advice worked, so, uh—thanks."

"Your situation is certainly unique. I'm curious to see how it all pans out."

"Er…me, too," I reply, not knowing what else to say.

"Cool. See ya around." He leaves me standing there as he whistles down the hall. My father was right, and if he were here at this moment, I may even consider admitting it to the old man. Tattoos and piercings are a red flag for weird.

When I'm about to beeline for my hall, Rigby approaches. Sheesh, I'm never going to get out of here.

"Hey, man. Was that Reed Devereux?" he asks, his toothpick hanging from his lip while he watches Reed walk through the crowd toward Benson.

I turn to watch him, too. "Yeah, I guess."

"What's he like?"

That's an odd question. "Um, well…he's as strange as Willow if that tells you anything."

"Dude, he's a legend!"

"Legend?" I question, still looking at the overly muscled Reed.

"He's one of the seven," Rigby says, like the guy is an MVP for the Cardinals.

"Reed's an Elite?"

"Oh, come on, man! Don't you know anything about this place?"

Guess not. I turn back to Rigby, not caring in the least who Reed is. As far as I'm concerned, he's just another Willow. "Listen, about Clara…" I say, wanting to clear the air.

He bites on his toothpick hard enough to flex his jaw, and with a new bitterness in his voice, says, "Yeah, about Clara. I thought you weren't interested."

"I'm not," I argue.

"So your date with her—"

"It wasn't a date!"

Rigby studies me for a few seconds. "She seemed to think it was a date. She still talks about it."

She does? "Rigby, you gotta believe me when I say I'm not interested in her. Honestly," I add, because he obviously isn't buying it.

"It's cool if you are." His tone contradicts his words.

"Rigby, I'm not! I went to Tate's," I blurt out before I can stop myself, having no idea where that came from.

"You what?" He's loud enough that a few people look our way. He grabs me by the arm and pulls me around the corner of the B hall. "You what?" he says with the same enthusiasm, but in more of a whispered hiss this time.

"I went to see her," I whisper back. "I know I shouldn't have, but I couldn't help it. I miss her so much, man. Being away from her is killing me."

"Dude, you're already dead."

"That's not funny," I say to his very lame joke.

"How'd you do it?"

"I displaced with my frame. She made it for me so it worked like a tocket." Evidently he hasn't gotten to displacement training yet. "A tocket is what takes you to your Tragedy," I explain.

"Oh." He's clearly not thrilled about me knowing something he doesn't. "You could get in some serious heat for that, right?"

I nod. "Willow caught me."

"Dude," he says sympathetically.

"Yeah. She wasn't nearly as understanding as you."

"I can imagine not. So you still have all your memories?"

"So far." My stomach does a nervous flip.

"Does Clara know?"

"No. Why?"

"Well, I was just thinking…maybe if she did, I would have a better shot with her."

"Maybe. But, dude, I can't go around around telling everyone."

"You're probably right. I hate to be a downer, but you know you're going to have to move on eventually."

I suck in a deep breath and pinch my bottom lip. "I don't know how I'll ever let her go. I love her too much."

He claps his hand on my shoulder. "Maybe you should talk to Jonathan. I mean, what if he could help you forget?"

I smack his hand away. "I don't want to forget!"

Rigby shoots a narrow look at a guy who's staring as he passes us, and then lowers his voice. "But it's necessary. Think about your Tragedy, man."

Ryder. If I let Willow down, I could never forgive myself. "I know. I just need more time to work it out. Promise me you won't say anything to anyone."

Rigby considers and then puts his toothpick back in his mouth, barely nodding. "We're cool."

"Thanks."

I look down at my calimeter when it buzzes and then push on the face, deflated because my chance to see Tate again is gone. "I gotta jet. Appreciate it, man. Really."

Ryder and Hannah unfreeze at the kitchen table. I

complete my reading while perched on the counter. It's nice having Hannah here. My muscles are grateful because she's a decent help when it comes to comforting Ryder. The unsightly holes peppering the yellow wall are a reminder of how broken Ryder is. They are also a reminder of how broken I feel inside. The weight of losing Tate and my parents—of never being able to have a conversation with any of them—feels heavier than ever. I wish I could patch the drywall myself.

Later in the evening, as written in Ryder's book, Hannah insists on sleeping over. This turns out to take very little convincing on her part and not a single block from me. With the two of them looking equally fatigued, Hannah curls up on the sofa while Ryder takes another turn in the recliner. Throughout the night and into the morning, I feel guilty for the disservice I am doing Ryder. My mind should be on him, not Tate. I know this, but I can't help myself. Seeing her has made the pull even stronger.

I block Ryder six times later the next afternoon when Mya, Lucas, and Lennon join the photo-collecting party for the upcoming funeral. Seeing so many family memories of the good times in their lives is enough to make me sad, and I didn't even know Troy. What stings the most is that Willow was absent for so many years. What she missed out on—it's just not fair.

By the time my calimeter sets me free, my arms and legs are trembling. I should code—I need to code—but I can't miss another opportunity to see Tate. And since Willow isn't in my room when I get back, I take that to mean I'm meant to see Tate. I race across the room and grab my frame, making sure to take my bag with me this time.

Tate's house is quiet when I arrive. A few Christmas decorations have been added to the kitchen and living room, but nothing compared to the winter wonderland of years past that could put the North Pole to shame. At one time, Tate shared her mom's Christmas spirit. I suspect Tate's newfound Goth phase probably has much to do with the lack of decor.

Edgy from the silence and not knowing where Tate is, I pace her empty room while my few free minutes tick away. I stop at Tate's dresser and push Willow's warning out of my head. That girl wouldn't know fun if it high-fived her in the face.

I force my eyes away from the disgusting, diseased me in the photo on the mirror and concentrate on one of Tate's rings. Remembering Willow's instructions, I focus my energy like I'm blocking. The sapphire-blue filter tints my vision. Squinting to focus the blue filter tight around the tarnished silver circle, I flick my finger against the ring. It flies across the room and hits the wall with a *ting*. Drywall dust rains down from the new dent in the wall.

Oops. Too hard.

I walk to the side of Tate's bed, bend down, focus again, and pull my filter in until the ring appears to be blue instead of silver. Pushing the ring with my index finger onto the palm of my other hand, I keep my energy tight and carry the ring across the room. I almost drop it when I pass the chair I always thought looked like a giant stuffed button, but I maintain my focus. My wrist flips to drop the ring onto the dresser and the tiny circle spins before settling.

Better.

The front door clicks open downstairs, and a deep voice says, "Can I come up?"

"Uh, sure," Tate replies.

I'm in the foyer an instant later watching an ugly badger-faced guy stand too close to Tate. He matches her in eyeliner, clothing color, and shirt size. The chain strapped to his jeans is conveniently long enough to wrap around his neck.

"Where are your parents?" he asks. What a creep.

"I don't know. Out somewhere, I guess."

"Oh, come on, Tate!" I scream at her. What is she thinking? And why isn't she with some preppy doctor-to-be instead of this guy?

Creep follows her up the stairs with me close enough behind to breathe down his neck.

"Nice room," he says on his way to the dresser. He flicks the corner of the photograph of me tucked into the mirror and rolls his eyes. Then he stalks toward her.

When she turns from her stereo, he pins her against the wall. My teeth grit together while hundreds of violent things I want to do to him play through my head.

He brushes his thumb across her lips. "You're beautiful."

"Thanks," she whispers.

My fingernails dig into my palms to keep me from snapping his thumb off. "Get away from her," I growl in a voice I don't recognize.

Obviously not hearing my warning, he kisses her.

I stagger into the dresser, feeling truly dead for the first time when she kisses him back. I keep both hands clamped over my mouth and look at the ceiling. This is what she wants? Him?

"I'm sorry, Patrick. I can't," Tate's voice says, and my eyes snap back to them.

"He's dead. You need to get over it. I can help you do that," he offers, putting his mouth on hers again.

She turns her face away and pushes her fists against his chest. "You need to go."

"Come on, he couldn't have been that great. Seeing you mope around all the time is getting old."

"Shut up!" Tate yells, now using all of her strength to shove him away.

He grabs her wrists and forces them over her head while she struggles and squirms under him.

I growl and spring. My fist, and then my body, ghosts through him. I soar through the wall and land in a pile of dead leaves outside. Stunned, I turn and look up at Tate's window from the front yard.

Oh, come on!

I jump, aiming for her drawn shades, and I am back in her room less than a second later. "Stop fighting me," he's whispering into her ear.

Panicked, my eyes dart around the room, stopping on the small dent in the drywall. An idea hits me. It's a shot in the dark, but it's all I've got. I use my mind this time to envelope the creep in my energy. I pounce and my body makes contact with his shoulder. Bingo.

When he hits the floor, the house shakes and a hairline crack runs halfway up Tate's wall. Saying oops would be a lie. I would have preferred to transform this guy into an inanimate object and welcome him into my world.

He and Tate share the same puzzled expression; then, he awkwardly stands and straightens his black T-shirt. His narrowed eyes are filled with a fury that doesn't even come close to mine.

Tate slowly moves along the wall, putting space between them.

"You're nothing but a tease," he hisses, and then, thankfully, he limps out of the room.

When he's through her door, I exhale in relief, and the filter I was holding around him dissipates. I follow him downstairs, and it takes all my willpower to keep my fists to myself. The photographs in the hall shake when he slams the front door.

Now really noticing the searing pain in my hands, I check out my palms on the way back to Tate's room, relieved to see they are unscathed. I expected blisters at the very least. I rub them on the tops of my thighs, and the imaginary flames slowly extinguish.

Watching Tate tremble on the floor and cry into her knees infuriates me. This is the path she's supposed to be taking? Why doesn't she have a Satellite? And who the hell has she been hanging out with?

I sit down, too, and try comforting her as if she can hear me. "Shhh." The more I whisper, the harder she sobs.

This makes me even angrier because I can't hold her—I can't save her.

When the door downstairs clicks open, Tate's head snaps up. She sucks in a breath and dries her eyes while I lunge up and brace myself in front of her. Someone's bounding up the stairs.

"Hey, can you help me with the groceries?" Elliott asks at Tate's open door. It only takes him a second to inventory her condition.

I jump out of the way before Elliott walks through me to sit by Tate. She leans into him like I, so desperately, wish she could do with me.

"Bad day?" he asks. She sniffs.

He fidgets with the laces on his faded blue Chucks. "Anything I can do?"

She takes a deep breath, trying to hold herself together, but says nothing.

"I miss him, too. I don't care what anybody says— there's nothing that could make me understand this. It sucks."

Tate swallows and vacantly stares, glassy-eyed, at her black Converse low-tops. "Thanks, El. You're the only one who gets it."

I hastily shut off my calimeter before remembering they can't hear the buzzing. Break can't be over yet, can it?

Elliott hugs Tate for a minute. "Quit being so lazy and help me out," he jokes, pulling her up.

My fingers squeeze the bridge of my nose and I try and get my emotions in check. I owe Elliott everything.

I pull my tocket from my bag, seeing no reason why it

shouldn't work. I say the command reluctantly, wishing I could stay here forever, but knowing I should probably never come back. Holding the granite rock, I'm pulled sideways through a blur of houses, trees, and mountains instead of being sucked upward. The feeling is unnerving, but I'm too numb to care.

———

The afternoon and early evening with Ryder are tough, just as his book said they would be. With the impending funeral, he's even more wrecked than yesterday. Every time his eyes lock on one of the photos of his dad spread out on the kitchen table, I think of my old man. Looking back on how fast my life went, I realize how many missed opportunities I could have used to build our relationship. I wish we had been closer. Maybe the emotional distance between us makes my grief lesser than Ryder's, or maybe not. The sadness I feel hurts like hell, I know that.

When the sun's gone and Mya's family and Hannah have gone home, the house is dark, aside from the small kitchen. Ryder's crumpling his fortieth piece of paper and chucking it into the growing pile on the floor. He lays his head down on his arms for a few minutes. Ready to take another shot, he picks up the pen, starts to write again, and then tears the page from the notebook. The paper ball joins the others on the tile floor. I still don't know why he's insisting on giving a speech at the funeral tomorrow.

Because his biceps are flexed, I block him when he

stands and paces the kitchen. He doesn't need to screw up his hand any more than it already is. When my mind is able to think through the electric current, I sever the command. Ryder's arms relax and he cracks his knuckles on his way back to the chair. After another shot at the notebook, his words start to flow. Finally, he's making real progress.

When the page is covered with black ink, I stand behind him and read what he's got so far.

My dad was the most amazing man in the world, and I know that each of you here today who knew him would agree. He was kind, generous, loving, and always put others before himself. His dedication to the food pantry, and the hundreds of people he's helped feed over the years, is proof of that.

He took pride in everything he did, especially in his career as a mechanic. He could fix anything. I never once heard him complain about having to go to work. He's taught me so much— not only about cars, but about life. He taught me to be accountable for my actions. He taught me patience and the value of good work. He taught me about the gift of charity.

He gave so much love to Mya and me that I thought it would be impossible for him to love anything more, but then Lennon came along. No words can adequately describe the day my dad first met his grandson. He cried harder than I've ever seen, and he didn't even care that Mya and I jabbed him about it. That was Dad—never worrying about what anyone else thought, always being true to himself.

He made the most out of the life he was given, even when he faced the loss of my mother. I pray that he is with her now.

My heart is broken. I will miss him more than words

can say. He was my best friend.

Ryder lowers the pen and puts his head down. I know he's crying because of his convulsing shoulders. Aside from that, he's completely quiet.

Behind him, I lean against the wall with my arms crossed. My dad was nothing like his. I'm not sure why this makes me so angry.

———

Because I'm bouncing back and forth between Ryder and Tate, the week flies by. Troy's funeral was, without question, my hardest day as a Satellite, and the days that have followed haven't been much better. To make matters worse, both Ryder and Tate seem to be going downhill fast. I've had better luck keeping Ryder from destroying things than Tate, although he's been crying a lot more. If I had to choose between destruction or tears, my current stance is that both equally suck.

Ryder's grandparents have brought pizza for dinner, but Ryder's been refusing to eat all week. So here he sits, zoned out and picking at the stringy cheese.

"Your dad wouldn't want you to carry on this way." Ryder's grandpa delivers this bit in a matter-of-fact tone that sounds just like Willow.

"Well, he's not here, so I guess he doesn't have a say," Ryder mumbles. If I'd known those words were going to spew from his lips, I would have blocked him to keep his mouth shut.

"I'm sorry," Ryder says a minute later when he notices he's made Nana cry.

It's hard to be angry with him. The poor guy is falling apart. The funeral just about did him in. I don't know that I was any better. The rectangular hole beside Willow's headstone affected me much more than I expected. Ryder's speech was brilliant, and the entire church bawled, including me. Ryder was lucky to have a dad like Troy.

When Ryder's grandparents leave, I sink into the super-comfy sofa while he talks to Hannah on the phone.

"I said I'm fine." Ryder's agitated movements contradict his words. He rubs at the back of his scalp aggressively and appears to listen to Hannah for a minute, but then his scowl surfaces.

"I wish everyone would stop saying that," he says, his voice rising. "He's gone, so how are things going to get better?" Then, ten seconds later: "What are *you* sorry for?"

I straighten up, scoot to the cushion's edge, and prepare to block.

Ryder moves to the kitchen and paces, saying lots of *mmm-hmms* into his cell phone. He says good-bye a few minutes later and tosses his phone on the counter.

I follow him into the garage and have to block him at the Craftsman tool chest. When his crying fit is over, he picks up different tools and weighs them in his hands until he's emotionally too weak to hold them. He places each one carefully into the rolling drawers until he gets to the hammer. I jump out of the way before the thing flies through me, not that it could damage me. The drywall, however, is not so lucky. Watching Ryder rips me up inside. I wish there was more I could do to help him. I'm grateful that he doesn't stick around the garage longer than five minutes, which, so far, is a record for him.

I owe his doctor big time for the sleeping pill/anti-depressant cocktail he prescribed and finally earn a break when Ryder falls asleep. I'm not a drug advocate, but this guy absolutely needs something to take the edge off. My only complaint is that when Ryder's on the sleeping pills, his snores thunder even louder. Tonight Ryder's chosen the sofa as his bed, leaving me the recliner, which is also too comfortable for its own good. If his bedroom didn't house his clothes, I'd start to wonder if he even had one.

While Ryder sleeps, the incident in the garage sticks in my head. Ryder couldn't hold the wrench longer than a few seconds. I wonder if my dad had trouble going back to work after my death. Heck, my old man hardly even talked to me— he probably went back to the job site five minutes after they put me in the ground.

Since thinking about my dad only raises my blood pressure, I spend the rest of the night worrying about Tate. Through the next day, I block Ryder when needed and count the minutes until I can see her again.

14. You weren't meant to find out this way

Now three months in, I've fallen into a decent routine. Things with Ryder are the same everyday: he snaps, I calm him down. I had expected his spirits to be improved by now, but he still misses his dad like crazy. When he's alone, he has crying fits that would give Ms. America a run for her money. Watching him upsets me quite a bit, either because I feel sympathy for him or because I'm angry that I never shared the same kind of relationship with my own father. Probably both.

At least Ryder has pulled out from his depression enough to go back to his classes. This is good for him, but terrible for me. Tagging along as he studies for his engineering degree—and in particular, attending his Ethics class—is grueling. I was never cut out for college. Sitting through lectures for long periods five days a week just about does me in.

Now that Ryder and Hannah are in a "Facebook-official" relationship, keeping Tate off my mind is harder than ever. It doesn't help that she's getting worse. Even Elliott can't bring her mood up these days. I haven't seen or heard anything more from the makeup-wearing creep, so that's a positive, at least.

Clara is still taking too much interest in me and not enough in Rigby. So far, I've done a decent job of maintaining my not-interested-in-romance stance with Clara, though.

Christmas was more than a little awkward. Having no idea about the traditions of Progression, thanks to my ever-helpful mentor, I did not come to Benson bearing gifts like the others. Clara gave Rigby the same gift she gave everyone else: a tin of her mom's famous peanut butter cookies. In return, Rigby gave Clara a sapphire bracelet. Clara gave me her drawing of San Francisco, complete with an over-the-top matte and frame. In return, I gave Clara nothing. I could have killed Willow, and then I could have died from humiliation. To make matters worse, said ever-helpful mentor made a point of hanging Clara's picture beside my bookcase. Every time I try to relax on the sofa, I feel like Clara is staring back at me.

Rigby was cool about the whole gift-exchanging incident, either because Clara seemed thrilled with her gift from him or because he's fully aware that I continue to see Tate. It's nice being able to talk to Rigby without having to censor my erratic behavior. Still, because of the weird Clara love triangle, uncomfortable doesn't begin to describe some of the breaks the three of us have shared.

I set my tray on the table and sit next to Anna. She was released from training a month after me. The remaining sixteen newbies were released after her. I was glad she wasn't the last. To this day, she has trouble keeping the details of her assignment to herself, so when she starts spilling, I close my eyes and shake my head. The small gesture is usually enough to shut her up.

"What's with everyone?" I ask, because Benson is noisier than usual.

"New Satellites are coming," Anna answers.

"Didn't we just get a group?" I say, stuffing half my sandwich into my mouth to play the part of a normal, rule-abiding Satellite. Being here during break is difficult with Tate filling my thoughts, but I figure it's necessary to avoid suspicion.

"Dude, that was three weeks ago," Owen replies.

"It's been that long?" I gulp down my Coke. Trying to act interested is almost as hard as being away from Tate.

"Time flies," Rigby says and resumes gnawing on his toothpick. He's sitting really close to Clara. Strangely, this bothers me today. Probably because I miss Tate so much; being away from her for twenty-four hours is about all I can stand.

"You really should code, man. You look like death," Rigby adds, watching me stuff a ham sandwich into my mouth and knowing full well why I'm eating so fast and why I haven't been coding.

Looking like death explains all the sympathetic stares I've been getting around here. I'm not surprised, as my weary body feels the sting of my muscles with every movement. I rub my eyes and vow to change clothes and run a comb through my hair soon.

"How's Willow?" Clara asks me.

"Beats me," I say through a mouthful of food.

"Haven't you seen her?"

Gulp (sandwich down, spaghetti to go). "Not lately. She's been with Troy a lot, I think."

"She was bloody beaming when I saw her last," Liam voices, but keeps his eyes on the table. I expect his assignment has gotten hairy because he's been quieter than usual the past few days.

"That's an understatement. If she's not careful, she's going to catch herself on fire," Owen says.

Clara perks up. "I can't blame her. I mean—have you seen Troy?"

Owen rubs his hand over his plastic hair. "Clara, you think everyone's hot."

"Not true. Take you, for example. And Grant's looking rough these days, too." She looks me up and down and grins. "But I'm still keeping him on the list." My cheeks get hot. Rigby's face gets hot, or at least red, too. I make a point to look away from him quickly.

"Hey, Owen's totally attractive!" Anna rebuffs, stealing everyone's attention so that I'm the only one who notices Rigby's disdain.

"Yeah, if you're into height-challenged guys." Liam almost smiles.

Owen answers the dig by smoothing his middle finger over his eyebrow.

"Have you met Troy yet?" Clara asks me, which shuts up the dogs.

"Mmm-hmm," I answer through a mouthful of meatball. When I ran into them four weeks ago, I had to play like I didn't know who he was. Mrs. Smiley, a.k.a. Willow, was acting even more eccentric and hyper than usual. She barely remembered my name when she introduced us.

"What's he like?" Clara asks.

I swallow some noodles. "He's cool. I could see myself hanging out with him if his wife wasn't such a nutcase."

"Speaking of Willow, do you think they're ever going to announce the new Elite?" Clara asks to no one in particular.

Liam takes a new interest in the conversation.

"I wish they'd get on with it," Owen says. "The suspense is killing me!"

"There's no way it'll be you, mate," Liam says. "They only pick Satellites who are good. Like me."

"Ha! Fat chance, bro!" Owen counters.

Rigby's expression is sour. "This Elite business is getting old. I wish they'd just announce it already so you can all move on."

"Thank you." I'm glad to know someone else gets it.

"You only say that because you're not in the running," Owen says.

Rigby frowns. "Why wouldn't I be in the running?"

Owen looks at Rigby like the guy just said the sky was green. "You're too new. They'd never pick someone with such little experience."

"Well, whatever. I don't know who'd want to be one, anyway. I'm perfectly content with the difficulty level of my current Tragedy."

"Nancy newbies could never handle the pressure." Liam's joking—I think.

"Oh, trust me, I could handle it," Rigby assures him. "I just wouldn't want to."

I brush a napkin across my mouth and push away my empty tray. "See you guys later." Thankfully, no one but Rigby and Willow has caught on to my disappearances, and Willow's subscribed to the "don't ask, don't tell" policy. Coding has proven to be useful, although not for actually coding.

In my hurry to find an abandoned hallway so I can displace, I only hastily glance at the new Satellites stampeding into Alogan. It takes me three full strides before it registers, and I whip around. Everything moves in slow motion; I've forgotten how to breathe.

I gasp when I finally find my voice. He looks up when I call his name, confirming that my eyes aren't lying. An invisible sledgehammer nails me in the gut and doubles me over. No! This can't be happening!

"Grant?"

No! It can't be!

"Grant, what's—"

"Elliott! What are you doing here!" I choke out wildly, and not as a question. "I don't...no...Tate!" My tongue is too big in my mouth. *No! Oh please, no!*

"Grant, is it really you?"

I try to catch my breath.

"Grant? What's going on?"

My senses are too blurry and muffled.

"Grant, calm down. Grant, look at me." I read Jonathan's lips while he shakes my shoulders.

"Elliott?" I ask, not recognizing my small voice.

"Grant, I'm sorry," Jonathan says. "You weren't meant to find out this way."

When his words sink in, I explode with anger. "No! This is a mistake! A horrible mistake! We need to fix this!"

"Grant, listen—"

"No! You listen! Send him back!"

"What's going on?" Elliott asks, watching our conversation as though it's a Ping-Pong match.

"Grant, please calm down. Let's discuss this privately," Jonathan says.

I shove my hand into my bag and displace as soon as I touch the frame, slipping out of Jonathan's grasp and falling into a numb free fall.

I spin around my old bedroom, surprised that I wasn't followed. I lunge without another thought, and the trees and houses I memorized months ago are blurred fifteen feet below me. I regret my hurry as soon as I step into the Jacoby's kitchen, into the massacre.

"No! Not my baby. Not my baby!" Mrs. Jacoby wails from the floor. Tate's dad holds his distressed wife and stares blankly across the room.

Tate gasps for air while Fischer absorbs the nightmare from the safety of her arms.

I react in the only way I can. "Haze!"

Calm, calm, calm, calm...

I stumble back in pain; the shock is worse than I've ever felt before.

"Block!"

Mrs. Jacoby's volume decreases, but sobs continue to rip through her.

"Haze!"

Calm, calm, calm...

My scars rip apart before I choke out the order to cease the current.

Tate becomes quieter, but then Fischer's cries ramp up. I stumble, both mentally and physically, before repeating the process one more time. Agony screams through my convulsing muscles, and I slump to the floor like the rest of the family.

When Tate's aunt and uncle make an appearance in the foyer, the hysterics resume. From the floor, I pull as much energy as possible, but the filter is just a light-blue tint.

"Haze," I murmur.

Calm, calm, calm...

I can't breathe. I can't focus.

"Block," I choke out. Tate barely reacts to my unimpressive persuasion.

"I don't understand. He was just rock climbing," Tate's dad says in a dead voice.

I don't have the strength to block; I don't have the strength to do anything. Instead, I endure a pain much worse. Tears sting my eyes while I focus on a chip in the tile floor and try to tune out the wailing from Tate's mom.

And Tate—what will this do to her?

My mind stops my thought and works again to find my energy. When I finally pull some, the blue ball is the most transparent it's ever been. I try for another block, but I am physically unable.

In pain, I push across the floor to Tate, and her crying slows. "Shhh," I whisper.

"Grant?" she breathes, so softly that no one else could have heard.

I try to use my energy to squeeze her arm as a sign that I'm there, but I'm entirely depleted. My blood boils in anger. I think of the Schedulers—of what they have done to Tate, to this family. How much can one person be expected to suffer?

I'm about to find out.

———

Bolting from my room to find Jonathan turns out to be unnecessary. He's already sitting on the sofa.

"Grant," he says calmly.

Wild-eyed, I shoot a look at Willow. Sure, now she decides to come around.

"Are you all right, kid?"

"What do you think?" I snap, well beyond pissed at this point. "I want to see the Schedulers."

"That's not possible," Willow begins, but she is hushed by Jonathan's raised hand.

"Grant, please sit. We have much to discuss."

"Frigging right we do! I want to see the Schedulers now!"

"That will not be possible unless you calm down," he says. I grit my teeth.

"Are you in control of your emotions?" he asks three

minutes later.

I nod my head, not trusting my voice.

"All right. Let's go."

Willow can't hide her surprise. The Schedulers must not make a habit of mingling with the Satellites. Funny, they have no problems ruining their lives.

Jonathan leads Willow and me in silence to the Orders hall downstairs. He bangs his fist three times on the unmanned golden desk. A bell chimes with each hit, and then a panel of marble recesses back and slides to the left, creating a doorway.

"Here we are," Jonathan says, motioning for me to go ahead. "After you."

I huff and walk past Willow, who's lamely gaping at the opening. The marble panel thunders closed behind us. Jonathan leads us out of the small lobby and through a maze of narrow corridors. If I wasn't so ticked, I'd find the old-school trim work in the bright, candlelit passages impressive.

One of the hallways finally opens into a large room. We approach two giant doors on the far side and Jonathan says, "If you'll give me a moment, I would like to announce our arrival."

Willow and I move five paces back so one of the doors can swing out. It closes quickly behind Jonathan, and the seeded-glass panels obscure what's inside.

Willow flings her arms around me.

"They can't do this," I say numbly.

She pulls back and holds my arms out to examine me, as if I could be injured. I consider screaming to her that I'm already dead, but I'm too drained.

"We'll figure this out," she says firmly.

"They can't do this," I repeat in a restrained voice.

"I can't believe we're here." She looks around, her eyes wide. "I've never heard of a Satellite meeting the Schedulers. Ever. This is major!"

"Glad I could help you out with that," I scoff.

"I'm sorry, that came out wrong. You must be sick about Elliott."

The knot in my stomach grows. Jonathan opens the door and pops his head around the side. "The Schedulers have been notified."

We walk into a space that's more like a coliseum than a room, except this coliseum isn't anything like the Roman Colosseum I've seen in pictures. This one is much more pristine, without the slightest hint of crumbling, and instead of stone bleachers, a double-tiered desk structure surrounds its perimeter. Unlike Willow, my expression remains level. At this point, I don't expect anything less spectacular from the ostentatious Schedulers.

Dozens of freestanding marble columns are joined together by arches to create a circular sort of wall that separates the desk structure from the overgrown, grassy field. A picturesque forest and mountain range surround us far in the distance. An evergreen scent drifts through the area and I swear I can hear a stream flowing.

Jonathan leads us to the center of the room, and I envision man-eating lions being released into the pit. At this moment, consumed by rage, I'd happily take on a dozen grisly animals and still come out the victor. We stand dead center, where the bright floor tiles form a bull's-eye within a sunburst pattern.

"The Schedulers will be here momentarily," Jonathan says, looking up at the scarlet tanagers perched along the thick arches.

When he shifts his gaze, I follow his eyes across the space to one of the arches. The archway swings out, and the grassy landscape beyond is replaced by a dark-paneled hallway. When an inordinate amount of people file through, I keep my face level, refusing to let Progression's magic impress me. I'm not sure what I expected—maybe monks' robes or judges' garb—but the group's regular, casual clothing throws me. I rub my thighs, and the scar on my knee prickles.

The mob settles into their golden chairs, filling both levels of the massive circular desk, and hundreds of eyes are suddenly on me.

"Thank you all for meeting with us on such short notice," Jonathan says to the alert audience. "As you know, this is Grant Bradley and his Legacy, Willow Beckmann. He would like to speak with you regarding a new arrival, Elliott Jacoby. Since this meeting has been convened at Grant's request, I will allow him to continue."

Following Jonathan's lead, I address the guy sitting in the center of the elevated portion of the inner desk. Well, not address per se, as that would require me to remain calm, and I feel my anger and frustration toward these people building steadily. "Elliott can't be here! You have to send him back!" I ball my fists, but that doesn't stop them from shaking.

A chair scrapes on the tile, and the man in the center of the group stands. "Hello, Grant. Let's start over, if you don't mind. I'm Landon, and these are my fellow Schedulers." He looks and talks like a politician, which pisses me off even more. "We have been doing our job for many, many years. Our planning is careful. It is precise. Let me assure you, we do not make mistakes."

"A mistake *was* made," I interrupt.

"I realize this is difficult for you, but as I said, a mistake has not been made," he repeats.

My blood boils and I clench my teeth. "Let me correct you. It's not difficult for me, it's difficult for Tate. She's been through enough!"

"Facing a great deal of adversity in a lifetime is not uncommon."

"We're not talking about a lifetime, we're talking about a few months! What is wrong with you people?" I accuse, spinning to see all of the staring, calm faces lined along the desks. I give Willow an apologetic look when my hand forcefully smacks against her arm.

"There are reasons for these events—a larger picture—though I realize that may seem unclear at the moment."

"Give me just one good reason," I growl.

"We cannot share this information out of respect for Tatum's privacy."

"You didn't show her any respect when you wrote her future!"

"Two deaths in such a short time is excessive. However—"

I cut him off. "Excessive?"

My teeth grind together and my mom's voice rings in my ear as if I'm nine again: "You'll only be defeated when you're heated." I almost laugh out loud. Partly because I can hear her singsongy voice like it was yesterday, but mostly because I think I really have lost my mind. "Has a mistake ever been made?" I ask in a calmer voice.

"Let me assure you that Tatum's future would not have been written as such had we thought she was not strong enough to handle it."

"You've got to be kidding me!" So much for my mom's advice.

"Please allow the events to unfold as they will. There are reasons."

"So there's no way you can send Elliott back?"

"I'm deeply sorry, Grant."

"What about Fischer? He's just a child! Did you even consider what this is going to do to him?" My voice raises with my blood pressure.

"Oh yes—Fischer. He is going to accomplish great things."

Landon's cocky smile infuriates me. I bite my tongue until the taste of iron runs down my throat. When the lesion heals, I bite again.

"I assure you that Tatum will come out of this as planned," he says.

"Let me assure *you* that if she doesn't, you're going to wish this was handled differently," I say, walking out of the circle. "Although I guess you already knew that, since you've written my future as well," I yell over my shoulder.

"Grant, I know this is difficult, but please have faith. We still need to discuss your extracurricular activities—" Landon's saying as I'm pushing through the door.

When I realize I need Jonathan to lead me out of this fun house, my fist attacks the wall. The wall wins. I should have learned from Ryder's mistake, but at least now I can understand his rage.

Jonathan and Willow step out of the room as I'm shaking the pain out of my hand. Jonathan eyes my red knuckles and then silently leads the way back. Willow grabs my arm and squeezes it. When our eyes meet, she looks away. Even the freak is at a loss for words.

Halfway through the maze, Willow leans closer to me and whispers, "They know you've been visiting Tate."

I should probably be more concerned about this, but I honesty don't care what they know. I hate them. If the Schedulers think I should stay away from Tate, then I'm going to see her even more. Those idiots don't have a clue what they're doing.

We finally get back to the lobby. Jonathan pulls down on one of the iron sconces like a lever, and the marble wall retracts and slides to the right. Jonathan follows Willow and me out and the panel closes behind us, leaving no trace that it ever existed.

"Willow, would you mind if I speak with Grant privately?"

Willow throws herself around me, but my arms hang dead at my sides. "It's going to be all right," she whispers before letting go.

Jonathan leans against the golden desk and addresses me after Willow leaves. "Grant, you must have faith that the Schedulers know what they're doing."

"That's slightly problematic for me. Certainly you can see my point," I sneer.

"I can, and I deeply sympathize with you." He does look sincere. "There is an issue we need to discuss. We've overlooked your visits to Tate in the hope that you would gain closure and say good-bye. But the time has come for your visits to stop."

Nothing like getting right to the point.

"You're not helping her as you think you are, and you're also putting Ryder in danger. You cannot be distracted. He needs you."

I stare at Jonathan hard enough that he should have a smoldering hole in his forehead, but I refuse to speak.

"Ryder's life course is at risk. I'm sure you've seen in his behavior—he is deeply struggling with the loss of his father. His grieving is beyond what we consider normal. Are you willing to face the consequences of failure? More importantly, are you willing to face Willow if something happens to Ryder?"

He's so not playing fair. I still won't answer him, though. I respect him too much to lie to his face.

"I'm not going to reprimand you any further, as I trust that you will make the right decision." He pauses. "I think it would be helpful for you to speak with Elliott. He was shaken up after your earlier encounter. Would you mind?"

I shake my head. Of course I want to see him, just under different circumstances.

"Thank you. I believe it will help him a great deal." Jonathan silently leads me to a small room off one of the hallways past Benson. "Please, make yourself comfortable. Elliott will be here shortly. If you'll excuse me," he says, squeezing my shoulder before leaving.

Staring at the jumping flames in the stone fireplace, I drum my fingers on the table to the rhythm of my racing thoughts. My foot stops bouncing when the door finally opens.

Physically, Elliott looks great—he's older and more built than I remember. Emotionally, he looks like he got hit by a bus.

"Grant, is it really you?" he whispers.

15. *You really are Captain Oblivious*

From Elliott's confused expression as he gapes at me, I probably shouldn't maul him, but in three strides, my arms are strangling his shoulders.

"Dude, you shouldn't be here. I can't believe this is happening," I say.

"Grant?" His voice sounds muffled.

I let him go so he can breathe. "Yeah, it's me."

"Where am I? What's going on?"

"Progression. You're dead, Elliott." I try to sound sympathetic.

"I got that much. I just heard the spiel from Fabio."

"Jonathan?"

"Yeah, I guess."

"So you know you're dead?" He's handling this well.

"Uh-huh. What's all this about being a Satellite?"

"Looks like you've been chosen, too."

"I don't understand."

"Neither do I. Have you gotten your Legacy yet?"

"No. Fabio asked me to come with him while the others were lining up."

"Your Legacy will be able to explain why you're here." The last thing he needs is my cynical explanation.

"My family. How are they going to get through this? And Tate." Just her name makes my stomach turn. "What's going to happen to her?"

His eyes burn into me for an answer. Not having one, I cross the room and avoid eye contact. "So, you're still rock climbing, huh?"

"Not anymore. Man, my mom must be a mess. I should have listened to her. It wasn't worth this."

There's no way I'm going to mention Mrs. Jacoby's reaction. "Don't beat yourself up too bad. That fall was out of your control." *And planned years ago by the monsters.* I keep this part to myself.

My calimeter drones just as Willow barges into the room. She's found the time to change into a glowing pink shirt that hurts my eyes. "Hey, Grant," she says, as if everything's fine. She extends her hand to Elliott. Her acting skills are scary good. "I'm Willow, Grant's Legacy."

Elliott pushes his eyes back into his head and shakes her hand. "*You're* Grant's Legacy?"

She winks at me. "Opposites attract."

"Apparently. Grant must hate you. He's way more like his old man than he'd ever admit, especially when it comes to his opinion of body art. Killer ink!"

I open my mouth to argue, but the two are already engrossed in their own conversation about Willow's self-induced, colorful scars.

After a few minutes, she remembers I'm still here. "Oh, kid—I almost forgot; you've gotta get back to your assignment. You guys will have plenty of time to catch up later. It was great to meet you," she says to Elliott before skipping out of the room.

"She seems cool."

Instead of adding my two cents, I say, "Come on."

Elliott runs his hand through his hair. It's exactly the same color as Tate's, and, though much shorter, it has a trace of the same curls, making my mind wander.

Elliott punches my shoulder when I dump him in line. "It's great to see you. You look a million times better than Cancer Boy." This was the nickname, much to Tate's disapproval, that Elliott gave me when I started to look creepy from my treatments. After the cancer took a disgusting toll on my body, he was about the only one who could talk to me like I had a disease instead of like I was a five-year-old. I respect him for that more than he'll ever know.

"I've missed you, man."

Before I can stop myself, I hug him again. "I've missed you, too."

After saying good-bye, I turn the corner to displace so I don't spook him more than necessary. Ryder and Hannah have already buzzed to life and are watching a movie.

My mind is preoccupied through the night and never-ending day. Luckily, I only have to block Ryder once. When break finally arrives, I bypass Progression altogether. Even though I want to see Elliott, I need to see Tate—to know she's coping all right. Screw the Schedulers. They're the reason for this whole mess. If they don't like my visits, then they'll just have to find a way to stop me. Maybe, if I'm lucky, they'll pull me from this whole asinine program.

Who am I kidding? My luck ran out months ago. Plus, saying I don't want to help Ryder would be a lie. Though our relationships with our fathers were very different, I feel a strong connection to Ryder because of our mutual loss. Maybe it's a stretch, but helping him through his grieving is helping me as well, and my feuding emotions of anger and sadness toward my dad have lessened a bit.

When I get to Tate's, her bedroom is dark. The blinds are closed and the air smells stale. My stomach flips nervously. Thanks to my night vision, my eyes need no time to adjust and I find her quickly. She's asleep in the big button chair. In contrast to the soft-green cushion, her eyelids are red, raw, and swollen.

The room shouldn't be this still. Why is the room so still?

I gasp for air when I figure it out. She isn't sleeping.

The word repeats with my thundering pulse: *Tragedy, Tragedy, Tragedy…*

I plow through the room in panic, stopping a couple of times to glance at her frozen body and listen for her breathing. When I finally realize there's nothing I can do here for Tate, I displace and run as fast as I can to Benson.

"Whoa! What's up with you?" Anna asks at my abrupt entrance.

"Nothing. Sorry," I answer, out of breath.

Like always, Clara has to get an eyeful. She scans my entire body before speaking. "You look like you've got the hangover from hell. Bad day?"

"You could say that. Have you guys heard of anyone

getting a new Tragedy?" I blurt out too fast.

The girls look at me like I've grown a third arm and disappoint me with their answers.

Paranoid, I sit in a chair and try to appear calm. "Did you know Tate's brother is here?" I ask to change the subject.

Clara bites. "Uh…yeah. I also heard you saw the Schedulers."

"It was no big deal." *Tragedy, Tragedy, Tragedy…*

"No big deal? Are you kidding me? Spill!"

Coming here was a huge mistake. "It was nothing."

Clara flips her hair over her shoulder. "You do realize that no other Satellite has ever seen them, right?"

"I seriously doubt that."

"None that I've ever heard of," she says.

"Maybe they've just kept their mouth shut. By the way, how did you hear about it?"

"Oh, come on. Everyone knows," Clara says. "You really are Captain Oblivious."

Anna chokes on her drink from laughing. Seriously? Girls and gossip go together like axles and wheels around this place.

"How many Schedulers were there?" Anna asks, wiping apple juice off her chin.

"A couple hundred, I'd guess."

"Wow! What did you say to them?" Anna asks.

"I asked them to send Elliott back."

Clara takes a bite of the carrot she stole from Anna's tray. "That's impossible."

"So I've learned."

"The Schedulers? Man, that had to be something," Owen says like he's impressed, sitting down with Liam and Rigby.

I don't answer and instead trace one of the dark knots on the table. *Tragedy, Tragedy, Tragedy...*

After shoving an entire cupcake in his mouth, Owen's muffled voice says, "Dude, you look like crap. I can't believe your bro-in-law is here!"

"Gross, Owen! Swallow your food before speaking, you swine." Clara gives him her most disgusted look.

"It's seafood." Owen drops his jaw to show her a mouthful of yellow cake. "Get it? See food?"

"Seriously, man," Rigby sneers with disapproval. "There are ladies present."

"Thank you!" Clara says.

Rigby sits up straighter and appears pleased that Clara has taken notice of him.

"Anyone hear who the new Legacies are?" Liam asks, shifting in his seat and looking down at his calimeter.

"I heard Liv is one. She looked totally bummed when I saw her," Owen says.

"Well, Lainie's stoked," Clara adds.

"I still don't get how someone could be excited about leaving all this."

"Owen, believe it or not, some people want to see their loved ones again," Liam says.

"Of course someone married would say that. Everyone I want to see is right here." Owen nips at Anna's ear.

"You were married?" I ask Liam.

"Yeah."

"For how long?"

"Nine years."

"Any kids?"

"A son. Finn," he answers.

This shocks me. Picturing any of the Satellites living normal lives outside of Progression is difficult.

"Finn was ten so we call him Liam's little love child," Clara jokes.

"How'd you die?" I ask.

He looks down at his entwined fingers and his voice is quiet. "I drowned."

Clara kicks me under the table. "Let's grab a bite. I haven't checked out what's new yet."

"There's some decent stuff in there," Owen says. "But it's not as good as the chicken," he whispers to Anna.

"Get a room." Rigby pulls a new toothpick from his shirt pocket. His raised spirits are no more, probably because Clara and I are getting up from the table together.

"You know, that's not a bad idea," Owen agrees, moving his eyebrows up and down at Anna before she punches his arm.

"Come with us, man," I offer to Rigby, wishing he'd stop seeing me as a threat.

"Nah, I'm good."

I want to push harder, but I let it go. Clara and I maneuver around the tables to the back of the room. I think about Tate with every step. *Tragedy, Tragedy, Tragedy...*

"I didn't want things to get weird back there." Clara

passes me a tray. "Liam doesn't like to talk about his death. He had some difficulty losing his memories."

Huh. Me too. "What happened?" I ask, trying not to sound too eager.

She misinterprets my question. "Liam was fishing with Finn and their boat got hung up on some nasty trees. When Liam dove into the water to free the propeller, his arm got caught in some debris. He couldn't get himself loose. Finn managed to get him untangled and back in the boat, but Liam died a few minutes later." Clara pauses before putting a plate on her tray. "Man, he was a mess when he got here," she says, more to herself.

"What about his memories? You mentioned he had difficulty losing them."

"They stuck around longer than usual, that's all."

"Does that happen a lot?"

"Not really." She bites her lip and eyes the egg roll and steak on my tray—mere props to avoid suspicion. I don't trust my queasy stomach enough to actually eat anything. "Good choices—although not so great together," she says with a sour face.

I look from her glossy lips to her salad that's too many shades of dark green. "Yeah, well...yours looks super filling."

I decide it's best to let Liam's memory thing go (for the sake of keeping my own secret) and we head back to the table. I barely talk, wondering if any of the Satellites in Benson could be Tate's. I wish Elliott was around so I could pick his brain while he still has his memories, but break ends without any sign of him.

Back on Earth, I don't catch up on my reading until Ryder falls asleep. As usual, my instructions are to keep him calm. His thunderous snores vibrate through the small bedroom. Surely a couple of minutes away from him couldn't hurt.

I dig into my bag and say the magic word when my hand finds the frame. The lightning speed no longer bothers me, nor does ghosting through the buildings, trees, and earth. Tate is all that matters. When the pull finally releases, I stumble against my old bedroom wall, shocked by what I witness.

"I miss you, kid," my dad whispers into a photo album, barely disrupting the still, quiet house. My breathing hitches. He's the only person who ever called me kid, aside from Willow. Why had I not remembered this?

Unbelievable. The old man is crying. Over me. This is news. He blows his nose on his stained handkerchief. I should probably feel sympathy for him, considering he's in such a state, but I feel strangely whole for the first time in a while. He actually misses me.

"I miss you, too, Dad," I say before I can stop myself. My heart swells because I mean it.

Then, remembering why I'm here, the wholeness I feel at seeing my dad's grief evaporates. I force my eyes from him, not wanting to leave yet, but knowing that I must. A second later, I'm soaring over blocks of dark houses spotted with glowing yellow circles. A sleet/snow mix swirls around me but never touches my skin.

I relax when I see Tate asleep in the chair, breathing

again. I kneel down and focus my energy around one of the curls resting on her cheek. I tighten the filter, and with feather lightness, I push the lock of hair away from her face. I shift the filter to the left, making her lips so blue that she looks like she has hypothermia. I pull in a deep, anticipatory breath and kiss her. I can't pull myself away from her peppermint taste. She feels so good, her lips so soft, that I linger around her mouth.

Her lips part slightly and curve upward, but I yank back and spin around when a throat clears.

"What are you doing here?" I demand. Seeing another guy stretched across Tate's bed irritates me beyond words.

Liam's speechless when he leaps up and paces to Tate's desk.

I stare in disbelief when my stupefied mind finally remembers what's happening here. "*You're* Tate's Satellite?" I blurt out.

"Thanks for the vote of confidence, mate," Liam shoots back.

"That's not what I meant. You just caught me by surprise."

I've never seen the guy so tense. He's looking around Tate's room like we're about to be invaded by martians. "The better question is, what are you doing here?" he asks.

"Oh, uh…"

"Yeah? Go on."

Dude, Liam, don't pee yourself. "I've got nothing. I should be with Ryder—"

"Whoa! Rules, man!"

Right. Apparently I'm destined to break them all. "This is Tate," I say lamely, because I can't come up with anything else.

He angrily shakes the book in the air. "Yeah, I got that much."

He's got her book! "Can I see that?"

"Are you dim?"

"More like defective." I look back at Tate. "I still know every detail about her, about our time together—everything." To claim my territory, I sit on the floor as close to Tate's chair as possible. "So, can I see it?" I ask, pointing my eyes back to the red book in his hand.

"No bloody way! And I don't care about your feelings. You need to get out of here! Now!" he adds when I don't respond.

"Clara told me about your death. She said you had a difficult time forgetting your past, too."

"Seriously, you've got to go!"

"Do you still have any of your memories?"

Liam looks around the room again in a panic and then huffs out a breath. At least his shoulders relax a little. "Just of my death," he says quickly, looking away.

"Yeah?" I hope my tone is encouraging enough that he will continue.

"Can't we discuss this later?"

"What's wrong with now?"

"What's wrong with now? Are you kidding me?" Liam barks.

"No."

"If I talk, will you leave?" He soooo wants me to leave.

I pretend to consider and then barely nod.

Liam starts talking fast. "Jonathan thinks the Schedulers wanted me to hold on to the memory of my death for some reason." His face still looks angry, but this time I have to wonder if his reason has to do with me. "I get to replay my son's reaction over and over whenever I feel like reminiscing."

"The Schedulers don't seem to be going for any kindness awards, do they?"

"Nope. Now will you leave?

I look back at Tate and ignore his question. "Don't get me wrong, I'm thankful that I still remember, but I'm a mess. I mean, I should be with my Tragedy right now and all I can think about is her. I worry about her every minute I'm away."

"She's going to be fine. I've got this. You can go now."

"Thanks." I say this only to be nice, because no one will ever protect her better than I can.

"Who's watching your Tragedy?" Liam's clearly appalled by my reckless behavior.

"You're right. I should get going," I answer, avoiding the question.

"Please tell me I'm not going to see you here again."

I grin.

"Seriously, man!"

I sober up when I look at Tate. "She means everything to me."

Whether on purpose or not, Liam's mood lightens. I can only guess this is because I've agreed to leave. "I'll watch over her like she's my own wife."

My eyes narrow. "Don't go that far."

"Kidding, bloke. Relax!"

I try to laugh, but it doesn't come out right.

———

I attend Ryder's morning Geochemistry class and learn more about element partitioning than I ever cared to know, all the while worrying about Tate. Certainly Liam's capable of protecting her or he wouldn't be a Satellite, I assure myself.

After weighing the consequences and mulling over Ryder's mood today, I decide I can safely leave him as long as he's with Hannah. As soon as she arrives for lunch, I bolt for Tate's.

When I walk through the kitchen wall, Tate's high-pitched shriek raises bumps along every inch of my skin. In a blur, I follow her screams up the stairs and jump over Liam, who's slumped over and trembling violently in the bathroom doorway.

My mind races, taking in Tate's skeletal, naked body slowly being swallowed by pink water. I hone my energy around a towel on the floor and bring it to her wrist, applying as much pressure as I can. She moans and her eyes roll back in her head.

"Tate, stay with me! Stay with me," I plead, leaning over the bathtub.

She looks at me—right at me—not like before. "I just

want to be with you," she whispers. Her eyes are so clear, so intense, that I drop the towel in shock and the pink water devours it. She moans again and her dad runs through my ghost body.

"Tate? Tate, what…oh God!"

The murky water swallows her when I step back. Mr. Jacoby pulls her limp body from the tub and wrestles a towel off the rod, haphazardly wrapping it around her. Tate sprawls across his lap on the small bathroom floor.

Please let her be OK, I plead over and over in my head.

"Tate! Come on, baby, look at me! Mary! Mary, call 911!" Mr. Jacoby yells.

I hear footsteps on the stairs and bury my head into the shower curtain, helpless. When her mom screams, I focus on the floor. My tears evaporate before they hit the muted, checkered linoleum.

"I'm so sorry," Tate says weakly.

"Mary, call 911! We need an ambulance!"

"Oh God," Mrs. Jacoby moans as she runs down the hall.

"Hurry," I plead. "Please hurry."

"We can't lose you, too, baby." When I'm able to look again, Mr. Jacoby is holding Tate tighter, quivering while he rocks her.

The door clicks open downstairs. "Mom? Dad? I'm home!"

Oh, for the love! Throw me a bone! In one bound, I'm down the steps.

"Haze!"

Go watch TV, go…

My mind is so anesthetized I hardly feel the voltage go through me.

"Block!"

"I'm gonna watch some TV," Fischer yells up the steps.

"That sounds great, Fish," Mr. Jacoby responds from upstairs, his voice cracking.

When I get back up to the bathroom, Mrs. Jacoby is wrapping a robe around Tate while Mr. Jacoby keeps pressure on the slices marring Tate's wrist. I look with disdain at Liam's broken body; he's still cowering on the floor. He has the nerve to look up at me with wild, terror-filled eyes.

"I've got her, Mary. Go stay with Fish so he doesn't see this," Mr. Jacoby orders when the sirens are just a few blocks away.

"Fish," Tate mumbles weakly.

Mr. Jacoby carries Tate past me and down the stairs, and I follow behind.

"What's going on, Mom?" Fischer's voice calls out.

Mr. Jacoby has to peel Mrs. Jacoby off Tate, which requires a difficult balancing act to maintain his hold on his daughter. "Mary, go!"

Mrs. Jacoby backs out of the foyer and does a decent job of faking strength. "Tate's not feeling well, honey, that's all. She's going to be fine, though."

I desperately want to believe her.

After Tate's strapped into the gurney, I bolt up the steps and pull Liam up by his shirt. "Explain!" I spit, slamming him against the wall.

"Grant, I'm sorry," he says through his shivering.

I slam him again.

"Grant, just listen! Please!" he begs.

"This had better be good," I say through my teeth, my face a half inch from his. I unclench my fists, and he slides to the floor in a heap of worthlessness.

"I—I was respecting her privacy," he stammers. "She was just going to take a bath. The next thing I know, she's wailing and slicing herself up. I blocked her eight times to get her to drop the razor. I didn't have anymore energy. I'm so sorry, mate."

"I'm *not* your mate," I say above him in a dead voice.

16. It won't stop hurting

A nurse hooks Tate up to an IV as soon as we're in the room and rattles off medical-history questions to Tate's dad. He can't answer half of them, while I can spew out every one. Another nurse is already at work cleaning Tate's cuts, which are even deeper than I feared.

A female doctor comes into the room and checks the monitor. "How are you feeling?" she asks Tate.

"OK," Tate utters in a dry, croaking voice.

"So, what's been going on?" Ms. Doc slips the stethoscope ends into her ears so she can listen to Tate's shallow breaths.

Tate shakes her head. "I lost my fiancé a few month ago…" She fidgets with a thread on her robe and swallows. Ms. Doc gives her a sympathetic look.

Tate turns angry then. The color in her face deepens to the shade of red that makes my heart stutter. She always flushed the same color during our make-out sessions, obviously for reasons other than anger.

"It wasn't a *breakup*, it was cancer," Tate growls, as if her clarification will wipe the look off Ms. Doc's face. Instead, the pitying expression deepens.

"And our son just died." Mr. Jacoby barely gets the words out, rubbing Tate's arm and blinking tears away. "It's been a rough few months."

Ms. Doc nods as if she could possibly understand. "I'm sorry." She takes the rest of Tate's vitals in silence.

"You're stable, but you've lost a lot of blood," she says to Tate when she's finished. Then she directs her attention to Mr. Jacoby. "I would like to discuss treatment options and admit Tate overnight for monitoring."

Tate expels an over-the-top sigh.

Mr. Jacoby ignores his daughter's nonverbal response. "My wife will be here soon. I'm sure she'll have some questions."

Ms. Doc nods. "I'll come back in a few minutes."

"We have a younger son. If you wouldn't mention anything in front of him, that would be appreciated."

"Certainly," Ms. Doc agrees before leaving the room.

Tate runs her tongue over her top lip, but her colorless lip remains dull and cracked. "I'm not taking their drugs."

"We'll talk about it later." I'm guessing this subject has already been exhausted. Her dad wraps his arm tighter around her. "We can't lose you too, baby."

I have to turn away when Tate starts crying, and my eyes squeeze closed even tighter when her sobs ramp up.

"It hurts so bad, Dad. It won't stop hurting. Elliott was the only one who understood," her voice muffles. "I can feel Grant around me sometimes. It's like he's still here."

I spin around, unable to hear what her dad's saying because I'm shouting, "I'm here, Tate! I'm here!"

Her high-pitched shriek cuts us both off. She covers her ears, screaming and hurling herself under the bed, bringing the IV tree down with her and almost ripping the tubes from her arm. Two nurses fly through me and try to calm her down.

The overwhelming truth has my hands shaking even more than the rest of my body. Jonathan was right. My being here isn't helping Tate.

It's making her worse.

———

The sun is still bright when I get back to Ryder's.

"Why are you being like this?" Hannah asks.

Even with his back to me, Ryder's defensive stance beside the fridge screams that something's wrong. My eyes jump from the wet stain on the yellow wall to the broken glass on the floor.

"Just get out!" he yells, seemingly at the countertop.

"I know you're upset…" Hannah trails off and wraps herself around the back of him. "Just talk to me."

He twists out of her grasp and she stumbles backward, looking wounded.

"I said, get out! And take that with you." Ryder directs his dirtiest look at a pamphlet on the kitchen table. "Grieving" is the only word I see on the paper cover before Hannah snatches the pamphlet and slams the door behind her.

Ryder belts out a frustrated groan. I block him before he opens up on the drywall like before; then I focus my energy again. "Haze," I order, projecting my thoughts for him to go after Hannah. When I break the connection, he grabs his keys.

I consider blocking him yet again so he'll slow down the car, but I don't. The faster he fixes this, the faster I can get back to Tate.

In Hannah's driveway he slams the breaks, barely missing the back bumper of her compact red car. He rolls his window down. "Get in!" he yells to Hannah, who's on the sidewalk digging through her purse.

Really, Ryder? No girl in her right mind would respond to that.

They stare at each other for a full minute before she stalks around his car and yanks the passenger door open. My jaw snaps closed, and I jump awkwardly into the backseat before she sits on me.

Ryder's tires squeal down the street while they both petulantly look straight ahead. He stops at a dead end and turns off the car. I finally get the nonsense expression my mom used about silence being deafening. I drum my fingers on the vinyl seat as the minutes tick by.

Ryder breaks first. "I'm sorry."

Hannah drops her head. "I just thought it would help. You've been so distant lately."

He has? I stare through the window at the now overcast sky, promising to pay closer attention…as long as he picks up his snail-like pace, that is.

"A self-help book isn't going to do me any good."

"It might," Hannah says, hopeful.

"Unless it can bring my dad back, it won't," Ryder says firmly, and I can see the corners of his eyes begin to fill with tears. I decide against blocking him, with the goal that his emotional state will soften Hannah, or at least make her more tolerant of his foul mood.

They sit in silence for a while until Ryder finally talks. "I just need more time."

"I'm sorry. I was only trying to help."

"You've got to let me handle this in my own way."

When she doesn't respond, he grabs her hand and kisses it. "I am sorry," he whispers.

When Hannah plants her mouth on his to accept his apology, I hurl myself out of the car and hang out on a stump in the snow-covered field. I'm so jealous I could scream! They're making out like wild animals while I'm stuck being dead. Meanwhile, my fiancée has added self-mutilation to her list of hobbies.

The happy couple comes up for air an hour later. Instead of riding in the backseat, I fly behind the car to clear my head. Not in the least bit breathless from the flight, I kick the toe of my boot against the curb while Ryder walks Hannah to her door. They say goodnight with their tongues because, apparently, they haven't gotten enough of each other yet.

Back at Ryder's, I take my chances and leave him unprotected for the handful of minutes before break. I go straight to the hospital, where Liam sits rigid and pale in the chair beside Tate's bed. Amidst the tubes and wires, Tate sleeps. The low murmurs of her parents talking with someone in the hallway compete with the beeping machine beside Tate's bed.

In a blur, Liam's across the room with his back pressed against the wall. "I'm sorry. I didn't know—"

"Shut up." I keep my eyes on Tate because I can't stomach looking at him. Every cell in my body wants to lay into him for being a failure.

Liam clears his throat and then says, in almost a whisper, "She's getting worse."

My jaw tightens and I fight to keep my voice level. "What do you mean?"

"I don't know. Nothing."

I force my eyes off Tate. "No, not nothing! What?"

Liam's chest muscles become defined under his thin shirt as he pushes himself harder against the wall. "You shouldn't be here. Your presence…this isn't the way things work around here."

Even through my anger, his worried expression makes me feel uneasy, like his reasoning goes beyond my breaking the rules. My presence is making her worse. Is that what he was going to say?

My calimeter buzzes, and the hospital room becomes so silent that it feels like it was screaming five seconds ago. Liam apologizes again and displaces, leaving Tate and I alone in the quiet, dark room. I brush my lips against hers, but her lack of breath makes me anxious.

"I love you," I whisper, trying to ignore the smell of blood and antiseptic. Frozen, Tate appears so peaceful. Certainly me being here couldn't have attributed to her suicide attempt. Could it?

———◇◇◇———

I consider coding during break when I displace back to my room, but my mind is too jacked up. I couldn't relax if I tried. Instead, I make coffee and spend the time on the sofa, staring at the shelves of picture frames and thinking about Tate. If she wasn't as frozen as Ryder right now, I could be with her. I hate the Schedulers for what they have done to her and her family.

When my calimeter finally buzzes, my mind is made up. Ryder was doing homework when I left him before break, so I should have at least an hour of him being preoccupied.

The hospital is further away than Tate's house, but by air I cover the distance in mere minutes. I ignore Liam when he moves to the far side of the stale room and I sit beside Tate on the mechanical bed. She's so thin that I almost have the whole uncomfortable thing to myself. I adjust my position so Tate's body is curled toward my chest and I watch as she scribbles on a music sheet.

Liam proves hard to ignore as he goes from pacing, to pulling at his hair, and then back to pacing. He stops mid-stride and shocks me by yelling, "Get out of here!"

I stare dumbly back at him. Does he seriously have the nerve to yell at me?

"Don't you realize how much trouble we could be in for this?" he says angrily. "Her book—" he begins, but then he stops himself and the worry on his face scares me.

Before I can respond, Tate chucks her pencil across the room, destroys the music sheet, and sits up so fast the tubes almost rip from her frail arms. She reaches for her purse on the bedside table and digs until she finds what she's looking for. Using the compact mirror, she ruins both eyes with more black makeup. She should have at least wiped off the remnants of the last layer. The black smudges under her eyes—upside down triangles—make her look like the most depressed circus clown in the world. After she returns the mirror and makeup to her purse, she digs for something else and pulls it out. *What's she doing carrying that around?*

"What's that?" Liam asks tensely.

"I bought that for her at the Arch. Just before my treatments made me too sick to leave the house," I say, more to myself, watching her turn the object over in her hands.

"Does she make a habit of carrying around snow globes?" Liam asks, which is a good question.

Tate holds the globe in front of her face, and the silver glitter swirls through the water around the tiny replica of the Saint Louis Arch. She juggles the globe in her left hand, tosses it to her right hand, and then launches it at the wooden closet door across the hospital room.

"Haze! Block!" Liam yells.

My vision goes black and a freezing chill courses through my veins. In panic, my breath quickens for the five seconds until I can see again. When my vision returns, Tate's sitting cross-legged and sobbing into her hands.

"This is what I'm talking about. She's off her bloody trolley. Sorry about the snow globe, but you need to get out of here!"

I take a steadying breath to decrease my adrenaline flow. Something feels wrong. I get up from the bed and walk across the room to study the mess that has Liam's attention. "What did you say?" I ask, staring at the tiny metal city in a puddle of water and broken glass on the floor.

"You need to go."

The sound of running feet in the hall coming toward us makes me talk faster. "No. Before that."

"Sorry she trashed your gift?" he says as a question.

I focus my energy and run my finger along the silver arch and mini buildings, confused. "I don't know what this is."

"Whatever," Liam sneers when two nurses push into the room. My guess is the women are looking through me right now, seeing the fragments on the floor, but I don't look up to confirm this.

Liam, now standing over me, looks confused. "You just told me about it."

I suddenly feel panicked. "What did I tell you?"

"Huh?"

"What did I tell you?" I ask again, more irritated because I have no idea what he's talking about. "Liam!" I demand.

He looks at me like I'm pointing a gun at him. "You bought that for Tate when you went to the Arch."

The city, now enclosed in my sapphire-blue energy and balanced on my finger, falls to the linoleum. The nurses never notice because they're too worried about sedating Tate, who's putting up a decent fight.

I think back to how I felt during coding when things went wrong.

"She's erasing my memories," I whisper. It all makes sense now. I'm not losing my memories; Tate's stealing them away from me.

Liam's questioning expression is replaced with one that says I've lost my mind. I'm starting to wonder myself.

"Every time she destroys something, I forget the memory connected to it," I explain, standing up but keeping my eyes on the glass fragments. "This can't be happening!" I growl, pacing between the closet doors and the hospital bed.

"I don't want to sound like Mr. Negative or anything, but when you're around, she's worse. It's like she can sense you," Liam says.

He's right. I know he's right; I see it, too.

"I didn't mean—"

I raise my hand to cut Liam off. "Just stop."

He opens his mouth to say something, but I displace before he gets a word out.

Back at Ryder's, I'm too terrified of what Tate is capable of to notice Ryder's pen scratching against the paper while he works on his Sedimentology homework.

<center>~~~</center>

After a quiet night of contemplating whether to visit Tate or not, I decide that I should stay with Ryder. I need to be more focused on him, I know, but Tate doesn't make this easy. She's all I can think about, which makes me feel even more guilty about what I'm doing to Ryder. He needs me, but I'm so distracted.

Ryder does well through the next day; his spirits are actually better than they've been in a while. I'm sure this is largely due to his excitement about making dinner for Hannah tonight. When he hung up the phone with her last night after making the plans, his smile was the first genuine one I think I've seen since being here. With everything that has happened, this significant gesture made me feel happy for a brief moment. Today, he appears as anxious as I am to get out of school in the afternoon.

Not able to stand the separation from Tate any longer, I displace while Ryder's strolling through the grocery store. Break is less than an hour away. Plus, he's humming. Humming! He'll be fine.

I get to the hospital, but Tate and her stuff are gone. I glance at the floor by the closet (now glass-free) before throwing my body through the wall and landing outside, three stories below. I jump into the air and fly over the houses to Tate's, praying that she's there. I don't relax until I see her.

"When did they release her?" I ask Liam, trying to use my nice voice.

"No! No more questions." Liam is obviously in an extra sour mood. "I'm not telling you anything. I've spent too many years working my tail off, and now there's finally a position open for an Elite. I'm not going to let a nancy like you ruin my chances of being selected just because you're choosing to break the rules."

Sheesh. What is it with everyone wanting to be an Elite? "I'll be the one in trouble, not you," I assure him. *And whatever the punishment is, it'll be worth it.*

Realizing I need Liam to help me, some of my anger towards him evaporates. "Please, man, give me something," I plead.

Liam appears to be having ethical issues. Or he's constipated. Probably the first, considering we're dead and no longer need the facilities. Finally, reluctantly, he asks, "Know anything about a concert?"

"Should I?" A brick settles in my stomach.

"Probably. She shredded some tickets earlier."

"At this rate, she'll have my mind erased in a week." I slide down the wall beside Tate. On the floor by her desk, she punches through a playlist on her iPod and ignores me because I'm dead. I'm dead! *Get it through your thick skull, man.*

What am I gaining here? There's never going to be a happily-ever-after for us. In truth, I'm here for me; I'm being selfish. There's a good possibility that my being here may cause her to erase me completely. If I can't see her anymore, at least I could have my memories. It's not a lot, but it's better than nothing.

Liam does a fantastic job of pretending I'm not here. So well, in fact, that I forget he's even in the room. Breathing in Tate's sweet scent, I close my eyes and imagine that I'm still alive with her.

A knock at the door pulls me out of my own head. The

door slowly swings in, and Fischer's head appears around the side like it's floating.

Tate pulls out one of her earbuds. "Hey Fish," she says in a croaky voice.

"Can I come in?" he asks.

She licks her dry lips. "Sure."

He walks over to her and I move out of the way before he sits on me—or, more appropriately, in me.

"I'm glad you're feeling better. I didn't like when you were in the hospital."

Tate yanks her black sleeve down to cover her bandaged wrist and puts her other arm around Fischer. "I know. I'm sorry." She pauses and pulls him closer. "I love you. You know that, right?"

"Yeah, I know. I love you, too."

"It's just you and me now," Tate says in a sad voice.

Fischer sniffs and leans his head against Tate's chest. "Wanna hear a joke?" he asks a couple minute later, his face brightening a little.

"Absolutely," Tate answers, trying to sound upbeat.

"Why was six afraid of seven?"

Tate already knows this one. She's told me the same joke before, but she plays dumb. "Don't know. Why?"

"Because seven ate nine."

Tate takes a deep breath and stares down at her brother. For a second, her eyes shine with life.

"Get it? Because seven eight nine. Like you're counting!"

Liam laughs first because Fischer is just too damn cute

not to laugh at. Then Tate joins in. Fischer, thrilled that his joke was such a success, cracks up with her.

Frozen, I watch her. Her whole face has brightened; it's a stark contrast to her black wardrobe. The glow lingers in her eyes like a spark ready to ignite dry kindling. She's stunning.

A tear runs down my cheek. She could get better with enough time. She could live again. This makes me so happy, yet so sad, all at once.

I push my calimeter to shut it up. Tate and Fischer become motionless and as silent the rest of the house.

No—stunning isn't a strong enough word to describe what Tate looks like right now, frozen in happiness. There's no word spectacular enough to encompass her beauty. I barely notice the frailty of her arms or her black fingernails.

Even Liam's spirits have lifted. "For what it's worth, you should be thankful you forgot about the concert," he says. "If the music she was listening to earlier today was any indicator of the show, it was a total chick-fest."

I laugh under my breath, partly because Liam is funny when he chills out, but mostly so I don't think about my insides being ripped apart.

Seeing Elliott during break makes Progression feel more like home. He's doing a decent job of hiding his real feelings toward his Legacy, Henry, but he can't fool me.

"Something funny?" Elliott asks when I chuckle to

myself. Every time he chews on the inside of his cheek, I know he'd rather be spitting a four-letter word.

"Nah, just thinking about Willow," I lie. Except that now that I've said it, I am thinking about her.

"How is she?"

I shrug. "Good, I guess. I don't see her much these days."

"That sucks. She seems cool." Elliott glances in Henry's direction.

Henry smoothes his cuff and picks an invisible piece of lint off his sleeve. "Ready for training?" he asks.

"Yep." Elliott stands and messes up Henry's hair.

"Hey, uncalled for!" Henry tries to put each piece of hair back in place. "Please don't encourage him," Henry says to Clara, Liam, and I when we laugh. Anna smiles at us from two tables over, where her and Owen are, quote, *on a date.*

"I thought you were uptight," Clara says to me after Elliott and Henry are gone.

"Funny." I smirk and then tell her and Liam that I'll be right back.

I jog out of the room and catch Elliott and Henry at the courtyard doors. "Hey, mind if I talk to him for a second?" I ask Henry.

Henry agrees and disappears behind the massive door.

"What's up?" Elliott asks.

"How are you doing with your memories?"

"It sucks. The ones of Mom and Dad are going the fastest. Any advice to make the transition easier?"

I shake my head. If he only knew. "Sorry."

"I figured as much. I'm sure this is tough for everyone."

"Do you remember if Tate had a black eye recently?"

He looks confused. "Why?"

I look around to be sure no one else is close enough to hear our conversation. "No questions."

Uncertain, he says, "Yeah, I remember that, but how'd—"

"Any chance you remember how she got it?" I ask before he can finish.

"In a fight, but—"

"What!" So much for keeping things on the down low.

"Tate ran into some girl who'd had a major crush on you. The girl told Tate you were a player and there was no way you were ever going to marry her."

What? "Who was she?"

He shrugs an I-don't-know. "Holly something or other, I think. Tate came unhinged on the chick. It took four people to peel her off."

"That's terrible." My voice is quieter and I shake my head. "I don't get it. She's not a fighter."

"Tate became a lot of things after…well, you know." Elliott pauses while I absorb this information. "You wouldn't believe the amount of guys that tried to get with her after you were gone. It was crazy-annoying. But Tate—oh man, you should have seen her. She got real creative with her excuses when she turned them all down. It was humorous, to say the least."

Humorous. I bet. I can't find anything funny about this. I knew the guys would be lining up for her, but hearing

Elliott confirm it makes me so sad I could cry. Eventually, she'll say yes to one of them.

"You have to know there will never be anyone else as good for her as you were." Elliott pauses and looks up at the giant carved doors. "I should probably get in there."

I pull my torn insides back together. "Yeah, big day— first day of training and all. I'm sure you're throwing Henry's whole schedule off."

"He's completely ridiculous." Elliott sighs and then passes through the doors. I watch him stop on the stone path before the door swings closed between us. I'm smart enough to guess his expression. No one can walk out to the courtyard for the first time without being blown away by its sheer magnitude.

"Everything cool?" Liam asks when I'm back to the table. Unless I'm imagining it, there's an undertone to his statement, like he's asking if we're cool. After considering for a few seconds, I nod.

While we play Sats, Clara shares a couple of stories from her past. I keep my mouth shut, because I still remember much more than I should. For now, anyway.

17. I'm all about doing the impossible

While displacing to Ryder's, I remind myself that Liam is with Tate, and then try to forget about his momentous screw up. Not that it matters, as my presence only seems to be making her worse. If only there was a way to keep Fischer on hand 24-7. I'd at least take comfort in knowing that Tate had a real shot at recovering.

I hang onto the frozen image of Tate in a jovial mood while I drop rapidly to the ground. Colorful streaks glow in the distance; other Satellites are plummeting back to their Tragedies, too.

I land in the passenger seat of Ryder's Shelby, and when the dash lights and radio flicker on, I notice our speed immediately. Gripping the dashboard—out of habit, I guess—I look over to Ryder. He swipes tears off his cheeks and then wraps both hands tightly around the steering wheel, leaning back in his seat like he's bracing himself.

I focus my energy into a tight blue ball and shout, "Haze!"

Slow down, slow down, slow down…

Before the paralyzing jolt hits me, I'm rocketing forward, ghosting through the Shelby's dashboard and then through the innards of the engine. My shoulder breaks my fall and my muscles tighten, prepared for the terrible pain that's sure to follow, but nothing comes. Kneeling in the slushy, melting snow, I spin around.

On no. *Oh no!*

The once beautiful Shelby is beautiful no more. I spring up and am standing next to the car's door in under a second.

I force my eyes away from the smoke pouring from the hood, away from the front of the car that's horseshoed around a massive oak tree, away from the windshield that looks like a spiderweb. Instead, I focus on Ryder, wishing I didn't have to look at him. There's too much blood.

This is all my fault. I've failed Ryder. I've failed Willow. Oh no—Willow. I feel so sick my head becomes groggy.

I need to do something—anything—so I form my filter around the crinkled door. With my energy focused, I am able to pry the metal away from Ryder's body, but I have to stop when someone runs to us from the house across the street.

Backing away from the wreckage, my hands tremble in fear. What have I done? An ambulance sounds in the distance, quickly growing louder, but not fast enough. Ryder's finger twitches, but this is the only movement he's made. He has to be all right.

I pace the sidewalk, keeping my stare locked on Ryder's hand, willing his finger to move again. It doesn't. More neighbors have joined the scene and are trying to set him free from the imprisoning metal. I dig my fingernails into my palms and feel sicker, knowing that I could pry the door open in just a few seconds.

The emergency vehicles come with more sirens wailing

in the distance. A few minutes later, the high-pitched scream of a metal-cutting saw makes me cover my ears. They reach in for Ryder's body and—

Whoosh!

As I'm yanked upward, the g-forces flatten my hair against my head and pin my arms to my side.

I land, trying to figure out what's going on. I never said displace. Why am I back here? And why are all the Schedulers staring at me?

"Grant, it seems we have quite a problem on our hands," Landon says from the raised portion of the circular desk.

"What's going on?" I ask Jonathan, who's standing beside me in the center of the circle. I spin around slowly, taking in the mix of disappointed faces and accusing eyes.

"What's going on is you have repeatedly left your Tragedy unattended!" Landon's voice is raised and unhappy.

"Then you should have left me alive!" I yell, equally outraged. "I'm not made for this. Everyone is so convinced for whatever reason that I am, but I'm not! I was made for Tate. I should still be with her, as I obviously suck at this Satellite thing. She was the only thing that ever made me good!" My last sentence is directed more at myself than at the Schedulers.

"On the contrary, you are an exceptional Satellite—but only when your head is in the game. This is precisely why memory loss is imperative. Your actions confirm that our decision many centuries ago was the right one."

"You're the reason why we lose our memories?" I

question.

"Not just me. It was decided by our entire panel"—he signals to the couple hundred-plus people surrounding Jonathan and me—"during the formation of the Satellite program, by way of majority vote."

Jonathan speaks for the first time. "Memory loss was not a unanimous decision."

"No, it was not," Landon concedes. "But I think we can all agree that allowing distracted Satellites into the world is a great disservice to our Tragedies." He pauses. "Yes, we have quite a mess on our hands, Grant. I don't know if you realize the amount of work that now needs to be done to get things back on track."

"Is Ryder going to be all right?" *Please say yes.*

Landon stares at me for so long that I turn to Jonathan, hoping he'll answer me.

Jonathan almost looks mad when he stares back at Landon. "Ryder is going to recover," he says, without turning to me.

"Which is going to be nothing short of a miracle. His body is broken beyond repair, and now, because of you, we have the grueling task of doing the impossible. There will probably be books written and, at the very least, television shows broadcast about his miracle story. Ryder's course doesn't include dying at this moment. Had you been where you were suppose to be, he wouldn't be dying at this moment."

There's nothing I can say. I failed. Period. I was such a jerk to Liam, and here I've done so much worse.

"I never, in all my years, have seen such—"

"I think he understands the situation he has created," Jonathan voices to cut Landon off.

But I wish Landon would finish whatever he has to say about me. However horrible it is, I deserve so much worse for what I've done to Ryder. Ryder! Willow's son! My responsibility! Afraid of yacking my guts up, I keep my lips tightly sealed instead.

We all stare at each other—Landon looking ticked, Jonathan looking doleful, and me feeling guilty as all get-out.

"What happens now?" I finally ask.

Jonathan crosses his arms. "You're going back to your assignment."

"Which I think is a mistake," Landon blurts out. The other Schedulers appear split—about half of them nod in concurrence with Landon, while the other half looks more pensive like Jonathan.

"That's enough, Landon," Jonathan asserts. "Grant, you will be going back to Ryder and seeing him through his recovery, first and foremost. You will not be going back to see Tate."

I swallow in panic. I haven't said good-bye. How can I leave Tate now? I've never said good-bye!

"I suggest you get back to Ryder now," Jonathan says as I internally panic. "You'll need your tocket," he adds a minute later, because I haven't made a single attempt to move.

"Right," I mumble, pulling the granite rock out of my pocket. I make the mistake of meeting Landon's eyes before I displace. He's clearly not a fan of mine.

Falling back to Earth, thoughts of Tate, Ryder, and Willow swirl through my head. I try to push Willow's image away, but even in my mind she's too stubborn to leave. When I land, the accident scene is in full swing. Looking again at the Shelby—because I don't want to look at Ryder, blood-covered and strapped to the stretcher—I can't believe what my inattention has caused.

I squeeze myself into the ambulance when Ryder is loaded and stare out the back window on our way to the hospital. The EMTs continue working on him, and already, the paddles have brought him back to life twice. If I didn't have the reassurance that he was going to live, I'd be even more of a mess than I currently am, which is saying something.

Hours later, we finally get settled into a room, and I do my reading. Things have changed quite a bit from before. Now my instructions are to, quote, *wait*. Mya, her own family, and her grandparents are here now, as well as Hannah and her parents. Ryder has more tubes coming out of his swollen body than a soda fountain machine. Options are being laid out for the family regarding the multiple operations that Ryder will need. Every time another scan gets brought in, prompting the scheduling of even more surgeries, my stomach lurches. When the doctors tell Mya that Ryder may never walk again, I throw up at the side of the hospital bed. The vomit, of course, disappears before hitting the linoleum. All the Schedulers said was that Ryder had to live. They never mentioned the quality of life he was going to have.

Since Ryder is in a drug-induced coma, there's zero

need for my blocking ability. My job now entails staring my mistake square in the face as the minutes tick by. Mya and Hannah refuse to leave his bedside. The night is long and uneventful, except when the story comes out about why Ryder was so upset.

According to Hannah, at the grocery store—when I wasn't there—Ryder ran into a friend, who also happened to be Hannah's ex-boyfriend. The guy, Mike, told Ryder that he and Hannah were still talking regularly and that he planned to get her back. Ryder went off the deep end, calling Hannah from the parking lot and chewing her out because he assumed she wanted Mike, too.

Since Ryder was being so irrational, Hannah canceled their planned dinner. This must have made Ryder even more upset, Hannah thought, hence the bad driving. Knowing how excited Ryder was about the dinner, the story makes sense. Hannah beats herself up, which makes me feel even worse.

The next day sucks. I wish Ryder would at least open his eyes or move his hand—anything that would prove it wasn't just machines making him appear alive.

When break comes, I don't want to leave, mostly for fear of seeing Willow. She hasn't been around much, but she has the insane ability of making herself materialize when she's least wanted. I'm dying to talk to Liam and find out how Tate is—and to apologize—but going out in public isn't worth the risk of running into Willow, so I stay in my room until my calimeter buzzes.

Back in Ryder's world, nothing changes. The time passes slowly, and he remains motionless through the night.

Mya and Hannah make up for his lack of movement by wearing paths into the hospital floor.

The next morning, three doctors and a team of nurses wheel Ryder off to his first surgery. The operating room is bright and smells like bleach. The lights make his badly bruised skin look even worse, and his face is unrecognizable from the massive amount of swelling. A large staff prepares the surgical tools and the three doctors who will be operating take their places.

What the—? I blink, sure my eyes are deceiving me as three ghosts fall out of the ceiling. They each stand behind a doctor, and then at the same time step forward so they are actually *in* the doctors. Knowing what it feels like to ghost through someone, this makes me cringe. Strangely, the Satellites stay in their positions and ignore me. I've never seen any of them before, although considering there's thousands of us, this isn't surprising.

"Hello?" I say, wondering why they are ignoring me.

No one answers. The guy closest to me moves his hand out over Ryder's body. Half a second later, the doctor moves his hand in exactly the same way so the doctor and Satellite are matched up. Weird.

"Hello!" I'm much louder this time. The other two Satellites move their hands, and their doctors mimic their movements. "What are you doing?"

Still no answer.

"Are these your Tragedies?" I wonder aloud, even though the idea doesn't make sense. No one in their right mind would spend so much time inside a body if they could help it.

I realize then what's happening. The ghosts are performing the surgery, not the doctors. Or, at the very least, they're guiding the doctors.

"Are you Satellites?" I ask, figuring no one's going to answer.

"We're Menders," one of them finally says in a deep, muffled voice like he's speaking from behind the doctor's surgical mask.

"You're what?"

"Menders. You created a real mess here," a female voice says in a not-so-nice tone.

"You're not Satellites?"

"What's up with this kid?" the third guy says, irritated. "We're Menders—like George and Ivy just said."

"But I don't understand."

"We're here to repair your damage—which is extensive," George says.

"Why haven't I ever heard of you?" I ask.

"Because we've never been needed for a Tragedy," the female, Ivy, says matter-of-factly. "Just like Satellites, we have our own department in Progression. I hope the Schedulers aren't making a habit of allowing people like you into the Satellite program. I've never—"

"Ivy, I think he gets it. Grant, please allow us to do our work now," the male ghost closest to me says.

I watch silently as they work, the doctors following their movements like machines on a one-second delay. The surgery takes a full six hours, plus some extra time to close

Ryder up. The Menders rise out of the doctors' bodies and disappear into the ceiling without saying a word to me.

I'm making all kinds of friends lately.

———∿∿———

Three days have gone by and I still haven't left my room during breaks. I'm not going to be able to hold out much longer. I have to talk to Liam. Not knowing about Tate is almost as bad as my daily exposure to my horrendous mistake.

Ryder's in his second surgery and the Menders are back, but now there are four of them instead of three. I keep my mouth shut through the operation, allowing them to hopefully fix what I've destroyed.

At the next break, I cave. Thankfully, Liam—minus Willow—is at the table when I get to Benson.

"Can I talk to you?" I ask, ignoring Clara, Anna, Owen, and Rigby. It's hard to tell if they know something. If so, they surely don't know the full extent of my failure. If they did, Owen and Rigby would be punching me right now instead of just staring. At least, that's what they should be doing.

Liam doesn't ask any questions when we walk across the room to a vacant corner and sit at a table for two. I steal a glance back at the table, noticing again that Rigby's arm is, rather comfortably, wrapped across Clara's shoulders. I remind myself that this shouldn't bother me and force my eyes to Liam.

"How's Tate?" I ask.

"Where have you been?"

"Around. How is she?" I ask again.

"She's doing better. She took Fischer to a movie today," Liam whispers while he looks to his left and right. Still afraid of being caught, I see. Mentioning that the Schedulers know about my visits is probably a fact better kept to myself.

"Has she destroyed anything else?"

Liam shakes his head and I relax. Finally, some good news.

I hate to ask, but I have to. "Do you think her improvement has anything to do with my absence?"

His expression answers my question. A mix of emotions swirls through my stomach. Tate is better off without me.

"Why haven't you come around? Not that I'm complaining or anything." Is it possible that Liam knows nothing about Ryder? I can only hope.

"I've just been busy. I was thinking I'll take some time off—you know, to give you a break." Every cell in my body screams in rebellion, but I know this is what I must do. I've messed up too badly with Ryder. Plus, my selfishly motivated visits are only hurting Tate.

Liam may as well be jumping up and down. "Really?"

"Really. Look, Liam, I'm sorry about coming down so hard on you when…well, you know."

Liam shifts in his seat. "Don't sweat it. I deserved everything you said and worse for messing up like I did."

I stop myself from flinching by looking down at the table. His mistake was nowhere near as abhorrent as my failure with Ryder. Part of me wants to tell him about my colossal blunder, but living with the full brunt of my guilt is what I deserve. If I unload this on him, he will probably downplay how awful the situation really is and the last thing I need is someone lying to me.

"No offense, mate, but I'm glad you're taking some time off from Tate. I think it will help. Plus, I was up to here"—he raises his hand over his head—"with your blatant disregard for the rules."

"Point taken."

———

A few more weeks go by, a few more surgeries, and Ryder finally wakes up. He's disoriented for the first couple of days and has difficulty coming to terms with how much time has passed. My work as a Satellite comes back into play. Now I'm usually not blocking Ryder because he's upset about losing his dad (though occasionally that's still the case). Instead, I'm blocking him because he's frustrated about his worthless body and his memory loss—both of which I can totally sympathize with. Fortunately for him, his memories are slowly returning. A large number of blocks have also been needed when he thinks about the loss of his Shelby. The car that held so many memories of time spent with his father was destroyed because of me. I'd rather have toothpicks stabbed under my fingernails than feel as guilty as I do.

I keep Ryder as my top priority, though I still think about Tate day and night. I refuse to see her, not only because the Schedulers would have my hide (as much as I hate them, seeing what's been needed to fix Ryder has softened me a bit), but because she's better off without me. She has always been better off without me.

—————

Now, two months later, Ryder has been released from the hospital. After hours of physical therapy, he's walking with the help of crutches, which I regard as a miracle (or, more appropriately, the amazing work of the Menders). To top that, he's expected to make a full recovery.

Not seeing Tate has been almost as bad as the physical pain I caused Ryder, and I remind myself that the hurt I feel is nothing compared to what I deserve. Liam has been decent towards me, feeding me a few updates about Tate here and there. He now has no problem stating that her improvement is a direct result of my absence. This stings even more than not seeing her.

None of the Satellites know about Ryder and my epic fail, which is a complete surprise, considering the way gossip travels around this place. For this, I am grateful.

I'm not sure if Willow knows what I've done to her son, but I've come to terms with having to face her, simply because I miss her terribly. On my way to Benson, I cross my fingers that she'll be there.

"Hey, man, wait up!"

In the corridor, I stop and turn at the sound of Owen's voice. He's in the lobby, jogging to catch up.

"Hey, Owen, how's it going?"

"Good. You?"

Seriously, do his assignments ever bother him? "Fine, I guess."

"So, ah, you eating today? I mean...you eating today?"

"Why are you acting weird?"

"What do you mean?" He nervously swipes his hand over his black hair. "OK, I may be acting a little strange. Sorry. It's just that I have a surprise for you. Well—I mean, Anna and I have a surprise."

"I don't like surprises."

"Keep an open mind, man. You might like this one."

"Doubt it."

"Just come on." He picks up his pace through the lobby.

"Where are we going?" I ask, half jogging.

"You'll see," he calls over his shoulder.

He almost loses me through the crowds of Satellites, which may not be such a bad thing. I don't have a great feeling about this. He's way too happy.

He stops, and I stare over him at the courtyard doors. "I'm not spending my break in training," I say firmly. "I want to eat."

He vice-grips my biceps muscle when I turn to walk away. "Trust me, man."

He looks too much like a used car salesman to be trusted, but he's obviously not going to let me leave without a fight. Against my better judgment, I follow him.

"Please tell me what's going on." I look around the

empty field. My eyes stop on the grassy area twenty feet past the bleachers. "What's that?" But I already know full well what *that* is.

Owen ignores me—in fact, he won't even look at me—and walks over to the red flannel blanket.

"Dude, I'm totally not into you," I say when he sits.

Owen cracks up. "You're not too hot yourself."

The door bangs closed at the top of the path and catches my attention. "Oh, come on, man!" I hiss to Owen. Please tell me this isn't happening.

"Open mind," Owen says under his breath as Anna and Clara walk down the sloping path.

"You're dead."

"No kidding?" Owen finds too much humor in turning my threat into a joke.

I bite down on my tongue extra hard while watching the girls approach. Anna even has the nerve to be carrying a picnic basket.

"What's going on?" Clara asks.

"Yes, Owen, please…enlighten us," I sneer.

"Oh my gosh, you guys are so cute together." Anna kneels beside Owen and pulls out four plates, napkins, a loaf of bread, a big ceramic bowl with a lid, and four Cokes from the basket.

Clara shares my sentiment and even her tone is one I would choose. "You're kidding."

"Double date!" the bulldog shouts. "Great idea, right?"

Great idea? Is he nuts?

I try not to look at Clara, but I fail. Her face is the color of the blanket. "We don't have to do this," she says to me.

"Really?" I ask, finally optimistic about something.

Her expression falters for half a second, but she recovers quickly. "Sorry, guys, I know you meant well, but this wasn't the best idea."

Anna doesn't bother hiding her disappointment like Clara. Ugh. Girls never fight fair.

"It's fine." I try not to sound angry and sit on one of the corners of the blanket. "It's just a meal between friends, right?" Because this is so nothing else. It can't be anything else.

Clara hesitates, but then sits on the only spot left on the small blanket. With her knees together, she folds her legs to her side, the only ladylike way to sit on the ground in a skirt. Her obvious discomfort proves she knew nothing about this either, which I find reassuring.

Anna goes to work, dishing spaghetti onto the plates. Owen breaks off a large chunk of bread and passes the remainder of the loaf to Clara. Then he proficiently shoves the entire piece into his mouth. As if that wasn't disgusting enough, he proceeds to talk while chewing.

"Nice day out, huh?" he says. At least, that's what I think he says.

Clara's frozen, holding the loaf of bread out in front of her. Her repulsed expression is comical, and I can't help but laugh. The sunlight shines off the blue stones on Clara's bracelet, and my laughter halts.

"Owen!" Anna scolds. "We've discussed talking with your mouth full."

"Oh. Right," he mumbles, still chewing. "Sorry."

"So, what's new with you guys?" Anna hands a plate to Clara and another to me. My stomach flips. The question, though innocent enough, sounds too much like Clara and I are a couple.

I grab the bread from Clara and shove a piece into my mouth to keep from saying anything that would upset Anna —and probably Clara, also.

"Not much." Clara seems more comfortable now. "I noticed the new group that came in yesterday. Did you hear Jessie is a Legacy?"

Anna hands Owen an extra napkin. "Is she the tall blonde girl you introduced me to a few months ago?"

"Mmm-hmm," Clara says, using her fork to push the spaghetti over to make a small space for her piece of bread.

"Was she happy about that?" Anna asks.

Owen snorts. "Dude, is anyone ever happy about that?" Red spaghetti sauce drips down his chin.

"Owen, not everyone wants to do this forever," Clara says.

He's completely dumbfounded. "Why not?"

Clara looks bored. "We've had this discussion so often —you know why not."

"I know. I still don't get it though. Who wouldn't want to do this forever?"

Me! Thankfully, my mouth is now full of gourmet noodles and sauce so I don't have to speak

"There are very few things I'll agree with you on— ever," Clara stares at the sauce still on Owen's chin, "but I have to admit, you're right. I don't know why someone wouldn't want this forever."

"Maybe so they can have their own life," I interject, before I can stop myself.

The three of them look at me like I just stepped out of a spaceship. Naked.

"Seriously," I continue. "You all had lives before this. Why wouldn't you want them back?" I just don't understand their thinking.

"We'll get our lives back someday when our loved ones die," Clara says. "That doesn't mean we have to give this up. We could be Lifers and have both."

"But why would you want to do this forever?"

Anna uses her fork to push the red noodles around her plate. "Because we're helping people."

"And because our work is hardcore, man," Owen chimes in. "I love a challenge. The fact that I get a new one everyday is epic!"

"You were an adrenaline junkie when you were alive, weren't you?" I've met a dozen guys just like him, mostly carpenters, always out for the next big rush. Shoot, even Elliott was constantly doing ridiculously dangerous crap.

"Totally," Owen agrees. "One of the few things I remember from my life was bungee jumping. When I displace, I'm always waiting for the moment when I'm jerked back up by my feet."

"You're not right."

Anna and Clara think this is funny. I think they're all seriously sick if they prefer this life over being alive. I will never be like them. I will never get over losing Tate.

Thankfully, the subject changes to the new foods that arrived with the latest recruits. Owen's particularly fond of the carrot cake, though he makes sure to add that nothing is as good as the fried chicken. His constant reminder about his favorite food is seriously old. Then things get weird because Owen and Anna get all gushy. They even kiss. And then kiss again. Clara looks away from me and twists a piece of her blonde hair. I wish I had more bread to shove in my mouth.

"So, snowmobiling, huh?" Clara asks, probably trying to break the awkwardness, since Anna and Owen are off in their own little world of romance.

"Yeah. You ever done it?"

"I don't remember." She thinks her answer is funny. "I grew up in Connecticut. They have some cold winters, so maybe. Although, I previously mentioned my parents not letting me do much. So probably not."

"Would you? I mean, if you had the chance?"

"Absolutely! I'll try anything once." She pauses. "You look surprised."

"It's just that—I mean, you seem so…proper."

"Proper?" She says it like I just called her ugly.

"Sorry. It's just that you have good manners and all." Did I just say that out loud?

"That's because you see me in the company of Owen. Everyone has good manners next to him."

Owen pulls his tongue out of Anna's mouth long enough to respond. "Hey!"

"She's right," Anna says, but then she sighs as if she doesn't mind that Owen was brought up in a kennel.

"Yeah, I guess you've got a point there," I agree. Clara's actually pretty comical. And her smile is amazing. *No, not amazing. Stop it, man!* I scold myself.

As if knowing of the chink in my armor, Clara reaches into her bag and pulls out her lip gloss.

"Peppermint," she says humorously when she sees me staring at the tube. She has no idea how much of a weakness that scent is for me.

She slides the clear stick over her lower lip first. Is she moving in slow motion on purpose? She adds some gloss to her upper lip and finally presses both lips together, sliding them back and forth enticingly.

"Earth to Grant," Owen sings.

I snap back to reality and give him a glare. I wish he wasn't dead so I could do the honors. He snatches up a piece of bread he dropped earlier on the blanket and chucks it at me, hitting me in the forehead.

Clara, who was oblivious to my previous lip fascination, is no longer. For the second time, her face is as red as the blanket.

"Should we call it a day?" she says to her brown sandals.

"Yeah, I should code before getting back to my assignment," I lie.

The three of them buy my excuse and stand. While I'm putting the plates in the basket, Anna asks, "What are you doing?" I don't know she's talking to me until she repeats herself. "Grant, what are you doing?"

I want to say, *"What does it look like I'm doing?"* but

instead, I answer, "Cleaning up."

"Why?" Owen asks.

My hand freezes in the basket when I get it. Then I'm sure my face turns as red as Clara's was. The three of them confirm this by laughing at me. Talk about feeling stupid.

"Sorry. Habit, I guess." I stand, but look down at my feet.

"Dude, you're a loser," Owen jokes, taking Anna's hand. They begin walking past the bleachers toward the stone path.

Clara and I follow a few steps behind the happy couple. "I thought that was cute," she whispers.

My face grows even hotter. I'd give anything to displace right now.

When we're inside, things become even more awkward. "So, ah, thanks for the meal." I shift my weight from one foot to the other.

"Don't thank me." Clara smiles and I swear she leans forward. "I had nothing to do with it."

"Oh—right. Well, I guess I'll see you later."

Her smile loses some of its juice. "I had a good time."

"Me too." I'm not sure if I'm just being nice when this comes out. No, I did have a good time.

Clara swipes her lips together like she's spreading the lip gloss around again, and her eyes move to the right. Something from behind pushes me. I lose my balance and trip forward. Clara takes this wrong, and—oh no!—pushes her peppermint lips against mine.

I want to pull back, but the taste keeps my feet—and lips—firmly planted. Clara's lips feel so much like Tate's, but so different at the same time. Probably because my eyes are wide open in shock, reminding me that this is not Tate.

What are you doing! I scream in my head. Finally, I do step back, not sure why it took five more seconds after my mental scolding.

Clara looks pleased by our exchange. I, on the other hand, am trying with great difficulty to keep my cool.

"Thanks," I say lamely. "I'll see you around." I turn and walk away as fast as I can without looking rude. *Thanks?* Did I seriously just thank her?

I'm in the elevator two minutes later, unsure how I even got here. I brush my fingers over my lips and then lick my bottom one, tasting peppermint. My stomach twists with the realization that I just kissed Clara. And I don't think I hated it.

Rigby's going to kill me.

18. She almost burned the house down

I know it's risky, especially since I'm sure the Schedulers are going to know immediately, but I have to see Tate—now more than ever. What happened with Clara…I don't know what to think.

When I land at Ryder's, I gauge his mood. This is easy considering he's taking a nap, just as he was when I left him before break. Now or never, I decide, and dig through my bag for the picture frame I haven't used in months.

I say the magic word and go rocketing across the Earth. While I zoom through the trees and mountains, nerves make my stomach tighten. What I'm doing is wrong—and so unfair to Ryder.

Standing in my bedroom feels strange, like it no longer belongs to me. I push all thoughts from my head except for one—Tate—and then I fly to her house. The sun is shining and the large, blooming trees hide most of the lawns below.

The muted violin notes coming from inside Tate's house drift through the back yard. I'm in a rush to get to Tate's room, but I still find myself stopped and staring at Fischer in the kitchen. He must have shot up six inches since the last time I was here. Unbelievable.

I take the steps two at a time, even though I could fly if

I wanted. Climbing them makes me think of the days when I was alive. Nothing wrong with a little fantasizing.

I walk through her bedroom door and Tate continues to play. I can't will my legs to move even though I desperately want to close the space between us. She is beautiful, more stunning than she's been in a long time. She's even wearing a brown sweater with dark jeans. Though I'd prefer an even broader color spectrum, this beats the black trash she was wearing before. Her makeup is lighter, too, allowing more of her true beauty to shine. With Tate's violin as the soundtrack, my reeling mind conjures past images of Tate and me in happier times like an old home video. Dizzy and in fear of falling over, I swallow and try to regain my balance.

"Really?"

My head snaps to the far corner of the room. In those few seconds of being entranced by Tate, I had forgotten all about Liam. Sitting on the floor beside Tate's desk, he has stopped juggling a red bouncy ball. His deflated tone matches his expression. "I thought we were over all this."

I ignore him and turn back to Tate as she finishes the song. She stills, leaving her bow on the strings. She closes her eyes and sucks in a deep breath.

"Tate," I whisper when I find my voice.

She takes another breath like she's trying to calm herself. Then she moves the bow across the violin again, playing a faster, almost angry sounding song.

Being here, seeing her—it makes me question how I could have liked Clara's kiss. This is where I belong.

I sit on Tate's bed, watching her play, ecstatic about how

much better she's doing. I need to come back more; I should have never stopped. I refuse to look at Liam, knowing he would disagree with my revelation.

Tate finishes her aggressive song, and I know I should go. Maybe if my trips are short, the Schedulers will never know about them. I walk over to Tate, breathe in her scent, and whisper "I love you" into her ear. "I'll be back soon." This makes me feel so much better about leaving.

Liam's disapproval is laced with expletives that are still rolling when I displace. With a mouth like that, he'd give my father a run for his money.

Ryder's still sleeping when I get back to his house. I pulled it off! I do my reading like a good Satellite and settle in for a quiet night of dinner and a movie. I even laugh through the comedy. Yes, this is a good day.

Later the next day, I step outside to wait in the breezeway while we're at Ryder's grandparents' house. The family photos gracing the walls only drive home how badly I want to talk to Willow because I really do miss her. Plus, with Ryder doing better, if Willow does know of my epic fail, hopefully she can forgive me.

Finally, Ryder hobbles out of the house with Hannah hovering over him. He tries brushing Hannah off when she offers more help than he needs down the steps.

I fly behind Hannah's red car on the way to Ryder's house, wishing I could feel the warmth of the bright sun on my skin. About a mile from Ryder's place, the brake lights shine and the compact car makes a U-turn. Confused, I follow behind until we finally stop. A cemetery visit seems odd, especially since Ryder's book never mentioned it.

Hannah tries to help Ryder out of the car, but he refuses her assistance. He gets himself supported on his crutches and says he needs a few minutes alone. Suddenly, goose bumps run along my skin.

I recognize the feeling as soon as my vision comes back. Hundreds of miles away, Tate just destroyed something—a memory.

I take a deep breath, convince myself that Liam can handle Tate, and remember what happened the last time I left Ryder unattended. Reluctantly, I follow Ryder to the twin headstones, still fighting with myself about choosing him over Tate.

Prepared to block, my calimeter cuts me off and Ryder turns to a mannequin in front of the graves.

Damn!

Unable to hold out any longer, I dig into my bag for the frame and displace, hoping to catch Liam. When I'm finally to Tate's, the burning smell in the air causes my mind to race, and Elliott's empty seat at the kitchen table makes me flinch. But then I see her, and the world is right again.

Tate's familiar beauty freezes me—oh, how I missed her!—and I stand rooted to the tile floor, as still as she is. Sitting at the table, she hasn't touched her plate of food. This bothers me, since Fischer and Tate's parents are almost finished with their meal.

My yell for Liam is answered by silence. I stare at Tate, wanting so badly to touch her, yet afraid that if I do, I'll never leave. I wonder if this is what it's like for a drug addict after they get their fix. It kills me to go, but I have to find Liam to know what she's destroyed.

I'm out of breath by the time I get to Benson. "Has anyone seen Liam?"

After looking at me like I'm a lunatic, everyone at the table shakes their head in unison.

"What's his room number?" I say it so quickly that my words almost trip over each other.

"Eight twenty-seven. But why—"

Halfway out of the room before Owen can finish asking his question, I have to spin and run back. "What's his last name?" I wheeze between breaths.

"Moore." Owen, along with everyone else, is still wearing the same confused look.

I sprint out of Benson, across the lobby, and down the M hall. My knock goes unanswered, along with my incessant door pounding, so fifteen minutes and a lot of stares later, I'm on my sofa, busting to talk to someone. Where the heck is Willow, anyway?

I check on Ryder before going to Tate's, mostly because I'm scared that if I see her again, I'll never leave. Ryder unfreezes, awkwardly leans on his crutches to get closer to the twin grave markers, and pulls a granite rock from his pocket.

"Hey, guys. I just needed to tell you that I'm happy, thanks to Hannah. That's what it's about, right?" He pauses. "She's great. Dad, you knew her, so I'm sure you agree. Nana and Gramps love her as much as I do." He takes a deep breath. "Basically, what I'm trying to say is, don't worry about me. Enjoy each other." He kisses the rock and places it on top of Willow's headstone. "I love you."

I snap my mouth closed, and, for the first time, the urge to follow Ryder is gone. Still, I don't leave his house until he's snoring loud enough to wake the neighbors. It's only seven in the evening, but his pain medication puts him to sleep with the infants and elderly of the world. Hannah's still here, too, which assures me that he will be all right in my absence.

Tate's sprawled on the wrong end of her bed when I get there. She adjusts her earbuds and nods to a beat I can't hear.

"Hey, man," I say. Freaked out, Liam drops Tate's book. "She destroyed something, right? I blacked out on my assignment."

He's obviously ticked that I've come back here, but after a sigh, he finally talks. "A photo album."

"How'd she do it?" I manage. Feeling sick to my stomach, I try to wrap my head around all the memories she eliminated in one shot.

"Fire. She's quite the pyro. She almost burned the house down."

I join Liam on the floor—which he seems none too thrilled about—and focus on the hairline crack in the wall. As the sun sets, the room darkens and the crevice gradually disappears. I can't help but think of Tate, how she is stealing herself from me, disappearing from my memories, and there's nothing I can do to stop her.

I jump when Fischer screams in the next room, but Liam doesn't even flinch. The house becomes still again. "He's been having nightmares lately," Liam says in a dry voice.

Tate's swollen eyes prove what I already know. My visits to her have been for selfish reasons, and they are doing nothing to help her move on. I have to let her go.

I wipe away a tear before it rolls down my jaw.

———

During break, I jump at the knock on my door and anxiously bury Tate's frame—which I've been death-gripping for the past twenty minutes—into my bag. "Come in!" I yell from the sofa.

"Hello, Grant." The person I was hoping for was Willow. Instead, I get Jonathan.

"How's it going?" I reply. Resting my head back, I decide I'm keeping the atrocious (but oh-so-comfortable) sofa. If Willow asks, I'll tell her it's because it's too much trouble to move.

"Quite well, thank you. Mind if I sit?"

"Nope. What's up?" I ask dully.

"I'm here with good news." When I don't say anything, Jonathan continues. "Your assignment with Ryder is complete."

I try to keep my face even. Does he know I just went to

Tate's?

"I realize Ryder's assignment did not go exactly as planned, but I am very proud of how you've stepped up the past few months. I know this transition has not been easy for you." He pauses, making me shift in the sofa. He knows something—he has to.

"Everything OK?" Oh yeah, he totally knows.

I can only nod, not trusting my voice.

"Hmm," he replies. *What does that mean?* "We will exchange assignment books in the Orders hall during your next break. I expect Willow will join us to celebrate your success; she's passing the torch, so to speak. You will have a week off to rest and familiarize yourself with your next assignment."

I keep quiet, not knowing what to say. Is he going to bust me right here?

"You're welcome to stick around Progression. You've certainly earned a day off. But if you'd rather, you can spend your final day with Ryder. Oh—also, because his assignment has closed, his book will now detail his full future, ending on the day of his passing. When you have some time, I suggest reading it. It's an important part of the process for Satellites and should bring closure to your assignment."

I can't stop thinking of Tate.

"You know, Grant, I am always available if you need to talk. No topics are off limits."

I think about Elliot's empty chair at the Jacoby table and hope a subject change will clear my conscience. "Actually, I do have a question."

"Yes?"

"How are Satellites chosen?"

"Every Satellite possesses a key chromosome that undergoes breakage and reverses its gene sequence at conception. We call this a chromosomal inversion. This rearrangement causes an abnormality in the brain, one that Satellites rely on daily: the ability to block. Incidentally, you are one of very few Satellites whose chromosome is not only inverted, but thicker as well. Over a century has passed since we've seen this in one of our Satellites."

"So I'm a freak?" I ask, almost laughing because I think of Willow.

"Quite the contrary. This anomaly makes you an excellent blocker—one of the best we've seen in many, many years. Certainly you can see how this talent makes you an asset to our team."

I want to argue that he's wrong, that I don't belong here, but know it would be a pointless fight. So instead, I get right to it. "Have there ever been two Satellites who knew each other in life?"

"Ah. You're speaking of Elliott."

Duh. I bite my tongue to keep from saying it aloud.

"No. This is a first for all of us." He pauses like he's waiting for another question, but I stay silent. "Is that all?"

I nod.

"Until tomorrow evening, then." He stands and crosses the room, stopping at the door. "Grant, in regard to your extracurricular activities…"

Oh no, here it comes.

"I do know everything that goes on around here. I understand your internal struggle quite well. I am allowing you a...well, let's just call it a free pass."

What? "What?"

Jonathan continues facing the door. "It is time to say good-bye. I am giving you the opportunity."

"What about the Schedulers?" What the heck is wrong with me? Who cares about the Schedulers! I've never listened to them before.

"I'll worry about them. But Grant"—he turns now—"just one time. That's it."

The door clicks closed. Did that really just happen? He wants me to see Tate?

No. He wants me say good-bye.

———

I'm torn when my calimeter buzzes, but I end up grabbing my bag and displacing back to Ryder because I know I'm not ready or able to say good-bye to Tate yet.

I hang out, leaning on the wall in Ryder's bedroom for what could be the final time. Hannah lounges on his bed, messing with his iPod despite the fact that she's here to, quote, help him pack. Ryder balances on his crutches and stuffs his duffel bag with bulky clothes for the upcoming spring weekend getaway in the mountains with Hannah and Mya's family.

"I can't wait to see Lennon," Hannah says.

"I know. He's growing like a weed."

"Your face lights up every time you talk about him. It's super cute." She leans up and kisses his cheek.

"You want kids, right?" he asks.

"Absolutely. You?"

"Definitely."

"So you've thought about it?"

Ryder shoves two more pairs of socks in the bag. "Yeah, sure."

"Have you thought about it with me?"

"Maybe." He leans his crutches against his dresser and falls on Hannah, playfully tackling her on the bed.

"How much have you thought about it?" she muffles from under him.

"Enough." His mouth skims across her cheek to kiss her ear. I turn away, preferring the eye candy of my dingy boots instead of the lovebirds.

"Well, if it's a boy, we're naming him Simon."

"Oh?" Ryder challenges.

"Yes. That was my grandfather's name," Hannah adds matter-of-factly.

"Fine, I can live with Simon. But if it's a girl, we're naming her Willow."

"I can live with Willow. I hope you're planning on making an honest woman out of me before we have all these babies."

"I'm thinking about it. Ouch!" he groans, and I lift my head.

Hannah apologizes, shifting carefully under him. Then, because saying sorry must not have been enough, she elaborates with a kiss that includes lots of tongue.

Tired of the make-out session, I'm about to leave the room, but then Ryder awkwardly gets up and resumes packing. Hannah pulls her phone out of her back pocket and turns her attention to marathon texting.

Ryder pulls a small velvet box out of his top dresser drawer and hides it in his bag while Hannah's attention is on her phone. A second later, I'm in the narrow hallway, gasping. I claw at the collar of my hoodie, desperately trying to release its hold on my throat. *Breathe, breathe, breathe,* I think, crashing against the wall.

I want so desperately for that to be Tate and me, but—unfairly—that's not the future we were destined for. Ryder's life is finally coming together while my own is unraveling, thread by thread. Our common tie of losing our fathers seems so far away now, making me feel even more alone. I catch my breath and slide down the wall.

I need to let Tate go, for her sake. She needs to move on—to build a life of her own—but how will I live without her? What am I saying? I'm not even alive. She is, though. If she tries to take her own life again…I can't even let my mind go there. If she died, knowing it was my fault would destroy me, no question. The guilt I felt from my mistake with Ryder was nearly unbearable, and he lived.

I stare at a dark knot in the narrow hallway floor, willing myself to come to terms with the BS hand I've been dealt. I hardly notice Ryder and Hannah walking past me or his voice carrying from the kitchen downstairs. What I do notice is the air turning to ice and blackness swallowing me.

When I stumble into the kitchen, Ryder's putting a plate in the sink and Hannah's finishing off the last bite of a sandwich. Apparently, I've been passed out awhile. I scour the house for my bag, find it in the living room, and displace. My flight to Tate's is a blur.

"What happened?" I yell, bursting through her bedroom door.

Liam jumps three feet in the air. "Dude, a little warning next time!"

"Sorry." I check on Tate, who's in the big button chair using her laptop (or staring blankly at the screen, anyway). "What happened?"

He nods toward three CDs on her desk, and there's zero enthusiasm in his voice. "I saved those."

I walk over dozens of broken discs, my boots not disturbing a single one, and squat down to look at one of the square booklets.

"Mean anything?" Liam asks.

Like I even need to answer. I don't bother looking at the other booklets or the mirrored shards scattered across the carpet. Instead, I tick through the cases on her desk. "Christmas. Just because. Birthday," I say, listing the occasions when I gave these to Tate.

"You've got a good memory."

"Until she destroys it." I point to the Van Morrison case. "She danced around my room to Brown Eyed Girl when I gave her this one." In any other time and place, and under very different circumstances, I'd laugh at the memory.

"What's with all the CDs?"

I watch Tate zone out behind her computer. "She loves music."

"Couldn't come up with anything more original to give her, huh?" Liam jabs.

I'm thankful that he's not trying to kick me out. "I mean, she *really* loves music." My boots pace soundlessly over the broken discs. "I swear she was more excited about getting these CDs than she was when I gave her the ring."

"Maybe you should have given her a better ring." Liam reads my somber expression. "Kidding!"

I pinch the bridge of my nose and close my eyes, realizing this is my free pass.

"I'm sorry I couldn't salvage more. I was distracted by one of Fischer's outbursts. Listen, you need to get out of here. I mean it, man. She's plummeting downhill and it's because of you!"

"Is Fischer getting worse?" I ask, ignoring his not-so-subtle request to leave and parking myself on the floor close to Tate.

Liam stares at me for a full minute, fuming. Eventually, he gives up and finds his own spot across the room. "He's averaging about two episodes a day, plus he has the recurring nightmares."

After a long time I break the silence, saying the words before I can stop myself. "I'm going to let her go." I have to let her go. My fingers twist together. Can I tell her good-bye? And mean it?

Liam's lifted expression is enough to tell me he's relieved. "Look, mate, I know it's going to be brutal for you, but it's got to be better for her. She's veering away from her book again."

"Can I see her book?" I ask, already knowing the answer. "Come on, man—this is my last visit, I swear. I just want to see what her life has been like without me."

At first, he looks like he's going to say no frigging way. Then, surprisingly, he gets up, walks past me, and reaches across the bed. He looks down at the red book and pulls it close to him like he's not quite sure this is a great idea. Eventually, he surrenders.

"Why not? Nothing from the past few days is relevant at this point, anyway." He drops the book onto my lap and resumes his position on the floor. "But if you tell anyone, I'll have your neck."

I want to question him, but my stupid mouth won't form any words. Nothing from the past few days is relevant?

I open the book, still shocked that he gave it to me, and skip over the hand outline. "You saw her past."

"Yeah."

"No smart comments you want to throw out?" I can't help but grin.

"Oh, I have plenty, but I figure I'll cut you some slack because you looked like such rubbish there at the end. Even worse than you look now."

I shake my head. "It wasn't pretty."

"Not bad on the engagement, though."

Liam, laying on his back now, stops juggling the silver

something-or-other so he can turn his head toward me. "I'm serious! It was quite brilliant. She never saw it coming. Still, I can't believe she said yes to a nancy like you."

"Whatever."

"Her dad was brutal, mate."

Amen to that. The man strung me along for a full ten minutes before giving me his blessing. Whenever he announced our engagement to someone, he'd share the story, commenting on his great acting skills and talking up how nervous I was. I have no doubt he had planned to tell his tale at our wedding.

The night I proposed, I took Tate to some cheese-ball restaurant where a carpenter had no business being. The whole setup (which is embarrassing now) was a total cliché. Not that it mattered. Tate, in true form, killed my plans. She didn't even notice how nice the place was because she spent the entire dinner talking about Fischer getting bullied at school. She was hot when she got worked up. Her flushed face, though red in anger, drove me even more crazy. I reached into my pocket at least two dozen times, but the right opportunity never presented itself.

When we got back to her house, Fischer begged Elliott and us to play a game, and then he begged me to be on his team. Like Tate, I could never say no to that kid.

"What is the most common last name in the world?" Tate asked, reading from the little red card.

"Chang!" Fischer shouted.

"No way, Fish, it's gotta be Smith," I correct him, trying not to be offended that this nine-year-old was looking at me like I was a moron. "All right," I finally agreed. "Chang."

"Chang, it is," Elliott said.

"Oh, buuurrrn!" Fischer yelled to Elliott. He was on a path to be as cocky as his older brother, which was comical.

I bumped his small fist. "Good job, Fish. I got this one," I told him when it was our turn to read. I picked up a blue card and looked directly at Tate. "This is a tough one. You sure you're ready?"

Tate snorted. "Whatever. Just read the question. You two are so going down!"

"You asked for it." After a theatrical deep breath, I said, "Will you marry me?"

Tate's laughter stopped. She stared at me with her jaw unhinged. I set the card down and stood, reaching into my pocket.

Fischer snatched the card off the table. Before Elliott could shush him, he shouted, "Hey, it doesn't say that!"

When I got down on my knee, I completely blanked on the perfect speech I had memorized. So, in a very inarticulate way, I spewed out the worst proposal ever. "Tate, you could do so much better. Every day I wonder why you're with me." (If that's not romantic…) "Even though I'll never be able to give you the life you deserve, as long as any part of me exists I will love you. So much more than you'll ever know."

My hands were soaking hers with sweat and my heart was pounding. "Tate?" I finally asked when she didn't answer, thinking (a) I just made a complete fool of myself, and (b) she finally did realize she was too good for me.

She laughed at me through her tears. "What was the

question?"

I smiled bigger than I ever had before. "You're impossible! Marry me!"

I'm brought back from the past by a voice in the present.

"You all right, mate?"

I use my palm to wipe my eyes, but I can't answer Liam.

"What is that?" I ask when I find my voice.

Liam is decent enough to ignore my moment of sissiness and stops juggling the object in question. He holds the plain silver ring between his thumb and index finger. "It's her tocket," he says casually, resuming his juggling. He doesn't mention the *I promise* engraved on the inside, and I wonder if he knows that's the ring I replaced with a better one—one that actually included diamonds.

I raise Tate's book and skim through more pages. Over the past months, she's been helping Fischer cope with the loss of Elliott…and playing music…and making new friends in—

"Group therapy?" I question.

"It's made a huge difference," Liam says.

I read on about the things she's been doing in my absence. I've selfishly needed her to need me, but she's beginning to move beyond my death.

My eyes freeze on a paragraph from two weeks ago, and feuding emotions slosh in my gut like oil and water.

"What's up? You're bloody pale."

Forgetting that Liam is still here, I blink back my tears,

though there's nothing sad about her going back to school. Her major is what stings. Social work? I mean, obviously she would be great in that field, but music and art have always been her two loves. Seeing her life go down such a different road proves that she will be moving on without me. She is destined to become a different person—one I do not know. "Social work?" I whisper to myself. *Breathe, breathe, breathe…*

"Maybe you should give me that back." Liam catches the ring and leans forward like he's going to get up.

I grip the book tighter in fear that Liam will swipe it from me. I will myself not to throw up and continue reading. He cuts me a break, going back to tossing the ring.

"We've got to keep her on track," I say when I reach today's entry in the book. "She needs to go back to school." More than anything else, I want her to be happy. She deserves to be happy. My sanity is a small price to pay.

"You'll be an amazing social worker if that's the path you choose," I whisper to Tate while she types on her laptop. "You'll be amazing at anything you do."

Feeling Liam's stare, I turn away from Tate to find him looking at me like everyone else used to when they found out I had cancer.

"She can still have the life she deserves." *Without me.* "I have to let her go." I have to. For her. My mind goes back to the day we spent fishing, the way she watched that little boy. What if her future includes being a mom? What if I steal that away from her? "I can't stand in her way anymore."

"Stop looking at me like that," I say to Liam after thirty

seconds. "This is hard enough. Your sympathy isn't helping."

"You're right. I'm sorry. I know it's difficult, but it's the right thing. You're not supposed to be here, and I'm not even saying that for fear of getting in trouble. You're messing with her destiny."

Having no argument, I keep my mouth shut. Tate's typing is the only noise in the still room. I watch my thumbs race around each other. I can't look at her. My heart can't come to terms with this yet.

"So, keep her on track, huh? Certainly sounds easy enough," Liam says a few minutes later in a more upbeat tone.

"You have to." I look at Tate when she shifts positions in the chair. "Please. And if there's any way to keep her from destroying all of my memories along the way…"

"Brilliant. I'm all about doing the impossible."

Under different circumstances, I would probably find the sarcastic delivery of Liam's statement funny. "You seem like the type who prefers a challenge."

Liam mumbles something to himself. I stare at the single word, *break,* typed on the page after today's events that never happened. I'm unable to turn to the blank pages that follow. They are empty spaces to be filled with a life without me.

When I stop thinking selfishly, I know that moving on without me is the right path for Tate. If I'm being honest, I've always known—a girl like her should have never been with a guy like me. The scales were always tipped too much in my favor. I was just a carpenter, for crying out loud. I was a fool for thinking she could have been happy with the mediocre life I would have given her. She deserves the world and nothing less.

I try to ignore the emptiness spreading outward from my chest like a stain and toss the book back to Liam.

I kneel in front of Tate, pull in my filter, and kiss her forehead. "You have a whole life ahead of you. I'm only letting you go because I love you. Do you hear me? I love you!" My tears burn like acid. I try to blink them away, but they won't stop coming.

She closes her eyes and breathes slowly.

I stare at the shape of her face, her small nose, her full bottom lip, the peach-shaped freckle on her left cheek—all the details I memorized years ago. I inhale, hoping to remember her scent forever. "Good-bye, Tate."

I look away from her when I stand.

Liam's not in the room anymore, but I know he can hear me. "It's done."

I whisper the command and grip the stone so tightly that my veins threaten to burst out of my forearm. My soul rips apart as I'm being pulled across the dark Earth.

Feeling even sicker than after my worst chemo treatment, I shrink into the far corner of Ryder's bedroom and focus on my knees. Ryder and Hannah, curled together in peaceful sleep, breathe rhythmically in the black room. Meanwhile, I can't stop shaking; I'm dying all over again.

Not until late the next morning am I able to force Ryder's assignment book open.

At the exact time I finish his final chapter, my calimeter

buzzes. Ryder's upcoming weekend and his engagement to Hannah is a slap in the face—a reminder of what I've just lost.

19. You guys look like you're lost

As my first step toward a so-called destiny completely out of my control, I pour a cup of coffee strong enough to put Willow's to shame and head down to meet Jonathan.

Just before I get to the Orders hall, Willow approaches from the opposite direction. God, it's good to see her face.

"Hey, freak! Where the heck have you been?" I shout to her, but there's no enthusiasm in my voice, despite my effort.

As she gets closer, it's obvious something's wrong. "Willow? What is it?" My pace quickens until I'm jogging. "Willow?"

She clutches my arms like she needs me to keep her balanced. She opens her mouth, but nothing comes out.

My muscles turn to concrete. "Talk to me! What's going on? Is Troy all right?" I'm desperate for her to say something, anything, so I know she's OK, but she only stares blankly through me. Does she know about my mistake with Ryder?

"Willow?"

"It's Tate," she chokes.

Her unexpected words pummel me. "What about Tate?" Unsure if the question came out of my mouth or if I was just screaming in my head, I plead, "Willow, tell me!" when she says nothing.

Her fingers tighten around my arms and she looks down at the floor. "She's been declared a Rebellion," she whispers, so quietly I almost miss it.

"Breathe, Grant! Breathe!" Willow's voice sounds like a distant echo.

My coffee cup shatters on the tile floor. I follow behind it, shattering as well.

———

"Shouldn't he have come to by now?" Willow's muffled voice says.

"Give him a little more time. It's important that his body protects his mental wellness."

"He's been out for so long."

"Patience, Willow," Jonathan says from far away.

I open my eyes and try to focus. Willow and her frizzy dreadlocks are just an inch from my face when the black hole swallows me again.

———

"What are you thinking about?" Tate asks, tracing her hand on my bare chest while we're stretched across my bed.

"Nothing," I lie. No way was I going to tell her I was thinking of my approaching death. "What are you thinking about?"

"Kids." She rolls her engagement ring around her

finger with her thumb.

"You're back on that?" I try not to sound angry.

"You know I want kids," she says into my neck.

"I know, but we've talked about this. I can't give you any until my treatments are finished," I reply, already knowing my treatments will never be finished.

"I can still dream about it." Her voice is harder.

"What is it with you and kids, anyway?"

"Not just kids. Your kids," she clarifies, softening again.

"I don't see how that makes a difference."

She props herself up to look at me. "I want a piece of you."

"What—like a memento when I'm gone?"

"Grant!"

"I just said what we were both thinking."

"I'm not thinking that! What I mean is, I want a baby with you. I want to create a life with you. Something permanent."

"Something my disease can't take away." I wipe the tear from her cheek. "I'm sorry," I whisper.

She lays her head back on my shoulder. "I love you."

I focus on keeping my breathing even so she won't notice the panic rolling through me. I'm going to lose her.

———

"Willow?"

She stops pacing and leaps over the trunk. "Jonathan, he's awake!" she yells over me. "Are you all right?"

I push myself into a sitting position on my sofa. "How did I get here?"

"We carried you. Kind of."

My brain is so foggy, I must not be hearing her correctly.

"Well no, not really. We dragged you. How are you feeling?"

I reach up to be sure that my pounding head is still connected to my body. "What happened?"

"You passed out."

When the replay with Willow flashes through my brain in slow motion, I spring up so fast I trip over her. "No!"

She slams her shoulder into me, and I fall back into the sofa.

"I was dreaming! Tell me I was dreaming," I plead when I finally find my voice.

"I'm so sorry," is all she says.

I hear Jonathan's pacifying voice behind me. "Grant, please try to remain calm."

"I don't understand…" I trail off, not even sure what to ask.

"Tate has strayed a great deal off course. We've been monitoring her since her episode in the tub." Jonathan sits in the chair by the sofa and watches me for a reaction because he knows I was there.

"What episode?" Willow interjects.

"Tate tried to take her life," he answers evenly.

I ignore Willow's shocked, abnormally silent response and ask, "What happens now?"

"The Schedulers are making the necessary arrange-ments to pull one of the Elites off their current assignment."

"You're going to be shorthanded," Willow states.

"We'll manage," Jonathan says.

"Put me on Tate's case."

"Willow, you've completed Programming. You can't go back into the field now. You know it's against the rules."

"Break the rules then. Jonathan, please! I'm the only Elite who has experience with a Rebellion. Let me help."

"I'll see what I can do. In the meantime, I need you to stay with Grant."

Willow nods.

"Grant, we are working diligently to get Tate back on track. We do not need any unnecessary interference," he says firmly. "We'll get to your new assignment in a few days." He pushes himself up from the chair and starts toward the door. "I'll touch base with you both soon."

"Where's your bag?" Willow demands when Jonathan's gone.

I look around and shake my head. "I'm not sure."

Willow darts around the room before finding it in the closet. She jerks the zipper open and starts rummaging. "Where's your frame?"

"Huh?"

"Your frame!"

I shake my head again.

"They already got to it," she mumbles to herself.

"Who?"

"The Schedulers. Seriously kid, do you have to be so

predictable?"

"What?"

Willow bites into her fisted hand and stares at the rack of T-shirts. "They knew you'd go back."

"Who?"

"The Schedulers! Shut up and let me think!" she yells.

Confused, I snap my mouth closed while she wears a path in the closet's plush carpet.

"There's got to be something," she says to herself, continuing like a madwoman for a couple of minutes. She smacks her forehead and plants her feet. "Oh! You were still visiting her, right? Please tell me you were!"

Sure, now she wants me to break the rules.

"Don't look so surprised. I'd be more shocked if you weren't, considering your consistent disregard of the rules. Who was her Satellite?"

"I don't understand—"

"Who was it? Come on, kid, we're burning daylight here!"

"Liam."

"Liam? Really?" She looks surprised for a few seconds and then exits the closet. "Come on!"

I run to keep up. "What's going on?" I ask when we're in the elevator.

She silences me with her finger, which remains frozen in front of her lips until the elevator doors open. She bolts through them before GPS Jeanette can get her words out and doesn't slow down until we're in Benson.

I find Liam first and point to the back of the room.

Willow spots him, too, and pushes through the crowd.

"Liam!" she hollers, breathing heavy. "I need to talk to you." She glances around the table. "Privately."

Liam and I follow/chase Willow down a long hallway into an unfamiliar part of the building. She holds a door open and Liam steps into a room.

"Privately," she reiterates, shoving her hand against my chest and slamming the door between us.

"Willow!" I yell, jiggling the handle. I pound my fists on the door, but the thick wood mutes the effect. "Open up! Come on, you little psychopath!"

Liam's muffled voice raises, but I can't make out his words. I slam my palms against the door, slide down its length, and fume.

I spring up when the door starts to open. "Willow, you've got some—"

"She's raving mad!"

I push past Liam and spin around the empty room. "Where is she?"

"She took my tocket and displaced."

"She what?"

"She's a lunatic!"

"Tate's tocket?"

Liam paces through the room without answering.

"Liam, what do you know about Tate?"

He studies me before checking the hallway and closing us in the room. "I don't know what happened. She frigging swan dived over the bloody edge."

I fall into one of the leather chairs, puzzled. "It doesn't

make sense. What happened when I left?" My volume increases. "Tate was fine when I left her!" I accuse.

"She was fine. Until you left." He looks down and shakes his head. "It's like she knew you weren't coming back. As soon as you were gone, she went psycho on her room. Her dad restrained her, but when he let her go, she bolted. She knocked Fischer over on her way out. Her parents tried to catch her. Dude, she's really fast!"

"She was a sprinter in track," I say dryly.

"Well, I imagine she did quite well."

"Mmm-hmm," I murmur in frustration. What have I done? First Ryder and now Tate. I'm a failure all around.

Liam stops pacing and shuts off his calimeter a second after I silence mine. "Bloody hell. What am I supposed to do now?"

"We'll go to my room. She'll have to displace back there."

"No. That's your room now."

"Then where?"

"Programming," he says.

Why can't anything around here be easy? "OK, how do we get there?"

He gapes at me before making a gagging noise that I can only assume is a laugh. "You're kidding?"

I stare equably back at him. "We need to catch her when she returns, don't we?"

"Are you mad? We can't go to Programming!"

"Why not?"

"Because we can't!"

"Well, that sounds like an excellent reason. You need your tocket back, right? Come on."

He follows behind me, mumbling, "You've lost your marbles. We don't even know how to get there."

"Just come on."

Glad to put my focus somewhere other than on Tate, I lead the way down the long hall until we are in the lobby and then peer into Benson's corridor. I pull Liam around the corner of another hall and signal him to be quiet.

Henry walks out of Benson, smoothing his shirt cuffs. When he's halfway through the lobby we follow, with me pushing Liam along with persuasive looks. Henry turns left by the courtyard doors, and we keep a silent pace behind him. When the maze of never-ending hallways opens into a larger room, Liam and I peek around the corner like kids.

Henry walks past the seating area and twists one of the candlesticks to the right. He steps around the now recessed wall and the decorative wood panel closes behind him.

"Let's go back. We're going to get into serious trouble," Liam whispers.

"No way. Besides, we'd never find our way out," I note, walking into the room.

Liam is not happy. "I can't believe I'm doing this."

"You can wait here if you want." I turn the candlestick Henry just used.

Liam looks around the room like he's considering. Then he huffs and follows me in, murmuring "bloody hell" along the way. The wood panel bangs closed behind us. Three hallways branch off the metallic, ceilingless room.

"How are we going to get out of here?" Liam whines.

I shrug a shoulder and play "eenie, meenie, miney, moe" like Fischer would. The hall to the left wins.

When a guy walks by us, I clear my throat to warn Liam to play it cool.

"Yo," the guy says. After he passes, Liam blows out air.

"Relax, man."

"Unlike you, I don't enjoy breaking the rules."

"I don't remember any rule about this."

He groans and hurries to keep pace with me.

At the end of the hall, I spin around and push Liam back. When I mouth the word *Jonathan*, his eyes nearly pop out of his face and I don't doubt he could use a change of boxers.

I hear a woman's voice speak first. It's Wynn from training. "If she stays, then we must delay the process. It has been written that the decision for the seventh will be announced today."

"Her experience will be a great asset. I feel it is worth the risk," Jonathan says cryptically.

"But the course of the next Elite will…"

Their voices fade, and I motion Liam down the opposite way.

"This is crazy," he hisses.

I ignore him and turn again, following the growing voices. A few people pass us, but no one seems suspicious.

In a circular room laid out like the stone well that took me through Ryder's past (but actually welcoming, with more drywall and less rust), Henry disappears into one of the doors. The girls on the sofa are too engrossed in a magazine to even notice us.

A voice behind us makes Liam jump out of his clothes. "You guys look like you're lost."

"Jordan, you're going to give poor Liam a heart attack," I say coolly, after Liam peels himself off the ceiling.

"What are you doing here? You could get in some major heat if someone sees you."

"Looking for Willow," I answer.

Jordan studies us. "Come on."

We follow Jordan down a hall that looks like all the others and opens to another round room. He steps around two guys wearing Virtual Reality-looking headgear before taking us through one of the ten ornate doors.

Jordan walks across the tan room and moves a notebook from the futon to the coffee table to sit. "How'd you get here?"

"We followed Henry. We could use your help," I explain.

He looks impressed. "What's up?"

I stare up at the cloudless blue sky and collect my thoughts before vomiting the entire story—everything. When I'm finished, Liam lies and says Tate's breakdown wasn't my fault. He then adds a few choice words about Willow.

Jordan already knew the Rebellion part, of course. Keeping secrets around here is a joke. "What do you need from me?"

"We need to catch Willow when she gets back. Any idea where she displaces?" I ask.

"Sure, to her room. You're in luck. It's just across the hall."

Liam scopes a J-shaped chair in the corner and relaxes a little. "Dude, I didn't know you were a gamer." About time the guy loosened his panties up.

"Totally. You?" Jordan asks.

"Uh, yeah! I'm addicted to Elite Seven."

"Have you figured out mission four?"

Aggravated, I clear my throat.

"Apparently Grant's never played before," Jordan says to Liam, directing us out. We cross the circular room, and he opens a seemingly random door. How he can tell all these identical doors apart is beyond me.

"You all right, mate?" Liam asks after we enter Willow's room.

I stop laughing, but my head still shakes when I fall into a dreadful, putrid-orange sofa. It's as comfortable as mine. Figures.

"I gotta go. You should be uninterrupted until Willow gets back," Jordan says.

Liam reverts back to freak out mode. "You're not going to mention this to anyone, are you?"

Jordan shakes his head. "It's cool."

"Thanks," I say.

Jordan closes the door behind him. Liam moves Willow's guitar and stretches across the faded rug in its place.

I rub my thighs and try not to think of Tate. "Should we take bets on when she'll return?" I ask, mindlessly watching the birds dart across the clear sky.

Liam stops juggling a red bouncy ball and looks at his calimeter. "My guess is, we're gonna be here awhile."

I sigh, and Liam resumes tossing the ball.

After twenty minutes, I cross the room and open the cabinet above the sink, helping myself to a mug and some coffee. I doctor it with sugar and return to the sofa.

Even though I couldn't care less, I ask Liam, "Any word on who the next Elite will be?" I'll try anything to keep my anxious thoughts at bay.

"Uh-uh, but I hope it's me. If we're caught and this messes up my chances, I am going to have your neck."

I half laugh.

"You think I'm kidding?"

"Nope. I believe you." And I do. He is so not happy with me. "What is it with everyone wanting to be an Elite?"

"Oh, come on. Don't tell me you wouldn't want to be one."

"No frigging way."

"You're off your bloody rocker, mate."

"Seriously, are your regular assignments not tough enough?" When the words fall from my mouth, the image of Tate in the bathtub burns in my eyes. I squeeze them closed and concentrate on my breathing.

"Sure, but being an Elite means you've arrived, man. There's nothing—" Liam stops talking and we both jump when the door opens.

"Here, man. It's probably going to be a while," Jordan interrupts, tossing Liam a pair of binoculars.

"Ace! I totally owe you!" Liam says, like he's just been

given the keys to a Lamborghini.

"It's cool. I'll grab 'em from Willow later."

"Want to play?" Liam asks me after Jordan closes the door.

I shake my head.

"Smashing!" He starts strapping the atrocity around his head.

I look up at the sky and think of anything that will keep me from playing worst-case scenario, starring Tate.

"Dance with me," Tate said, pushing herself up from the bed of my truck. The gravel lot was empty, and we hadn't loaded our mountain bikes yet after a day of riding on the Katy Trail.

"You know I can't dance," I half joked. "And besides, there's no music."

She pushed the top half of her body through the truck cab's open back window, and a second later, country music was coming from the speakers. She wrapped my arms around her waist and pushed herself against me.

"The song's a little too fast, don't you think?" I whispered.

"Just hold on to me."

We stood there, barely moving, through the rest of the song and the commercials that followed.

"I love you." After the words were out, I regretted them. Not that I didn't mean them (God, I meant them), but it was too soon. It hadn't even been three months.

Tate pulled back, clearly ticked. "Why did you say that?"

"What?" This was best answer I could come up with.

"Why did you just say that?" she demanded.

"I'm sorry. It's too soon, I know. I shouldn't have—"

She placed her finger over my mouth to put me out of my misery. "Did you mean it?"

"Of course."

She studied me and then caught me off guard with a kiss. When she pulled away, I thought, *Here it comes, she's adding "desperate" to the list of reasons she can do better than me.*

Instead, she whispered, "I love you, too."

My heart sprinted when she kissed me again. When she pulled back this time, we were both out of breath.

—⁘—

"You say something, mate?" If he wasn't already dead, I would kill Liam for interrupting my replay from when life was good. He gauges my expression, shrugs, and pulls the hideous goggles back down.

I cross the room for a refill while Liam sways and karate chops the air. Suddenly, ice shoots through my veins and my coffee spills onto the counter, black as the hole that engulfs me.

—⁘—

"Grant! Wake up, you nancy!"

My eyes blink open to find Liam inches from my face, snapping his fingers. "Good morning, sweetheart. It's about bloody time!"

I rub my head. "Huh?"

"You were out cold, mate."

When I sit up, Willow materializes behind Liam. I open my mouth, but Liam cuts me off. "You!" he yells at Willow. "If you ever do that again, I swear I'll kill you!"

"Simmer, dude." Her deflated tone matches her face.

"Are you all right?" I ask.

Her eyes meet mine, and then she looks away. "Oh, jeez."

"What happened?" Liam demands.

"It's bad. Really, really bad." Willow's eyes dart to me for half a second before holding steady on Liam. "She destroyed everything. *Everything*, Liam." She rubs at the creases on her forehead. "Even her ring," she whispers.

"Her ring?"

An invisible weight causes Willow's shoulders to slump even more when she answers Liam. "Her engagement ring."

They both turn to me with oversize eyes, like they're waiting for me to say something. I can't imagine what they're expecting. I don't even know what the hell they're talking about.

20. Why couldn't you have shut up like this months ago

From my sofa, I try to tune out Willow and Jonathan's not-so-quiet argument in the hall. They've been at it since Jonathan unhappily lead us out of Programming and back here. Their cryptic conversation hasn't evolved much in the last hour.

"But it is important. He needs to know," Willow's insisting.

"No, he doesn't. This is the natural order of things."

"He's different. You and I both know it."

"The transition took a little longer for him, that's all. Willow, you're missing the point. This is a good thing. He will no longer have the unnecessary distraction."

Willow grumbles something I can't make out and then yells, "It's different! His memories weren't forgotten naturally like ours. She erased them!"

"Maybe you're too personally connected with this assignment. It may be best that we bring in someone else—"

"No!" she interjects. "No one else."

Long pause. *Please let them be finished.*

"You need to pull it together, for the sake of both parties."

"Fine! I'll handle it," Willow huffs.

My head snaps up when the door opens. After gauging her mood, I know better than to even consider opening my mouth.

Willow stomps to the kitchen and her head disappears behind a cabinet. I join her, but put the counter between us just to be safe. She slams two mugs down, fills them, and shoves one in my direction. Coffee sloshes onto the black marble but it vanishes a second later.

"You have no idea how frustrating this is for me," she states.

I stare back at her, knowing anything I say can and will be used against me.

"Dang it, Grant! You've gotta remember something about her?"

I give her my best "I have no idea what you're talking about" look.

"Gah! Think about it! Tate. Tate Jacoby. She was your fiancée—your soul mate, for crying out loud!"

I smile placidly. "Please tell me you don't believe in that crap."

Whoops. Now she's *for real* pissed. "Who are you?!"

"I think you need to get your head checked," I suggest.

Her volume raises. "My head is fine! It's yours that's jacked. Come on, kid; it's Tate we're talking about here. Tate whom you broke almost every rule for. Tate whom you couldn't stop connecting with. You've got to remember something!"

I'm seriously questioning her sanity. "Sorry. Can you

calm down long enough to tell me why we were all in Programming?"

"You're impossible!" she growls and storms out the door.

I shake my head. In the words of Liam: "She's gone bloody mad." I drum my fingers on the counter and check my calimeter. Almost break. Finally.

I grab a table for the others when I get to Benson. The room seems even larger when it's quiet and empty. My thumbs race around each other while I wait.

And wait.

And wait.

Mental sigh. It's going to be a long week waiting to start my next assignment.

Finally, the masses come. "Oh, Grant," Clara says to me, like I'm a sick cat or something.

Not her, too. "Yeah?"

From across the table, she trails off. "I, uh…"

"Oh my gosh, are you all right?" Anna almost pushes my chair over when she throws herself on me.

I peel her arms off my neck and catch Owen's stare. My eyes dart to the others, who give me similar cautious looks. "What?" I demand.

Rigby holds his toothpick in front of his gaping mouth. "What's up with you, man?"

"Nothing. What's with you guys?"

Rigby shrugs, turns a chair around, and sits between Clara and a new guy. The others follow Rigby's lead, sitting down and keeping their eyes on me. No one even bothers introducing the new Satellite. *Rude.*

"You've all gone postal," I mumble under my breath.

Everyone looks away, trying to act casual—except for Liam. His glare emanates pure hate. If looks could kill…well, no, that one doesn't work anymore. If looks could kill again, I'd be a goner.

"I'm getting something to eat," I say to the table of lunatics.

"I'll go with you," Anna offers, rising from her chair.

When we're in the buffet room and I'm filling my tray with everything I can grab, Anna says, "Grant, I'm worried about you."

"Aren't you going to eat?"

She shakes her head. "Honestly, I don't know why everyone's tiptoeing around it. We've all heard what's going on."

"And what, exactly, is going on?" I ask peevishly.

"Tate's a Rebellion." Anna's volume is low and she looks around the room like she's just said a bad word.

"And?"

"And she's your fiancée," she hisses.

Not this again. "Seriously, Anna, you've got to stop believing the gossip. Trust me, I'd remember if I had a fiancée." I push her chin up and her jaw clinks closed. "What happened to keeping assignments private, anyway?"

"We're all worried about you."

"Well, don't be. I'm fine. Couldn't be better, actually. Now, can I get my food? I've got a quiet week ahead of me and would prefer to take advantage of the company."

She says nothing else and leaves the buffet with just a bottle of water. I, on the other hand, am carrying two overflowing trays of food and intend to eat every last bite. I catch Rigby at one of the meat tables; I'm glad to have an opportunity to talk to him.

"Hey man, how's it going?"

He eyes my trays. "Not bad. Hungry?"

"Nah. So listen, I wanted you to know…" I pause, not sure how to continue. May as well put it right out there. "I kissed Clara."

He clenches hard on his toothpick and remains silent.

"I'm sorry. I'm not sure what happened."

He doesn't look too keen on accepting my apology. "What about Tate?"

Ugh. Not him, too. "Please tell me you don't believe that Tate crap like everyone else?"

"You told me all about her!" he accuses, like I'm the one that's crazy here.

This whole place has gone mad! Not wanting to get into a heated argument with so little time to be around the others, I set one of my trays down, ready to clear the air. "Are you ticked about Clara?"

"Yeah I'm ticked about Clara! You knew I was interested and you kissed her anyway?"

"It just…happened. I didn't plan it or anything."

Rigby's anger escalates.

"Look, I'm not interested." Am I?

No! I can't do that to Rigby. I don't have time to play *Love Connection*. I'm a Satellite, after all, soon to have a new

Tragedy to watch over. This isn't high school. Though now that I think of it, I don't remember much about high school at all.

"But you kissed her," Rigby reminds me.

"It was a momentary lapse of reason."

"You're quoting Floyd now?"

I grin, impressed that he got the Pink Floyd reference. "Is it working?"

"No. And just so you're aware, if you are interested, I'm not backing down," he threatens.

"I'm not interested," I reiterate, hoping my voice sounds convincing. After a good, old-fashioned stare down, we both wordlessly concede and make our way out of the food room.

The conversation back at the table dies when Rigby and I return. I'm like the sideshow freak no one wants to be caught looking at—except I do catch them.

When Rigby sits, he hops his chair closer to Clara and shares his Hollywood smile with her. She pushes her hair behind her ear, turning away from Rigby, and glances sideways at me. Not wanting to see Rigby's reaction, I put my focus on my trays of food.

After a few silent, awkward minutes, I swallow a piece of steak and drop my fork loudly. "Listen, I don't know what's up with you guys, but if this is about Tate, my so-called fiancée"—my fingers make mock quotations—"there's obviously been some miscommunication. I don't know her, I've never known her, and if she happens to be a Rebellion, well, then good for Willow for scoring herself the assignment of the century."

I return my attention to my plate and cut another piece of steak. The new guy stands so abruptly that his chair falls behind him. He kicks it angrily and marches out of Benson.

"What's with him?" I ask, and then shove a forkful of mashed potatoes into my mouth.

I don't get an answer, just a lot of wide-eyed looks. Even Owen is flaking out on me.

"Seriously, dude, that's cold," he whispers.

"What?" I demand.

"He doesn't remember Elliott," Liam grumbles, more to himself. "She erased those memories, too."

Curiosity gets the best of me. "Who's Elliott?"

"Tate's brother," Owen explains in a quiet voice. I didn't know Owen even had a quiet voice. "Seriously cold, man," he repeats, shaking his head.

I stop chewing and hate their accusing glares. "How was I supposed to know?"

Clara gives me the stupid sick-cat look again. She really is *Sports Illustrated* hot. Deciding I should stop staring at her, I focus back on my food and eat in silence. Finally, Owen and Rigby strike up a conversation about some new video game.

By the end of break, the others are almost acting normal. Except for Liam, who has said nothing.

"Aren't you headed back to your assignment?" I ask him when everyone else vanishes.

"Seriously, bloke, you don't remember her at all?"

I suppress my irritation, though I'm miffed that we're on this topic again. "No."

He looks as frustrated as Willow was earlier. "I was Tate's Satellite. I was there when you visited her. You may not remember her, but she's real. The two of you, your relationship—it's all real."

I hope my expression conveys how ridiculous he sounds.

"She erased your memories. I saw her do it firsthand."

I stare back at him, trying to gauge how someone seemingly sane could believe this. "I guess she did a good job, then," I finally reply.

His eyes look desolate when he squeezes my shoulder. After he releases me, he whispers "displace" and vanishes.

I push out my chair, hoping some time-killing idea will strike me on my way to my room.

"Jonathan!" I yell loudly so my voice travels across the vast lobby. He turns at the sound of his name.

"Jonathan, wait up!" I shout, jogging to him.

"Hello, Grant."

"Hey," I say, a little out of breath. "Is there any chance I could get my next assignment now? Because here's the thing: I'm going crazy. I need something to do."

He considers my request for a moment. "There's an urgent matter that needs my attention first. Can you meet me in Orders at the next break?"

Ugh. Next break? "Sure," I end up saying, because it's not like I can argue with the guy.

I glance at the courtyard doors when he's gone. Any place is better than my room, so I spend the rest of the day sprawled on the lawn. Time couldn't possibly move slower.

Unable to wait a minute longer, I arrive at Orders before break starts and lean impatiently against the golden desk.

Eve, the whacked-out girl who gave me my first assignment, approaches and pops a pink bubble. "Grant?"

I nod. Please tell me she's not going to question my name again.

"Jonathan sent me," she explains, smacking her gum.

Apparently, no one ever told this girl it was rude to stare. "Okaaaay?" I draw the word out so she gets it.

"He sent me with a message. He cannot meet you today. Something urgent came up." She talks like she's reciting a script. "Meet him back here in two days."

"Two days!" I bark. She pops her gum. "Can't you just give me my next assignment?"

"Sorry, I'm just the initial girl."

"The what?"

"The initial girl," she states again, as if I'm supposed to get it this time. "The girl who gives the *initial* assignments."

I wait for her to say more, maybe a "Duh!" or something to that effect, but she just stares and pops another bubble. Finally, she asks, "You seeing anyone?"

"Excuse me?"

"Do. You. Have. A. Girlfriend?"

"Oh. Uh…no."

She cocks her head. "Want one?"

"Sorry, I'm not in the market right now," I stammer, pushing by her to get away as fast as possible.

"Well, if you ever change your mind…" she calls after

me.

I walk directly to my usual table in Benson, thankful to be away from her. Sheesh, the way things have been going around here, Progression may as well be Match.com. After I endure stares from Rigby, Clara, Owen, Anna, and Liam, the atmosphere around the table returns to normal. I'm dealt into their game of Sats. Deflated, I tell them about having two more whole days to kill.

"You should totally try gaming, man," Owen suggests.

"No, you shouldn't," Anna argues, eyeing Owen.

Owen brushes her off. "Seriously, it's way cool! You're welcome to my headgear if you want it."

"Maybe," I reply noncommittally.

"It's in my room—number seven twenty-three in the K wing. Help yourself."

"Thanks. Anyone seen Willow?" I check the archways, wishing I could make her appear.

"She's pretty busy right now." Liam's apparently still ticked that I'm not buying his made-up story.

"Think she'll be coming for break?"

Liam's scowl deepens. "Doubt it."

"Have you seen her? Is she OK?"

"How do you think she is?" He pushes up from the table and stomps out of the room.

I shake my head and return to the card game before the others have to leave as well.

—~~—

The next two days crawl at a snail's pace, only slower. In a desperate attempt to kill the remaining half of the second day, I take Owen up on his offer and try the gaming thing. After laughing at his floral sofa (which is even uglier than mine), I grab the absurd binoculars sitting on his coffee table, strap them around my head, and take a deep breath when the lenses power on.

I'm shocked to see Willow as one of the character options in *Elite Force Seven*. There's no way I'm pretending to be that kook—or the tatted and pierced Reed for that matter—so I choose a giant guy named Billy instead. Using my body as the controller, I memorize and repeat the displayed movement sequence that allows for a successful block. It takes some getting used to (and I'm sure I look as stupid as Liam did playing it), but the game is surprisingly decent. I should have been playing it two days ago. After mastering three levels, my calimeter buzzes. I pull the binoculars off and drop them onto Owen's cushy leather chair on my way out.

I'm relieved when I turn the corner to Orders and see Jonathan at the end of the long hallway. He smiles. "My apologies for the other day. Something pressing came up unexpectedly."

"No problem." I'm just glad to finally be getting my next assignment.

Jonathan looks past me. "Ah, here she comes."

Carrying herself as though her energy has been snuffed out, Willow forces a smile and pulls me into a tight hug. She steps back and scans me. She's such a mom.

"How you doin', kid?"

I hug her again, realizing how much her absence has bothered me. "I'm good. Bored as all get-out, but good," I say into her hair before letting go. "How are you?"

"I'm all right." She pulls her dreads into a ponytail. "I totally need to code, but thankfully, my assignment is complete."

"She's pretty amazing," Jonathan beams.

"Oh, stop!" She pretends to be embarrassed. Jonathan and I laugh, knowing that could never happen.

"Now that you're both here." Jonathan turns to the wall behind the desk expectantly. Shelves of books fold out of the dark wood panels, reaching so high they disappear. A golden ladder slides from the right and settles around the middle of the bookcase. Jonathan steps through the walkway that was part of the desk just two seconds ago and grips the ladder. "Your book, please," he says to me.

I grab Ryder's book from my backpack and hand it to him.

He looks up the ladder. "Be right back."

"I told you he was traditional," Willow remarks after he's out of sight.

"You call that traditional?"

"Well, maybe not the magic wall, but the bookshelves, definitely. It suits him nicely, don't you think?"

I don't answer because my eyes are too busy searching for him. When he finally returns, he's carrying a book the same size as my last, but this one is dark purple instead of red.

"It is my pleasure to present you with your first Elite

assignment." Jonathan's words get delayed somewhere between his mouth and my head. I look at Willow a minute later when they sink in.

She beams back at me and pushes up on my chin, forcing my jaw to refasten. "Congratulations, kid."

"You have been selected, out of a grand pool, might I add, to join our Elite team of seven. Congratulations," Jonathan says.

"Really?" is all I can manage.

"Yes, really! Why couldn't you have shut up like this months ago? It certainly would have made my job easier."

I'm too stunned to jab Willow back. "I'm taking your place?" I ask, still not believing it.

"I had a good run. May as well give someone else a shot. Although I seriously doubt you'll ever possess my awesomeness." She winks at Jonathan.

"With this great title comes greater responsibility." Jonathan's eyes move to the book in my hand. "This next assignment will be extremely demanding. I trust you to keep your focus."

"Yes, of course."

"I look forward to many more years of your service." He pauses, adding the dramatic effect that he always seems to pull off. "Well, you'd better get to it." He shakes my hand, wishes me luck, and strolls down the hall.

Me...an *Elite*? I'm not entirely sure how I feel about this, though I can't deny that I'm a little stoked. Still, to have been selected over so many others who are much more deserving, I can't quite wrap my head around the idea.

"Come on, I'll walk you to your room." On our way down the hall, Willow fidgets with her sleeve like she's uncomfortable. The volume from the lobby increases with every step. "I guess this is it, huh?" she eventually says.

"What do you mean?"

"We're not going to be seeing much of each other anymore."

I put my arm around her as we snake around small groups of Satellites in the lobby. "We'll make time," I promise, kissing the top of her head when she leans against me. "After all, someone once told me, when you're a Satellite, it's forever."

She stops when we reach the B hall and turns to me. "Thank you."

"For what?"

"For protecting Ryder. I know it was you."

"How?"

"His tocket. I knew when my memories fully came back. I owe you so much."

"You owe me nothing," I say, meaning it.

"No, I do."

We resume a slow walk down the crowded hall.

"What's he like?" A tinge of sadness plays in Willow's voice.

"He's great. Really great." I think about his accident and wonder why I was unable to stop it, and then become fearful that I'll give away how badly I failed. "And Mya," I say quickly, "she couldn't be more like you if she tried. Well, except she's less of a weirdo."

Willow pushes against me with her shoulder.

"I do have a question," I say.

"Hmm?"

"What's with all the granite?"

She smiles. "It's always kinda been my thing. As a kid, I would sneak away to the beach a few blocks down the street from our house. I'd climb on the granite boulders, imagining I was an explorer looking in the dark shadows for their secrets." She pauses. "Imagine the history they hold— submerged by the sea part of the time, left to dry when the ocean retracts. They remain solid, while the world moves and evolves around them."

I dig in my pocket, pulling out the small stone tocket. "And this one?"

She takes it from me and rolls the smooth rock over her fingers. "Troy collected these for me. He filled an entire garden with them, if you can believe that. This one"—she holds it up in full view—"was my focal point through Ryder's birth." She places the rock back in my hand. "Take care of that one for me."

I agree, knowing she's not referring to the stone. "How come you don't have a New England accent?"

She steps into the elevator. "I'm as Midwest as you are, kid. All the way from Iowa. You and I were practically neighbors," she jokes. "My family moved to New Hampshire when I was eight, but I never picked up the accent. It's bizarre, right?"

I shake my head and laugh. Willow calling something bizarre brings three words to mind: *pot, kettle,* and *black.*

She hugs me tightly when we get to my door.

"Want to come in?" I ask.

"Nah."

"I have coffee," I say in my most persuasive voice, hoping to change her mind.

"Thanks, but I need to get going. Troy's probably bored out of his mind."

"Ha! More like dreading your return."

Her expression is much too serious and her lingering stare makes the space between us zing with awkwardness. "I'm gonna miss you."

"Shut up!" I hug her again. "It's not good-bye."

"It feels that way."

"It's just a chapter closing."

"Are you going to be all right?" she asks. "Elite…that's a big deal."

"I'll be fine," I answer, but I could swear there's a glint of doubt in her eyes.

"I'll see you around, kid."

I nod. "You'd better."

Before the elevator doors close, she leans around them and sticks her tongue out at me.

"You're so annoying!" I yell to her.

"Darn right," she sings back before the doors slide together.

I walk into my room and drop my backpack on the counter. With a cup of coffee in hand, I settle onto the sofa and open the dark purple book to prepare for my first Elite assignment.

Epilogue

"Hey, Jonathan—got a minute?" Willow asks.

"Certainly." Jonathan excuses himself from a pair of Satellites and walks with Willow to the edge of the field. "What's up?"

"I wanted to talk to you about Tate."

"Yes, how is she?"

"Doing better. She just enrolled for fall classes. Here's the thing, though. She's changed. A lot. It's like she's wiped her own memories, too."

"Her memories are intact; she's just moving on," Jonathan assures. "We should all be happy about that."

"And what about Grant? His memories weren't filed away like ours. What if she erased them permanently?"

"We'll cross that bridge when it becomes necessary. Please remember—Grant's memory loss is essential, now more than ever. You know how difficult Elite assignments are. A distracted mind is inadmissible."

Willow's shoulders fall a little. "I know. Well, I'd better get back to Troy. Today we're venturing to some jungle in South America," she says with displeasure. "It's totally his idea."

The corners of Jonathan's eyes crinkle when he laughs.

"That sounds nice."

"No, not nice! The humidity does nothing for my hair." Willow twirls a dreadlock around her finger and uses as much drama as she can muster.

Jonathan's laughter increases. "I'll be around if you need me."

Willow begins skipping away, but then stops. "Jonathan!" she yells across the field. When he turns, she shouts, "Grant and Tate—things are going to work out OK for them, right?"

Jonathan raises his hand in a silent farewell. Willow accepts his smile and wave as an answer and bounces through the courtyard doors.

To be continued…

1. It's the name of the game

Willow

"You wanted to see me?" I wish my candlelit dinner with Troy wasn't being interrupted.

"Yes, thank you for arriving so promptly, Willow." Jonathan stops a few feet from the K hall in the grand marble lobby. "I am in need of your assistance with an assignment."

Anxiety hits quick, making my heart rate spike when my mind ticks through all of my Tragedies. "For who?"

"I am saddened to say, Tatum Jacoby. She is careening off course once again."

Tate. I'd bet the farm she is off course. Things like this tend to happen when the natural order gets altered. "But you said…never mind. What's going on with her?" *Aside from the fact that she erased all of Grant's memories* is what I want to say, but don't.

"Grant's inherent memory loss is a natural part of the process," Jonathan says, using his unnerving mind reading ability—he can deny having this gift all day long, but I'll never believe him.

"We both know the way his memories were erased was not natural," I taunt.

"Despite how his memories were taken, losing them was essential, especially now that—"

"Now that he's an Elite," I mumble, knowing Jonathan is right. Probably, anyway.

"As a member of the Elite team, distractions in our work can be treacherous. Wouldn't you agree?"

I hesitate before nodding. Regular Satellite assignments are strenuous enough. The kid has no idea how agonizing the road ahead is going to be. "Working towards the greater good," I say with phony enthusiasm.

Jonathan smiles. "That's the spirit. I would like you to accompany Liam on Tate's assignment until we can get her advancing forward again."

"I'm guessing you need me to go now?"

Jonathan nods and squeezes my shoulder.

So much for my chicken marsala, and more importantly, my husband-time.

"Thank you. You are one of our most exceptional, though you mustn't need me to tell you that."

How is it that this guy knows flattery always brings him forgiveness? "Oh, come on Johnny, you say that to all the Satellites," I tease. "Am I expected in training?"

"Unless you feel the need, I think you can manage without. I'm here if you need anything. Good luck."

"Will you get a message to Troy that I'll see him at break?"

When Jonathan nods, I thank him and dig in my bag. When my fingers find Tate's gold necklace, I whisper, "Displace," and fall through the dark marble floor of the lobby. On my way down to Earth to save another Tragedy, I think of Troy. At least he will understand. God love my husband. He's more than a girl could ever hope for and I'm somehow lucky enough to get eternity with him. Not a bad trade for missing out on a few years of my mortal life.

I breathe deeply to pull the zooming wind into my lungs and then I grin. Being a Satellite will always be a close second to being with my husband. As the houses below quickly approach, I still find it difficult to believe there really is something better than this. Six months ago, before I was reunited with Troy, I didn't believe it myself.

When Liam almost jumps out of his Sketchers from the shock of my landing, I can't help but snicker.

"Bloody hell, woman!"

"What's up?" I ask beautiful, British Liam. Shocked expressions always look silly on him. He should really lose the hat; his wavy, sand-colored hair is too perfect to be covered. I shift my eyes toward Tate. "I hear our girl is still going all mental-ward on us."

Tate appears normal enough, minus the black jeans, black tee, and black make-up. The protruding ribs aren't overly flattering either. Not that I can blame the poor thing, having lost first her fiancée and then her brother within a few short months. If she knew Grant and Elliott were both Satellites and that she would see them again, it would make my job a lot easier. Until then, Liam and I will have to keep her slogging on through life. "She's still on the black kick, huh? Pity. She wears color so much better."

"Her attitude is as dark as her clothing. I can't believe I'm saying this, but I'm glad you're here. I could certainly use the help."

"I can see that. Have you been coding during breaks?"

"Yeah, but my relaxed state is usually diminished within the first ten minutes of being with her." At the same time Liam says this, Tate cranks her radio up to ear-piercing volume. "Here she goes again," Liam shouts over the noise.

"I got this one," I yell back and focus on pulling in my filter. When my energy is formed into a pretty, purple ball floating in front of me, I say, "Haze," and then send my thoughts to Tate through the film than has enclosed the two of us.

Turn it down.

Oh, it hurts! My body clenches in pain. *Labor, Willow, labor!* Remembering childbirth always snaps my mind back into the game.

"Block." The connection between Tate and me is severed, making the vapory filter fall to the carpet in droplets before vanishing.

In my head, my arms raise in victory when Tate spins the volume dial down.

When she switches her attention to the family photograph on her nightstand, I ask Liam, "Has Elliott forgiven Grant yet?"

Liam shakes his head. "I can't blame Elliott. The bloke put down his sister."

"He didn't really put her down. According to Clara, Grant just said something along the lines of 'so what if Tate was a Rebellion.'"

As usual, Liam isn't buying my downplaying attempt.

"All right, his tone probably wasn't super-sweet."

"A *Rebellion*, Willow. The worst-case-scenario for a Tragedy, and Grant pretty much told the girl's brother he didn't care. Don't forget, he and Grant were almost brothers themselves. It was cold."

"I understand Elliott's point, but in the kid's defense, his memories of her are gone, so he really didn't know what he was saying."

Liam lets out a loud breath.

"I guess this means you're still mad at Grant, too?"

"I had to endure watching Grant here, remember?" He points his eyes at Tate. "He broke every rule we have to be with her, even leaving his own Tragedy—whom he should have been watching—unattended."

I wince, knowing my own son was left unprotected while Grant was making illegal visits to Tate. Liam continues and paces around the room. "She erased his memories one by one. She destroyed all the reminders of him from her life: photographs, music, even her clothes."

"I know!" I immediately regret my sharp tone that was merely a result of wishing he'd stop with the rehash. "I'm not cool with how his memories were wiped from his mind either; it's not the way they were supposed to disappear, but there's nothing we can do about that now. The fact is they're gone like they should be, like how it is —or was—for all of us. It's not his fault and it's not fair of you and Elliott to blame him."

"He's changed," Liam says in a quieter voice.

"We all changed when we became Satellites, Liam. It's the name of the game. You forgot your life, I forgot mine. That's what Programming is for: to return our memories when our loved ones join us. You weren't so quick to lose your memories either, and as I recall, you were able to keep more of them than a lot of people around here." Oh Lord have mercy; I wish I could take the words back as soon as they are out.

Liam squints his eyes and his hand freezes on his ball cap. "Do you think I want to remember my death?"

"No, I'm—"

"Do you think I want to remember the look on my son's face when he pulled my body from the water?" Liam shouts.

"No! I'm sorry. But how about the alternative, Liam?" I yell back before I'm able to calm myself. "How about not remembering you had a son at all? How about not remembering you died while giving birth to him?"

We both retreat to our respective corners, speechless.

"Just try to cut the kid a break, Liam," I finally say. "Being a Satellite isn't always an easy road. If it were, there'd probably be a lot more of us."

I take the next block, which is better than any apology I could give him. His grateful expression says so.

Grab your paperback or ebook of Elite today at www.Amazon.com and continue with Grant and his friends on their journey through the afterlife.

Acknowledgments

I am indebted to those who continue to sprint alongside me through this journey. First and foremost, to Dan: Thank you for concealing your sighs every time I carry my laptop to the dining room or back porch. No matter how absurd my ideas are, you always support me. For that, and many, many other reasons, I love you.

To Mom, Connie, Monica, Russ, Wendy, Joe, Lindsey, Anthony, and Jenny, who, even after muddling through the earliest drafts of this story, continued to root me on: Thank you for your feedback, and my apologies for the numerous typos. I am just an artist, after all.

Dawn, in the very early phases of this project, you said, "So what if no one ever reads it? Your boys will find it one day and be able to say, 'My mom wrote that.'" Thank you. This has been the most encouragement anyone could have given me.

A great big thanks to my editor, Amy, for polishing—and I mean polishing!—this manuscript and offering excellent advice that did not include rewriting a new story. To Katie and my CreateSpace publishing team: Thank you for making this dream a reality for a girl who, just two years ago, knew very little about writing a novel and even less about publishing.

Last, but certainly not least, to Heather: No words can tell you how much I've appreciated you through this process. The number of books you read in a week is freakish, and for that, I am grateful! You've read more drafts of this book to count, discussed story ideas, characters, publishing, marketing, editing, book covers, etc., and still, by some miracle, you continue speaking to me. If that's not a friend, I don't know what is. I hope there's a vacation in our future! Thank you, thank you, thank you, thank you, thank you...

About the Author

Lee lives in Missouri with her husband and three sons. She received a BFA with a Graphic Design emphasis from Lindenwood University in 2000. She spends her days as a graphic designer for a billboard company that makes having a day job not so terrible. You can usually find Lee hanging out with her boys—preferably by a body of water, hidden behind her laptop, or conversing with her dog, Dixie. Satellite, Lee's first novel, was selected as a quarterfinalist in the 2012 Amazon Breakthrough Novel Award contest. Visit www.leedavidson.net for social media links, book updates, and more.